THE
UNBROKEN
LINE
of the
MOON

THE VALHALLA SERIES · BOOK 1

THE UNBROKEN LINE *of the* MOON

A Novel

JOHANNE HILDEBRANDT
TRANSLATED BY TARA F. CHACE

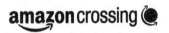

Text copyright © 2014 by Johanne Hildebrandt

English translation copyright © 2016 by Tara F. Chace

The Unbroken Line of the Moon was first published in Swedish as *Sigrid: Sagan om Valhalla* by Bokförlaget Forum in 2014. Translated from Swedish by Tara F. Chace. Published in English by AmazonCrossing in 2016.

Published by Amazon Crossing, Seattle

www.apub.com

ISBN-13: 9781503939080
ISBN-10: 1503939081

Cover design by Shasti O'Leary Soudant

Printed in the United States of America.

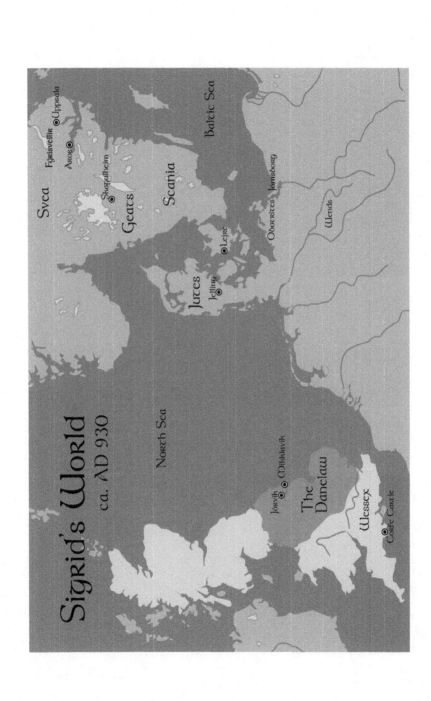

Sigrid's World
ca. AD 930

Svea

Uppsala
Aros
Fyrisvellir

Skagulheim

Geats

Scania

Baltic Sea

Jutes

Lejre
Jelling

Obotrites
Jomsborg

Wends

North Sea

Jorvik
Oliklavik

The
Danelaw

Wessex

Corfe Castle

Sigrid the Haughty, one of Scandinavia's most powerful and legendary women, lived in the tenth century. She was widely recognized for her intelligence, her strength, and her deep faith in the Norse gods.

All that is left of her brutal and dramatic life are fragments of stories and traces of facts that contradict each other. Few have heard what really happened when she saved Scandinavia from darkness. This is Sigrid's saga, which should never have been forgotten.

PART ONE

ᛈ

Sigrid hurried through the dark of night toward her mother's burial mound, her heart hopeful. The darkness had transformed the oak forest into another world, the dark tree crowns whispering their greetings. Only the outlines of slumbering cattle and slaves were visible in the fields. The woods rustled with ghosts, trolls, and beasts.

To give herself strength, she prayed to Freya: *Vanadís, protect me.*

It didn't help much. Fear tingling down her spine, Sigrid broke into a run. Her grandmother and the elders would be furious if they knew she'd snuck off the estate again, and if her luck was really against her she might be captured and carted off by one of the Scylfings' enemies. Still, she had to try, because tonight was her only chance.

Sigrid clutched her bag to her heart and scrambled up the steep slope of the burial mound. Only when she was safely on the top did she stop to catch her breath. The treetops and fields glowed in the moonlight.

The lights from the halls of the twelve gods lit up the heavens. Sigrid searched until her eyes found Folkvang, Freya's home, guarded by the six valkyries.

"Watch over me, Ur-Mother," she whispered to the shimmering lights as worry gnawed at her belly. "Erce, grant me some of your timeless sorcery so that I can open the gates to the afterworld."

She bowed to the moon, Máni, who was being chased across the sky by Hati the wolf. Then she took a wavering breath. It was time to do what she had come to do. Without hesitation, she pulled up her skirt and squatted down in the moist grass that grew on the burial mound so that her blood, filled with life force, ran onto the ground.

Step one.

"Hel, hear my prayer. Let my mother rise from Niflheim, where she now dwells."

Her hands trembled as she opened her bag and took out a fistful of flower petals that she had picked in silence by moonlight. Carefully she strewed them over the grass.

"Mother, hear your daughter. Come to me," she pleaded.

Step two.

The response came as a warm wind, which took the flower petals and carried them away from the mound, out over the sea where the dísir danced in the haze that wafted over the water. Those ghosts of fate whispered a thank-you and then continued their quiet song about what the future would bring. Sigrid shivered as the darkness gathered around her.

In preparation for this, she had bartered for a spell stick, a piece of wood with a magic spell that would make Hel open the gates of Niflheim. Now she carefully took it out and rubbed the blood from her womb onto the piece of wood bearing the runic incantation and then looked around expectantly. Those she summoned were closer now. She could see the shadows moving around her. Her heart pounded in her chest as those who had gone before gathered, hungering after her youth. She could sense her mother among those pale shadows. Soon she would finally get to see her.

Her hands trembled as she dug up the dirt with her fingers and buried the spell stick. That was the third step, according to her dream.

Her sacred night had come, when she bled for the first time. She was filled with sorcery and could use the spell stick to open the gates to the afterworld. Sigrid took a deep breath of cool night air and shouted into the night:

"I am Sigrid. Hear my blood."

Her heart was ready to burst in her chest.

"Mother, come out. I command you!"

Her voice echoed over the burial mound, over the fields, and over the sea, where the dísir were dancing, all the way to the vast forest where the beasts dwelled. A black bird flew up with a complaint, but after that, only silence.

The shadows pulled back, and the whispering dísir quieted down.

Sigrid looked around. Her mother was supposed to come to her. Why hadn't it worked?

"Where are you?" she pleaded, placing her hands on the ground.

Her mother was in the mound, burned in her nicest dress, wearing pearls and twisted silver.

Why didn't she come? Stifling waves of disappointment washed over Sigrid. She had held this hope for so long.

"Why have you forsaken me?"

The sound of her voice echoed over the mound, but there was no answer.

It was over. Sigrid's head drooped. She had bled and prayed to Vanadís just as she was supposed to. Why was she not permitted to see her mother just this one time, to learn why she had survived when her mother had not?

Why?

Sigrid curled up in the damp grass, longing cutting at her chest.

She remembered her mother's fear when the Svea had attacked the estate, also her mother's body on top of Sigrid to protect her, the heat of the fire, the smoke, the smell of blood, and the screams of the dying.

"Don't be scared," her mother had said before her body became so heavy Sigrid could barely breathe.

What happened after that was shrouded in darkness, small sections of the tapestry that unraveled as she tried to pin them down. Someone carried her from the flames. Safe arms?

Grief welling out of a half-healed wound, quaking sobs shook Sigrid.

Vanadís, I beseech you, let me know.

Sigrid looked pleadingly up at Valhalla in the sky. Folkvang glittered as if Freya herself were looking down at her from her hall, Sessrúmnir, filled with dísir and heroes.

"Help me, and I will serve you for the rest of my life," Sigrid said.

Just as she said the words, a light left Folkvang and fell toward earth. Sigrid sat up, the hairs on her arms and the back of her neck standing on end. It gleamed as it slowly traveled across the heavens, a burning chariot driven by a dís on her path to the world of mankind. Sigrid followed the light with her eyes as it journeyed west. The light twinkled and then vanished.

Sigrid gasped for breath. What in the name of the goddess was that? Had she really just seen that? She reached for her cloak and wrapped it around her body, shivering.

What if that was an omen? Her heart skipped a beat. In the sacred Freya lay, which had been sung to her so many times, Kára the dís is sent to Gunhild to assist her in the battle against the Rus and she arrives like a light from Folkvang. Sigrid was directly descended from Freya in an unbroken line . . . Valfreya must have sent a valkyrie to protect and help her.

A trickle of blood ran down Sigrid's thigh as she stood up, looking at the starry sky twinkling above her. That had to be it. She had promised herself to Freya and in response the Radiant One had sent her a dís. It was more than she could have ever dreamt.

Everything you wish for, you will get, the wind whispered to her tenderly, embracing her.

An irrepressible joy filled her chest. She had been selected by the most glorious of goddesses on her blood night. She had been sent the most powerful of omens.

I thank you, mistress. From this moment, I will serve you in everything. My life is yours.

She bowed her head and prayed until Sól rose from the underworld in her gleaming chariot and her brother Dag took over the world.

Sigrid welcomed the new day with her hands raised to the clear blue sky and her heart filled with a new wisdom. She knew which path she would take now. She knew that the secret power was hers.

ᚾ

Wolf time, blade time, grief time. Darkness pours over the world, and the end of an era approaches. Three priestesses of the old way—with gray-white hair and tattered clothes, supporting themselves on staffs—peer somberly into the fire and glimpse images, amidst the flames, of the days to come.

Midgard, Niflheim, Jotunheim, all nine worlds rip apart as the old gods are destroyed. The temple at Aros, dwelling place of the gods, is consumed by flames. Trees fall, fields are poisoned, seeresses die screaming. Hordes of people trudge over piles of bodies in the infertile fields. They kneel passively before a cross, begging for salvation and grace.

"The new god's priests shackle the minds and hearts of men," the eldest of them said.

Mangled bodies, new ice, dancing bears, a bride's words in bed.

"Ragnarök," whispered another. "The victory of the cross worshippers, the fall of Valhalla. Then the goddesses have left us."

"No, not yet," the eldest said, raising a rune-carved staff crested by a hawk.

The fire blazed up. Now it showed new images. Chieftains and kings from near and far, some Christian, some believers in the old religion, knelt before a young man in a king's cloak with the wreath of victory on his head.

The young king raised his sword to the skies and the mark of Thor glowed on his wrist.

The priestess grunted contentedly and took a step closer to the fire.

"There is still hope. Who is this king of kings? Erce, Erce, show me."

A young woman appeared dimly in the dancing flames. She knelt and stretched her arms to the night sky as a black shadow loomed over her. The images came faster now. The woman lay dead on the ground as the darkness drank her life force. She died in bed with a swollen, pregnant belly. In a hall she was killed by a sword, the baby in her arms. Time after time the curse that lay over her succeeded in taking her life.

Then the images vanished, and the fire once again burned calmly in the night. The three priestesses stood silently pondering what they had seen until one of them began to speak: "Fragile are the threads that weave the life-cloth of that unborn king. The future we saw is far too uncertain."

The eldest of them nodded and said, "Powerful forces will extinguish the life of the child's mother even before he is born."

"We must make a sacrifice to protect the mother," said the third. "Only her child can save us from this darkness. She must have the strength to live."

The three turned around, supporting themselves on their staffs, and returned into the night as the fire faded and died.

Þ

Sweyn was running so fast his feet hardly felt the ground. Branches whipped his face and his shield thumped against his back. Still, he picked up the pace when he caught a glimpse of the Saxon's gray clothes between the trees.

His enemy's steps grew heavier now. The man had tossed aside his shield, helmet, and sack of loot during the pursuit. Exhausted, he tried to climb up a steep slope but slipped and fell.

Sweyn was there in a flash, his sword drawn. He was ready to fight. Sweat poured down his body, and his legs ached, even as his pounding heart grew calmer.

The warrior stood ready with his short sword. He was old and thin, and his body looked frail. His face was bright red and glossy with sweat, and his eyes were fearful. He wore neither chainmail nor cuirass, and his gray clothes were stained with blood and soot from the butchery in the village. Sweyn took a firmer grip on his sword hilt and smiled at the man who was about to die.

"You could have saved us both this forced march through the woods," Sweyn said, and spat on the ground.

They had sailed for days from Jómsborg to protect the village of Mikklavík. But by the time the Jómsvíkings finally reached the village, it was too late. Only days before they arrived, Mikklavík was burned and abandoned, which was a heavy shame to bear. When Sweyn had spotted a couple of stragglers who had lingered to plunder one of the outlying farms, Sweyn and his fellow soldiers had taken up the chase right away.

Sweyn's foster brother Åke had felled one with an arrow, and now Sweyn had caught the last one. The other Jómsvíkings came running up from behind, huffing and puffing, their footsteps heavy, like a herd of wild boars.

"You run faster than Alsviðr, boy," Ax-Wolf panted, doubling over and wheezing as he tried to catch his breath. The redheaded Ax-Wolf was the size of a giant, and he did not enjoy running through the woods and fields in full battle armor. Åke and Ax-Wolf's brother, Sigvard, panting and bright red in the face, positioned themselves behind the Saxon with his weapon drawn.

The Saxon surveyed the situation and then lowered his short sword. Sweyn spat on the ground again, his thirst tearing at his throat.

"Whom do you serve?" Sweyn demanded.

The Saxon stared at him with a defeated look. He knew he was going to die soon yet still remained silent.

"Who sent you to burn Mikklavík?" Sweyn continued.

Just then the Saxon lunged.

Quick as a snake, he slashed his sword at Sweyn, but Sweyn was skilled from years of training and acted without thinking. One quick blow and the Saxon's severed sword hand dropped to the ground. The warrior's scream could have come from a woman. He sank to his knees, staring in horror at the bleeding stump where his hand had been.

Sweyn lowered his sword, his heart pounding. He had almost been caught off guard.

"Tell me whom you serve. Otherwise you'll lose the other hand."

The Saxon's face had already gone gray and his body was shuddering as the blood gushed from his wound. Soon the death tremor would take the man, and then they wouldn't get anything sensible out of him.

Ax-Wolf probably had the same thought because he trudged over to the warrior and punched him hard in the mouth.

"Who sent you to burn the village?"

"The king," the Saxon whispered, his mouth bleeding. "We cleansed the village of the evil that has cursed the fields with failed crops. God will reward us."

The Saxon stared blankly at his stump. The blood ran slower from his wound, and his body trembled much more.

"We're not going to get any more out of this one," Ax-Wolf said. "If he still had his hand, he could have prayed to his lone god."

Sigvard and Åke took a couple of steps back as Sweyn raised his sword, carefully measuring the angle with his eyes. Ax-Wolf was watching him. The blow had to be clean, otherwise Sweyn would be derided for a long time.

The Saxon stared resignedly straight ahead and whispered softly with his pale gray lips.

Sweyn's blow sliced into the man's neck so the blood sprayed. The Saxon fell to the ground and tried, rattling, to inhale as he drowned in his own blood.

Ax-Wolf grunted, and sounding pleased, he said, "Not bad for a Jelling bastard."

These words were high praise and Sweyn smiled as he wiped his blade with the rag he carried in his belt. The Saxon died in a pool of blood. It boded well for the rest of the military campaign that Sweyn had succeeded in killing the king's man. If he killed enough men, he would secure his reputation before they returned to Danish soil.

He needed to do that before he met King Harald.

"What was all that business about evil among the Mikklavík residents?" Åke asked.

Ax-Wolf squatted down and started searching the dead man for anything worth taking.

"The king probably needed a scapegoat," Ax-Wolf said, brushing off Åke's concern.

Åke scratched his cheek. Sweyn knew that his foster brother Åke was terrified of ghosts and wights and wouldn't give in so easily.

"What if he was right? What if there is evil in the village?" Åke said nervously.

"What does it matter as long as we get good loot?" Sigvard said as he pulled the shoes off the dead Saxon, lighting up when he found a coin hidden in the straw inside.

Ax-Wolf and Sigvard stood up and started walking through the forest.

"Don't pay any attention to that Saxon cross worshipper's empty words," Sweyn said.

"Maybe you're right," Åke muttered.

Sweyn cast one last look at the body and then returned with his brothers-in-arms to the ruins of Mikklavík. If he were lucky, he would soon find more enemies to defeat.

ᚠ

She was going to get in trouble, but that didn't matter. They would all be happy when she told them Vanadís had blessed her. Sigrid's chest swelled with joy as she followed the path by the meadows where the mares were grazing with their foals as well as the cows, their calves scampering around and playing. Rising above the fields and pastureland, the thatched roofs of the farms and the clay-daubed white walls glowed in the dawn sun. The carved dragons topping her father's magnificent, newly built formal hall jutted out high above the roof so that every farm and hut in the surrounding area could see them and appreciate the importance of the Scylfing dynasty.

Sigrid smiled at the warmth and inhaled the scent of flowers and clover.

Thank you for your abundance and beauty, Vanadís, and for the dís you sent to be my guardian spirit.

Slaves were clearing weeds from the cultivated fields. Hilding was already at work at the smithy, and the sounds of his hammer followed Sigrid up the hill past the piggery and the kitchen garden to the farmhouse.

"Where have you been?" Jorun asked, stepping out of the shadows at the end of the longhouse.

Sigrid slowed down. Her cousin's arms were crossed over her dress apron and her thin lips, pressed so tightly together, formed one sharp line on her angular face.

Sigrid couldn't help but laugh. Jorun was certainly going to be surprised to learn about the miracle that had happened. Sigrid had prayed to Freya that she would become a seeress, and her prayer had been heard: a dís had come to earth.

"Hurry up," said Jorun before Sigrid had a chance to speak. "They've been looking for you for half the night. A messenger arrived last night."

Jorun's serious tone wiped the smile off Sigrid's face.

"Why? What's going on?" Sigrid asked, already bracing for the worst.

Both her father and her elder brother Ulf were attending the Thing, the local governing assembly. Had there been a battle on their way home? Was one of them injured? Or dead?

"Your father will be here soon. He's bringing powerful guests. You must be ready to welcome them. That's all I know. You have to go see your grandmother right away."

Sigrid exhaled. Well, if that's all it was, there was no big hurry. Relieved, she walked into the central courtyard that was surrounded by the old house and the wooden longhouse with its freshly thatched roof. The buildings were built close together for warmth and shelter from the wind.

Everyone seemed to be getting ready for the feast. Old Halte was decorating the doors of the formal hall with birch leaves, and Cooking-Róta was yelling at one of the servant girls in the cookhouse, where a wild boar was roasting over the fire. The scents of boiled fish, freshly baked flatbread, and smooth porridge lay heavy over the courtyard. The warriors, all combed and well dressed, sat in the shadows under the warden tree that defended the estate from bad luck.

"Hurry up, otherwise Allvis is going to be even madder," Jorun said. She took Sigrid's hand and pulled her toward the wooden benches in the shade of the old house, where her grandmother, Allvis, and the other elders were sitting.

The women stopped talking when they spotted Sigrid approaching. They were wearing their finest dresses, and their nicest head-cloths were bobbing up and down as they leaned over to each other, whispering among themselves.

Whatever was going on, they were displeased with Sigrid. She could tell that by looking at them. Even her father's mistress Åse, who was rocking her little daughter, gave Sigrid a look of disapproval. But soon, thought Sigrid, they would all be thrilled about the fate she'd been given.

Sigrid smiled at her grandmother, who slowly got up from her seat. The old woman was wrapped in a gray cloak despite the morning already being warm. Her dress was held together with old-fashioned bronze shield bosses. She mostly resembled a feeble bird, with her furrowed face and her skinny body, but Sigrid feared her mood for good reason.

"Where have you been?" Allvis asked.

Sigrid took a deep breath and said, "At my mother's grave. And when I—"

"You look like you slept in a dung heap," her grandmother said, cutting her off. "Your maidservants, Jorun and Alfhild, will clean you up and make you beautiful. And get going with it."

"Why is it so important how I look?" Sigrid asked, giving the old woman a puzzled look. Usually no one even cared if she was there or not.

Then her father's wife, Gunlög, came out of the great hall wearing one of her finest dresses, the blue one with the embroidery and the shimmering silver brooches at either shoulder. She hurried across the courtyard.

"Thank Frigg she's here," Gunlög said. Then she stiffened, and Sigrid braced herself for some criticism from Gunlög's sharp tongue, but she only sighed. "Go wash up immediately," she ordered.

"This is what happens when you let her run around the woods and fields like a slave girl," Sigrid's aunt Hilda muttered.

Gunlög glared at the plump widow and then said, "You try reining her in, if you can." And then to Sigrid she added, "Hurry up, girl. They'll be here soon."

Sigrid frowned. The road was empty. She had a clear view of the furrowed pathway as it threaded its way past the neighboring farms before disappearing into the woods that stretched all the way to the Sea of the Vanir. Everything was quiet except for Strutulf's youngest, who was leading the sheep over to the oak grove. Sigrid pulled back the hand that Jorun had been holding and calmly looked Gunlög in the eye.

"I'm not leaving until someone tells me what's going on," Sigrid said.

Her grandmother and Gunlög exchanged looks.

"Your father found a husband for you," her grandmother finally said. "Your suitor's envoy will be here soon."

Sigrid shook her head in surprise and blurted out, "I can't get married! I was just chosen to become a seeress." She'd received the sign. She'd seen the dís descend to earth. She was meant for something more than becoming a housewife.

Her grandmother blinked at her. There wasn't the smallest sliver of patience left in her.

"No more talk like that," her grandmother said, her voice like the crack of a whip. "The daughter of the chieftain of the Scylfings was not born to run around in catskins and predict farms' futures."

Her grandmother had no idea what had happened. She hadn't had a chance to hear about the blessing Sigrid had received.

"Last night at my mother's burial mound, Our Lady sent me an omen. A wonderfully beautiful dís came down in a burning chariot." Sigrid's eyes teared up as she thought back on the miraculous thing that had happened. Smiling, she held her hands out to the women sitting on the benches. "It was the most beautiful thing I've ever seen. Don't you understand? It was like when Kára came down to Gunhild to give her the victory over the Rus. I've been chosen. I've been blessed by Freya."

Sigrid was met with only silence, and her smile slowly faded. Gunlög looked away with that sneer that Sigrid had learned to hate. Helvig shook her blotchy jowls and started fiddling with a thread on her cloak. The old women sitting nearby stared at Sigrid. Their mouths were all agape and their eyes skeptical. Jorun stood, turned away, as if she weren't paying attention to what was being said. Only Åse smiled at Sigrid as she stroked her baby daughter's downy head.

None of them realized how significant the omen was. That much was clear. Sigrid turned again to her grandmother, who was on such good terms with the gods. Surely she would understand?

"Aren't you happy for me?"

Allvis scratched a fleabite on her neck before clearing her throat and saying, "The sign you received surely foretold the marriage proposal." Sigrid recognized the gentle tone she had used so many times before to reprimand Sigrid as a child.

That wasn't it!

"Vanadís wouldn't send a powerful omen like that for a marriage proposal," Sigrid scoffed.

"You'll say otherwise when you know who the suitor is. Now go get dressed." Her grandmother gave her a friendly look, which was unusual coming from Allvis.

"They're coming!" someone cried from the bottom of the hill.

Her grandmother jumped up and cast her eyes down the road.

"Go get yourself ready, right away!"

Sigrid frowned with disappointment. She would go change, but this was not settled. That was for sure.

◆ ◆ ◆

A suitor.

The domestic servants were already lined up in the courtyard, waiting for Sigrid's father, Toste, and his party, when Sigrid took up her place by her grandmother's side, having washed and changed in a great hurry. The more she thought about it, the more petulant she felt. She would never have expected her father to talk to someone about marriage without asking her first. He was plotting behind her back. And no one wanted to talk about the omen she'd received.

Sigrid gritted her teeth as her grandmother adjusted the braid that Alfhild had hurriedly put in her hair. Then her grandmother inspected the red dress with the blue embroidery Sigrid had put on. A band of colored stones hung between the shoulder clasps, and her mother's silver necklace chafed her throat.

"This will do, but quit looking so angry," her grandmother said drily. "A husband is a privilege that not everyone receives."

Sigrid scoffed.

"Who is he?" she asked but received only a headshake in response.

Sigrid did not believe for a second that her grandmother did not know all about this. Like a spider in a web, Allvis controlled everything and everyone. Father would never do anything without asking her advice first.

Well, the man must be a nobleman at any rate; otherwise Toste would never bring him to the estate. They were Scylfings after all, the most powerful dynasty in Geatland. Their family owned almost half of the eight large estates and thirty-nine hundreds. A suitor would need to measure up to the family's wealth, and Sigrid couldn't understand who that would be. Ideally, they shouldn't drag in an old man with a limp prick and toothless gums. Gyrild had married a man like that, and he had insisted that she join him in his funeral pyre to accompany him to the afterworld when he died. Instead she divorced him and was now living as a pauper at her sister's house.

Things had gone just as badly for Sif. She tended the farm while her husband was off at war. When he returned many years later, he brought a new wife with him, and Sif was supposed to treat her as if she were an equal. Now Sif lived like a servant in her own home. Sigrid shivered. It was hard to think of a fate worse than that.

The sound of the hoofbeats grew louder, and the horses neighed their greetings, receiving answers from the enclosed pastures along the road. Sigrid took a deep breath.

"Remember that you bear the family honor," her grandmother said. "If you buck and are willful, I will make sure you get a husband uglier than a troll."

Sigrid straightened up with a sniff and looked toward the two oaks that stood on either side of the road.

Father was the first to enter the courtyard. Tired and dusty from the journey, he held on to Sóta with one hand and raised the other in greeting. The horse's chest was lathered in sweat, so they must have ridden hard during the day. The horse's saddlebags bulged with everything Toste had bartered for at the Thing in Skedlöse. They must have stopped at Vara, because his leggings looked new, as did the belt he wore over his tunic.

Sigrid's brother, Ulf, rode in right behind him. Ulf was so lazy that he never walked if he could help it, and his horse's head drooped with fatigue. Some of their father's hirdmen followed on horseback. Behind them came the strangers.

Sigrid craned her neck to see better as warriors from an unfamiliar hird rode into the courtyard. They were magnificently dressed in byrnies and vigilantly scanned the domestic servants, as if they suspected Old Halte might pounce on them. Their shields bore no markings, which was unusual. Warriors generally liked to show whom they fought for.

A moment later, two noblemen rode into the courtyard. Sigrid's heart beat double beats. One was a young warrior with a broad smile who was shamelessly inspecting the womenfolk. The other was older, with a graying beard and a wrinkled face. He dismounted his horse and brushed the dust off himself with an expression of profound relief.

The cut of their cloaks was foreign, so they weren't Geats, that was for certain. Nor did they wear their hair long like Danes. Sigrid bit her cheek. Where in the name of the dís were these envoys from?

She watched impatiently as her father passed his horse off to Old Halte and then strode over to her. His beard was gray with dust, and his eyes twinkled with satisfaction.

"Well?" her grandmother asked. "Was it a successful journey?"

Father wiped the sweat off his brow with his sleeve and then smiled broadly and said, "Better than expected."

Allvis nodded at Sigrid and said, "Talk to your daughter."

Toste put his arm around Sigrid and led her over to the benches against the longhouse, away from listening ears.

"What tribe are these envoys?" Sigrid asked. "Where are they from?"

"They come from Svealand," he said. "They're King Erik's men."

Sigrid stared at her father with her mouth agape. The ground swayed beneath her feet, and she sank down onto the bench.

Svealand was the enemy. That was the kingdom of the Svea. The Scylfings had been at war with them for two generations, and the Svea frequently won. Geat farms had been burned down, whole families killed. The Svea had wiped out entire bloodlines. Only in the last two years had the Geats had any victories at all. Anund the Strong had managed to rally several families, and together they fought the Svea trespassers. But the Scylfings had not joined Anund yet. Far too much bad blood had flowed between the houses.

"The Scylfings no longer have any quarrel with the Svea. We reached a unanimous decision at the Thing to make peace with the Svea and join them in fighting against the House of Anund."

Sigrid tried to collect her thoughts.

Is this your will, Vanadís?

"What are the terms?" she asked hoarsely, even though she already knew the answer.

Toste lit up, as if this were the best part of the whole thing.

"The peace was secured through marriage," he said proudly. "I offered you as bride to King Erik. You will be the queen of Svealand."

Sigrid took several long, deep breaths and looked out over the courtyard where the two envoys were walking by. They eyed her with curiosity as if she were one of her father's mares.

Is this what you foretold at my mother's grave?

Her grandmother had sidled her way over to them. She sat down on the bench now and eyed Sigrid coolly, ready to give her a beating if she put up a fuss.

Toste's hand was rough and warm as he squeezed Sigrid's arm.

"Do you fully understand what this means?"

Sigrid responded, "That Svealand wins, and you will become the most powerful of the Geats."

The marriage would weaken Anund. Toste would become the most important Geat, with family ties to King Erik of Svealand and support from Harald Bluetooth, King of the Danes, for whom Toste served as a thane.

"You have been very cunning, Father."

"You will step into a queen's shoes and be married to a king. Surely a young girl couldn't wish for anything else?"

Sigrid's laugh sounded bitter.

"Last night our mistress called me, Father. My destiny is to become a seeress. I have received the greatest of omens."

Toste pulled his hand over his blond beard and looked at his mother.

Allvis responded tersely, "A portent of this marriage, nothing else."

Toste nodded and said, "Yes, that must be what it was."

Sigrid made a face. Did they really think she was so feebleminded that she didn't notice the contortions they were going through to get her to do what they wanted?

"Try to remember, daughter, the most sacred temple to the gods is in Svealand, and as queen of Svealand you will be the foremost of the seeresses, Freya's top maidservant. Seeresses and priestesses will kneel to you."

Sigrid grew quiet for a moment and looked up. These words enticed Sigrid.

That's all I've ever wanted, to be able to serve you.

Then she shook her head. Her father had an answer to everything, even this.

"You think I want to marry the man who killed my mother?" she asked.

The pain was visible in Toste's eyes before he turned away. Then he took her hand and held it to his heart. She could feel it beating beneath her fingers.

"I loved your mother. Every day since she died I have wished I could have been there with you. All the same, if this isn't done we could lose everything. As Erik's peace queen you will turn defeat into victory, give life where there was once death and battle. It's true that the Svea killed Allfrid, but is that enough to turn down this offer, which could save everything we know and hold dear? Do good men have to die because you don't want to lie with a man who is said to be handsome and good? Do other mothers and children have to die in the flames because you are too proud to live a life of wealth and be loved and revered? Remember that you are a chieftain's daughter, a Scylfing. Your life doesn't belong to you but to your family, and this is the sacrifice that is required of you."

Sigrid looked at him, at the wrinkles around his eyes, at the gray patches in his beard and hair. Her whole life he had been her security and role model. He loved her most of anyone. It was impossible for her to say no to this. This was the duty she was born to.

"Is there nothing I can do to get out of it?" she whispered.

For a fleeting instant she saw pain in his eyes, but then there was just resolve.

"If you don't agree to this, you will bring shame to us all, and I will become an oathbreaker."

Sigrid lowered her head. Her father was right, and there was nothing she could say about it. She knew her obligations all too well.

"What do I need to do?" she asked.

"Talk to the envoy Erik sent. Show what a valuable gem you are."

Sigrid smiled joylessly. At sunrise she had believed she was blessed by the greatest of her foremothers, that Freya sent her a dís for protection. Now half a day later, her father was all set to marry her off to the man who had killed her mother. Was her grandmother right? Had the omen meant that she was going to become a peace queen in Freya's name? It couldn't be a coincidence that her suitor's men came so soon after the omen.

"You can't find a better marriage than that," her grandmother said, scratching again at the fleabite on her neck, this time so hard that it started bleeding. Crossly she wiped the blood off with her cloak.

Sigrid chewed on her cheek. What if Freya didn't want her to get married? The radiant Freya lived in Folkvang without a husband, and was rich, powerful, and respected by the Æsir, who feared her sorcery and temper.

I beseech you. Give me a sign if this is your will.

A shriek from the sky made Sigrid look up. Way up in the clouds, which lay like a veil over the clear blue sky, a falcon circled.

Thank you, mistress, for your guidance.

Sigrid stood up and nodded to her father.

"I will do what you say."

If this was the will of the gods, she would yield and obey.

R

There wasn't a house left in Mikklavík that hadn't been consumed by the fire. Sweyn surveyed the devastation as he walked through the village with his three brothers-in-arms. Ravens fought over the charred bodies. A woman held her baby even in death, a spear driven through both of them by someone out of his mind with rage. Cracked skin, burned lips, toothless grins. Corpses full of ax cuts, their blood mixed with the mud.

Sweyn scoffed at the cowardice they observed. If only they had reached Mikklavík a day earlier, the king's men would have faced their Jómsvíking swords instead of the local farmers' axes. Then there would have been an honorable fight, not this slaughter.

Sweyn looked away from a child, no more than two, whose skull had been crushed with an ax. The stench of burned flesh and death tore at his throat. Curse on Harald and his weaklings who couldn't bring themselves to fight real men in battle. Instead they were so spineless that they went after dishonorable spoils.

"We should have carved the blood eagle on that Saxon," Ax-Wolf muttered somberly, kicking a charred cooking pot. "It seems that he got off far too easily."

Ax-Wolf looked like a big troll, stepping over the clothes and kitchen utensils that lay strewn in the mud after the pillaging. He swung his ax back and forth, as if warding off invisible enemies.

Åke nudged Sweyn in the ribs and pointed at young Alfred, who was sitting beside a dead woman who lay half naked in the mud. He placed his cloak over her body, his face as stiff as a death mask.

"He couldn't have had a worse homecoming," Åke said.

Sweyn shook his head. Alfred had come to Jómsborg early in the month of Gói bearing a message from his father, Osmund, the chieftain of Mikklavík. Everyone who saw the sails knew it must be a matter of life and death, because only a fool sails across the sea in the ice and cold. Sure enough, when Alfred stood in Palna's hall, he explained that his father wanted to hire the Jómsvíkings to protect their village.

"King Harald's men are burning Danelaw villages and slaughtering anyone with Danish or Jutish blood. They say we are pagans and that our heathenness is causing crop failures throughout all of England," Alfred had explained to Palna, chieftain of the Jómsvíkings. Alfred had offered him a significant amount of silver if he protected Mikklavík.

It was an easy decision to make. Sweyn's foster father, Palna, and Osmund had fought together in the past, and Palna felt he had a debt of honor to repay. The winter had been long and uneventful, and there were good prospects here for both fighting and plundering. They had all cheered when Palna agreed, and for Sweyn it was a wonderful opportunity to travel to England. He had only killed three enemies and would need to slay many more to make a name for himself. Today he had killed his fourth, but killing a straggler who stayed behind to plunder didn't give anyone honor. It was dishonorable that they had arrived in Mikklavík too late to confront King Harald's men. He would have welcomed a true battle.

Ax-Wolf stopped abruptly and picked a broken comb up out of the mud. He wiped it off on his leggings and then stuffed it in his bag.

"Meager booty is better than no booty," he said contentedly.

"If you comb your filthy beard, maybe you'll find that knife I lost last winter," his brother Sigvard teased. The short, sinewy Sigvard grinned up at the redheaded giant.

"All you'll find hiding in my beard are those poor young maids who fled from your measly manhood," Ax-Wolf responded good-naturedly.

The seeress Beyla, Palna's sister, poked her staff around in the dirt. She wore a cloak with fox heads draped over her shoulders. Ax-Wolf's laugh made her look up, and she glared at him, instantly silencing him. Beyla interpreted the gods' signs and was a great sorceress. She understood the hidden world and knew the will of the valkyries.

"Don't mock the dead with your small-mindedness," she said now.

Ax-Wolf looked around uneasily for spirits from the afterworld and then muttered, "I'm not mocking them. I just want to cheer them up."

Beyla's gray braids swayed as she shook her head.

"Did you get your plunder?" she asked Sweyn.

He bowed his head and received a nod from the seeress before she turned her back to them.

Palna was over by the well with the rest of the men. They were standing around a little girl with a cracked skull. A straw doll was still in her hands. Her blond hair had been trampled into the mud. An older man lay beside her wearing a chieftain's cloak and a Norwegian-style beard.

Palna tossed aside his own gray cloak. Like a sinewy wolf, hardened by hunting and ordeals, he squatted down beside the dead man. His jaws were clenched; a scar that glowed red ran straight across his face.

"So we meet again, old friend," Palna said, pointing to a scar on the dead man's arm. "Osmund took the blow that was aimed at my head with his bare arm. I hoped I would be able to repay him today, but the gods wished it otherwise."

The Jómsvíkings stepped aside, letting Alfred through to his father's body. Alfred dropped to his knees, his face so pale that he looked like he was dead himself. They had all heard about Osmund. Alfred had braved the winter to sail to them in the north. Then he convinced the Jómsvíkings to come all the way to Mikklavík, but although they hurried they were too late. Now Alfred's father and all his kin were dead.

They stood in silence while the men accompanying Alfred pushed their way in to see Osmund, their dead chieftain.

"My father was an honorable man, a credit to the family," Alfred said hoarsely, looking up at the warriors who had gathered around him. "May God grant me vengeance."

Palna stood up and contemplated Osmund's body.

"Your God won't help you, but our swords can," Palna finally said.

Sweyn and Åke exchanged glances. This sounded promising.

"That Saxon I killed said the king had sent them to cleanse the land of evil, because there were witches in Mikklavík," Sweyn said.

Palna nodded thoughtfully and waved over the ealdorman from Alfred's retinue, an old, gray-haired man with a stooped back.

"Have you had forces of darkness in the village?" Palna asked.

The old man shook his head and then explained: "There's famine from crop failures, and people are blaming King Edward. The church is still on his side, but noblemen are increasingly looking toward the widowed queen Elfrida and her son and saying that he is the legitimate heir to the throne. The king sent men into the Danelaw to plunder monasteries and churches and villages for the riches he needs. King Edward blames the pagans for the crop failures and says that he is enacting God's punishment on those who brought misfortune over the land with their heresy."

Palna smiled sarcastically and said, "While he fills his sacks with riches. It seems as if this King Edward is very cunning, which is a trait to admire."

Palna looked over to where the ships lay pulled up on the beach while running his thumb over the scar on his face. Sweyn recognized the gesture. He tensely watched every movement, hoping and praying there would be a battle.

"Can we find this cunning king?" Palna asked finally.

"That's an easy thing to find out," Alfred said as he got up, his face grim with his desire for revenge.

Palna looked at his brother Gunnar, who nodded in response. Only then did he cross his arms and look at his Vikings.

"Honor and glory require us to avenge what has happened in this village," cried Palna. "Let us sail south and show this king the true wrath of the Northmen."

Sweyn eagerly raised his sword and along with his fellow soldiers hooted in triumph. It was going to happen. They were going to deal with the Saxon king. Finally Sweyn would get to fight a proper battle against a worthy opponent. He would finally be able to make a name for himself.

Sigrid stood in the dark courtyard, peering in the formal hall's double doors, which were open on this warm night. The men at the long table ate greedily from the platters that had been set out. The light from the torches reflected in the bronze shields on the wall, spreading a soft light over her local relations who had washed and dressed in their finest clothes to dine at Toste's table.

The men from Svealand sat nearest her father, who occupied the seat of honor, awaiting her arrival.

"It is hard to understand how you can be so calm," said Alfhild, smoothing Sigrid's cloak. "Aren't you nervous or excited?"

The servants had been speaking of nothing else but the suitor, and in Alfhild's mind Sigrid was already queen of Svealand, seated on a golden throne surrounded by princes and princesses. Alfhild meant well, but sometimes she was like a little child.

"I follow the will of the goddess," Sigrid said and straightened her necklace, the most beautiful thing she owned.

Sigrid was going to be displayed to the prospective buyers, like one of her father's splendid mares. With her head held high and her hair neatly braided, she would traipse into the hall, prance around, and be appraised. That was the fate that had been woven for her, and she ought to be excited about the position she would gain as the king's bride. Yet she felt neither happy nor sad. Sigrid chewed on her cheek, feeling the pain bring her closer to reality.

"If you marry Erik, I suppose we'll all have to grovel before you," Jorun said under her breath. Jorun had always dreamt of landing a rich husband and being mistress of her own farm, and she tried to pique the interest of every nobleman who came to the farm in the hope of ensnaring him.

"Remember that the Svea killed my mother," Sigrid replied. "The sweetness of power leaves a bitter taste."

"Oh, we've all lost someone. You're not alone in your anguish," Jorun responded, pursing her lips the way she did when she was really mad.

Sigrid stared blankly at the two kinswomen who were her maidservants. It was like they were blind to who she was and everything that had happened. They saw only their own dreams and aspirations. They didn't understand that Sigrid was no longer the person who had gone to her mother's burial mound the night before.

Vanadís had changed everything, and soon both her maidservants and her whole family would see that.

The marriage to Erik, with all its enticements of power and wealth, was the fate that the gods had chosen, and there was nothing that either Sigrid or anyone else could do about it. The only thing that had any meaning was the wonderful bliss she felt in the presence of the dísir and Freya. Everything else was shadows and light.

Sigrid sighed and looked at her two young maidservants.

"I'm doing this to prevent more people from dying, not out of desire or joy," she said. "Remember that."

Then she walked into the hall to join the feast.

◆ ◆ ◆

The men fell silent as Sigrid walked through the hall, her eyes locked on her father. He sat in the ornately carved seat of honor with the familial dynasty's two building staves, one on either side. All chieftains had their mark carved into the wood, and dragons curled around the names. Their ancestors stretched all the way back to Frey, who founded the dynasty at the dawn of time.

Sigrid's father, looking magnificent with his combed beard, blue shirt, and Frankish cloak, stood up and watched Sigrid with pride.

"Sit next to your father, my precious treasure," he said, gesturing toward the smaller seat on his left.

The men from Svealand followed every movement as Sigrid sat down, showing as much dignity as possible.

The older of the two men stood up and bowed slightly. His face was narrow behind his blond beard, and his eyes were alert yet kind. He wore a blue tunic with beautiful silver embroidery and a chain hung around his neck with a key on it.

"I am Axel," he said, introducing himself. "A kinsman of Erik Eriksson, the highly esteemed and beloved king of Svealand."

His delivery sounded different from what Sigrid was accustomed to, almost as if he were singing the words.

Axel nodded to his younger companion, who sat directly across the long table from him. He was a handsome fellow, his hair and complexion just as fair as Axel's, but he looked very strong, with broad shoulders.

"This is Orm, Erik's lead warrior and good friend."

The young man stood up. As he bowed, his face lit up with a smile.

"You are both welcome to Skagulheim," Sigrid said.

"We're honored to be here," Orm said. "Your beauty, extolled by many, is greater than anyone can do justice to."

Sigrid smiled to herself. The name *Orm* meant snake, so she supposed she ought to expect him to be a smooth talker with a serpentine tongue.

"A pretty face weathers with age," Sigrid replied. "Surely you seek more than mere beauty in my father's hall."

Orm's smile widened. He was truly handsome, with his blond beard and his broad shoulders, and she appreciated that he could ensnare both women and men with his slippery deceptions.

"True, but such a beautiful maiden as yourself is already more than King Erik had hoped for."

"Then maybe my father will be able to negotiate a bride price without difficulty," Sigrid said, nodding at her father, who seemed pleased at her dignified manner.

She leaned back in her chair and waved over a slave woman, who hurried forward with a tankard of mead. Sigrid took the mead and once again fixed her eyes on the two messengers.

"Tell us about your king," she requested.

The messengers exchanged surprised glances. Surely they had expected Toste's daughter to be foolish, but Sigrid was not planning to be sycophantic or overly dainty. Nor would she show the repugnance she harbored toward them. Tonight she was Freya, and she was not afraid of anything.

Axel spoke. "He is the most elegant man in Svealand, a good man, kind and just. No one has anything negative to say about Erik."

Now Sigrid knew for sure that they believed her feebleminded, a young maiden from the sticks who greedily gobbled up every word spoken and accepted it as true.

"Surely there are a few members of the Hafse clan in the North who do not hold your King Erik in such high regard, since you sent them to the afterworld and then burned their farms," she replied.

She shouldn't have said those words, but it was like they'd popped out of her mouth on their own. It was dead quiet in the hall for a moment, and then the men at the long table began to laugh. The warriors hit the table with their fists in approval.

Orm bowed first to the warriors who were his former enemies and then to Sigrid.

"Erik is a highly esteemed warrior. No one in Svealand is held in higher regard by chieftains or free men. He is victorious and fights with the courage of a bear. I am proud, as are the other warriors, to have given the eagles food at this great man's side."

There was no conciliatory spirit in the silence that spread through the hall now. Sigrid looked down into her mead and tried to swallow her rage. In her mother's name, she should slit the throat of this messenger for his swagger. And there wasn't a Scylfing man in the hall who wasn't thinking the same thing.

Axel stood up and with a gesture had Orm sit back down on the bench.

"I apologize for my companion's words. He speaks as the king's most loyal friend, and surely no one can fault him for being attached to his friends."

Sigrid nodded for him to proceed.

"What you say about the war is correct. Honorable vengeance has sent far too many to the afterworld. Entire clans have been killed in battles in Svealand as well. But there has never been any enmity between the Svea and the Scylfings. Like us, you are sons and daughters of Frey. We are kinfolk, not enemies."

His candor earned many nods of approval throughout the hall.

"Lovely Sigrid, both you and Erik are scions of the venerable Folkunga bloodline, and that is why I stand before you in this hall. Our king needs you as his peace queen. Then harmony and good can prevail once again."

Axel raised his tankard.

"It is said that the only thing greater than your beauty is your intelligence. Today I see that you are a queen in thought and action, and I speak for my king when I ask if you will marry King Erik and sit beside him on the throne of Svealand."

The words had been spoken now and could never be taken back. Sigrid drank some mead and leaned back in her chair, watching the men watching her. They all knew she had to say yes. All the same she couldn't do it here. To consent now would affect her bride price.

"Does your king honor the old ways?" she asked.

"Erik is sworn to Frey, and Svealand's king must host the sacrifice every year, otherwise he will be burned by the Thing. That is our law."

That was reassuring.

"Is he wealthy?"

Axel's face broke into a broad smile.

"There is no Svea who owns more."

Toste leaned forward and joined the conversation. "With her inheritance from her mother and with my gifts, my daughter owns eight farms and a hundred of land. She is to retain these, married or not. Will your king consent to this?"

The two messengers exchanged a glance.

"We can certainly promise that, but it will affect the bride price," Axel responded.

Let the negotiations about the cost of the mare begin. Sigrid suppressed a sigh as Toste ran his hand over his beard and pretended to be contemplating the issue.

"Forgive me, my beauty," Axel said and turned to Sigrid. "It was not my intention to bore you with men's talk."

She regarded him calmly. Everything going on in this hall was filled with lying, cheating, and maneuvering.

"The farms are mine, and I am the one guaranteeing the agreements that are made," she said.

Axel waved to one of his hirdmen who was standing by the wall holding a wooden box. The warrior hurried over to Sigrid and dropped down to his knee before her and then opened the lid of the box.

Sigrid looked down at the most beautiful piece of jewelry she'd ever seen, a half-moon–shaped disk of heavy silver inlaid with several rows of red stones. There was a beautiful pattern of intertwining dragons curling around each stone, with no beginning or end. Even the chain was formed of small figures, and the whole thing fastened by the sacred couple embracing each other.

Sigrid had never seen anything so ornate, but she carefully concealed her delight at the extravagant gift, surely worth several hundreds.

The warrior held up the necklace to Toste and the men at the long table.

"Thank your king," she said quietly, receiving approving looks from everyone for her self-control.

Axel smiled, and Sigrid could clearly tell that he wasn't fooled by her attempts to appear indifferent to the gift. The messenger cleared his throat and then spoke again.

"These are the words Erik asked me to deliver: *Nothing would please me more than to have you as my bride. I swear to respect and honor you.*"

Sigrid bit her lip to keep from laughing. Erik was not much of a poet. That much was now clear to everyone present.

"Perhaps the maidens of Svealand are driven out of their minds and into lovesick swoons by pretty words and beautiful jewelry, but I am a Scylfing daughter, and it will take more than that to woo me."

Toste had meticulously instructed her to be cunning in negotiations. Selling herself was like selling a horse or a slave. What someone was willing to pay determined everything. If you paid a high price for a filly from a good family, you would give her tender care and ample food so she could have strong, healthy offspring.

Combined with her father's and the rest of her family's property, Sigrid's wealth in land and farms included almost all of western Geatland. When Erik married her, he would control this land. Although she had to marry Erik, she knew he would value her more if her bride price were high.

Even now she could see that Axel and Orm regarded her with greater deference than when she had entered the hall. She had to make sure it stayed that way. It was the only way to get them to respect her.

Sigrid nodded graciously and said, "Your king is generous."

"We hope that he will also be your king," Orm replied ceremoniously.

The whole hall awaited her response now, and it was so quiet she could hear the mice breathing. Sigrid took a deep breath and slowly put down her mead cup. The power she held in her hands was unexpectedly agreeable.

Ulf looked quite exhilarated, as if he could already start celebrating his sister's becoming queen of Svealand. The warriors sat way down at the end of the long table. These men and many more would have to fight against Svealand if she didn't go through with the marriage.

"I'm pleased by what's been said of King Erik," she said and got up from her seat. "Now I will consider your words carefully before I give my response."

She left the hall with her head held high, feeling the floor sway beneath her feet. At least the proposal was over with now. Sigrid shivered and pushed aside her nagging sense of uneasiness.

She had to have faith.

I follow your will, Vanadís. If this is what you wish, I will follow your path.

X

"I hope they have a lot of silver behind those walls so I won't be freezing my nuts off for nothing," whispered Åke, who lay semirecumbent by Sweyn's side in the rain.

Sweyn gazed somberly up the hill where a stone church towered above them like a dark shadow in the rain. It had a yard on one side and a building surrounded by a wall on the other. At the bottom of the hill toward the ocean there were some farms but no sign of any people. Even the cattle were staying indoors to avoid the cold rain that lashed the fields.

Sweyn changed position, feeling the water soaking into his breeches and shoes. The thicket they were lying under did not provide much shelter. The rain bent the leaves down and soon his cloak felt like a wet hand on his back. And it didn't make him any happier that they were watching the only place they knew for sure that neither the king nor his men were.

Six ships, the Jómsvíkings' five dragon boats plus Alfred's ship, had sailed south to find the king of England and take revenge on him for Mikklavík. It was an audacious idea, almost insane given how few men they had, and therefore also glorious. If they managed to catch the king's hird off guard and kill King Edward, the Jómsvíkings' renown would grow, and they would be even more celebrated in song. A warrior couldn't wish for more.

They had tracked the king to Corfe Castle in Wessex. Palna had tasked Eyvind, one of the six ship captains, with watching the castle. After that he had assigned the warriors from his own ship to watch a monastery on the outskirts of the village, which they could raid to fill their coffers. The Jómsvíking leaders often gave the best assignments to the crews of the other ships to keep them loyal.

Since Sweyn and Åke were the youngest, they had to do the jobs no one else wanted. So they had been lying in the wet, staring up at the monastery forever, looking for signs of warriors and riches. The only thing that had happened so far was that two poor, scrawny figures had begged at the gate and a couple of religious men in long, gray tunics had entered the church.

"Pain and cold are bracing," Sweyn whispered, trying to think of something besides the wetness. Distraction was the only way to endure. He had certainly learned that.

"If the others go into battle without us, I don't know if I'll be able to stand it," said Åke.

Sweyn clenched his teeth to keep them from chattering.

A Jómsvíking had to be a man, and if he didn't behave as one he would take a vicious beating from his brothers. There were warriors who had lain still for days to get the lay of a place. Ax-Wolf was full of stories from his youth, like the one about Yng, who had frozen to death by his side without saying a word while they were watching a mountain pass near Tromsø.

Sweyn tightened his aching hands into fists and looked out at the hills undulating like waves of grass down to the sea. The English countryside spread its legs like a bawdy bitch to all who desired her. If Guthrum hadn't turned his back on the gods, this whole land could have belonged to the North.

Guthrum had unified the various Scandinavian chieftains into one kingdom, the Danelaw, and ruled almost all of Britannia. Only here in Wessex had King Alfred succeeded in holding the Scandinavians at bay, so Guthrum had brought his men here. The raid started out badly. The Danes lost 120 ships at Swanage, and then chieftains Ivar and Ubbe went home.

All the same Guthrum carried on and attacked Alfred's castle in Chippenham. But Alfred managed to get away, and even though he didn't have many warriors, he first conquered Guthrum's hird and then besieged the castle that had been taken from him.

Guthrum, King of the Danelaw, shamefully gave up after two weeks. He abandoned the old beliefs and allowed himself to be baptized. The Scandinavians' grip on the island had never been as strong again.

It was hard to fathom why Guthrum was so lacking in honor that he would first give up and then turn his back on the gods. A Jómsvíking should have fought to the death.

Sweyn twisted the oath ring on his arm. There were few things he was as proud of as what it represented. King Harald Bluetooth had built five ring fortresses and filled them with warriors who were sworn to defend the kingdom of the Danes and Jutes. Jómsborg was the most prominent of Harald's fortresses, and that was especially thanks to Palna, because there was no better fighter or more worthy leader than Sweyn's foster father.

Men came to Jómsborg from far and wide, filled with hopes and lofty opinions of their own fighting skills, but few were worthy of wearing Palna's oath ring. A Jómsvíking had to be equally skilled with the sword, ax, and spear. Some of them who came were too clumsy, others too frail since they had been sitting at long tables instead of running, swimming, and making their bodies strong. Many had to leave because they were weak of mind.

Sweyn twisted his oath ring again. He had fought, bled, and suffered since childhood to wear the oath ring. Never had he been as proud as when Palna gave him the ring, which qualified him as a full Jómsvíking. He had his foster father to thank for everything, and all he wanted was to one day prove himself worthy of Palna's faith in him.

The church bells started ringing in heavy, low peals that echoed through the roar of the rain. Then a low rumble was heard in the distance. Sweyn looked hopefully at the gray-black clouds and smiled as the noise of the sky chariots grew. Thor was here and his einherjar. The most faithful of the gods had arrived to stand by their side. There would soon be battle.

ᛈ

Te deum laudamus, te dominum confitemur.

The holy sisters prayed before the simple wooden cross. Their head coverings bobbed up and down and made them look like hatchlings popping up from a sea of stone.

Emma knelt at the very back of the church with the servants and waited for the prayers to end. Her legs ached from the cold floor and she was so tired it was hard to stay awake. Matins was the hardest of the day's seven fixed-hour prayers, and she still had a hard time getting up in the middle of the night to pray and then work the whole day after that, with prayers and mealtimes as the only breaks.

"To work is to serve God," Sister Hedvig used to say, and Emma was certainly forced to venerate him day and night.

When the prayer was over, she would go to the cookhouse and help prepare the first meal of the day. Then it was time to go to the building outside the walls where wayfarers were granted shelter for the night. After giving them water and a small piece of bread, she would sweep the dirt floor, spread out clean straw, and then hurry back for morning prayers and then proceed with the rest of the day's duties.

Emma looked at Jesus hanging on the cross. Sister Hedvig said Jesus had had mercy on her sinful soul and that work would drive the devil out of her body. It might take a lifetime of penance before her soul was cleansed of sin, and then she could receive the virgin's grace. Emma had been trying to make it come true, had been trying for almost a year. She suppressed another yawn and felt her sleepiness swallowing her up. Soon her head lolled forward.

She was startled awake when the prayers ended. Her legs ached as she stood up, and she took care not to touch any of the other servant girls as they followed mistress Gyrwynne out to start their daily work. She heard Megan whispering something to one of the other girls.

The gate in the wooden palisade that surrounded the nuns' dwelling house was a light shadow in the cold, gray morning. Rain splattered as they hurried shivering along the path, into the courtyard. Some of the girls pushed closer to Emma. Then Megan's smiling face popped up, right next to her.

"Devil's little whore-child," Megan whispered and pinched Emma's breast, hard—quickly so that mistress Gyrwynne wouldn't see anything.

Emma slipped in the mud but didn't let on how much it hurt.

Megan sneered, like a demon with her wet hair plastered to her rosy cheeks. None of them hated Emma more than she did.

"I'm going to drive the devil out of you tonight," she said.

The other girls stared at them, fully expecting to see Megan strike Emma with her cane and force her to crawl on the ground in humiliation.

Emma swallowed. She should kill Megan, by stabbing a knife into her face until it was a bloody pulp, and then pee on the wound. But that would be a sin and she would burn for all eternity for it.

Her heart pounded harder in her chest. If she could only get out of here! Sometimes she studied the wayfarers who stopped at the guest-house and hoped that one of them would take care of her, but they were all just as poor as she was. Failed crops and food shortages had driven many people onto the roads. If Emma left the nunnery, she would surely starve to death.

"Leave me alone," Emma said, looking up at Megan for the first time.

Megan made a face and continued to taunt Emma. "You may have fooled the sisters, but I see what you are: a filthy whore. I see the devil in you."

Emma pushed a lock of wet hair out of her face.

The rain had already soaked through her shoes and dress. Now she was going to be cold for the rest of the day.

"If the devil was in me, I would have sent you to hell."

Before Megan could respond, mistress Gyrwynne called that she was going to get the vegetables. Megan ran into the warm cookhouse. Emma watched her disappear and then went to fetch some firewood.

A year earlier as she had walked up the hill to the nunnery for the first time, Emma thought she had arrived in heaven. A monk named William had taken mercy on her when she was begging in the streets. Her owner, Acca, had beaten her up earlier that same evening because Emma had pleaded with him not to offer her body to men that night. When the monk saw her wounds and swollen face, he gave in and brought her to the nuns in the hope that they could save her soul.

Emma went to the woodshed and started loading the basket with pieces of wood.

The monastery was by a village near a castle on a hill overlooking the water, and was much bigger than she'd imagined. On one side was the monks' big building, protected behind high stone walls. The nunnery was smaller and made of wood, surrounded by a simple wooden palisade. The stone church sat between them.

On that first day, Sister Hedvig had brought Emma to the cookhouse and seen that she was given food and a place on the floor to sleep. Since then Emma had worked very hard to pray to Jesus Christ the savior. It wasn't so bad in the beginning. The other servant girls shunned her, but she had a roof over her head, received food every day, and no longer had to raise her skirts to all the men Acca sold her services to. She'd been given a new frock and a head-cloth that completely hid her hair, and the work tired her out so much that she didn't have nightmares anymore. It would have been all right if it hadn't been for Megan. Emma had received the first surreptitious pinch last winter and since then things had grown worse and worse. Emma was used to being beaten, and the men who had groaned and emptied themselves into her had sometimes hit her, but to have a girl just a few years older than herself harassing her was more than she could bear.

She prayed to Jesus and Mary for help, and sometimes when no one was listening she prayed to the gods she had prayed to as a child, to Thor and Freya. So far none of them had responded.

Her back ached when she lifted the full firewood basket and carried it across the muddy courtyard into the warmth of the cookhouse. Mistress Gyrwynne was kneading dough. Megan sat on a footstool peeling turnips and sneered malevolently when Emma stepped in.

Emma set the basket by the oven and put some wood on the fire.

A curse on that fat Megan and her fingers.

The flames leapt up with a crackle. She ought to set fire to the cookhouse and then see how the flames devoured the monastery with a roar. Megan would scream in pain as her skin burst. She would bellow until her lips turned black. This place was hell on earth, so why shouldn't they all burn now?

"Don't sit there dawdling," mistress Gyrwynne yelled.

Emma jumped and stood up. Soon she would let the flames take the nunnery. This plan took root in her breast and filled her with joy. Soon they would die and she would finally be free. Emma giggled and hurried back out to the woodshed.

H

The night was auspiciously dark, concealing the six ships where they hid in the bay. Sweyn had made his way back and now stood at his foster father, Palna's side on Ranfaxe's prow and listened for the last scouts. Åke, Ax-Wolf, and the others stood behind them, at the ready. If they brought good news about King Edward, the attack would begin. Sweyn rested his hand on the hilt of his sword and squeezed it hard. He had made his offering to Thor and prayed for the opportunity to cut down England's king. He hoped Thor would grant him that favor. Hope was all he could do, for the moment.

The ship rocked beneath their feet, and the only sound was the soft lapping of the waves. No one said a word. Rán's treacherous daughters could carry sound far, and the enemy must not be forewarned. Like Mjölnir the Jómsvíkings preferred to strike without warning. Finally a faint splash was heard, and dark shadows waded toward them from the beach. The archers had already pulled back their bowstrings, watching the scouts closely until they climbed aboard. Palna waited impatiently for the three men to catch their breath.

Finally one of them, Stigbjörn, looked up at Palna.

"The king was murdered yesterday at Corfe Castle. The dowager queen stuck a sword in him herself. His retinue left the castle, and there aren't any noblemen or warriors left."

Sweyn made a face. Damn her for usurping his chance at honor and revenge now that they had finally found King Edward. They were just as late getting here as they had been at Mikklavík.

He could tell Palna was dissatisfied in the darkness. They all needed this battle. The ship's warriors already bore the valkyries in their chests, and they demanded blood.

"Where is the queen?" whispered Palna.

"Even she has fled, inland with her son," replied Axe, one of the scouts.

"By the dripping poison of Loki," Palna swore.

Whispered grumblings could be heard behind Sweyn. He knew the other men were just as frustrated as he was.

Palna rubbed the back of his neck and peered out at the water before facing his men.

"What's at the church?" he asked.

Sweyn grinned. So, his shivering in the bushes hadn't been in vain.

"Besides the nunnery there are two noblemen's estates, three smaller houses, and a village next to the bay," Sweyn reported. He drew the positions of the buildings as he spoke. "There are plenty of spoils."

"Soldiers?" Palna asked.

"Of the capable ones, no more than thirty."

Sweyn held his breath while Palna thought it over and then nodded.

"Spread the word," Palna announced. "We will go toward the monastery and attack when we reach the beach. I will go first with my men. The plunder is free for the taking."

Sweyn nodded eagerly. *Finally.*

"Oars in the water," Gunnar ordered and raised his arm and then released the dragon boat over the dark water.

Palna put his hands on Sweyn's and Åke's shoulders and said, "Remember this when you are leading men into battle. If you don't release the wolves to take their plunder, they start to bite each other. And the first one they turn on is the one leading them."

Sweyn nodded and looked expectantly at the lights in the bay.

"Are you ready?" Palna said.

Sweyn's mouth felt dry. This would be his first real battle. At the other two, he had fought in the rear echelon, against enemies already weak with injuries. Now he and Åke would follow Father in the lead, against proper warriors, sword to sword.

"You've trained us well, Father," Åke responded. "Well, me anyway. Things might not go quite as well for my brother here." He laughed tensely.

"I'll show you what I'm worth," Sweyn said.

This was his fate. He had been born screaming to Thor to let him fight and now it would happen.

Sweyn checked his armor, ax, and pants over and over before he put on his helmet. May Thor give his arm strength. His heart pounded as Ranfaxe slid through the water toward land like a noiseless spear. His sword was still clutched in his sweat-dampened hand, and the power of Thor streamed through his body. Soon the valkyries' hunger would be sated with blood and death.

Åke stood by his side, manly. His face was pale in the moonlight. A drop of sweat ran from his brow. Sigvard smiled quietly and placed one hand on the gunwale. He had fought the most battles of them all, and he entered them now with the same ease as if he were on his way to a feast.

The warriors stood silently behind them on the boat. Brothers-in-arms were brothers-in-arms.

In the moonlight behind them the dragon ships raced over the water. You could not find more lethal warriors in the world than the Jómsvíkings.

Palna stood on the prow with a piece of Osmund's bloody cloak tied around his arm. Tonight they would take revenge for what had been done to the chieftain of Mikklavík. Tonight the souls of the dead would be liberated so they could travel to the afterworld.

Silent oar strokes pulled them toward shore. The village lay silent, no movement visible among its buildings. Palna raised his sword, warning that the attack would happen soon.

"Cut the back of the legs. Slice the tendons so they can't run away," Ax-Wolf said softly behind Sweyn.

A moment later, Ranfaxe touched bottom. Palna lowered his sword, and as one body all the warriors flung themselves over the gunwale, waded through the water, and ran toward the houses.

A watchman spotted them and started screaming, a shrill howl that roused the entire village. Sweyn pulled the ax from his belt, weighing it in his hand. He measured the distance with his eyes and threw.

It was a clean hit. The blade struck the back of the watchman's head, and he keeled over dead. Sweyn heard the valkyries' shrill shrieks in his head as he strode over and pulled his ax back out of the man's head.

"Good throw, little guy," Ax-Wolf called to him.

Sweyn smiled at Åke, who slapped him on the shoulder. Then they ran onward. They heard battle sounds from the men from the other ships. The local men approached, running through the darkness with axes and pitiful little knives. Ax-Wolf and Sigvard rushed toward them with a roar.

Sweyn dispatched his opponent with ease. He deflected the man's ax with his shield and swiftly struck him on the back so he sank down. Then Sweyn raised his sword and lopped off the man's head. Two down. Quickly he turned around. Åke had already killed his opponent, while Ax-Wolf and Sigvard were fighting side by side next to a larger house. Without exchanging a word, Sweyn and Åke ran over to join them. Sword against sword, they howled out their rage.

When the last of the enemy was killed and lay dead on the ground, Sweyn heard Sigvard cry out. The warrior was pointing to a body, signaling with the death cry that one of their own had fallen. Alfred lay on the ground. He had come to avenge his father and family and had himself gone to join his ancestors.

"It was an honorable death," Ax-Wolf said, bowing his head in respect.

Warriors from sly captain Ingolf's ship kicked down a door, and they all pushed their way into a large hall. The men who awaited them there rushed toward them, axes raised. Every death cry, every cry of pain filled Sweyn more with battle fervor. The warriors were black shadows in the darkness. He cut down everything that moved. He parried with his shield, dodged, and struck again and again.

Then everything grew quiet. With a hammering heart, Sweyn lowered his sword and wiped the sweat from his brow while searching for his men.

Åke was ransacking a chest with an insane smile on his face. Since the men were dead on the dirt floor, everything was theirs for the taking. There was no honor in plundering living men. Ax-Wolf tipped over tables and chairs, searching for any more cross worshippers to slay. Sigvard dragged out a woman who screamed and tried to hide. He slit her throat with a laugh. The woman died with a rattling gurgle. More women sat huddled in a corner. Screaming and whimpering, they attempted to hide children and half-grown boys.

Sweyn raised his sword. He had killed eight, more than he had hoped, but it wasn't over yet. The time for pillaging was not yet here.

"Take the slaves," Sweyn said to two warriors from Ingolf's hird.

After that Sweyn raised his sword and bellowed out his lust for battle.

"Onward!" he yelled.

Åke, Ax-Wolf, and Sigvard dropped everything and ran to the door. Like a pack of wolves they ran side by side, looking for more fighting.

✝

"Take cover! Take cover!"

Emma set down the bucket of water and walked out into the courtyard.

Sister Hedvig and three other nuns hurried toward the church. They were yelling for everyone to follow them. Mistress Gyrwynne and Megan ran toward the gates along with the servant girls. Then the church bells began to ring.

Her heart pounding, Emma saw the women running across the muddy courtyard while the hens flapped their wings and scattered in every direction and the pigs squealed anxiously in their pen. Liberation from purgatory had arrived. The deep chiming of the bells filled the dawn.

Emma looked at her hands, permanently stained with dirt and covered in calluses, and smiled in astonishment. The moment she had so fervently wished for had finally arrived. The angels of death would send Megan to hell where she would burn screaming for her sins. They would be slaughtered like animals and consumed by flames.

Emma jumped when Sister Elfrida grabbed her hand.

"Come, child. God will protect us," the elderly nun said and pulled her toward the doors.

They could hear screams and battle cries coming from the village. Several houses had been set on fire, and two horses galloped away across the meadows in a panic. People were running up the hill, looking for protection. Women with babies in their arms, children, and old people rushed into the church, shaking and crying.

"They're killing everyone. They're killing children. How can they kill children?" cried a woman with a bloody gash on her arm.

Emma could hardly believe it. Six ships had landed on the beach by the bay. Her heart was pounding so hard she could scarcely breathe.

She grabbed a girl whose face was black and blue, her dress bloody at the crotch.

"Are they Vikings?" she screamed.

"They're demons! They're killing everyone," the girl cried.

The girl pulled free and pushed her way into the church. It was far too crowded in there for everyone to fit, and screams echoed inside the stone walls. Emma's legs trembled as she eagerly watched the dark wave of doom washing toward them. The stench of fear and urine stung in her nose. Soon it would be over.

"Seek shelter in the chapel," one of the monks shouted.

Sister Hedvig extended her hand to Emma.

"Help me protect our flock," she said and gestured to a group of women to follow her.

Emma grabbed hold of two elderly women and followed the nun. They ran into the monastery, past a garden to a little building that was half-sunk into the ground. The monk William, who had brought her to the monastery, stood by the door.

"Take shelter here. God will protect you."

He helped an older woman down into the darkness, and a woman followed her with a child in her arms and another holding her hand.

Soon villagers were pushing to get in. Emma backed away a couple of steps as the aversion in her grew.

This was no place to seek shelter. A prickling premonition shivered through her body.

"Go to God's house, my lamb. God will protect you there," the old monk Ambrosius called, showing still more people into the darkness.

His eyes glistened with glory, and suddenly Emma knew she had to run.

She took another few steps backward, to the cloister behind the colonnade that ran along the building, and then turned around. Behind an open door she saw the monks running around in a hall, their arms full of papers, goblets, and candlesticks made of gold and silver. They ran toward a wall and then disappeared into an opening in it.

A moment later, a pair of strong arms grabbed her. Ambrosius and another monk, a fat stranger, dragged her toward the little house.

"You have to take shelter!"

Emma fought for her life. She kicked and bit their hands, but they didn't let her go.

"We're all going to die. Soon we will wander in paradise," Emma whimpered. Again she tried to break free of the two men, but she couldn't.

"We'll protect you, child," Ambrosius said, and they dragged her down the steps to the chapel and shoved her into the darkness.

Emma tripped and fell flat on the dirt floor. No sooner was she on her feet than the door was bolted behind her.

"No! Let me out!" she screamed.

"Quiet," a voice urged softly. "You'll lure them here with your noise."

Emma turned around, her pulse ringing in her head like the church bells outside. Sister Hedvig stood beside a stone altar in the little chapel. Women and children crouched on the floor around her. A few men rocked back and forth as they prayed. There was a narrow opening over the nun's head that let in a tiny bit of daylight. It was too small for Emma to escape through. The ceiling was sturdily built from wooden beams and straw. She was trapped. On the verge of fainting, she sank to the floor with her back to the door.

The church bells had stopped ringing. Even the smallest of the children were quiet, sitting in their mothers' laps. Like gray shadows they waited in the darkness while Sister Hedvig knelt before the altar and prayed to God.

Then they heard a woman's shrill scream, which stopped abruptly.

Fear was like an icy hand. It was all her fault. She was the one who had wished fire and death upon these poor people, and now she was going to die with them. The Vikings would kick open the door any minute and slaughter them. Emma joined Sister Hedvig's whispered prayers.

"Holy Mary, Mother of God. Pray for us sinners now in our hour of death."

There was nothing she could do, nowhere to escape to. They heard sword strike sword outside. Men's death cries fell suddenly silent. Sister Hedvig crossed herself and then stood up with a bundle in her hand. Her face was calm and there was no fear in her eyes. She serenely pulled out three knives and passed them out to the mothers around her.

"Go to God with strength. Spare the children from being violated before they ascend to paradise."

Crying, one mother put the knife to her daughter's throat. The girl couldn't have been more than three or four, but she still screamed for her life when she felt the metal against her throat.

"Don't do it," Emma cried.

The woman started to sob. Then she dropped the knife on the floor and hugged her daughter.

"Let go of your fear, Emma," Sister Hedvig said. "Rejoice and surrender yourself into God's embrace." Her voice was calm and peaceful.

They heard a crackling sound, and smoke started to find its way in through the roof. The building was on fire. Soon they would be engulfed in the flames. Crying, Emma curled up in a corner. God was punishing her for wishing fire and death on the people here. Now she was going to burn with them.

Sister Hedvig stood by the altar with her hands held high. Her face, with the yellow eyes of a demon, was contorted. She laughed at the people's death screams, licked her lips with a long snake tongue. And suddenly Emma understood. This monastery was the devil's work. These holy, noble people were demons who lured in innocent souls in order to devour them. Rage grew inside her.

"I curse your false God!" she screamed.

The fire had taken true hold of the roof now. Flames were spreading over them. Sister Hedvig smiled serenely as she lifted the candle from the altar and threw it at the straw, which immediately flamed up with a roar.

"And I curse you, you devil!" Emma screamed.

The demon disguised in false piety had lured them all to their death. One woman stood up screaming and tried to put out the fire but the others remained seated, paralyzed, as the smoke curled around them.

Damn these Christians and their faith in God. Damn the heretics.

"I reject God, Jesus, and the Holy Spirit!" Emma cried and then coughed until she was in tears. The heat was starting to become unbearable, and sweat poured down her body. "Hear me, gods of my forefathers, help your daughter," she yelled.

Around her, people screamed as they caught on fire. Many of them crowded around the little window, trying in vain to get out.

Wheezing, Emma inhaled the smoke and screamed again: "May the gods help me! I demand it in the name of my ancestors!"

That very instant she felt a peculiar silence envelop her. The screaming and the noise of battle and the all-consuming flames disappeared.

Emma was floating in a peaceful darkness where there was neither heaven nor earth. Here there was no dread, no fear, no sin or joy. There was only time spiraling slowly onward through infinity.

She was rescued. Like an unborn baby she rested in the safety of her mother as the infinite pulse rocked her to settle her and filled her with a blessed tranquility.

"My child," said a strange voice, so barbarous and powerful that infinity was shaken to its core.

A female being hovered in front of Emma, dazzlingly radiant in shimmering light and terrible in the power emanating from her in heavy waves.

Emma drank in this power. Brutally it filled her, penetrating deep into her soul. Like a fire it burned away what she had been and was going to become. Then the being opened its mouth and transformed everything into a roaring boom that flung Emma screaming back into the chaos between life and death.

I

The oaks whispered greetings as Sigrid walked through the unfamiliar woods. Beams of sunlight pierced the canopy of leaves like golden spears, and her dísir, almost completely transparent in the light, hovered at her side and urged her to follow them. Sigrid smiled at the playful creatures, sheer as air, and let them lead her deeper into the trees.

Soon she stood at the edge of a glade and watched a man pick up a little boy, not more than a couple of years old, and spin him around and around so he was hiccupping with laughter.

The man grinned at the boy's delight. This man was young, not much older than she was, and had the broad shoulders of a warrior. His angular chin and piercing eyes were so familiar to her, as if she'd always known who he was and had always longed for him. Sigrid smiled at the man. He was hers; she knew that now.

He set the child down on the ground and ruffled his hair so lovingly that Sigrid felt a twinge. Then he pointed to her while whispering something to the child.

The boy's face lit up in a smile and he ran toward Sigrid on his wobbly legs. His little feet were bare under his yellow frock, his hair so blond it was almost white.

Sigrid squatted down and held out her arms to the child. *My son,* she thought, her heart aching with love. *You will be the greatest of kings. Your name will echo throughout the whole world and will be remembered until the end of time.*

Oh, how she longed to hold that soft, warm body in her arms. The ache burned in her body. But the child stopped before he reached her outstretched arms and looked at her seriously.

"Be careful, Mother. They want to kill you."

Sigrid sat up in bed, her heart pounding. It was only a dream, no matter how real it felt. In the early dawn light she could just make out her kinswomen sleeping in their beds. The bearskin in front of the fire, the clothing chests sitting by the wall, the embroidered tapestries hanging on the wall. Everything was the way it usually was.

Even if it was just a dream, it had brought with it a warning. Sigrid's face was damp with sweat when she ran her hands over her cheeks. Her head ached from all her thoughts, hopping around like a flock of fleeing frogs. It used to be that almost nothing ever happened and her days were full of boredom. Now there was so much happening she was at her wits' end.

Sigrid took a deep breath and lay down on the bed's feather bolster. She needed to rein in her mind and her thoughts, trust in Vanadís, and not wander around like a chicken with its head cut off.

A fly buzzed in the wooden rafters as she forced herself to breathe calmly. Her heartbeat slowed as her thoughts settled and the meaning of the dream became clear.

The dream was a sign that Vanadís wanted her to marry Erik. That had to be it. Sigrid ran her fingers through the warm fur by her belly and felt anticipation flash through her body. Svealand's king was better-looking than she'd expected. She smiled at the memory of his laughter as he played with the child, their son, the boy who would be the king of kings.

He is your gift. Thank you for the sign you granted me, and for your warning.

Sigrid's smile faded. The child said someone wanted to kill her, but this wasn't the first time that someone had hoped to snuff out Sigrid's life.

With you protecting me, I am not afraid.

The daughter of the Scylfing chieftain had many enemies, and none of them had managed to kill her so far, despite their attempts.

Life was fragile, and living meant fighting to remain in this world. Sigrid had seen two younger brothers and a sister come into this world, and she had loved and protected them. The sister and one of the brothers had fallen ill and wasted away from natural causes. Neither of them had made it to their first birthday.

After the Svea had burned their house and her mother and her remaining younger brother had died in the flames, the neighbors had found Sigrid alive, crying in the courtyard. She would never stop wondering why she alone had made it out, and the others had perished.

She got out of bed and dressed angrily, determination taking root in her chest. Just let them come, the enemies, forces of darkness, and traitors; they would not manage to kill her so easily. If she'd learned anything, it was that she must fight for her life.

The outdoor gallery was dark as she walked down the stairs to the hall, where kinsmen and servants were still sleeping on the benches lining the wall. The door creaked faintly as she snuck out into the courtyard and hurried over to the outhouse.

At the hill of the gods, in the temple to Thor, the priest was blowing on his horn welcoming a day of peace and good crop growth. Cattle lowed and sheep bleated as slaves drove them out to pasture for the day.

Dogs barked in the distance, probably out hunting with Strutulf. Sigrid pulled her dress back down and exited the outhouse.

The aromas from the oven drew her to the cookhouse, where Allvis and her slaves were preparing the first meal of the day.

Axel, the tall stranger from Svealand, sat eating on the bench outside the cookhouse, a piece of bread in one hand and a bowl of milk in the other. He quickly got to his feet when he spotted her.

"I hope you slept well."

"Very well," she lied. Sigrid had very little desire to talk to the Svea warrior.

With a courteous nod, she entered the little building where Allvis was baking flatbread over the fire.

A servant noticed her and, wiping sweat from her flushed face, held out a bowl containing a whole pile of cooling freshly baked rolls and buns.

"I can bring you some honey if you'd like," the servant said and poured milk, still warm from the cow, into a cup.

Sigrid shook her head and took a bite of the bread. Then she left the warmth of the cookhouse and returned to the cool morning air.

"It can't be easy marrying the man responsible for your mother's death," Axel said thoughtfully as she walked by him. "In your eyes we must be brutes."

Sigrid stopped and looked at the messenger in surprise.

"I lost my son Ivar to a Geatish sword last summer," Axel continued. "He was my pride, and grief still keeps me awake at night."

"May he enjoy Valhalla," she said softly.

His son would have lived if he'd stayed away from their land.

"Ivar died at his farm in Svealand when he was bringing in the hay. The Hafse clan came through the woods seeking to avenge a victory the Svea had previously had in their lands. No side is without blame in this war."

Axel's voice was low and sad. Sigrid suddenly had a hard time swallowing.

He continued: "I wanted to avenge his death when my king asked me to come here and seek peace and a wife among the Scylfings. And so now here we stand. I wanted to tell you that I understand better than most if you're not completely thrilled to travel north with us."

Sigrid sat down on the bench and eyed the Svea messenger warily. His words were frank and clever, and if he had traveled all the way here to propose to her for his king he had no reason to wrong her. To the contrary his job was to protect her life. Sigrid decided to trust him. She needed a friend in Svealand and now that she knew that Vanadís wanted her to marry, she was more than curious about her husband-to-be.

"Tell me about Erik. And tell me the truth without any smooth talk or ballads about heroic deeds."

Axel laughed softly and set his cup of milk on the bench.

"He's maybe fifteen years older than you, skillful in battle, and strong the way a Svea king must be. And he values honor foremost in both women and men. If Erik decides to do something, he will do it in the most manly way. Few can resist his will once he's decided on something."

Sigrid smiled, imagining Erik. In her dream he had been the same age as her, but aside from that she could certainly believe that everything Axel said fit. He would be the father of her son. The tenderness she felt for the child still ached in her heart. Everything would be fine. They were meant to be together.

The door to Toste's great hall creaked, and Åse came hurrying across the courtyard to the women's building. She was still Toste's favorite mistress even though she was starting to get old. Normally, when one of the mistresses had a child, it would be left out in the woods to die, but Toste had adopted their little girl. He even still occasionally shared his bed with Åse. His devotion to her pleased Sigrid very much.

"How many mistresses does Erik have?" she asked.

Axel smiled slightly.

"Two that I know of, and he has two children with one of them. The mistresses don't measure up to you in any way, either in lineage or beauty. I've known Erik since he was a boy, and I know that he'll be captivated by your beauty and strength."

Sigrid nodded. She'd never had any feelings for a man and had a hard time understanding the fawning lack of sense that overcame Jorun and Alfhild whenever they looked at handsome warriors. She couldn't fathom why they strutted around for them, putting on fake voices.

"I will be satisfied if your king honors me," she said. Sigrid already knew her own worth.

Axel shook his head and clicked his tongue disapprovingly.

"Never say such a thing. The wife of Svealand's king must always demand the best."

They smiled at each other and now Sigrid knew for sure that this messenger was her friend. Their moment together was interrupted when Ulf called to her. Her brother came across the courtyard in rapid steps.

"The old folks want you to come," he said.

"It was fruitful speaking with you of war and mistresses," Sigrid told Axel, smiling slightly at Ulf's astonishment.

Axel stood up and bowed to Sigrid.

"It's my pleasure to serve you," he said.

After that Sigrid walked to the great hall.

"War and mistresses?" her brother asked, raising his eyebrows. His eyes looked tired under his leather hood. After the night's feast, his face was just as swollen as his gut. Sigrid smiled but didn't respond to the question.

"Is *everyone* gathered?" she asked. She didn't relish facing the old folks and listening to their nagging, especially if Toste's wife was going to be there.

"Yes," Ulf said with a nod. "And she's already dripped poison into several ears."

They stopped by the door and exchanged glances.

"Father is going to disown her," Ulf said. "She hasn't given him any children."

"That won't help you or me this morning," Sigrid replied and opened the door.

Father sat at the long table, his head hanging, looking red and bloated but cheerful after the evening's revelry, celebrating the conclusion of several days of negotiations.

"The Svea are pleased with you, and the bride price they offered is better than what I'd planned to request," he said happily.

Toste's brother Björn grunted in satisfaction from where he sat shoveling porridge into his mouth from a bowl, his long hair hanging around his face. Grandmother sat down at the end of the table surrounded by the women of the estate. Like a flock of birds, dressed in gray, aged but with the sharpest of tongues, they watched Sigrid attentively as she approached the long table. Gunlög stood among them. She kept to the background, but Sigrid knew that was just an act.

"What did you pay?" Sigrid asked her father, sitting down on the bench across from him.

Toste shook his head as if he could hardly believe it was true.

"One hundred—Skogsvík up by the border to Norrskogen, the worst land we have."

Sigrid could not help but smile. Erik must really need the Scylfings if he wasn't demanding more.

"Can I keep my hereditary estates if he and I separate?" she asked.

"Yes, and all the gifts you're given." Toste ran his hand over his curly beard, just as blond as the hair on his head. His eyes gleamed with his eagerness to marry her off to the king of the Svea, but even if the matter was settled, Sigrid wasn't planning to bend completely.

"Can I take my children with me if I leave him?" she asked calmly. She was going to be mother to the king of kings, so she had to protect her son.

Toste's smile vanished. Clearly this hadn't occurred to him.

"Are you thinking about leaving your husband before you've even met him?" her uncle Björn muttered.

"The law of the Geats says that my children are mine until the age of seven," Sigrid said. "That must be part of the agreement. Father, if you do not protect my rights, I plan to do so myself."

Her grandmother chuckled contentedly at her impertinence, but the old folks behind her started whispering.

"It's bad luck to talk about such things. She will bring ill fortune upon herself," one of them said.

"Yes, a maiden mustn't haggle over her own bride price as if she were shopping at the market," another said.

Toste pretended not to hear and merely shrugged.

"It's a reasonable request," he said. "I'll see that it is as you wish."

Sigrid nodded. Her father was usually never this communicative about negotiations. He must have really enjoyed having Åse in his bed last night.

"This is not going to go well," cried old Yrsa in her creaky voice. She stood up with difficulty and looked around. Thin gray wisps of hair clung to her gaunt face, and her saggy jowls hung like sacks around her toothless mouth. "The wench is wild as a two-year-old on slippery ice. She will never manage to become a dignified queen; she'll bring shame and misfortune to the Scylfings. You mark my word."

Sigrid sighed as several of the other old folks agreed with Yrsa. Now the laments began.

"Do not speak about things you have no knowledge of!" Toste's wife Gunlög scolded. She turned around and gave the old folks an angry look. Only then did Gunlög step forward to stand behind Toste and say, "Perhaps this does require more consideration. Sigrid is a wild little girl who runs around barefoot in the woods and thinks goddesses are talking to her. Jorun is older and seems a better choice for queen."

You treacherous snake. Don't think I don't know who incited Yrsa's and the other old folks' complaints!

Sigrid gritted her teeth. Ever since she realized that Sigrid did not bend to the will of others, Gunlög had been trying to thwart her.

"Maybe you ought to have your own child and be quiet about things that only affect my father and the Scylfing family," said Sigrid. That jab hit its mark. Gunlög pouted and stepped back. The old folks patted her arm, but Toste drank from his cup and pretended yet again not to have heard.

"They want Sigrid, not Jorun," Toste said.

"The matter is decided and won't be discussed any further," Sigrid's grandmother said, not seeming displeased that Gunlög had been reprimanded. "When will the festivities occur?"

Toste looked away. His mother eyed him for a long time.

"They want us to travel to Svealand immediately," he finally admitted.

"That's insane!" Grandmother shouted, hitting the table with her fist, making everyone in the hall jump. "She's not ready to get married. The maid has neither clothing nor dowry chest. We haven't even held her blood party."

Toste cringed at his mother's anger, but shrugged.

"Those were their terms, that we leave at once."

"Clothes don't matter. In this case something else is more important," Sigrid said, calmly regarding her father and her grandmother. "In her mercy, our lady Vanadís sent me a warning in a dream last night. It warned that someone wanted to kill me."

Björn raised his chin from his porridge and stared blankly at her through his long hair. The elders whispered among themselves while Toste shook his head in concern.

"Warning dreams must be taken seriously," he said. "Each and every one of us knows that, just as we know that that oathbreaker Anund has much to gain from your death. If you die, the Scylfings cannot conclude their transaction with Svealand, and that swine Anund would be pleased if he succeeded in killing Erik's queen."

Sigrid bit her cheek. Then it was as she'd thought.

"We must thank Freya for her warning," Toste said. He leaned across the table and took Sigrid's hand. "We will be traveling with our hirdmen, many strong warriors, who will protect you with their swords. If I must, I will watch over you day and night and make sure you do not meet your mother's fate."

Sigrid saw how serious her father was, and she did not doubt for a second that he would give his life for her.

"If the children are brought into the agreement, I will marry King Erik," she replied.

"I told you the girl would do her duty, did I not?" Grandmother mumbled, relieved.

Her father's face broke into a grin and he squeezed her hand so hard it hurt.

"Thank you. You will be the most prominent member of our family."

Sigrid smiled acceptingly at her father. Now that she had seen her destiny in the dream, she knew that he was right. A great destiny awaited her.

"I think not just the most prominent in our family, Father. I will be the greatest queen in this world and the next."

Because I know this is your will, Vanadís.

Ax-Wolf swung his long-shafted ax at a Saxon, who skittered out of the way. Sword in hand, the soldier was not young. He was experienced in battle, judging by the scar just visible under the dirt on his face. Yet he did not notice he was being driven toward the wall, where Ax-Wolf would soon end the game.

Next to him, Ax-Wolf's brother Sigvard killed a warrior with one sword thrust to the belly. He twisted the blade and watched calmly as the warrior died.

Sweyn looked around. The band of armed men that awaited them at the monastery was far too small for these Vikings. They needed more men to send to the afterworld. Sweyn stood by an outlying farm surrounded by a high wall of black stone. There was a gate behind him and in front of him a large two-story stone building. Palna and his warriors had already entered it, and more men followed him.

A passage ran between the building and the wall, wide enough for two men to walk down it side by side. Several people could hide in there.

"Follow me," Sweyn yelled, running toward the passage with his three brothers-in-arms.

They emerged into a little yard in front of a stable. Two guards deserted a gate in the wall, fleeing toward the barn.

Screaming, Sweyn overtook one of the soldiers with his sword raised. The fear showed in the man's face as he leaned forward with his ax to block the bite of Sweyn's blade. The counterblow came at Sweyn's throat and he batted it away easily with his shield. Before the sound of iron hitting wood had faded, Sweyn slashed his sword at the warrior's leg, and it sliced deep into the flesh.

The man sank to his knees shrieking, and Sweyn slashed at his throat. The blade penetrated halfway through the man's neck and he fell to the ground, where he twitched, made a rattling sound, and then died.

"Sixteen!" he boasted to Åke who pulled his ax out of the other guard's skull, his eyes gleaming with victory. This was going better than he expected.

"Ten," Åke said petulantly. He knew he would never catch up now.

Ax-Wolf stepped over to the body of the guard Sweyn had just brought down, looked him over, and grunted.

"Not a clean chop," Ax-Wolf commented.

"And yet dead all the same," Sweyn said, wiping the sweat from his brow and looking wearily at his teacher.

"If he'd had any fighting skill, he'd have gone for your heart. You should have cut the leg like I told you. You also should have sliced his head off in one blow, considering your arm strength."

Sweyn shot Åke a cross look. Ax-Wolf the giant never complained about Åke's battle skills. All the same, Sweyn had to concede that Ax-Wolf was right. He could have fought better.

The gate their dead opponents had been guarding opened. Sigvard raised his hand to them and yelled, "Follow me!"

They ran through the gate, into a garden. On one side rose the wall and on the other side there was a colonnade running along a residential building where the Vikings had already started their slaughter. At the far end a fire raged, and death screams could be heard from the flames.

Ever vigilant, Sweyn walked past the stone benches, around a pond that was surrounded by bushes shaped like birds or crosses.

"Be on your guard for the priests," Ax-Wolf warned. "Some are mighty gods who can cloud people's minds and make them obey their words." Then he set off toward the fire.

A fat monk was kneeling in front of a little stone house, half sunken into the ground. The roof was on fire. The flames had spread to the rafters. Singing could still be heard from inside the building, but soon it was interrupted by coughing and screaming.

Sweyn shook his head, baffled.

"They're burning themselves?" he asked in genuine surprise.

Ax-Wolf pulled the monk to his feet. He was a fat, bald little man who struggled in terror, like a trapped animal in his fist, saying something in a foreign language. Then the monk started laughing like a fool and stretched his hands to the sky.

Someone was pounding on the door from inside the little stone building. Thicker smoke rose from the burning roof, and wails of the dying could be heard from inside. Sweyn squeezed the hilt of his sword and looked around.

"The monk must be sacrificing those people to his god," Ax-Wolf said, watching the struggling man in surprise. "He should not be permitted the pleasure."

Ax-Wolf nodded to Sigvard, who quickly unbolted the door and tried to open it. But people were pushing on it from inside, and he could only open it a crack.

Ax-Wolf heaved the portly monk out of the way and then put his shoulder to the door. Fingers found their way through the crack; death screams and crying could be heard from the fire. With a roar they managed to get it open far enough that a woman, burned black, managed to climb out, followed by others.

The screaming monk reached for them and bellowed deliriously, saliva pouring out of his mouth.

"Make that native shut up," Sweyn told Åke, who promptly stabbed the monk in the face and the stomach so he sank to his knees, bleeding.

Then he was quiet.

Burned women climbed over the body of the bleeding monk to get out of the building. An old woman with half her face covered in blisters clutched a dead child in her arms. She stood outside the building, staring vacantly at nothing. Others rolled around on the ground to smother the fire on their bodies. An unrecognizable body, charred black as overcooked pork, dragged itself across the ground and then died.

The people in better shape stared confusedly at the praying monk as if they had no idea what to do. The ones who were charred black made Sweyn feel sick. The smell of burned flesh lay heavy over the courtyard. The whole building was on fire, and the flames rose high above the roof.

"Father is not going to be happy about this," Sweyn said, without letting go of the monk. "It would have been better if Ax-Wolf had let them burn. Most of them are going to die anyway."

Åke made a face and said, "Ax-Wolf may be good at finding fault, but he's not so good at thinking clearly."

Åke stopped talking, watching as Ax-Wolf strode over to them and spoke to the monk in monk language.

"He says we stopped them from getting to paradise, and that now instead they will burn in hell until the end of time," Ax-Wolf reported scornfully.

"They have to be burned alive by a monk to get into their paradise?" asked Sigvard.

Ax-Wolf shrugged, unconcerned. "Christians," he said, as if that explained everything. "What else would you expect of people who only have a single god, nailed up on a cross?"

Sweyn shook his head and watched Palna flanked by warriors approaching through the smoke. Palna looked like a terrible wolf, his chieftain's cloak fluttering like eagle wings, as he surveyed the locals. This did not bode well.

"What by the stinking tooth of Balder is this?" Palna bellowed.

Even though Ax-Wolf was almost twice as big as Palna, he cowered before his chieftain.

"The monk was offering a sacrifice to his god, so I ruined his satisfaction," Ax-Wolf mumbled.

Palna's face contorted in rage. "Have you lost your senses? Do you even remember why we're here?" He turned to Sweyn and Åke to reprimand them, but just then a girl with one arm covered in burns came gasping and stumbling toward Palna. The chieftain grabbed his sword and raised it to strike the girl.

"The gods sent you to save me," she said in a recognizable Scandinavian lilt before her frail body was overcome by a violent fit of coughing.

Palna lowered his sword. The girl had curly blond hair under all the soot. Her light-blue eyes were wide open and shone with a craziness that was even more unhinged than the monk's.

"You speak the Danes' tongue," Palna said.

"I was born in Jórvík. My father was a Viking," she said, and spat on the ground.

"We could get a nice price for her," Sweyn said, and Åke nodded his support.

"I will pay you generously for saving me," the girl said.

Palna looked at her in puzzlement and said, "If you have silver, you hide it well."

She touched her burned arm and grimaced in pain. People had already started dying on the grass around them. Only a few were still screaming loudly. Some who had survived the fire were trying to help the injured, but most of them had fled.

"I know where the monks hid their wealth," the girl whispered. "And I can show you, on two conditions."

Sweyn and the others exchanged glances. As Odin himself said, women's words cannot be trusted.

Palna crossed his arms over his chest and said, "Let's hear it."

"I want you to take me home," she said.

Palna looked at his brother. Gunnar shrugged his assent.

"And the second?"

"Let me kill the monk," the girl said. "I would really like to repay him for the trip to paradise he tried to give me."

Her smiling face was full of mania. But revenge and silver were both languages Palna understood. Without hesitating, he pulled a knife from his belt and handed it to her.

Sweyn still had a firm hold of the monk, and Ax-Wolf watched the monk expectantly.

"This is something we're all sure to remember," said Ax-Wolf.

ʃ

Emma wrapped her fingers around the beautifully carved handle of
the knife that the blood-spattered Viking leader placed in her hand.
Pain tore and ripped through her arm where her skin was burned and
blackened. But the fire had not left her; it still raged with its godliness
bestowing a strength that was not of this world. The veils she'd had
before her eyes had been burned away, and for the first time she could
see clearly. Everything around her was a lie. The church was of the devil's
making. It twisted people's minds and made them forsake things and
kill in the name of the false god.

Freya, her heavenly mother, had sent her back to this world—
reborn from rage and filled with her holy spirit—to fight the evil the
cross-worshipping heretics were spreading through the world. She
understood that now.

The tall Vikings, strong-armed destroyers with their weapons in
hand, were her weapons. They had come over the sea, raped her screaming mother, and begotten Emma in blood and shame. And now they
had returned to pull her out of the fires of purgatory.

The fat monk whimpered and shook in Sweyn's firm grip. The
monk's belly swayed under his cassock, a knotted rope tied as a belt

below it. Sweat ran down his dirty face, and his bloated cheeks wobbled as he prayed to his imaginary god. Emma drank in the fear in his eyes as she approached him, enjoying the strength the knife in her hand seemed to give her.

Without hesitating she sliced open his urine-soaked cassock and took a firm hold of his prick and balls. He screamed like a pig, his forehead soaked in sweat, as he begged and prayed for mercy. But Emma had none to give. She cut for the stinking men who had driven their filth into her, for the innocent children who'd been killed in the flames, for the devil who lived in the false soul of this man of God.

The knife was sharp and it didn't take much to carve off the hanging rags of skin. She held them up in front of the monk and laughed at his shrill shrieks as he pissed blood.

"Enjoy my revenge," she said, stuffing the bloody skin into his screaming mouth.

Then she yanked the fat monk out of the warrior's hands and dragged him with her. Her strength was unbounded as she dragged him over to the burning building.

"May you burn in hell," she said, kicking him into the flames.

He fell face-first into the fire.

The clothes and skin burned off his belly immediately; even so, he was able to crawl, screaming, away from the fire as the heat made his skin bubble. Emma let him almost escape the flames before kicking him back in. His howling ceased, and he twitched and floundered a bit before he was completely still.

Emma inhaled the smell of burned fat as strength surged through her. Triumphant, she turned toward the Vikings, wiping off the blade of the knife on her dress.

The warriors watched her in silence, a few with disgust on their faces. A redheaded giant of a man with an ax as big as her arm was the only one who grinned cheerfully.

"Well, he must have really pissed you off," he said, causing the others to burst out laughing.

The Vikings stood among the dead and wounded people at the monastery and laughed as if this was the most entertaining stuff they'd ever seen.

"May the powers protect us from Freya's wrath," the Viking's leader said stiffly, his voice filled with respect.

Emma placed the knife back in his hand and tenderly wrapped his fingers around the bloody handle. She saw the desire in his eyes, felt it like a warm wave washing over her body.

"Come," she whispered, walking toward the room where she'd seen the monks hide their things.

The building was built entirely of stone, with little windows. It was furnished only with small tables and benches. The monks had disappeared into one of the walls, but all that was visible there now was a set of shelves with papers on it. Emma pointed to the wall.

"I saw them going in there with their arms full," she said. She had only caught a brief glimpse, so she wasn't completely sure. The Vikings would not be merciful if she lied.

Two warriors grabbed the shelf and tried to tip it over, but it was secured to the wall. The redheaded giant pushed his way forward, and the warriors moved when he raised his ax. It took him two blows to open a hole in the wood. Then the others pulled chunks of wood away to enlarge it. Emma felt the leader's eyes on her, expectant and hopeful.

"There's a hole in the stone back here," called one of the men, and more wood was chopped away.

Sure enough, there was an opening in the stone wall. Emma inhaled the smell of piss and fear that seeped out of the low opening.

ᚲ

Sweyn raised a torch and peered into the narrow passage. It was so low
that he almost had to double over to enter it. The passage sloped steeply
downward and after four spear lengths it ended behind some crouching
monks, dressed in brown.

Sweyn took a couple of steps closer and raised the torch.

"By the eight legs of Sleipnir!" he said in amazement. "Their god
is generous."

Behind the monks who sat whimpering and trembling there was
a pile of candlesticks, goblets, and crosses made of silver and gold, a
fortune greater than he could ever have imagined. Palna would be able
to pay the geld taxes to the Jómsvíkings for many years to come and
build new ships.

"We're richer than Skaði's frost giants!" Sweyn cried out.

"Move," Sigvard ordered.

Sweyn pressed against the wall, smiling, and Sigvard squeezed by
with difficulty. Without much fuss, Sweyn grabbed the monks and
forced them to crawl back up and out of the passage toward his companions' waiting swords. When the last of the anguished monks had

crawled past Sweyn, he was able to proceed. He raised his torch to survey their treasure.

Sigvard's eyes gleamed as he held up an ornamental silver chalice on which hunters with bows in their hands were chasing a stag. The workmanship was so beautiful that the figures almost looked alive. There was a gold cross, inlaid with colorful stones in a curling pattern. There was a large dish with a Viking dragon pattern curling around its rim. And those were just the things lying atop the hoard.

"I thank their god for this!" Sigvard bellowed, and everyone roared with laughter as he began passing the items back up the passage.

Sweyn could hardly believe that the wealth he held in his hands existed. Never had he dreamt they would find anything like this. Sigvard pulled out a small wooden chest.

"Take this to Palna immediately," he ordered.

The box was heavy in Sweyn's hands as he stepped out of the tunnel into the stone room.

Several warriors had come to the room to see what was going on and were immediately stunned by the treasures and admired them with great interest. Palna stood by one of the small tables, watching the whole process with a contented look. The blond girl stood by his side and stared, her mouth hanging open.

Sweyn placed the chest on the table next to Palna, opened the lid, and saw coins, jewelry, and gemstones.

"We're rich, Father," Sweyn said, beaming.

Palna's mouth twitched. He was having a hard time controlling himself and not showing his great pleasure; that much was clear. Instead he picked up a necklace made of joined silver plates and inspected it closely.

"The All-Father must have sent you to guide us," Palna said and placed the chain around the neck of Emma the emasculatrix.

She didn't even look at the valuable necklace, staring transfixed at Palna instead, her eyes burning with madness and lust.

"No, it wasn't Odin. It was a goddess who led me," she said in such a flat tone that Sweyn took a step back from her.

Palna picked up a little golden brooch that depicted Odin's horse, Sleipnir, running on his eight legs. A ray of sun shining through one of the narrow windows made the gold sparkle.

"How many?" Palna asked.

Sweyn stretched his back and replied, "Sixteen, all told."

"You've killed one enemy for each year you've lived," Palna said, nodding contentedly. He placed Sleipnir in Sweyn's hand. "I honor the glory you won in the field."

The men who stood around them, Gunnar, Ax-Wolf, and a few others, agreed. Sweyn's proud heart swelled and ached in his chest.

"Thank you, Father," Sweyn said. "You trained me well."

Sweyn looked down at Odin's eight-legged horse and ran his finger over the gold. He ought to say much more, to honor Palna and the Jómsvíkings, but eloquent words ebbed away and he stood silent. With relief he felt Åke's hand on his shoulder.

"I couldn't find myself a better brother and friend in this world or the next," Åke said. "And as a warrior I would rather encounter Garm loosed from his chains at Gnipa Cave than you."

"Well said," cried Ax-Wolf.

Ingolf, one of the ship captains, pushed his way forward to Palna and nodded contentedly at the loot.

"The tide will be turning soon," he said.

Palna looked at the four ship captains in the room.

"There's nothing more to be gotten here. We have taken the vengeance we sought. Gather your men, load up your slaves, and set fire to their temple."

"Is this slave yours or can I have her?" Ingolf asked, pointing to Emma.

The sticky-fingered Ingolf was widely known for his greed. He sometimes reached for possessions rightfully belonging to others.

"The one who led us to this treasure must not be repaid with slavery," Gunnar said.

"An oath made to a stranger is worth nothing," Ingolf said. "I want her. She's not a free woman. Tell me your father's name, wench."

"My mother is Danish," Emma said, stretching her back. "Her father died fighting Harald Crow. My mother never knew my father's name, but he was a Viking in a raid. They were camping at Jórvík for the winter."

Ingolf grinned and said, "Some unknown Viking driving his cock into your mother does not make you a free woman. Although perhaps our honorable chieftain wants to keep you as booty for himself and not share you with his brethren."

"Watch what you say," Sweyn roared, grasping his sword.

Ingolf laughed and said, "Oh, I forgot. Your father didn't want to recognize you either."

"All the same," Sweyn retorted, "I have not one but two fathers, and at least I wasn't begotten by a poor wretch who was so drunk and stupid he drowned himself."

The warriors all laughed. They often made fun of Ingolf's father for drowning drunk in a barrel of mead.

"You can all forget about the girl," a low voice said. "She belongs to me."

Everyone fell instantly silent and turned around. The seeress Beyla, the death witch, had entered the room unnoticed, supporting herself on a staff. Her gray hair hung in braids around her still-beautiful face, and her eyes were dark with rage.

"Has your manhood blinded you?" she roared so her words echoed through the room. "Do you not see the dís concealed in her body, the dís that has given you wealth and will protect you in battle? Are you trying in your inexhaustible foolishness to put a slave's shackles on a girl sent by the gods?"

The seeress spat on the floor and brandished her staff at Ingolf.

"You must sacrifice generously tonight to Our Lady Freya, for she will not look mercifully on your blasphemies."

Ingolf paled and backed away.

"Instead you should be asking what the girl wants," Beyla said.

"They promised to take me home to the North," Emma said, her eyes still gleaming insanely as she looked from the seeress to Palna. "That's all I want."

Sweyn had never heard of a woman voluntarily asking to travel with the Jómsvíkings before.

"She really has no idea what's in store for her," Åke said with a sneer.

But Beyla nodded her head to the girl in deference, and when she did that everyone was expected to follow suit.

"Promises to the valkyries must be kept, Chieftain Palna," the seeress said contentedly.

Palna did not appear displeased.

"She will have protection at my hearth. Men, grab the spoils and burn the rest. We sail north."

ᛉ

"Do you know how to carve runes?"

The oak trees of the sacred grove sighed expectantly as the thirteen foremost Scylfing women formed a circle around Sigrid. They all wore masks of wood or leather depicting the dynasty's most powerful foremothers. Sigrid bowed her head as twilight fell around her. The concoction she'd drunk before being brought to the grove for the ritual was beginning to dissolve the boundaries between the nine worlds. Suddenly she felt like laughing.

Sigrid bit her cheek hard and forced herself to stand up straight and participate.

"Yes," she replied in a firm voice, "I know the signs Freya gave to Odin as he hung on Yggdrasil and sacrificed his eye in Mímir's Well."

Do you know how to decipher them?

Do you know how to color them?

Do you know how to use them?

As she responded to the ritual questions, she let her hand stroke the heavy cloak they had placed over her shoulders. The glorious achievements and deeds that had been stitched in the cloak came to life in that moment. Houses were burned, battles were waged, giants were banished, and foremothers swayed the gods. An instant later the swarm of visions had calmed.

Do you know how to pray?

Do you know how to offer a sacrifice?

Do you know how to send them?

Do you know how to destroy them?

These were the easiest of questions. Sigrid knew how to slit the throat of a sacrificial animal so the carotid arteries were exposed and could be cut away. She also knew how to stick a pig in the heart while saying the right words to consecrate the animal. She had carefully learned how to section the body correctly, setting aside the proper pieces of flesh to give to individual deities and noble-born guests. She knew which rites to do, and at what time of year, so that the powers wouldn't abandon them, good crops would prevail in the fields, and there would be peace.

When the answers were given, the women quieted and sat down on the circle of stones in the middle of the grove. Unmoving masks, unfamiliar in their stiffness, came to life, and the faces of the foremothers could be glimpsed in the wood and leather.

Over at the farm, a dome of light was visible from the fire where her engagement was being celebrated. Relatives had come from far and wide to say good-bye before she made the journey north. The foremost chieftains crowded into her father's great hall. Torvald Scylfing with his red-haired son, Harald, Tibrand from Alfheim and his brother Isar, Annfinn from Frökind, and many others were there. They had greeted her with respect and pride.

"Only a true Scylfing daughter would dare to travel to Svealand to secure the peace for her people," old Ubbe had whispered into her ear.

"You honor us," Torolf of Raskvík had said.

"You're making a great sacrifice to guarantee the peace," his wife, the stately Ebba, had added.

Even her maternal uncle Sten was there, and it had meant a lot to her to be blessed by her mother's family.

"This great achievement will never be forgotten. The sacrifices you are making will never be lost in Mímir's Well."

Aunt Ulfhild, who had been a shield maiden in her youth, spoke now in a loud, shrill voice as she got up and walked to the middle of the sacred grove. There she began to enumerate the Scylfing dynasty's most powerful women. In olden times Freya had saved Alfheim from war and the plague that a nasty seeress sent. Then came Saga, who bore four daughters, two of whom became queens in Thule, and their daughters in turn became priestesses, shield maidens, and resourceful women.

Queen Yrsa of Svealand was captured by King Helge Halvdansson. He brought her to Lejre, where she became his wife. They had a son together, but when he was three years old Queen Ålov came to Lejre and recounted that King Helge was Yrsa's own father and that she herself was her mother. When Yrsa found out she'd had a child with her own father, she traveled back to Svealand immediately, where she reigned as queen until she died.

Then came the furious Hyndla, the seeress who had defended her people by burning King Eystein and his men.

A house rises from the rocks
Like a ship o'er the waves
Its rafters hewn from trees
That swayed upon the slopes
Like kelp surging with the tide
Fire swells in biting curls
The homestead is a sea of flames
The house becomes a blazing ship
Sinking on the crew within
And at the helm a burning king

The enumeration ended with Ulfhild recounting her own story about how she defended her hundred as a shield maiden.

"Do you swear to remember each and every one of these women you are descended from?" Ulfhild asked.

Sigrid bowed her head in reverence. She was but a slender thread in a great tapestry that stretched back to the dawn of time.

"I swear it," Sigrid answered.

There was a rustling at the edge of the sacred grove and from the corner of her eye she saw little gray creatures that were curiously watching what happened. The grass rocked under her bare feet and started shimmering red and blue. A handsome, bare-chested man with stag antlers on his head appeared through the trees. Happiness was seeing the beauty of the Hidden.

"Do you swear you will put the honor of the family line ahead of your own life?" Ulfhild asked.

Sigrid put her hand on her heart and bowed her head in affirmation.

"Then you must take the oath," Ulfhild said.

Sigrid's heartbeat was strong beneath her hand. This was the oath that each of the family's women had sworn all the way back, ever since their foremother Freya stepped into the flames and burned to death so that she could ascend to Valhalla. Now it was Sigrid's turn to step into line.

"By my blood and my lineage, I swear my loyalty to Freya and the Scylfings," she whispered. "You are my life. You are my everything."

A warm breeze swept through the trees and the Mistress was standing beside her and she took Sigrid tenderly into her arms. The hairs on her arms and the nape of her neck stood up in Freya's presence.

Beloved Freya, my mother, my sister, and my everything, blessed be your greatness.

"May I be killed and cursed for eternity if I break this oath." Her voice trembled with emotion and love.

The foremothers stood up and started walking counterclockwise around her as they chanted incantations.

"Bless her, Mother Freya. Protect her with wind, earth, fire, and water. Take her, Great One. We give her to you."

Sigrid gasped, feeling enchanted as the veils between the worlds and time fell. The thirteen who had gone before chanted new incantations that filled the air with sorcery. Some women were tattooed with spirals on their cheeks. A young woman with curly blond hair, like herself, had curling snakes on her arms and eyes as blue as the sea. She smiled so beautifully that Sigrid's eyes filled with tears of joy.

I am you. We are united in eternity.

Sigrid swayed and allowed herself to be swallowed up by the Hidden while the foremothers danced around her. The branches of the oak trees undulated playfully in the wind. Laughter in the distance mixed with the rhythmic rumble of the drums. Sigrid held out her arms and let Our Lady Freya's blessedness engulf her.

I am yours, Mighty One. For all eternity.

ᚴ

"Make room so the boy can sit," Asbjörn called out as Sweyn approached Palna's hearth.

Almost everyone had gathered to eat the fish they had grilled over the fire and to remember those who had fallen in the battle. Sixty of the finest men who had rowed, lived, fought, and prepared to die together nodded amiably and gave Sweyn appreciative looks as he sat down on the log next to Åke.

Åke passed Sweyn a fish wrapped in a leaf. The difference in their standing now that they had proven themselves worthy in battle could not be greater. No one asked them to gather wood or dig a latrine. When Sweyn came back from his watch shift, someone had even gathered birch boughs for his bed and prepared it.

His heart swelled when he looked at the men around the fire.

Uncle Gunnar was sharpening his ax and talking to Rolf and Haakon, who both came from Vestland. Like many others from the North, they had fled Christianization. They signed on with Palna, who secretly clung to the old beliefs, the true beliefs. Inge sat on a rock by their side and ate greedily from his bowl. He was born in Jutland and after a long period of discord with his father, he had left the farm and traveled to Jómsborg on his own, where he had begged and prayed to be admitted. Now he fought with the scarred Sverre who had been kicked out of a Frankish royal family but had found a new home in the brotherhood of the Jómsborg Vikings.

Sweyn had fought his whole life to earn their respect. He nodded gratefully to Palna. The light from the flames danced over the chieftain's disfigured face, every bit as solid as if it were carved in stone.

Palna was a hard man, merciless in his training. Sweyn had cursed many times when Palna forced him to practice with his sword and ax until his hands were swollen and covered with wounds, and his body ached so badly that he couldn't sleep. Every time he had made a mistake with his sword, every time his swimming or running hadn't improved, he had been punished without mercy.

Palna had been harder on Sweyn than his own birth son, Åke.

"A Jómsvíking is stronger than all other warriors, and you must be the best of us," Palna had said as he beat Sweyn to punish him for his mistakes. "A Jómsvíking always speaks the truth and never lets his brothers down. He does not steal, never lies with another man's wife, and never speaks ill of his fellows or quarrels with them."

The rules had been drummed into him with a fist until Sweyn never made a mistake again. Now he had succeeded in completely satisfying his foster father, and nothing made him prouder than the recognition he now saw in Palna's eyes.

Ax-Wolf sat down next to Sweyn with a heavy thud.

"I enjoyed a couple of the slaves. They were quite pleasing. You young stags ought to go see for yourselves, instead of sitting here hanging your heads. The choice is yours, as long as Sigvard isn't still out there fornicating."

"Being inside a slave after you isn't really that tempting," Åke replied.

"No, I can imagine," Ax-Wolf said seriously. "No one can tell if you poke a twig into something that's been stretched out by a log."

He tipped his head back and guffawed so his belly shook, and several of the men seated around them joined in the laughter.

"Chieftain, people say we're going to set up camp for the winter in Jórvík," Ax-Wolf said. Then he leaned forward, snatched a piece of fish, and stuffed it into his mouth.

Palna smiled faintly at the men, who had grown silent. But instead of responding, he turned to Sweyn and said, "Tell me, if you wore my cloak, what would you decide?"

It was another leadership test among many his father had given him. The warriors leaned forward. They all wanted to hear his answer. He wouldn't make any mistakes with this one, because the answer was easy.

"King Edward has been murdered, and England is without a ruler. I would set up camp for the winter somewhere in the Danelaw, gather an army, and then take back the kingdom that Guthrum so infamously lost. In battle we don't hide from the noise of the weapons. We must hold our heads high when the ice of battle seeks to split skulls. We should strike now when uncertainty prevails, before the powerful men unify and stand strong."

The men around the fire nodded. Even two of the ship captains showed their approval.

"What do you say about this, Ingolf?" Palna asked.

"What Sweyn says is wise," Ingolf began, thoughtfully stroking his beard, "but it would be tough to rely on the foreigners for cover in battle when we instead could be fighting side by side with our brothers. With the riches we've found, we can build more boats and gather the best of men to return in the spring with an army that can conquer all of England."

Damn that sticky-fingered wretch. Sweyn suppressed his anger with difficulty. If they showed manly courage, they could easily conquer this land. And yet Palna nodded contentedly at Ingolf's suggestion.

Then Palna spoke: "The grain rot in England's fields and the crop failures will be even worse this year. What would be wise is to let the Saxons and Angles weaken from starvation for another winter and then overpower them with a force greater than any other."

Sweyn clenched his fist but bent to his foster father's will. No one bested Palna when it came to battle and military strategy.

"We sail for home tomorrow," Palna said. "It's time for you to stand before King Harald Bluetooth and demand your birth right as Jelling."

Then Palna turned to Gunnar and started discussing the route home.

Sweyn pushed aside the last of his fish. He wasn't hungry anymore.

"Father won't let anyone rest on their laurels," Åke said quietly, but Sweyn didn't respond.

The thought of standing before his birth father made his gut ache. Harald had drunkenly and violently forced himself on Sweyn's mother one night in Jómsborg. When Sleep-Åsa became pregnant, the king had said that anyone at all could have fathered the child. However, Palna knew, as did everyone in Jómsborg, that even if the mother was poor, she was an honorable woman who was good as her word. He tried to persuade Harald to recognize the child and when he scornfully refused, Palna swore to raise Sweyn as his own son and shoulder the obligation that Harald Bluetooth had disgracefully refused.

When Sweyn was six years old, Palna tried again to get Harald to adopt him, but the king refused then as well.

This would be the third time Sweyn had stood before Harald, and this time he was old enough to plead his own case. If he didn't succeed now, it could mean a far-ranging downfall, for him and for Jómsborg.

As Jarl of Jómsborg, Palna had been forced to have himself baptized, but in his heart he was loyal to the old gods, and he often made sacrifices to them. Skilled warriors fleeing from forced Christianization were welcome in Jómsborg despite King Harald's decree to kill them. Palna stood firm in his belief that everyone was entitled to his own faith, in open defiance of his sworn sovereign. So far Harald had looked the other way. He had made plenty of silver by hiring out the Jómsvíkings' swords, and he likely feared going to battle against them.

King Harald didn't know that Palna and several other jarls and chieftains had hatched a plan to overthrow him, allowing Sweyn to take his place leading the Danes, Jutes, and Scanians. From childhood, Sweyn had heard that he'd been born to sit on the Jelling throne and, like his birth father's father, Gorm the Old, rule as the protector of the Danes.

But first Harald had to be convinced to recognize Sweyn as his son and a member of the Jelling dynasty.

This burden weighed on Sweyn's shoulders like a heavy cloak, and none of the joy and pride he had felt earlier remained. *It'll work out,* he told himself. A man must follow his destiny. If things went badly, he would feast in Valhalla instead, and that wouldn't be so bad either.

↑

The warriors stood in silence around the funeral pyre, where they'd placed those who had fallen in the battle at the monastery. The light from the torches illuminated their tense faces as they waited to light the pyre so the dead could follow the smoke up to Valhalla.

Emma cocked her head to the side and regarded the Vikings with affection. During the days they had sailed north, the men who had been described in the abbey as demons and heathens, possessed by the devil, had treated her with greater deference than she had ever known before in her life.

Beyla had attended to her and looked after the burns on her arm. As the dragon ship rode the waves, the seeress had carefully explained the Viking world to her. The first rays of sunlight that shimmered over the sea were from the dís of light, Sól, who drove her chariot Álfröðull over the vault of the sky to bring light to mankind. Her chariot was pulled by the horses Árvakr and Alsviðr and chased across the sky by the wolves Hati and Sköll.

The wind that filled the sail came from the eagle Hræsvelgr, the Corpse Swallower, beating his wings from his perch at the top of the world tree, Yggdrasil. They sailed over the realm of Rán, the sea goddess, and were forced to appease her nine daughters to gain free passage across the water.

Emma drank in the wise woman's knowledge. In the Vikings' world there was no judging God or tempting devil. Thor ruled over land, sky, and seafarers. He helped the humans hold the giants away from the outlying lands, and when he struck with his hammer, lightning flashed in the sky. Odin was the wise one who reigned in Valhalla. The white Heimdallr watched over the bridge Bifrost, and Frigg watched over the hearth.

They were mighty, unpredictable kinfolk, whom you had to stay on good terms with in order to triumph against the chaos that threatened to tear the world apart.

"Freya's dísir protect the warriors. They are terrifying and powerful beings," Beyla had said, looking at the white cliffs that rose from the sea.

When she said these words, Emma felt for the first time that the otherworldly presence was speaking to her. Like a mother feeling a baby quicken for the first time, like a fish in your belly, she felt the power of the dís within her.

You are mine.

The words were like a wind that sweeps howling over a deserted moor, and Emma willingly bent to the will of the dís who possessed her. When Emma was in the borderland between life and death, the mother of the universe, older than time itself, had blessed her. This was the strange witchcraft that had caused her to be reborn.

Beyla now raised her hands and invoked her mistress Hel to aid her in the offering she was going to make. The seeress's face was painted with the death goddess's symbols, so powerful that they glowed in the twilight.

"Eggthér, we will put out the fire," she said softly. "Eggthér, we will put out the fire."

The words caused the being in Emma to howl with anticipation. Soon, soon it would happen. She shivered when Beyla walked over to

Megan, who was kneeling on the beach, bound and naked. She was one of the prisoners they had unloaded from the ship when they pitched camp, yet another gift to Emma.

Megan had screamed when they fetched her, prayed that God would rescue her from the devils who ripped off her clothes and raped her, again and again. Megan, who in the abbey had hit Emma and stuffed her cold fingers into all of Emma's openings and called her a bastard, had ended up lying naked, bleeding, and broken on the ground, and Emma had found revenge sweet.

Megan now sat shivering in her own urine in front of Beyla, who raised the sacrificial knife and invited the goddess in. It was close now. The being inside Emma stormed with her hunger for blood.

"Dear, good God, save me from the devils," Megan cried. "I beseech you, hear my prayer!"

Her big breasts swayed heavily against her belly as she twisted and turned, trying to get free, shadows and light dancing over her wide-open eyes. Emma moved in front of her with the bowl that would catch the blood.

Megan seemed to snap out of it, tears running down her cheeks.

"Good God, don't let them do this to me," she said, her voice trembling.

Emma smiled as the shadows darkened around her. Her mistress, the dís possessing her, was waiting to be set free. The power grew so mighty that she shivered.

"You're the devil. I can see the demon in you," Megan cried.

Emma laughed quietly as Beyla took up position behind the sacrificial offering and yanked her head backward so her throat was exposed.

"We give you this slave to serve you in the afterworld," Beyla told the warriors who had died in the battle. Then she began reading the death spell. The light from the funeral pyre danced over Beyla's painted face, so ghastly in its power. In one slow slice she slit open Megan's neck, and the blood, the sacred, life-giving blood, pulsed into Emma's bowl below.

The feeling of release was immediate. The powerful being within her drank the life force that flowed into the bowl and broke the fetters that had chained her in this world.

Beyla released her hold on Megan and let two warriors lift her onto the pyre, where she died, rattling and gurgling. The warriors brought their torches to the pyre and lit it ablaze with a roar.

Emma stretched out her arms as the storm raged within her body.

"Take this power and drink of its strength," said Beyla. She dipped a sprig of maple into the bowl and splashed the blood over Emma, who was now enveloped in wind. The remnants of her that were human crumbled away and disappeared like dust as the unknown raged inside her.

"Tell me your name!" yelled Beyla.

The ground beneath her pulsed with a timeless heartbeat. The giants on the beach guarded the gates to the kingdom of Hel where the dead dwelled. Rán watched quietly as her nine daughters swam around her, screaming with hunger. The fire ogres greedily devoured the funeral pyre while the smoke rose to the sky where the gods twinkled like stars.

"Kára," the being inside Emma bellowed as the wind transformed into a raging storm, tearing and tugging at all their clothes.

Insignificant and frail, Beyla knelt down, groveling before her feet. Beyla's gray hair whipped around her face, and her cloak soared like a sail. The men shielded their eyes and cowered from the wind.

Kára pulled back, and the wind stilled around them. The waves that had pounded the beach grew calm. Emma collapsed to the ground, her body shaking from exhaustion. Kára still filled her mind, crowding Emma out and raging against her body's weakness. It was like a snake had coiled itself around her head and body, chilly and damp, a superior power that tore her mind to shreds.

A moment later Beyla helped Emma sit up and leaned her against the cool stone.

"Withdraw, Mighty One, otherwise your vessel will break," Beyla said calmly, stroking Emma's cheek.

Kára howled inside Emma but pulled back, and suddenly Emma could breathe again. She wolfed down the air, wheezing, filling her lungs while Beyla hugged her and rocked her as tenderly as a mother.

"What's wrong with her?" Palna asked, squatting down beside Emma, watching her with concerned curiosity.

Beyla stroked Emma's hair and then tenderly kissed her head.

"Nothing. The gods have sent us what we prayed for, my brother. This is the dís who will save Valhalla for us."

ᛒ

The straight tree trunks held up a light-green roof. Rays of sunlight cut through the leaves, like glowing spear shafts, down to the ground. It was covered with a thick carpet of leaves that muffled the horses' steps as the line of warriors and carts followed the trodden path. A creek ran alongside, merrily laughing at their hardships.

The Alva Woods were widely known for their beauty but only now did Sigrid realize how singularly beautiful they were.

"There's the old Gyrild memorial," Ulf said, pointing to a tall painted stone bearing twisting runes so old they could no longer be made out. "So we'll surely reach Uncle Rune's place safely before dark." He urged his horse on so it would keep pace with Sigrid's mount, Buttercup. "It appears that Anund doesn't have the courage to attack our hird," Ulf said, relieved. "Have no worries, sister."

Sigrid smiled wryly. Ever since they had left the farm, the warriors had been assuring her she was safe. But she was not afraid of Anund's warriors or anything else anymore, not since the foremothers had embraced her. The unhealed skin on her wrist where she'd been tattooed still ached.

The intricate design showed lines enclosed in a circle, indicating how the Mistress sustained their world with both arms and legs. There was a smaller circle in the middle, representing the fertile, swelling belly as the source of all life. On either side there was an arrow: one pointed up, symbolizing the valkyries Freya sends into battle, and one pointed down, symbolizing Freya's welcome to all family in the afterworld.

Kneeling in the sacred grove, groggy and surprised, Sigrid had come to when the tattoo on her wrist was almost complete. The concoction she had drunk had made her wander through the worlds, and Grandmother had said that she could never tell anyone what she saw. Sigrid couldn't have put the bliss she had felt into words even if she'd tried. It was far too overwhelming.

When the tattoo was done, she returned to the estate, a full-fledged adult woman. The good-byes and tears of relatives and servants and even slaves had awaited her there. Saying good-bye to them all had been easy because she knew now that it was her destiny to leave.

I am safe in your bosom.

"I'm looking forward to taking a break," she told Ulf.

Toste had been pushing them hard, and they had taken only one break. But they hadn't spotted any of Anund's men, and their journey through the woods and valleys had been peaceful.

Warriors rode around her, still ready for battle, but more serene than they'd been when they left the estate. They chatted as they walked or rode along on their horses. Axel wore a helmet that covered his entire head and nose, a chainmail byrnie that rattled over his leather armor, an ax in his belt, and a sword at his hip. Orm was next to him, wearing the same battle gear, but his horse also wore leather armor over his neck and chest.

The carts creaked as the oxen pulled them along the path, and Sigrid saw Jorun and Alfhild walking farther back in the long phalanx of carts and warriors. There were so many people you might think they were an army.

A squirrel watched the passersby with curiosity until it scurried up a tree trunk, just like Ratatoskr, who ran up and down the trunk of Yggdrasil, spreading hostile words among the world tree's denizens.

Soon they would reach the ship, which lay moored at Toste's brother Rune's home. From there they would sail west across the open sea all the way to the Danish town of Lejre, the largest known trading post, where the great king Harald Bluetooth had one of his royal estates. Toste had business with the king's men, and he wanted Sigrid to acquire the most beautiful clothing and ribbons she could find at the market.

"Anything you want, you will get," he promised her.

Then they would sail north to Aros, where she would meet her future husband King Erik of Svealand for the first time, the man she had seen in her dream. She stroked the mark of Freya on her wrist, and her heart filled with love. This would truly be a grand tale to tell the son she was going to have.

A stag watched them from among the trees. She followed the animal with her eyes as it ran from them in long bounds, and then her eyes locked on to something dark moving through the trees. For a heartbeat she thought she could make out a woman with a painted face squatting on a stone. An instant later the vision was gone, and there was only the sunlit woods. Sigrid furrowed her brow as a sense of foreboding ran down her spine. Every forest was home to so many beings: forest dísir, the seductive hulders, the souls of unburied children called mylings, various nature spirits and wights, and beings for which there were no names.

"I saw something, over there," Sigrid whispered to Axel and pointed into the trees.

"A spy?" he asked, moving his hand to the hilt of his sword.

Orm and the other warriors around her scanned the area vigilantly, ready for battle.

"Something else, a woman," Sigrid responded.

Axel surveyed the woods as they proceeded. Something had changed. The birds that had welcomed the day earlier had quieted, and there was not an animal in sight. It was as if the forest was holding its breath in anticipation.

"I will gladly meet flesh-and-blood warriors, but supernatural creatures are another matter," Axel murmured.

Heavy gray clouds were starting to block out the sun, and soon the travelers found themselves riding through a dark half-twilight. Buttercup whinnied uneasily and tossed her head. Sigrid shivered as her sense of foreboding grew. Something malevolent was watching her. She felt that clearly.

Keep me from evil, O dazzling, radiant Freya.

The warriors farther ahead began yelling to each other and pointing to a little hill shaped like a contorted monster that had tried to leap away, but was turned to stone instead. There was a gully below, and a thick gray fog was billowing over the edges, coming up from the bottom of the gully, like water boiling over from a cauldron.

The fog rushed over the ground with a speed that could not be of this world. All the horses started whinnying. Buttercup danced around so much that Sigrid could hardly stay on the horse's back.

"Battle sorcery!" Alex yelled. "Close ranks!"

Orm pulled his sword as if that would help against the mists that were rushing toward them. The men surrounded Sigrid with their swords and axes raised. The next moment they were engulfed by the damp fog, and everything went quiet.

Axel, who was only an arm's length away, looked like a shadow. The riders ahead of Sigrid seemed like dark patches in the gray. She clung to Buttercup's mane as hard as she could, her heart trying to leap from her chest. The sounds of hooves and horses' snorts sounded muffled. It was as if they were in some border region of the afterworld.

"The enemy will attack soon," Axel said calmly.

They wanted to kill her. Sigrid held tight to her horse's mane. They would cut open her belly and crush her skull. She wanted to throw herself to the ground and beg for mercy, but her body was immobile, frozen in fear.

"We'll take the battle here," Axel cried.

Two hands came around her waist. Someone lifted her off her horse, which fled into the mists, and then pushed her head down so she was squatting, surrounded by the backs of the Svea warriors as they formed a protective ring around her. Her legs trembled, and she could hardly keep herself upright as she listened in the mist.

A short whistle shot through the air, followed by a tormented moan and a heavy thud. Dark shadows appeared and disappeared in the fog. More screams could be heard now, both ahead of her and behind, followed by the ringing of blades striking each other.

"Stick together!" Axel yelled. "They're going to try to separate us."

Her heart hammered in her chest and fear made her sink to her knees. This was unacceptable. Sigrid took a deep breath and put her hand on the mark of Freya on her wrist, drinking in its power. She couldn't let herself be eclipsed by fear when she needed her strength most.

I have faith. You will protect me, Vanadís.

A horse bolted past like a dís in the night. The warriors shot arrows into the fog. A shadow came out of nowhere and attacked one of the Svea men accompanying them. Twice their blades met before the shadow disappeared back into the fog again.

"I don't see anyone," Orm yelled tensely, striking at the blade of a warrior who quickly vanished into the gray.

Shadows flickered; men fought and then vanished into the mists. Like wasps they swarmed around the Svea, who protected her. They struck and pulled away, time and again. Sigrid closed her eyes.

Help me, Vanadís. You have to help me now.

She clung to the ground and felt her body calm down and her mind clear.

The enemy was surrounding them. They came from every direction, and she even heard them up in the trees. A nearby scream came from somewhere very close.

Sigrid clenched her fists and finally Freya gave her a flood of blessed rage, which rushed through her body and swept away her fear. Damn these warriors hiding in the fog, who didn't have the balls to come fight them man-to-man. She was not going to die here, not now. Freya was protecting her. Sigrid got to her feet and stared into the fog.

"In the name of Freya, my foremother, I curse you!" she yelled so loud that all the warriors shot glances at her.

Sigrid raised her marked wrist to the sky and enjoyed the strength from her fury.

"Mother, come and aid your daughter! Vanadís, save me! I command you. Send the damned all the way to the caves of Hel."

"Shut up, you're attracting them this way," a warrior warned her, but Sigrid's fury was so strong that she would not be stopped.

"May you be cursed in the name of Vanadís!"

That very moment a gust of wind blew through the trees. It caressed her cheeks before picking up strength. Sigrid laughed out loud. Her prayer had been heard. Not even the darkest sorcery could keep the fog on the ground.

"Storm dís, I beseech you, show your power, and I will repay you amply."

Sigrid didn't have a chance to say any more words before the wind grew in strength. With her hair whipping her face, she watched the wind drive the fog away with its rage. It was a blessed miracle!

Cowardly fighters hiding in the fog couldn't hide anymore. Easily identified by Anund's mark, there they crouched just arm lengths away, shielding their unshaven faces from the dirt and leaves whipping around. The mother goddess had answered Sigrid's call!

Sveas and Scylfings started mercilessly slaying Anund's awestruck warriors. Orm lunged and beheaded a scarred warrior and then a moment later slit the throat of another. Sharp steel sliced people's flesh as it hunted for new fodder. The Sveas' armor dripped with blood as Anund's warriors helplessly fell to their swords.

Spears were thrown at those who attempted to flee. As if propelled by the wind, the spears bored deep into the cowards' backs.

Toste's warriors came running with their swords raised, and Anund's men could no longer put up any resistance.

Mighty goddess, thank you in all your strength for taking pity on me, your humble servant, in my hour of need. My life is yours.

The wind gave Sigrid's cheek one last caress before fading away. She shivered and touched the mark on her wrist as the sun broke through the crowns of the trees and warmed the ground where the dying and wounded screamed in pain.

Father came running along the path, his armor hanging open and thumping against his chest, and his sword still in his hand. He slowed down, relieved, when he saw that Sigrid was uninjured.

"Where's Ulf?" Sigrid asked him.

"Farther ahead, uninjured though the same cannot be said of many others," her father responded gloomily with an approving look at Axel, who had not strayed from Sigrid's side. "May the inglorious Anund be eternally damned for hiding behind a seeress's sorcery. If the wind hadn't picked up and driven away the fog, we would all have been massacred, blinded by Mist."

The valkyrie Mist had aided Anund's warriors in battle. The seeress that Sigrid had glimpsed must have been powerful if she could summon Mist to her.

Orm pulled off his helmet and, still out of breath, wiped the sweat off his face, smearing blood spatters across his face and into his beard.

"It was really lucky that your daughter got Freya to send us that wind," Orm said.

Toste cocked his head and gave Sigrid a questioning look.

"I prayed to Freya, and she sent the storm dís," Sigrid said with a happy smile.

Toste furrowed his brow. Then someone called his name from a distance.

"We must offer a bountiful sacrifice for this kindness," he said quickly and then hurried away to the man who had called for him.

Sigrid took a deep breath, the triumph simmering in her blood.

Warriors walked through the woods, thrusting spears into still-writhing fallen enemies. Other warriors attended to their wounded fellows or carried the dead toward the carts. Jorun and Alfhild helped a man with an injured leg. Sigrid walked into the trees to take a closer look at the devastation.

"Don't trouble your eyes with what's out there," Axel told her.

Sigrid shook her head. Did he really think she was going to hide from what had happened?

"A Scylfing never shirks," she replied and bowed her head to Erolf from her father's hird, who was solemnly carried to the carts by his comrades.

May he find joy and peace in the afterworld.

One of Anund's fallen fighters lay a stone's throw away, his eyes staring vacantly. He couldn't have been any older than she was. Sigrid bit her cheek. It was the first time she'd seen an actual enemy from Anund's clan. They were the sworn enemy of her family, but he looked just like one of them.

Lives had been lost for her sake. All because she was going to marry a man she'd never seen. Sigrid gulped when she spotted a man with his belly slashed open. Pale blue intestines billowed out onto the ground from his gaping wounds.

Nausea turned her stomach and she vomited, nearly on top of the dead man. Axel gave her a thoughtful look, and she quickly turned her back and strove to suppress her discomfort.

"The valkyries' cruelty is not beautiful to behold," Axel said.

Sigrid couldn't reveal weakness now, not after the mercy she'd been shown, not when the goddess had taken lives to protect her, not when everyone's eyes were on her. The storm dís had saved them. Without her they would all be lying dead on the ground.

Sigrid sought and met Axel's eyes again. "They do what must be done, as we do," she said.

Just then Toste came running up the path looking hounded.

"We have to move on," he yelled, pointing to the dark smoke rising into the sky beyond the treetops. "Rune's farm is on fire."

M

Palna was talking to his brother when Emma stepped into the tent. Both men quieted and watched her expectantly. The smell of uncertainty was so strong that it was hard to breathe, but she saw the desire in Palna's eyes and felt it just as clearly as the heat from the fire.

"Your payment," the chieftain said, tossing a leather pouch to her, which she caught neatly.

Emma glanced absentmindedly at the silver pieces. In her previous life, she would have done anything to own such riches; now she hungered for something completely different.

Kára's presence was strong inside her. Like a raging river during the spring melt, Kára flooded every part of her mind and caused a hunger greater than Emma had ever felt. Like a ravenous animal, the forces tore at her body.

Palna reached for a wooden cup and watched her expectantly.

"My faith in the old ways has shown me many things, but I've never seen anything like what happened by the bonfire. Are you human or dís?"

Emma inhaled the pungent scent of his manliness. A scar ran over his chest, likely from a sword blow he had sustained. A burn mark the size of her palm was also visible on his shoulder, and at his waist a scar covered a sunken hollow in his flesh.

"I'm both," she said, pulling off her dress to stand naked beside the bed.

"Think this over carefully, brother," Gunnar said warily. "No one knows what she may entice you to do."

"I'm sure I can handle whatever she's got," Palna said, leaning back. He undid his breeches and pulled out his cock, paying no attention to his brother as he left the tent. The hunger—the pushing, ravenous hunger—engulfed Emma in its darkness, and without hesitating she straddled him.

"May Frey give me strength," Palna panted, sinking down by her side. His body was full of wounds and bite marks, as if a wild animal had devoured him.

Emma leaned over him and slowly licked off a drop of sweat that was running down his thigh. Then she lay down on her back, her heart pounding in her chest. Sweaty and exhausted with pleasure she felt Kára withdraw, sated.

Everything is as it should be.

Emma leaned forward and kissed Palna's scar. His vitality was like glowing coals in her, fueling her strength and bearing the burden of the Wild Stormy One within her.

"I'm tired as if I've already gone to the afterworld. What have you done to me, valkyrie?" Palna's face was gray from exhaustion.

"The best I could," she smiled.

When Acca used to sell Emma's services to men, she could only lie still and wait for the pain of their sweaty pushing and groaning to end. With Kára inside her, she had conquered the chieftain, ridden him, and controlled every action as she drank in his vitality.

And yet he was grateful and tenderly stroked her hair.

"Is my sister right when she says that you were sent from the hidden realm to aid us in our struggle against the Christian cross?" he asked with gravity.

Emma lay down on her back and peered up at the hides that made up the tent fabric above her head. It was a big question, but Kára was silent and offered no answer.

"The Most High will always be at your side," Emma finally said to soothe Palna's curiosity.

The words pleased him, and he kissed her hand.

"Tell me about your father," he said.

Her father? Emma licked Palna's fingers. They tasted like salt from sweat and her.

"He was a Viking who raped my mother, despite her being of Danish blood."

"That kind of thing happens in war."

He tenderly stroked her breast and let his hand continue on down toward her abdomen. Emma felt Kára awaken, and she hungrily moved her breast toward his mouth.

"Do you know how old you are?" he asked before closing his lips over her breast and biting her so she whimpered.

"I think I'm fifteen."

He changed breasts and started playfully nibbling so that enjoyment sped through her body.

"And you were born in Jórvík?"

She sighed, annoyed. Why did this matter?

"No, in Mikklavík by the border of the Danelaw. I tell people Jórvík because no one's ever heard of my village. There was a war and the Vikings had come to take back the land that had been lost. My father raped my mother in the village and then I came to the world."

Her mother had hated her for the disgrace of what happened. She had hardly fed her and hadn't been able to look at her, no matter how much Emma begged and cried from hunger.

Palna released her breast. A trickle of blood ran from the scratch marks she'd made on his back. Red-hot with life, the trickles found their way down to his waist. She carefully licked up this life force, groaning as the taste filled her mouth.

Palna got up and poured himself a cup of mead.

"Did I do something wrong?" Emma asked, wiping her mouth as the intoxication from the blood filled her.

Palna didn't answer, just looked at the wooden cup in his hand.

"Mikklavík was burned to the ground," he said briefly. "Everyone is dead."

Her mother was dead. Emma lay back on the animal skin rug and tried to remember her mother. She could clearly picture the hatred in her mother's face whenever she reached out her childish arms, and how she had turned away when Emma was sold to Acca. She also remembered her siblings, their warm, heavy bodies in her lap, their arms around her neck, and the way they smelled as babies.

"Were the children dead?" she whispered.

Palna nodded.

Emma tightened her lips. "Things will be better for them in the afterworld," she said.

"True," Palna responded, and took a swig of mead.

He just stood there, frozen. It was clear to Emma that he was hiding something.

Palna has visited Mikklavík before.

A stab of disgust surged through Emma.

"What else are you hiding about my home village?" she asked.

Palna cleared his throat and emptied his cup in one go. "I fought in Mikklavík when I wasn't much older than you are now. What we did in that village was not honorable. We were wild after having lost many of our brothers."

Emma sat up with Kára's roars of laughter echoing in her head. Slowly she began to comprehend the significance of what he'd said.

"You were one of the men who raped my mother?"

Palna looked at her wanly. Then he shrugged, as if the whole thing were unimportant.

"It was a long time ago. Worse things have happened."

Emma took a deep breath, sucking the air in through her teeth. Her thighs were still wet with his seed. She had ridden him greedily, hungered to have him inside her. Shame filled her with more disgust.

"Did I just bed my own father?"

Palna studied her.

"No, that's hard for me to believe," he finally said. "You don't look anything at all like my daughters."

That doesn't mean anything.

She huddled up and clung tightly to that consolation, as paltry as it was.

"How many of you were there?" she asked.

"Lots. Father gave us a real beating afterward for desecrating Danish blood. It wasn't something I was proud of."

He'd raped her mother. Her mother and her siblings were dead.

That doesn't mean anything. You're mine now, Kára said.

Palna sat down on the bed and stroked her naked thigh while Kára, whispering, swept away her shame and sorrow.

"No point in thinking about the past," he said. "Better to enjoy the delights of the present."

Emma grabbed his hand and looked him in the eye. "How many of you were there?"

"A lot. I don't remember who."

He got his hand free and slid it up between her legs. Emma moaned reluctantly.

More, we need more.

"You're not related to me by blood, I swear," Palna said.

Kára surged through Emma like a wave and lifted away all reflection, and like someone drunk she spread her legs and let the dís open her arms.

ᛗ

The din of battle approached relentlessly along with the smell of smoke from Uncle Rune's burning farm. Sigrid clenched her teeth and walked on beside the carts carrying the wounded. There was no doubt in her heart that Freya would yet again give them a victory and that they would reach the ship. That's not what was bothering her like an unhealed wound, but rather how Anund's men had attacked them.

Jorun sat with Stig from Toste's hird and tried in vain to do something about the gash in his chest. All the while, she waved away the flies buzzing hungrily around the blood that seeped through the bandage on his leg wound. Alfhild gave three other wounded men water and urged them to drink even though they didn't want to. Her face was gray, either from fear or from the stench of the men's wounds. There was no trace of her usual gaiety. The oxen trudged ahead slowly as the carts' wooden wheels bumped along the path. The warriors continuously scanned the surrounding area, ready for the battle that would soon come.

Beyond the treetops the dark smoke rose to the clouds. They would be there soon.

Toste had ridden ahead with his warriors to help his brother while Axel and several of the Svea faithfully remained by Sigrid's side. They said that they would be strong enough to overcome any warriors who attacked, but Anund had carefully planned his assault, and he seemed to have good information about their journey.

Sigrid urged Buttercup, who trotted along behind her, and picked up her pace so that she caught up to Ulf, who was still riding even though his horse was tired.

"What if one of us has ties to Anund," she said under her breath.

Ulf scoffed and shook his head. "You speak as if you understood the business of men. None of the Scylfings would betray their own people."

"How do you know that?"

If Ulf were a quicker thinker, he would have realized that the whole idea was worth considering and entirely possible. Many Scylfings had lost family members to the Svea and were not happy about her marrying King Erik.

"Because everyone voted for the alliance with Svealand at the Thing. There was no dissent among the chieftains; no one spoke out against the idea."

Ulf spoke to her as if to a feebleminded child, but Sigrid had never allowed herself to be silenced by him.

"If you were deceitful enough to serve Anund in secret, then would you speak out against all the chieftains at the Thing, or would you remain silent and listen so that you could give Anund the information he needed?"

"There is only one way to Rune's place. Anund may have had men keeping an eye on us who saw us leave home. With a fast horse, the spy could give plenty of notice."

Sigrid nodded. What Ulf said was possible, apart from one thing.

"A spy would never have been able to ride through our lands without being seen. The farms are too close together."

Ulf shook his head and urged his horse on so it trotted ahead and moved up the line, away from her. Sigrid sighed.

Grant us wisdom, Vanadís, because some of us could really use it.

"I think there's a lot of merit to what you say," said Axel from behind her.

Sigrid turned around in surprise. She had spoken so quietly that she hadn't thought the messenger would hear her.

"What should we do about it?"

The din of the battle was louder now, and the smell of smoke spread through the trees. The scouts they had sent on ahead came galloping back down the path.

"Wait and watch," Axel said and put his helmet back on. "There are more pressing matters right now."

He rode off to meet the scouts.

"Are we going to die?" Alfhild called from the cart.

"No, but we're getting close to the fighting," Sigrid answered and mounted Buttercup.

"They're going to kill us all. We're going to end up like him."

Alfhild made a gesture toward the wounded warrior she had been tending. He now lay dead, his eyes staring vacantly. Soon she began to cry, cowering beside the body. Jorun took her hand to comfort her as if that were going to help.

Sigrid clenched her jaws. The last thing they needed right now was crying and blubbering.

"Pull yourself together, Alfhild. The goddess is protecting us. You must believe that."

"How can you say that when it's not true?" Alfhild said, looking at Sigrid as if she were crazy. "If she's watching over us, how could she let him die?"

"Watch your words, kinswoman," Jorun told Sigrid. "Not everyone has your strength and faith," Jorun said, putting her arm around Alfhild's shoulders and glaring at Sigrid.

Sigrid shook her head. How could anyone lose their sense and resolve on this day of all days? Their lives had been saved. What more of a sign did they need?

"If you're going to cry, then do it silently," she said and urged Buttercup onward.

She rode over to the men who had gathered by the edge of the woods farther up the path.

"It's over," Ulf told her without taking his eyes off the hillside below them.

Sigrid took a deep breath and looked out over the devastation.

Rune's farm sat on a peninsula that jutted into the river. A tall wooden palisade, burning on all sides, surrounded several houses that seemed to have escaped the flames. What was burning instead were the buildings outside the palisade, a few wooden scaffolds by the shore, and two ships down by the water. The smoke lay thick over the clear blue river, like fog on an autumn morning, and no other ships were visible. Without ships, she thought with worry, their journey was over.

But they had won the battle. Sigrid saw bodies in the grass but no fighting going on anywhere. The Scylfing warriors and other fighters she assumed must be Rune's people were walking toward the gates in the palisade.

Sigrid wiped the sweat from her brow. Victory was had, but at what price? With a heavy heart she followed the men down the hillside and over to the farm while the carts followed with difficulty.

Standing beside his brother Rune, Toste was sweaty and red in the face after the battle. His ax and armor were stained with blood, as was his beard, and beneath the sweat running over his face there were cuts and gashes. His shirtsleeves were torn open, and he had a small wound on his arm, so small that he didn't seem to notice it.

"Once again we have driven the enemy away, and we didn't lose a single man," Toste announced, and the warriors around him raised their axes. Like a pack of dogs they barked at the sky.

When they quieted, Toste once again looked at Sigrid, his eyes dark with anger.

"I swear in your name, daughter, that after I return to Skagulheim, each and every member of Anund's clan, women and men, will be dispatched to the afterworld. My sword will not rest until it is done."

The men yelled even louder, raising their axes to the sky. Sigrid simply touched her heart in response, showing that she was moved by his oath.

"Thor will give you victory, Father," she replied and coughed as the wind turned, bringing a cloud of acrid smoke with it.

She sincerely wished that all of Anund's brutes would be destroyed. Only now did she comprehend the scope of their ill will and their thirst for Scylfing blood.

"How will we get to Svealand now that the ships have burned?" Sigrid asked. If they couldn't continue their journey, Anund would have won all the same.

Rune, who was both younger and taller than his brother, started laughing.

"Oh, we managed to row most of the ships across the inlet. They're waiting safely over there for your journey. This isn't the first time they've attacked us, and we're all too familiar with their flaming arrows and appetite for my vessels."

Sigrid took a breath of relief. That was good news. She praised Rune's cunning, as her fury at Anund grew even stronger. He had no reason to attack the Scylfings, and yet time after time his men came looking for battle. They were butchers, brutes that hid behind the skirts of a seeress.

May your valkyries slaughter them all.

"May Anund and his kin be cursed for all eternity," Sigrid said, looking Rune in the eye. "May you exterminate them until no one remembers their names anymore. Sing of my fury, and let all remember how they failed to kill me today."

Rune bowed his head in respect.

"Your name will be heard at our next battle against them, my kinswoman."

A yell made Sigrid turn her head.

"Speaking of fury, you still haven't met my wife, Ylva," Rune said and smiled at a plump matron striding toward them with a grim look on her face. Her gray dress was stained with blood and soot, and her hair hung loosely around her blotchy red face, but it was hard to tell whether her ruddiness was from anger or from exertion.

"Rotten men, isn't it enough that you let the outbuildings burn down? Now you're making the girl stand outside the gate without offering her either water or shade." Without waiting for a response, Ylva stopped in front of Sigrid and gave her a concerned look. "Your face is white as snow. No wonder, after everything you've seen. Come with me now, and let the men tend to their own."

She took a firm hold of Sigrid's arm and led her through the open wooden gates of the palisade and into the courtyard. The house was half the size of Skagulheim and had a thatched roof. There were only three outbuildings but more fenced-in paddocks, where farm animals paced anxiously as people rushed past. Slaves better nourished than those back home ran with water sacks to put out the last of the fire burning in the palisade. A wounded warrior's comrades helped him walk into the longhouse.

"You can get a little peace and quiet over here," Ylva said, ushering Sigrid to a garden by the side of the main house.

Between the hop vines, medicinal plants, and herbs there stood a wooden bench, where she pushed Sigrid down to sit. Ylva yelled for a slave, who came running right away with a cup of water and a cloth woven from the finest linen so she could wash her hands and face.

"Poor girl, you're just a child, after all," mumbled Ylva while Sigrid cleaned herself up and was given a cup of milk to drink. "And to think they're going to drag you all the way to Svealand." Ylva shook her head and grunted. "Men and the things they come up with."

Sigrid leaned her head against the sun-warmed wall of the house and inhaled the scent of flowers as exhaustion washed over her in waves. The rest of the retinue entered the courtyard, and horses and oxen were unharnessed. Alfhild and Jorun stood by the carts and looked around awkwardly. Ylva put her hands on her hips and sternly scrutinized them.

"Are you Sigrid's?" she called. "Why are you standing there lazing around? Take her things to the inner room in the house. Child, show them where it is."

A slave child quickly hurried over to Sigrid's kinswomen, grinning.

"You don't manage your servants very well," Ylva scolded. "That bodes ill for the cloak you will shoulder up north. Keep after them and never let them idle, that's what I always say." Ylva sat down on the bench next to Sigrid and eyed her with concern. "Toste is crazy to send you north with only two worthless handmaids. I'd better set them straight and give them a talking to. Now if only this whole thing ends up being worth your long journey so there'll be peace in these parts. The gods know we've had our fill of fighting with Anund."

Ylva patted Sigrid's cheek with moving tenderness. Sigrid swallowed and forced herself to smile, though her body felt like collapsing.

"Oh, you young thing," Ylva said, concerned. "It pains me that you have to go through all this without your mother at your side. If you were one of my children, I would never have married you off to any Svea, that's for sure."

Maybe it was Ylva's care, the long ride, the battles, the storm dís, the premonition, or all of it together, but suddenly tears started rolling down Sigrid's cheeks. In vain she tried to hide the shame behind her hands, but Ylva hugged her and stroked her back.

"You cry, young lady. Just get it out."

Sigrid shook her head. She couldn't help blubbering like a feeble-minded slave, low on sense and born to serve. Angrily, she wiped away her tears.

"A Scylfing never cries."

Ylva sniffed scornfully and said, "What kind of nonsense have they been drumming into you over in Skagulheim? Did Allvis say that? Of course she did. That old woman was born with a heart of stone, and I know how hard she brought up my Rune. It took me years to make him human again. How can she make you a full-fledged member of the family and then turn around immediately and send you off to live with strangers who are far from honor and integrity?"

Ylva ran her hand over the mark on Sigrid's wrist and shook her head with concern as she tucked a few wisps of hair that had come out of Sigrid's braids behind her ears.

Sigrid wasn't planning to speak ill of Grandmother. Instead she rinsed her face with the cool water.

"I saw a seeress in the woods," Sigrid said. "She made the mist swallow us."

"Then you're really blessed to be alive, because the hag you met is powerful," Ylva said with an astonished look.

Sigrid smiled wanly.

"Nothing can withstand the dazzling Radiant One. She listened to my invocation and sent a storm dís, who drove Mist away so our men could see the enemy and fight."

Surprise and disbelief were clearly visible in Ylva's eyes, and she sat for a long while in silence.

Then she cautiously asked, "Have you spoken to Our Lady before?"

Sigrid couldn't help but laugh.

"Yes, every day for as long as I can remember. On my blood night she sent me the dís, Kára, who descended to earth. She drove away the fog when the battle was at its peak."

"Anything else?" Ylva asked, and Sigrid nodded eagerly.

"She sent me a dream about my husband. He was holding a child who was going to become the king of kings, and the boy called me Mother and warned me that someone wanted to kill me. That's all."

Ylva stood up. She paced back and forth in front of the bench.

"Have you spoken to Allvis or any of the others about this?"

"I explained what happened at my mother's burial mound," Sigrid said with a shrug. "And she knows that Freya watches over me."

"Gracious Mother," Ylva muttered and paused. She plucked a leaf off the hop vine.

"We're shipbuilders and farmers, and I don't know any more about the Hidden than that the fields give us a good harvest if we sacrifice faithfully. But my mother talked about her sister. When she got her period, she started to be able to see into the Hidden. And Grandmother, who had good sense about most things, wanted to send her to three priestesses who lived by themselves on a farm in the district so that she could learn the old ways there. My grandfather refused and my aunt remained on the farm, alone with her visions, portents, and spirits. It got to be too much for her mind, which broke and clouded. One day she was gone and when they saw her again much later, she was filled with darkness and using her witchcraft to do ill."

Ylva nodded gloomily when she saw Sigrid's expression.

"Yes, she was the one you met in the Alva Woods—Ragna, cursed be her name. She serves Anund now and uses her witchcraft against her own family." Ylva stroked Sigrid's cheek. "Maybe you've also got the talent. You can never get away from the gift, but if you're left alone with it, it will become a curse. And alone is just what you've been."

She sounded so tender Sigrid thought she would burst into tears again.

"I follow the goddess's will," Sigrid said, "to marry Erik and become mother to the greatest prince of them all."

She had no choice; there was no other way to go.

"They've really succeeded in controlling you both in heart and mind," mumbled Ylva. "That is a great destiny to shoulder. May you not go astray along the way."

Sigrid wondered what Ylva meant. How could she go astray with Freya herself guiding her? Before she managed to say anything, Ylva noticed a servant girl cautiously approaching them.

"What are you staring at?" she asked the girl.

"The bath water is warm, matron."

"Well, just say so, then. You can go help with the food now." She dismissed the girl with a wave, and she ran off toward the cookhouse. Ylva watched her go and then shrugged. "Only a seeress can give you the advice you need now. The powers prevail, and the Norns weave the fates of mankind. What must happen happens, and if Vanadís is watching over you now, you don't need to feel afraid."

She stood up, stretched her back, and grimaced. It had been a long day for everyone.

"On the other hand, food you need, and a warm bath. Come and we'll find your incompetent maidservants and see if they can find you a clean skirt."

Sigrid followed her aunt Ylva, her questions multiplying. Yes, only a seeress could give her answers, but where would she find one of those?

ᛁ

"Rarely is a sleeping man victorious." Sweyn woke with a start from the hard kick. Without thinking, he grabbed his sword at his side and stood up, ready to face the enemy.

Åke stood in the darkness and laughed. "Calm down," he told his foster brother.

Sweyn took a deep breath and looked around at the ship. The warriors were still sleeping between the oarsmen's benches, snoring loudly. A light gray fog lay over the sea, and in the distance they could make out the full sails of the other ships. Everything was as it should be. Sweyn exhaled and drowsily rubbed his eyes. His tongue was swollen, and his mouth tasted like a pigsty.

"Father wants to talk to you," Åke said.

"There's no need to kick my leg off for that," muttered Sweyn.

"Rough night? You look like Garm's been chasing you around Gnipa Cave."

"What does Father want?"

Åke shrugged. Then he lay down on Sweyn's bed and closed his eyes.

Ranfaxe rocked beneath Sweyn's feet as he walked toward the stern. Gunnar was at the tiller, which he usually manned until dawn. No one was better suited to commanding the ship overnight than Gunnar.

Palna stood next to his brother, looking out at the sea. When he heard Sweyn approach, he turned around and looked him over. Signs of age and the burdens of life showed clearly on Palna's scarred face. Even so, few if any could beat him at single combat or in battle. Sweyn was ready to follow him all the way to Niflheim if he demanded, for there was no one he held in higher esteem.

"Are you ready to face your birth father?" Palna asked.

Sweyn calmly looked his father in the eye and replied, "I'm not afraid of him."

Palna and Gunnar exchanged glances.

Gunnar shook his head and said, "Thank the gods for your youthful ignorance, because there's no better shield."

Gunnar gestured toward the oarsman's bench closest to him, where the food was laid out. Sweyn sat down and took a little of the salted meat and tore off a piece of black bread.

"The Jellings are very powerful, and even if age has been hard on Harald, there's no certainty this will work. If you can't persuade him to give you what you want, all the plans we've so carefully laid will fall away."

Sweyn nodded and concealed the anxiety that burned in his belly.

"I know what must be done," he said.

Palna stuffed a piece of bread into his mouth, eyeing him seriously.

"Will you rein in your temper?" Palna asked.

Sweyn nodded yet again.

"Remember that you do not stand alone," Palna said and put his hand on Sweyn's shoulder, an unfamiliar gesture. "You are a credit to me, both as a son and a warrior. I look forward to watching you fulfill your destiny."

Ranfaxe lurched beneath them, leaping forward over the waves. The sun chariot had been pulled almost up out of the sea, and a faint light fell on the ships that followed them. Their full gray sails carried the mark of the Jómsvíkings, the hammer and the roaring wolf, the most dreaded crest in northern seas.

No one was their match when it came to strength or battle, but even so, Sweyn felt doubt chafing in his chest. He was a bastard, without wealth or standing, while the Jellings were the most powerful of all Danish families. To stand before their leader, a king widely renowned for his strength and cunning, would be no easy matter.

"I'm ready to fight to the death for you," Sweyn said. "But King Harald has three legitimate sons whom he highly esteems. The elder brothers, Erik and Haakon, are already vying for their father's title."

"Are your brothers better men than you?" Palna asked with distaste. Hesitation was not something he wanted to see. A Jómsvíking was bold and feared nothing.

Sweyn took a deep breath of the salt-saturated air, and despite not knowing the answer, he told his foster father no.

"Then take what you want with the right of might. Remember to keep your anger in check. Harald is obligated to recognize you as his son and give you what you desire. That is the victory we seek, no other."

Palna looked out at the sea where the sun had risen now. Land was just barely visible in the distance—their land, the land of the Danes, Sweyn's future kingdom. The breeze carried their boats toward Lejre at full sail. The waves, like powerful seahorses, galloped eagerly onward over Rán's fathoms, bringing them closer to the shore.

"Today the game begins," Palna said. "Maybe our protective dís will lead you to victory."

Sweyn glanced gloomily at Emma, who was huddled farther up in the boat, rocking back and forth, her eyes wide, a manic smile on her face. That wasn't the help he needed. Let him not err in this. Let him not disappoint Palna.

◆ ◆ ◆

Kára sang along with the morning dísir who slowly danced around the boat. Those ethereal beings, barely visible in the half-light, were now stroking the sleeping warriors, now swirling up again, dancing playfully with each other.

She urged the wind, which easily filled the sail and carried the boat forward. She appealed to Rán's nine daughters, who stirred beneath them.

Sisters, carry me carefully onward.

A chorus of otherworldly voices chimed in from the depths in greeting.

Though Emma's head ached, she gazed at the Hidden with fascination. When the veils were lifted, she could see the Norns' weaving. In that tapestry, all life and havoc spiraled through time and the universe. Humans, so arrogant and frail, were just brief sparks in the rainbows of light and darkness that flowed through the nine worlds.

She was everything and nothing.

A frail container that had been blessed.

A fiery band of pain tightened around her skull and burned so that Emma moaned, her body shivering uncontrollably. She wrapped her cloak around her and shuffled closer to Beyla, who slept curled up against some sacks.

"Help me, I'm in so much pain," Emma pleaded.

The seeress grunted discontentedly and reluctantly opened her eyes.

"My head feels like it's splitting in two," Emma whimpered. She almost started crying from the excruciating pain. It was like knives stabbing through her hair.

Beyla rubbed her eyes and said, "Everything has a price." She yawned widely and then stretched, reaching for her rucksack, and pulled out a wooden bowl and some little cloth-bound bundles.

"I had a feeling this would happen," Beyla mumbled and started mixing herbs with a dark sludge in the bowl. "A dís is too large to be contained in an untrained mind."

One of the warriors got up from his bed and stretched before walking over to piss over the gunwale.

Palna was talking to his son Sweyn at the stern of the boat. He looked pale and haggard after the night Emma had spent with him. Emma knew Beyla had advised him not to sleep with her anymore, lest Emma siphon off more vitality than he could spare. It didn't matter, she thought. She rubbed her temples, trying in vain to drive away the excruciating pain.

"It should steep for longer, but this will have to do. Drink," Beyla said, handing her the bowl of viscous sludge. Without hesitation, Emma drank it all. She almost threw up from the bitter dirt taste and swallowed until her stomach stopped tossing and turning.

"Thank you," she whispered, wiping away the sweat that appeared on her forehead. "What's happening to me?"

Beyla gathered up her bundles and carefully placed them back into her sack.

"Don't ask what you already know."

Emma looked down at her clenched, dirty fist. Neither her body nor her mind was up to bearing the wild, raging Kára for long. The dís's strength was too great to be borne in a human vessel. Both the bad and the good would get worse until Emma fell apart.

"What can I do?" Emma pleaded, huddling under her cloak.

"You are an empty sack, a tool the dís is using," Beyla said, giving her a look of compassion mixed with scorn. "Feel joy and gratitude for having been chosen."

Emma pulled her hands over her face and tried to drive away the throbbing pain.

"Why did she choose me?" she sobbed.

Beyla sighed heavily, as if Emma were a simpleminded child.

"I will soothe your pain and your madness, and I will help Kára with her cravings. But only the dís knows what she wants. As you will, too, eventually, once you've learned to interpret the Great One's will."

Emma shuffled across the rocking deck and curled up by the seeress's side. She pressed against the older woman and asked the question to which she already knew the answer.

"Am I going to lose my mind?"

"You already have, girl," Beyla said, drowsily patting her hand.

Emma started to cry. She clung to the seeress's hand and watched her with pleading eyes.

"Am I going to die?" she whispered.

"No," Beyla answered. She looked around the ship where the warriors were still sleeping between the oarsmen's benches, rocked by the endless waves that carried them northward. Then she turned her gaze to Emma, regarding her tenderly.

"Don't you realize that you already are dead?"

᛭

Sigrid clung tightly to the gunwale as the ship pitched and heeled at full sail. It was like riding a balky horse in stormy weather, and while everyone else seemed to enjoy getting splashed in the face with salt water, she wanted nothing more than to feel the ground under her feet and sleep peacefully in a feather bed, far from these cramped quarters and the unpredictability of the sea.

It shouldn't be long now. The Danes' kingdom rose from the sea around them. It was flat and lacked the mountains and big forests they had back home. Fat farm animals grazed in the grassy meadows and in the tilled land, rye and flax bowed in the wind. In the middle of all this stretched the countless houses of Lejre.

"That's really a sight for the gods," Ulf murmured.

Sigrid quietly took in Lejre. More ships than she could have dreamt of crowded at the wharves or lay pulled up on the beach, and the workshops, dwellings, and shops were so thick that you couldn't tell where one building stopped and the next one started. The royal hall was on a hill; it was a large longhouse surrounded by more buildings than she could count. Next to these were the burial mounds where the Æsir kings, her own ancestors, were buried.

"Just wait until you see the shops. You can buy anything in Lejre, and the royal hall is the most luxurious in all Scandinavia." Her brother smiled widely. "We're really lucky to be here for the summer festival. They say it's something to remember."

Sigrid turned away from Ulf's happiness. Did he really think she desired fabric, wealth, and pomp? They'd almost been killed in the Alva Woods, and many good men had fallen fighting Anund's warriors. Every night before she went to sleep she pictured the dead, young men who'd died protecting her. She would carry that guilt for the rest of her life.

They had made it across the sea by the skin of their teeth. Today Rán's daughters were sweeping around the ship, threatening to pull them down to the monsters that hid in the wet darkness beneath them. Just as they were finally going to have solid ground beneath their feet, the next hazard was already lurking. Sigrid shivered and clung tight to the gunwale.

Lejre was a place filled with cross-worshipping strangers who would try to exorcise their minds with Christian incantations.

"They are apostates, so poor that they only worship a single god, and he's nailed up on a cross," her aunt Ylva had explained with a look of distaste. "If you meet one of their priests, don't talk to or look at him. They can take over your will."

Ylva had explained how they ate their dead god's body and drank his blood. She also said that they were forced to renounce all other gods and goddesses, so their god could take over their minds and control their actions.

"The Danes kill those who hold on to the old ways, so promise you'll be careful," Ylva had warned as they said their good-byes on the shore by Rune's farm.

Sigrid had promised and then given her aunt Buttercup as a gift of friendship. Buttercup had nudged her with her muzzle the way she usually did when Sigrid was feeling sad. Sigrid felt the tears come. If she had a choice, she would have stayed with Ylva. She made her feel safe. But Sigrid had to keep going and shoulder her fate. She took a deep breath of briny air and all the unfamiliar scents it bore.

"How will we protect ourselves against the Christians' incantations?" she asked seriously.

"King Harald may have banned the old religion among his people, but many of them still make sacrifices in secret," Ulf said calmly, grabbing hold of his cloak, which was flapping in the wind. "Strangers are entitled to their own beliefs. As long as you don't proclaim anything about Vanadís, there won't be any trouble."

Sigrid gave a doleful laugh and said, "So I'm supposed to deny my faith?"

Doing that would be renouncing life in this world and the next.

"You're not Sigrid Tostedotter anymore," Ulf said somberly. "You're Erik's bride now, the future queen of Svealand. As such, you must be careful in your words and your actions."

Sigrid couldn't help but smile at her brother's simplistic notions. The temple was in Aros, the cradle of the faith from where the gods' and goddesses' power shone over the world.

"I am going to be queen of a land where the old ways are at their strongest. How can I hide my belief?"

Ulf gave her a patronizing look and said, "The Svea and Danes have been enemies for generations. Even though a fragile peace prevails for the moment, war could break out again at any time. If the queen of Svealand openly challenges Harald's law against the old religion, you will be offending the Danish king's honor in your husband's name."

Sigrid glanced nervously toward Lejre, which was getting closer and closer. She clearly had a lot to learn. No matter where she turned, there was something unfamiliar and strange. Offending her future husband's honor was the last thing she wanted to do. After all, Sigrid was supposed to be his pride and joy. Fear seized her gut.

How was she going to manage everything and at the same time defend herself against the Christians' incantations? What if she made a mistake?

Beloved Vanadís, send me a seeress who can interpret your signs and tell me what to do.

"Father should have prepared you better," mumbled Ulf.

"Don't speak ill of Father. He raised me just fine, thank you very much," she said. She sulkily brushed aside a lock of hair that was whipping her face.

"We're all gifts that are given away to increase his wealth. You just haven't realized that yet. How could you, having been left to run around in the woods and fields with no one to look after you?"

"But you and Father are so close," Sigrid said, taken aback at the bitterness in her brother's voice.

Ulf had shadowed Toste in everything since he was a little lad, and she'd often been jealous of him for that. Her brother shrugged and looked out at the sea.

"We were close until I wanted to marry Ingeborg from Haglaskog. But Father decided that Jorid and her five farms would make a more propitious marriage. Now I'm engaged to an ugly woman and Ingeborg has married someone else."

Sigrid's astonishment grew. She had no idea Ulf was so upset about that.

"Marriage is the sacrifice we make for the family," she replied.

"That's Father's voice talking, not your own desires. Remember that Father married Mother for love, then he married Gunlög for her beauty. But he's selling us off to the person who benefits him the most."

Ulf's words were true and correct, yet they didn't sit well with Sigrid.

"You shouldn't say such things."

She cast an anxious glance at Toste, who was cheerfully chatting with Axel on the other side of the boat.

"The day you care about something other than the old ways and yourself, you'll have the right to speak," Ulf said, staring out at the water.

Sigrid clenched her teeth. What did he know about anything?

"It's unmanly to moan and pine for a maid you didn't get."

Brother and sister stood glaring at each other in silence when a yell was heard over the wind.

"There are ships behind us!"

Sigrid turned to see six mighty dragon ships turning into the bay, heading toward them at full sail. Father stood up and beamed at them as they raced over the waves. He pointed to the wolf painted on the sail and shouted into the wind.

"It's the Jómsvíkings! Palna is their leader!"

Sigrid looked up at the ships. She had heard about the great exploits of the Jómsvíkings her whole life. No warrior could defeat them. Their chieftain Palna was Father's comrade-in-arms. Twice they'd gone on raids to the west and come home with tremendous riches and amazing tales.

Now Sigrid would finally get to meet the man she'd heard songs about by the hearth. Alfhild and Jorun whispered together as they smiled at the ship, already yearning for the warriors.

Only Ulf looked gloomy, leaning on the gunwale, glaring at the ships as if they were full of enemies. No doubt it was hard for him to be surrounded by impressive warriors when he had a bulging belly and was slow with his sword.

"Are you so jealous that you can't even stand to meet Jómsborg's heroes?" she asked.

"Ships filled with Jómsvíkings at Lejre's summer festival can never lead to anything good."

Sigrid couldn't help but laugh. "You sound like an old man. You're jealous of all the manly warriors."

Her brother didn't get angry, just glared at her dejectedly.

"You know not what you say, little sister. Someday you'll understand better."

◊

"Seems like half the world is here for the summer festival," Åke said, shoving Sweyn a little on the back to force him to walk farther up the shore.

Boats and ships crowded the wharves. They were pulled up on the long, narrow beaches or lay anchored in the harbor. Most of them were fishing boats or belonged to the king, but there were also two Obotrite ships, two dragon ships from Trondheim, and three well-built ships that none of them recognized. One was intended for trade, but two were built for battle, even though they didn't have dragon heads on their prows.

"They were built in Gardarik. Those vermin from the east are finding their way everywhere. They can't be trusted," Sigvard warned as they stopped by the wharves to wait for the others.

The market square was ahead of them. Merchants selling fish, shoes, clothing, livestock, and seeds turned and stared at them. Smiths, potters, weavers, and shoemakers left their work in the nearby workshops and came out to gape at them.

"Jómsvíkings," a craftsman wearing a leather apron whispered to his son.

"They say they're the king's best warriors," one woman told another as they both pushed their way through to get a good look.

Sweyn put his hand on his sword hilt and stretched, trying to look as tough and manly as he could.

Palna stood on the wharf, giving his ship captains instructions about what to do with their crews and slaves, but he paused as a man approached the wharves with his retinue. Sweyn recognized him as Skagul Toste.

The two chieftains embraced with such noisy heartiness that Sweyn was almost embarrassed by their unmanly display.

The fair-skinned Skagul Toste resembled a dandy in his expensive clothes and the jewelry around his neck and wrists, but Sweyn knew he was widely respected for his cunning and swordsmanship.

"Is that Toste's son? He hardly looks like he could lift a sword," Sweyn said, nodding at a young man their age, just as garishly dressed as his father but with a receding chin and a belly that billowed out over his belt.

Åke laughed scornfully at the weakling.

"He also has a magnificent daughter," Åke noted.

Sweyn trained his eyes on the young woman who waited behind Toste, and in that instant it was as if Thor sent a bolt of lightning that incinerated everything inside him.

She was like a dís descended from Valhalla. Her hair was the color of ripe wheat and curled enticingly around her serious face. Her eyes were the color of a quiet sea, and she had lovely posture and looked strong as a valkyrie. Sweyn stared, heart pounding, until Åke jabbed him in the side.

"You look like a slack-jawed fool," he said with a teasing smirk. "She's not that magnificent."

Sweyn quickly looked away and grabbed his sword hilt again as he tried to pull himself together.

"Sweyn and Åke, come over here," called Palna.

Sweyn clenched his jaws as he walked over to his foster father. By Thor's magic belt, Megingjörð, how was he ever going to withstand this creature?

Sigrid had never seen so many people in her life. They thronged around her like a swarm of bees. Matrons walked around with baskets in their hands, children ran around shouting, merchants held up dyed ribbons and things for sale, a foreigner in strange clothing spoke with a maid dressed in a simple frock, a dark-skinned man led an ox, and some dirty, skinny children gathered around them asking if they had any food.

Women and men in dirty, tattered clothing stood beside noblemen with silver around their necks and luxuriant matrons with serving girls. Pigs, dogs, and slaves walked around freely. There didn't seem to be any order.

Sigrid's head was on the verge of splitting from all the noise, and the stench made her feel sick to her stomach. Even on the hottest of days, the muck pit back home didn't smell this bad.

Sigrid regarded the cross worshippers with suspicion. Surely they could already tell that she followed the old ways. They were probably wondering how they could lure her to their god with their crosses and fish. She put her hand on her Freya mark. They didn't dare go after her. They would never fill her mind with their spirit.

I know you're watching over me, Vanadís.

Father spoke cheerfully with the leader of the Jómsvíkings. Palna was shorter than Sigrid had imagined. He didn't have any bulging muscles, rather he was thin and sinewy. His head was shaved, and he had a scar running across his cheek.

"Why don't they have beards?" she whispered to Ulf. All the men she knew proudly wore their beards long, so it seemed weird that the greatest of warriors hardly had any hair on his face at all.

"In battle, enemies can grab your beard and hair, so they always wear them short."

Well, she could understand that reasoning.

"That redheaded troll has a long beard," she said, nodding at one of the Jómsvíking warriors who had gathered a little ways away, surrounded by people staring at them. The "troll" was a giant of a man, almost two heads higher than the others, and had a straggly red beard and bushy hair of the same color.

"That's Ax-Wolf the berserker, the one who killed twenty warriors at the battle of Oldenburg. No man can defeat him whether he has a long beard or not."

Sigrid stared at the giant and almost felt dizzy at the thought of what these men had accomplished. Imagine having so many tales told about you at people's hearths. No wonder Ulf and the hird were so uncertain around these warriors. The Svea were tall and strong, but their clothes looked garish compared to the Jómsvíkings'. For their part, the Svea wore their beards braided. Many wore chains around their necks, in addition to the oath rings on their arms.

Palna's warriors wore simple tunics, breeches, and cloaks in rough gray cloth. But their armor was meticulously oiled, as were their weapons and belts. Very few of them had even an ounce of fat on their bodies, and their arms bulged with strength.

The Jómsvíkings looked like a pack of wolves that all the tame dogs were carefully avoiding.

"You're afraid of them," Sigrid surmised.

"They live and die only for battle and their brotherhood," Ulf said. "No one can defeat them, and they serve whatever side pays them best. Not even King Harald can keep them completely in check. Yes, I'm afraid of them, and you should be, too, sister."

A young warrior stood just behind Palna's back, staring down at the ground. His blond hair hung in wisps around his chiseled face. His body was as tense as a dog's before an attack. He wore the rough tunic of a Jómsvíking but carried a sword at his hip, and an ax hung from his belt. His shoes were laced halfway up to his knees and his cloak was held over his leather armor with a simple iron nail. Sigrid furrowed her brow. There was something familiar about him, as if they'd met several times before and knew each other well.

Just then the warrior looked up, and their eyes met. Sea-blue arrows shot into her body and tore her chest to pieces. Her heart was beating so hard she could scarcely breathe. Those were the same dark blue eyes, and the same hands picking up that laughing child. The warrior smiled hesitantly, and Sigrid plunged toward the abyss.

Vanadís, don't do this to me!

The dream had been her comfort and strength in the face of her coming marriage. The dream was what made her believe the goddess wanted her to become Erik's wife. But it had all been ashes and delusions.

"These are my sons, Åke and Sweyn," Palna said.

Sigrid looked at the Jómsvíking in despair and forced herself to greet him as she tumbled ever deeper into the darkness. Sweyn was the husband the dream had promised her, and now everything was lost. She was going to marry the wrong man.

ᛗ

Sweyn forced himself to look away from Sigrid. She was going to marry the king of Svealand, and there was no honor in ogling another man's wife.

Relieved, Sweyn watched Toste say good-bye to Palna and then leave with his retinue. Sweyn had to pull himself together and prepare to face his birth father. Nothing else mattered. He turned around and his eyes met Sigrid's one last time before she disappeared into the crowd.

"Toste's daughter made you lose all sense." Åke put his arm around Sweyn's shoulders and playfully thumped him on the armor as they walked over to the others. "You were staring at another man's wife like a drooling village idiot."

Sweyn pushed Åke's hand away. Yearning for another man's woman was against the Jómsvíking code, and Palna would kill him if he chased after Toste's daughter. He had to quit thinking about her, the same way he quit thinking about the temperature when he was cold and food when he was hungry. It was simple.

Sweyn turned his head to look again, but didn't see her anywhere.

"Have you been out raiding?" asked a boy in a ragged tunic with a dirty face.

Sweyn nodded, glad to be distracted. Two young ladies batted their eyelashes at him and whispered to each other, their cheeks blushing.

"Did you kill very many enemies?" the boy asked.

Sweyn nodded again.

"How many?"

"That's enough, Ragnvald," an older man said, pushing the boy along. "Excuse the boy. His head is filled with stories about you men. It makes it hard for him to hush up and mind his manners."

"I'm going to be a Jómsvíking when I grow up!" Ragnvald cried and then ran away when the man shook his fist.

"We've heard worse," said Sweyn, smiling at the boy, who stopped defiantly a few arm lengths away.

"I bet you have," the man said, nodding somberly. "Allow me to offer you some of Lejre's best mead. It would be an honor to serve Jómsvíkings."

He gestured to a wench, who came running over from a barrel of mead with a full pitcher and some cups that he eagerly began to fill for the warriors.

Sweyn accepted a cup and drank thirstily before passing it on.

"You're always welcome to come drink here. I'm Sten Halte. I sell the best mead in the kingdom of the Danes, served by the most beautiful wenches."

There were benches around the barrel, where several men were already drinking even though the day was still young.

Away on the wharf the slaves were being unloaded. Women and children stood close together, while the men stood on their own with their hands tied. They looked around with vacant eyes. Sweyn turned away, disgusted by their weakness.

The king's jarl and his men came riding into the square from the far end of the market. The sight of the fat jarl rocking himself down off his poor horse and waddling over to Palna silenced the Jómsvíkings.

"I come with the king's greetings. He wishes the Jómsvíkings a warm welcome to Lejre."

No one totally believed the words, but Palna put his hand on his heart anyway in a gesture of respect.

"You have the king's permission to pitch camp on the battlefield," the jarl continued. His cheeks jiggled as he spoke, and sweat ran down his forehead even though the day wasn't especially hot. "King Harald also summons you and your people to the hall this evening, Jarl Palna."

Sweyn squeezed his sword hilt tightly. So, he was going to face his birth father before the day was out.

"We are honored and will be there," Palna replied.

The jarl wiped the sweat from his brow and anxiously looked at the warriors who surrounded him.

"The king looks forward to hearing the news from the west and receiving his gifts."

"I can imagine," Palna replied guardedly and turned to his ship captains. "You heard that, men."

People immediately started passing on the information, and Sweyn went to fetch their belongings. There was no turning back now. If luck weren't with him, he'd be dead before dawn.

ᚹ

O Freya, Mistress of Folkvang, speak to me. Why did you send me the dream with the Jómsvíking? What is your will?

Sigrid looked at the sellers holding up their wares outside their shops. What if the warning dream about Sweyn had been sent by the evil seeress Ragna or other forces of darkness? If that was the case, Sigrid would have to make certain that hag burned on a bonfire and her remains were cursed so she could never enter the halls of Niflheim. Or were these Christians filling her head with phantoms? Sigrid shivered.

I don't understand what's happening.

It couldn't be Vanadís's will that she marry a young Jómsvíking without any land or farm or standing.

"Pick anything you want," Toste said proudly, gesturing toward the swaths of the finest linen, which Jorun and Alfhild were already fingering.

"It's beautiful," she said to a dark-skinned man who held a pearl necklace up to her.

Premonitions and seeresses, dísir and battles. Her head ached, and sweat ran down her back. Sigrid stepped aside to get out of the way of some goats, and her shoe landed in a mound of manure. Alfhild started giggling.

"You be quiet," she scolded her kinswoman, who stopped immediately. "Father, I'm tired and need to rest."

She saw disappointment in Toste's eyes, but she wasn't up to flitting from shop to shop like a butterfly. Not now, when her world had just collapsed.

"You're tired, I understand," he said and then lit up in a broad smile. "Only the best for my queen."

"It's crowded. There are a lot of people here for the summer festival, so it may be hard to find lodgings," said the servant who showed them the way to one of the longhouses surrounding the royal hall.

He was an older man in a greenish-yellow shirt and white breeches, with lips pursed inside his black beard. He had tired eyes, as if he were weary of guests arriving and disrupting his important duties.

"Is it King Harald's choice not to honor the queen of Svealand with suitable quarters, or is it your own?" Toste asked, raising an eyebrow.

The servant looked worriedly at Sigrid and the rest of the group before clearing his throat and saying, "If you can wait, I'll see if I can find you something more suitable."

Then he hurried off.

"Soon you'll have the quiet you need," Toste said.

Sigrid sank onto a bench and looked gloomily at the Danish king's royal hall. Four of her father's great halls would have fit in that one longhouse. Several beautifully ornate doors depicted brightly colored images from events she was not familiar with. The dark roof featured variously colored wood tiles forming a coiling pattern, and on the ridge at the very top there were gleaming black dragon heads, so big that they made the ones atop her father's hall look tiny. There were several longhouses surrounding the courtyard, in which magnificently dressed foreigners and warriors hurried back and forth.

She was going to marry a man who was just as powerful as the Danish king. Soon she would rule over the kind of splendor they had here. Could she marry Erik if that wasn't Freya's will? Could she refuse a king if peace was at stake? A glowing band of pain tightened around her head, so tight she couldn't think.

"See our ancestors' burial mounds," Toste said to cheer her up. "Here lie Harald Wartooth, the last of the kings, and Skjold, Rolf Krake, Frode Fredegod, and the rest of the dynasty's forefathers. They fought giants, trolls, dragons, and monsters to conquer this land. Their courage and sacrifice made our family strong."

Father nodded to himself as he contemplated their preeminence.

"That's great," Sigrid said in a monotone.

"I wish I'd lived back then and killed a dragon," Ulf said. "Like when Beowulf brought down Grendel."

Toste laughed, stuffing his thumbs into his belt, and replied, "Beowulf was a braggart, widely known for his exaggerations. Grendel was just a dragonling and they're easy to kill. If he'd met the mother, it would have been another matter. You should fear the females the most."

Sigrid turned away from the men, who started bragging about various females that had been killed and how dangerous they'd been. Two men in long gray cassocks with shaved heads walked across the courtyard. They went into a wooden building standing on a little hill between two halls. It wasn't until Sigrid saw the cross on the door that she realized it was a house for the Christian god.

She shuddered uneasily.

May the mistress of the valkyries burn them all to ash.

Their very presence was sacrilege. The All-Father himself had lived here before he traveled on, and the descendants of his sons lay buried here in their barrows. She hunched over on the bench, her head aching and burning.

Help me, Vanadís. I wander alone in the dark. Show me the way.

A woman in a long brown frock walked toward them, her pace so rapid that her blond assistant could barely keep up.

"Hail, Skagul Toste," she said. "I'm still waiting for the gift you so generously promised me when I tended your wounds."

Long gray braids swung around the woman's face, which was neither old nor young. She didn't wear a seeress's blue cloak, but Sigrid saw the cat pelt on her belt. That was the sign of Freya, and she was certainly a priestess of the old ways, even if she didn't show it openly.

Sigrid stood and inhaled deeply with relief.

Thank you.

She should never have doubted.

"O Revered One, I seek your council," Sigrid said.

The seeress didn't listen to her, just kept walking toward Toste, who immediately sank down before her in respect.

"Forgive my impudence, Beyla. Before the day is over I will repay you amply for your kind deed."

The seeress nodded in approval at Toste's fawning.

"You will find me in Palna's camp," she said and turned toward his daughter.

She peered at Sigrid with a focused squint. Deep wrinkles formed around her gray wolf eyes.

Sigrid had met two seeresses in her life: the kindly Helgur, who visited their estate with her retinue of priestesses every year to prophesy about coming times and love troubles, and the malevolent Ragna in the Alva Woods. This Beyla didn't resemble either of them.

"I'm looking for the gods' advice," Sigrid said, receiving a stern glance and a disparaging snort in response.

"Then you should look for it where the old ways are not forbidden," Beyla retorted. She nodded slightly to Toste and then walked quickly away.

Red specks danced before Sigrid's eyes. That seeress couldn't just leave her! Sigrid needed help. Otherwise she was lost.

"I beg you. Whatever you request, you shall have it," Sigrid called after Beyla, but the woman didn't even turn around.

Beyla's blond assistant remained nearby.

"Beyla can't help you," she tittered, looking up at Sigrid in delight.

"Get out of here," Toste yelled, taking a step toward the girl to drive her away.

But the blonde shook her head and told Sigrid, "I can't leave you, not ever, my lovely."

Sigrid looked uncomfortably at the insane girl. Her curly hair hung over her face, uncombed, her eyes were vacant of life, and drool trickled from the corner of her mouth.

"Move along," Toste ordered.

"Calm down, I'm here now," she whispered.

With a grunt she grabbed Sigrid's arm and pulled her sleeve up until her tattoo was visible, as if she'd known it was there all along. And then she kissed it. As she did so, she screamed, making a choking noise that sounded like it came from the throat of a dying animal. Her eyes rolled back. Then she swayed before collapsing to the ground.

Sigrid yanked her arm back and pulled her sleeve back down. She took a step back, her heart pounding in her chest.

"What are you doing?" Beyla said, having suddenly returned and taken the girl's arm and helped her to her feet. "Get yourself together now, Emma," she commanded with gruff tenderness.

Surprise and happiness came over the blond girl's face as she stood up, drowsily watching Sigrid.

"I saw her pain, so I took it," the girl said with a giggle.

Sigrid shivered uncomfortably at the girl's insanity. But when she rubbed her hand over her forehead she realized her headache was gone, as if it had never been there.

She gasped. "What did you do to me?"

All she received in response was a lunatic smile. Beyla put her arm around the girl, who laughed like a drunk, and then scrutinized Sigrid closely as if for the first time.

"Maybe we should talk, after all," Beyla told Sigrid. "Come to me tomorrow when the sun is at its zenith. Then you will get the answers you seek."

"You *are* a seeress!" Sigrid said. So she had been right, in the end.

"Lower your voice." Beyla's whisper was like the lash of a whip. She took a firm hold of her protégée and led her away from the courtyard. Perplexed, Sigrid watched them until they disappeared behind the thatched roof of a longhouse.

Tomorrow she would finally get her answers. Then the gods would reveal to her what was in the tapestry.

Thank you, Revered One, for this blessing.

ᚾ

Beyla held Emma firmly as she left Sigrid, supporting her unsteady legs with her staff.

"What did you see?" the seeress asked when they were away from listening ears, walking toward the field where the Jómsvíkings were pitching their camp.

"I saw what is to come," Emma said hoarsely and smiled sadly.

Words could not describe how beautiful it had been to see the glowing grains of sand floating in Sigrid's womb. They spun like a spiral slowly through time while everything that once was returned again in a never-ending repetition of the world's creation and destruction. Around that there was a swarm of sparks that glittered and then died. People's lives were brief instants in the eternal cycle of rebirth.

When Emma had grazed Sigrid's wrist, she had seen right into the Norns' weaving: countless shimmering life threads that ran in and out of each other—meetings, births, and deaths—down into the afterworld and up again as a new life. Everything was connected. No person was ever alone, whether in this life or the next. Only then did Emma understand why Kára had chosen her and why she was still alive. The relief and fear melted together into a roaring boom within her.

"I saw the future, and Sigrid carries it in her womb," Emma announced.

Beyla eyed her sharply, waiting impatiently for her to go on.

"She's going to bear a child. If he is not born, the tapestry will tear, and our world will break up into Ragnarök."

Emma shivered when she realized how frail the threads forming their world were.

If the tapestry tore, the people of the North would suffer horrors. Hoarfrost giants would be set free, and Fimbulwinter would spread with crop failures and death. Beyond the winter waited plagues that would wipe out almost everyone. Wars would rage, brother against brother, and there would be slaughter in the name of the cross. Only this unborn, the strongest of kings, could hold the tapestry together by creating harmony where there was only chaos.

Beyla was deathly pale.

"What else?" she demanded.

Emma smiled sadly at the memory of the woman screaming in pain and mortal fear.

"I will be sacrificed so that the child might live."

ᚾ

This was it. Sweyn clenched his jaws so hard they ached and took a deep breath. His whole life had led up to this moment. He put his hand on his sword hilt and felt the calmness as his fingers closed around it. His brothers-in-arms stood by his side. He would prevail, and with the right of might he would take what was his.

Åke gave him a look of encouragement, and the ship captains all looked confident. Even Ingolf could be trusted at a time like this.

"As one?" he asked.

"As one!" they responded.

Palna turned toward the ornate doors of the royal hall and reminded them, "Be on your guard, men. In this hall we are on thin ice. As Odin says, *At every doorway before proceeding, study the shelter, look around the shelter, because one never knows where a foe waits sitting within.*"

"I've been waiting for this moment for a long time," Sweyn said with a grim smile.

"Well, let's find out what kind of mood the king's in today," Palna replied, head held high, and walked toward the doors.

Two servants opened the doors wide so the nine Jómsvíkings could walk right into King Harald Bluetooth's royal hall.

People said the royal hall back in Jelling was the biggest ever built by a Scandinavian, but the torchlit hall they stepped into now in Lejre was plenty grand with its high roof and walls covered in tapestries and shields.

The people inside were dressed in showy, expensive clothes, and they stopped talking when they saw the Jómsvíkings walk in. There were many warriors in attendance, some from King Harald's hird. Storbjörn the Strong, the Jarl of Trelleborg, was there as well as several other chieftains along with their retinues. Other men looked weaker and were draped in silver chains. They were no threat. The Obotrites stood off on their own, as did other groups of foreigners.

The crowd parted, letting the Jómsvíkings through to the king. King Harald sat on a carved throne gleaming with silver and gemstones at the very back of the room. On a post on either side there were pictures of his and the Jellings' great achievements.

King Harald Bluetooth was both older and shorter than Sweyn had expected. His hair was thinning, and his beard was braided into a thin dark-red braid. His face was a sickly gray hue, like you see in the dying, and was plump but wrinkled with age. Golden threads were woven into his cloak, and red silk stretched over his swelling belly.

An elderly woman with her hair up in an elaborate hairdo sat in the smaller chair next to him. That must be Queen Tova, daughter of Prince Mistivoi of the Wends. Next to her sat a dark-haired, frail young maiden, probably their daughter Thyre.

On the king's other side sat three men dressed as courtiers in elegant clothes. Two of them were Sweyn's age. If they were his half brothers Erik and Haakon, the third young man might be Torgny, the youngest of Harald's sons.

The Jómsvíkings stopped in front of the king's throne. They closed their fists, placed them over their hearts, and bowed their heads, the sign that they belonged to Harald and offered him their respect. Silently they waited for the king to speak.

"Greetings, Jarl Palna, strong arm of the Danes, chief of Jómsborg," Harald finally said.

He moved on his throne, with difficulty, as if both his back and his legs ached. Sweyn's heart thudded heavily in his chest as his hatred gave him strength. The old man, swollen there on his throne, fat and putrefied, was an embarrassment and an abomination.

The difference between Harald and the strong, scarred Palna couldn't be greater.

"It's good to see you again, my friend," King Harald said, and as he spoke his blue front teeth were visible. They had been filed to points and dyed to show that he was the greatest of warriors. "I've heard your journey was successful and that you bring news."

His cordiality sounded so insincere that it turned Sweyn's stomach.

Harald feared Palna and the Jómsvíkings. Their swords had helped him to increase his power among the Danes and the Jutes. Their victories had made him a strong king. Harald had used their blood sacrifices. They had created this swelling atrocity who slaughtered Vikings for believing in the old ways and poisoned the realm with his greed.

"England's King Edward has been killed," Palna said. "The dowager queen Elfrida's people murdered him when he was visiting her castle. The queen's son, a mere boy, now sits on the throne. Æthelred is the name of this beardless king."

The king burst out in an immense laugh that echoed through the hall. Everyone fawningly joined in.

"So Elfrida killed her own stepson? For an old lady to show such manly courage says a lot about the Saxons." Harald sneered and ran his hand over his braided beard. "God himself must have given us this opportunity."

Sweyn grimaced.

"We will speak more of this," Harald said, satisfied. "First, however, I'd like to see what gifts you've brought."

Sweyn took a deep breath as Åke handed him the chest. Now was the time. As agreed, he followed Palna forward to the king's high seat, opened the lid, and showed the king and queen the spoils. It was only a small portion of what they'd found in the monastery—they'd kept most of it themselves—but it was enough to make the queen and her daughter cry out in delight. Harald nodded in contentment.

"You have been successful, Palna."

"I have capable warriors," Palna responded, putting his hand on Sweyn's shoulder. "This one killed sixteen men with his sword, matching his age in years."

A murmur of approval was heard from the guests, and Sweyn placed the chest at the king's feet. Head held high, Sweyn stood there, calmly looking King Harald in the eyes. All his anxiety and hesitation were gone. Everything but the enemy and he receded.

Harald leaned forward, the cross he wore on a chain swaying over his fat belly, and scrutinized Sweyn.

"Your father must be proud of you. Tell me his name." With that, Harald stepped down into the hole Palna had dug.

"My mother is Sleep-Åsa, a poor but very honorable woman who is highly esteemed by all. You know her well because when you visited my foster father Palna's estate, you raped her. You, Harald Gormsson, are my father, though you have never shown any pride."

The hall became quiet.

King Harald, red in the face, stared directly at Sweyn, as the queen grabbed hold of their daughter's hand.

"Who are you to presume to call yourself my son!" Harald bellowed, standing up. He stumbled forward toward Sweyn, filled with rage, but Sweyn held his ground.

When his mother had tried to get away, Harald had beaten her half-unconscious and then begotten Sweyn in blood and shame. Staring back at Harald, Sweyn clenched his jaws, thinking of his dear mother, whom everyone knew was the sweetest and friendliest of women.

"Your mother can't have chosen your father with much thought. I suppose she was following her own lascivious nature," roared King Harald, and spittle sprayed out, and a stench of decay billowed from his mouth. "It appears that you're just an urchin, just as crazy as your mother."

Sweyn wiped the spittle off his cheek and calmly regarded the fat king. He ought to kill Harald here on the spot, open up that swollen belly and piss on his intestines.

"I may be an urchin, all the same it is your obligation to behave honorably. Give me three ships with crews so that I can shape my destiny. That is all I ask." Sweyn spoke so calmly that he surprised himself.

"Who do you think you are to demand something of your king?"

"It is my right as your son."

Harald raised his hand as if to strike him and Sweyn waited, head held high, to receive the blow, but before it fell, Palna stepped between them.

"If you give him three ships, I will do the same," Palna said.

Harald lowered his hand and looked around the room where his guests and courtiers were carefully following what was happening. Only now did he realize that everyone had seen what had happened, and that this was not to his advantage.

"You know the boy is yours. He looks just like you when you were young; you can't swear your way out of this," Palna said.

Harald looked insane, and Sweyn put his hand on the hilt of his sword, sensing the vigilant strength of his brothers-in-arms behind him. Harald's hird was already moving to surround them, prepared to engage if the Jómsvíkings drew their swords in the royal hall. A drop of sweat ran down Harald's lined forehead, down his wobbling cheek.

You poor cockless, tired old thing, Sweyn thought, already able to smell victory. *I am the wolf that will slit open your throat while you snivel and cling to your crosses. I am the force coming to take your throne and send you to Niflheim. I am the future, while you are a fat, feeble shadow of the past. I am the one who is going to stick a sword into you and smile as I watch you die.*

Out of the corner of his eye he saw the queen whisper something to her daughter, Thyre, who immediately stood up and walked over to them.

"Can't you see that he's just as handsome as you, Father?" Thyre said lovingly, putting her hand on Harald's arm.

She had dark brown curly hair tinged with red and a beautiful face. Everything about her was refined and delicate, and yet she was able to calm the king and restrain him.

"Do not meddle in the affairs of men, Thyre," he said, but the anger in his voice was gone, and she did not seem upset by his words.

Instead she cocked her head and studied Sweyn carefully with her sea-blue eyes.

"Palna's right, everyone in the hall can see that the boy looks like you. Why reject a warrior who does you credit?"

Harald's rage evaporated as if it had never existed. He chuckled and patted her hand. Thyre smiled beguilingly; like a seeress she had reined in the king's temper.

"Imagine me having a Jómsvíking for a brother!" she exclaimed. Thyre was married to Styrbjörn the Strong. Sweyn had heard that she was a rare beauty and charming, but he never would have believed this.

Thyre leaned over to her father's ear and whispered so quietly that the words were scarcely audible.

"If you give the boy the ships, he can help my husband in battle. Then you can send Palna to fight, too. Once we defeat the Svea, Styrbjörn can take the throne, and the Svea can finally be Christianized. God will reward you for this, Father."

Harald's eye twinkled.

"I'll think the matter over," he said, sounding dignified, and turned his back to Palna and Sweyn, as if they were no longer there.

Leaning on Thyre's arm, the king walked toward two large doors that opened into an even bigger hall. Only after he had left did Sweyn slowly exhale and wipe his sweaty palms on his breeches.

"That wasn't so bad," Palna said as his ship captains moved in around him, forming a protective wall.

"I should have killed him for calling my mother lascivious," Sweyn replied.

Palna grunted and said, "And just how is King Harald supposed to recognize you as a Jelling if he's dead? Let him *give* you the hammer that you will crush him with."

"It's good that Thyre intervened," Ingolf said. "Freya herself must have sent your sister to assist you."

"It was the queen's doing," Åke said. "She sent Thyre to soften the king's anger."

"That gift will not come without strings attached," Palna said, thoughtfully scratching the scar on his face.

"Will he give me the ships?" Sweyn asked.

Palna stopped scratching, and his face brightened a little.

"It will be hard for Harald to get out of this. He didn't reject you after Thyre called you her brother. Everyone in the hall heard that. It would be dishonorable for him not to give you what you've asked for."

Sweyn clenched his fists and brazenly returned the gazes of the people in the hall. While he knew that to rule he would have to fight the chieftains and courtiers who turned their backs on him, the friendly nods he received from some in the hall pleased and encouraged him.

Tore, the stately Jarl of Juteborg, was the first to step forward toward the Jómsvíkings.

"Palna," he tersely greeted Sweyn's foster father, who returned the greeting with equal brusqueness.

The jarls of Harald's five ring fortresses were serious rivals. For Tore even to come over to them was unexpected. All the same he turned to Sweyn.

"May you receive your share of the inheritance," Tore said and then left the astonished Sweyn with a brief nod.

Palna crossed his arms over his chest and shook his head.

"You've made an unexpected friend there. If dissatisfaction among the Jutes is high enough that you can get Tore and Juteborg to stand on your side, much is gained."

Sweyn nodded. As always, his father was right.

The queen and the rest of the nobility walked by and scrutinized Sweyn, most of them with distaste and anger. One of the three men who'd been sitting beside the king, however, nodded amiably.

"That's your half brother Erik," Palna said. "He's next in line for Harald's throne."

"Don't let his cunning fool you. Erik covets the Jellings' throne as much as you do," said Skagul Toste, who had just walked up to the Jómsvíkings, unconcerned. Eyeing Sweyn, Toste said, "You handled that well."

Sweyn smiled slightly and reluctantly looked around. If Toste was here, maybe his daughter was with him.

"What were they whispering in the back of the hall?" Palna asked.

"They spoke well of Sweyn's rights and ill of the Jómsvíkings' impertinence," Toste reported.

"Good." Palna grinned. "They'll be seeing more of that impertinence."

Sweyn turned his head and found himself looking straight into Sigrid Tostedotter's eyes.

She stood next to her brother and was more beautiful than Freya's daughter Hnoss, with her braided hair forming a wreath on her head and a gorgeous necklace glittering at her neck. Sweyn's heart skipped a beat as everything paled. Her bosom strained under her dress. Her lips were blood red. Desire for her burned in his body. He had to have her. This certainty grew to become just as strong as his desire for Harald's throne. One way or another, it would happen.

Λ

A king's son. Sigrid's cheeks grew hot as her eyes met Sweyn's, and she was filled with certainty and longing. For a moment she was back in the dream where he smiled and lifted their son into his arms. The child's carefree laughter echoed far away as she caressed the warrior with her eyes.

Sigrid gulped and turned away, her heart pounding in her chest. *Why must you torment me with this?* She took a deep breath. She was going to marry the king of Svealand and secure peace and strength for her family line so that Anund and his infamous dynasty could be slaughtered down to the last child. She couldn't go back on the promise she'd made and bring disgrace on herself, her father, and all Scylfings.

Dragons and strange creatures curled around the ceiling above her. The colorful tapestries on the walls depicted the great deeds of the king and the Jelling people. Light glowed from the torches burning in their holders on the walls and mixed with the light and air coming in from the open doors. It was a warm evening. The light danced over the images in the tapestries and made them nearly come alive.

Noblemen and chieftains with trimmed beards, sumptuous out-fits, and shiny jewels spoke around her. Sweyn wasn't even particularly handsome compared to them. He was a king's bastard son in coarse-spun clothing begging his father for ships, seemingly a pigheaded young warrior who lived off his sword. Sigrid's feelings were surely a delusion that would soon end, allowing reason to prevail once again.

Thyre Haraldsdotter floated across the floor as she wandered around talking to the guests in the hall. Her dark blue dress shimmered like the sea, and the jewelry around her neck was exquisitely ornate. Sigrid had never seen anything like it.

"So this is Erik's bride," Thyre said of her. "He's truly favored to have found such a young and beautiful one."

Tendrils of silver had been woven into Thyre's head-cloth, and her dress was cut to show off her breasts, which Sigrid had a good view of since she was almost a head taller than the elfin Thyre.

"I look forward to getting to meet my husband," Sigrid replied.

"You won't be disappointed. My husband's uncle is not at all a disagreeable man, even if he does persist in licking the sacrificial bowl of the pagans."

Around them men began to laugh, as if that were the funniest thing they'd ever heard. Taken aback, Sigrid looked at the women and men in their extravagant clothing, and anger awakened in her. How dare these cross worshippers mock Freya the Radiant?

"A king who does not bend to the new ways shows great honor, in my estimation," Sigrid said, stretching her back so that she towered over Thyre. "I anticipated many things about Lejre, but not that the king's kinswomen would mock the faith of Svealand's king."

Thyre immediately grew serious and put her hand on Sigrid's.

"I do apologize. I didn't intend to be disrespectful. Erik is a good man, and I can see that you will be happy together."

She turned Sigrid's wrist, revealing the mark of Freya to everyone.

Giggles could be heard throughout the room, while a few people looked with scorn at Sigrid's pride, the mark of her foremothers.

So this was the game they wanted to play. Sigrid slowly pulled her hand back without any change in her facial expression. If Thyre thought Sigrid would be demoralized by her artifices, she would be disappointed.

"Treating guests politely is another old custom that I see Lejre has outgrown. It was useful to meet you, Thyre Haraldsdotter, and see your true nature," Sigrid said. Her words transformed Thyre from an effervescent young woman to a dark dís.

"There will be no friendship between us, heathen," Thyre scoffed. "You will discover that soon. Do not think that I will bow my head to a farm girl who thinks her birth outranks my own."

Sigrid looked down at the king's daughter and smiled quietly. So that was where the ill will lay.

"Necks that are too stiff to bend break easily," Sigrid replied calmly.

Grimacing, Thyre turned and disappeared through a crowd of guests standing nearby, while Sigrid caught her breath. True, she had expected ill will and wicked arts, but this attack from the king's daughter was unanticipated.

"Congratulations, sister, you really succeeded in concealing your love of the old ways," Ulf said in a snide tone. "You've made yourself a powerful enemy before we've even sat down at the table. Grandmother would be proud of you."

Ulf had stood beside her and carefully followed what was happening with the usual sneer on his lips. Sigrid's hands trembled with rage. She quickly clenched her fists so no one would notice.

"Grandmother would have hit me if I didn't give as good as I got," she retorted.

"You managed that whole thing just fine. Thyre is rarely at a loss for words in any situation," said a young man with a candid expression, who came over to stand next to them. "Hello, I'm Olav Tryggvason from Gardarik, a stranger in this hall like yourself."

He gave her such a friendly and inviting smile that Sigrid's anger melted to vexation.

"Is it customary to treat a guest the way she did?" she asked.

Olav glanced at Thyre, who stood a short distance away, and then shook his head.

"I may as well tell it like it is, because it's not a secret. Thyre's husband, Styrbjörn the Strong, has a claim to the throne of Svealand. Styrbjörn's father, Olof Emundsson, was King Erik's brother, and the two of them ruled Svealand together. When Styrbjörn's father died, his uncle Erik became the sole ruler. Styrbjörn sat on his father's burial mound and demanded that he be given his rightful place on the throne of Svealand. Instead he was given thirty ships so he could go raiding and win his own kingdom. Styrbjörn wasn't content with that and is here in Lejre now to beg for Harald's assistance so he can go to war against Erik."

Olav knowingly raised an eyebrow.

"If he manages to convince Harald to support him they say your time as queen of Svealand will be brief, because Thyre will take your cloak."

So that's how it was. Sigrid bit her cheek. Then it wasn't so strange that Thyre harbored such disdain for her. Nor was it strange that Svealand's king was so insistent on seeking peace with the Scylfings.

"Thank you," she said.

Olav smiled broadly again.

"Besides, Thyre has always dripped poison in people's ears and loves to control men. Everyone has been talking about your beauty since you came ashore in Lejre, and Thyre is not one to tolerate a beautiful rival."

To her embarrassment, Sigrid felt herself blush.

"People will talk about anything," she mumbled and turned away to conceal her burning cheeks, and in doing so found herself looking straight at Sweyn's face.

Confound it. His dark blue eyes were sharp and stern, his jaws so tightly clenched that a muscle twitched in his cheek. Sigrid swallowed. He was standing so close that she could feel the heat from his body, and she lost her breath.

"It's hard to believe that you're a king's son," she said to Sweyn, taking a step backward. The words slipped out of her and she regretted them immediately, but he just smiled and didn't seem to mind.

"Harald seems to think so, too," he replied in a somber voice.

Sigrid blushed. She couldn't think of anything else to say and just stared dumbly at the Jómsvíking.

"Harald is going to have a hard time dodging his responsibility on this one," Olav said, stepping up to address Sweyn. "All honor for how you stood up for your right."

Sigrid exhaled, relieved.

"I see that you're well armed," Olav said, pointing to the sword that Sweyn wore at his side.

"It was forged by a Lombard smith from the purest Thule iron," Sweyn said, drawing his sword a little way out of his sheath so that Olav could examine its quality. Sweyn's arms were brown from the sun and strong. Two white scars glowed on his wrist.

"I spoke with a master smith who said there were two Ulfberht swords up here in the North," Olav replied. "I'd give my arm to own one like that."

Sweyn's face lit up and he said, "They say Ulfberhts are forged in dragon fire, and nothing can break them."

"The dragon fire is what makes the blade shine like that," said Ulf, who had been standing quietly next to Sigrid.

Soon the three men were comparing weapons and different blacksmiths and iron qualities. The ordinary conversation was a relief. Sweyn laughed at something Ulf said, and Sigrid's heart clenched. He looked just as happy right then as he had in her dream.

Give me strength to forget him, Vanadís.

"Esteemed Sigrid Tostedotter," someone said. Sigrid felt surprised to see an older servant bow slightly to her. "The queen would like to speak to you."

This was unexpected and might not go well. Sigrid pulled her hands over her hair and straightened her cloak. She didn't know what customs prevailed in this court or what the queen was after. Toste might have offered her some counsel, but she didn't see him anywhere. Ulf shrugged slightly in response to her questioning look.

"The queen is waiting," the servant said impatiently.

Sweyn turned away, but Olav was able to remedy her indecision. He leaned over and whispered softly in her ear, "Fear not, the queen is the nicest one in this court. Bow deeply, and let her speak first. Remember that you're equals."

The words made Sigrid stand up straighter. She supposed that if she hadn't let the daughter intimidate her, she shouldn't fear the mother either.

"Thanks, you're a true friend."

"Whatever you ask, you shall receive," Olav said with a playful bow.

With one last look at Sweyn, Sigrid turned and followed the servant.

The hall she entered was just as big as the one she had left and every bit as magnificent. The difference was the two long tables, the largest Sigrid had seen, where the servants were bringing out platter after platter of food.

Queen Tova sat on a chair by the window, thin as a bird in her beautiful dress, with a sad smile on her lips.

Sigrid bowed deeply.

"Erik has chosen his bride well: young, beautiful, and strong," the queen said in a lilting voice.

"I'm honored," Sigrid said.

The queen got up with difficulty, then took Sigrid's hand in her own and gently stroked it.

"I was your age when my father, Prince Mistivoi of the Wends, gave me to Harald to be his third wife. Oh, I was so scared to leave my beloved mother and travel to the North. Are you as scared as I was?"

Sigrid hesitated and remembered Olav's words about Harald possibly supporting Styrbjörn's claim to Svealand. Queen Tova's kindness might be a smoke screen or an act.

"I long to become Erik's bride," Sigrid lied.

"He's an impressive man and your connection is auspicious. You will be well received in Svealand."

The wrinkles around her eyes deepened as Queen Tova smiled. She was no beauty, but her dignity had great charm.

"I was also beloved by the Danes when I got married, but then my father led the Wends in battle against the Saxons, and he went back to the old ways, our forefathers' religion. Everyone turned against me because of my father's actions, even my husband and the Danes. So many things are out of our control."

Tova turned and looked at Harald, sitting in a throne at the far end of the hall, talking with three men. The king was upset, yelling and swearing at the men who were cowering before him. Powerful or not, he was an unappealing sight with an undignified way about him. The queen sighed quietly.

"My daughter Thyre inherited her father's bad temper. You must pardon her for what she said to you. Personally I bear you no ill will, rather I offer you my warm friendship."

Now Sigrid understood why the queen was being so nice to her, a simple chieftain's daughter from the land of the Geats. She wanted to be allies and secure her support. Sigrid had become so powerful that the queen of the Danes and the Jutes was currying favor with her. The realization was staggering.

"I accept your friendship gladly and return it in kind," Sigrid said.

"Nothing could please me more," Queen Tova said, taking Sigrid's arm.

Together they walked along the wall decorated with shields and burning candles.

"May you give your husband many sons. The homesickness gets better after the birth of your first child. It's a big comfort." Tova stopped in front of a cross that was hanging on the wall and waved her hand in front of her chest. Sigrid stiffened as discomfort seized her. For a brief moment she forgot where she was.

"Seek comfort in God and the holy virgin, beautiful Sigrid," the queen said gently. "Only she can grant you peace and salvation."

Sigrid eyed the frail queen with distaste.

Protect me, Vanadís. Don't let her false speech entangle my mind.

"I seek my salvation elsewhere," Sigrid said tersely.

Queen Tova nodded, as if she already knew that.

"I wouldn't have expected otherwise of Erik's bride, since Svealand still clings to the old ways. I pray God will guide you to renounce the false gods and seek salvation in Jesus Christ. Only He, and He alone, grants salvation. Don't you know in your heart that His love is the way out of warfare, blood feuds, and death? Only God grants victories."

The queen's face filled with an unusual look of happiness that made Sigrid draw back in discomfort. That must have been the lone god's spirit, speaking through the queen's mouth. Behind her back, Sigrid made the sign to ward off evil.

"Everyone is entitled to their beliefs," Sigrid replied.

"Wisely put," the queen said, nodding in approval. "Now I know that if a man of God arrives in Svealand, the queen will protect his life, because everyone is entitled to his own belief. Will you give me your word on this?"

Sigrid clenched her teeth as the trap snapped shut. Did the queen think she was a simple, naive girl she could trick with a promise of friendship and some pretty words? She had no intention of being the plank that the men of God, like rats, used to come ashore in Svealand.

"Only my husband can make such a promise. In whatever he decides, I will support him faithfully."

Such resolve wasn't what the queen was expecting. Tova's eyes grew serious, and she let go of Sigrid's arm.

"I will pray for your soul's salvation, my child."

Sigrid couldn't help but laugh.

"I will sacrifice to the gods for yours, Queen."

At that moment the doors to the hall were thrown open and the guests streamed in. Apparently it was time to sit down at the table. The queen straightened her back and once again looked genteel and dignified.

"I'm glad we had this time together, and now I know that you're not only beautiful but also clever. Tread cautiously. The cloak you will shoulder is heavier than you can imagine."

Sigrid nodded politely and said, "It's lucky that my shoulders are so strong."

Even the thinly veiled threats of a queen would not scare her.

ᚠ

Emma looked up at the rising moon, just one night away from full. The chilly light tore at her body like claws and made her pace restlessly back and forth in front of Beyla's tent.

The warriors had gathered around their fires to eat their suppers, and they were laughing and talking in the twilight. A somber voice sang a sad song about a beloved maiden who sought the peace of Rán's watery embrace.

Emma greedily inhaled the rank scent of masculinity and blood. She could feel each of their warm bodies against her skin, sense each heartbeat. Kára demanded life force and needed to satiate her hunger.

"Give me more of that draft to drink," Emma whispered to Beyla, who was sitting in front of her tent. "I'm being ripped apart."

She wanted to hover over the ground again, light and worry-free, but Beyla shook her head and said, "I can't give you any more today."

Emma understood that she was being punished for her silence about the vision, but she couldn't talk about it, not yet, not now when Kára's hunger was so strong.

The hunger was so many times worse than when she was lying with Palna; like a bottomless cavern it expanded. Soon it would destroy her.

She grabbed hold of the seeress's hair, yanking her head backward so her throat was exposed.

"Give it to me!" she hissed.

But there was no fear in Beyla's eyes as she gently loosened Emma's grasp.

"It's not my brew you need tonight. You can't satisfy yourself in this camp. Everyone saw how pale and feeble Palna was after you visited his tent. If you do the same thing to another of us, they will drive you away."

Emma tore at her face with her fingernails, struggling to gain control of the dís. *Don't do it. Don't do it.*

"Foolish old woman, you are nothing to me," Emma said.

"Hunt further afield tonight," Beyla said calmly.

Emma looked out at the lights glowing in the harbor. Without a word she set off running.

The benches by the market's mead barrels were full of men drinking and talking loudly together. Young girls scurried back and forth with tankards and dishes. A dark-haired wench sat on a warrior's lap and playfully tugged on his beard while the host watched them both closely. Emma's prey needed to have the right scent; nothing else would do. She ambled slowly past the benches and pretended not to notice the men's catcalls.

"Come sit by me, honey."

"Show us what you've got under your gown."

"Look at her eyes—she's crazy."

"Those are the best ones."

There was no one to pick up in this hall. Irritably she continued onward, stopping to look into the alleyway between two buildings. A man was standing in the alley, moaning as he drove his manhood into a woman with her gown pulled up. He wasn't the right one either.

Disappointed, she proceeded to the other side of the market square, where there were more men howling in the evening air. A young man with a brown beard was standing by a table talking with several men. Without hesitation, she walked up to him and stood so close that her body touched his.

"Follow me," she said.

He took a step back while his buddies laughed.

"Get out of here, I'm not paying," he said.

"I'm not looking for money," she said, grabbing ahold of his thigh. "I need you."

The man hesitated, but just for an instant, before he set his mead down on the table with a smile.

"Well, in that case I'll be happy to accommodate you."

ᚻ

"I have a relative in Svealand whom I swore I'd visit. Perhaps while I'm up there, you'll offer me a meal in your hall," Olav yelled across the table to make himself heard over the pipers and lute players.

Sigrid put down the cup of wine she had been drinking, feeling a little ill. This was the third time the drunken Olav had brought this up.

"You'll always be welcome in my hall, Olav of Gardarik," she told him again, but he'd already turned away and was following a busty servant girl with his eyes.

She should have been more than honored to get to sit at the king's table and dine in his hall. But the meal was lasting forever, and everyone was bellowing around her. She could hardly sit still, feeling anxious to know what the next day would reveal. She snuck a glance at Sweyn, who was sitting farther down the table.

He said something to the warrior next to him, and they laughed together. Then he leaned over his plate and their eyes met yet again. The pipers began a new song, and a man started clapping, and soon everyone was clapping in time. Sigrid couldn't help but smile at Sweyn. Immediately he looked down at his plate as if she didn't exist.

"Don't encourage him," Ulf said. "You're acting like a bitch in heat." He was so drunk he slurred his words.

"Mind your own business," Sigrid said with a snort.

Ulf had been going on and on about his long-lost Ingeborg all night, and she didn't want to hear any more.

"I know more about this than you do," he said.

His elbow slipped as he tried to support himself, and he almost spilled his wine. Not that it would have been very noticeable, because the table was covered with pools of wine and mead and piles of chewed bones in between the dishes of boiled meat and vegetables.

"More about looking like a fool? Yes, you're right about that, my brother."

She'd already had too much, but Sigrid made a face and drank the acidic wine thirstily. The sight of the dish full of gray cooked meat turned her stomach, and the heat in the room suddenly became insufferable even though the doors were open to let in the cool night air.

An older woman a little ways away stood up and left the table. Sigrid gulped as the nausea lurched within her.

"I'm going to follow her out," Sigrid said.

Ulf prepared to keep her company.

"You stay here. The lady is more suitable company for what I need to do," Sigrid said and left the bench without waiting for Ulf's response.

The wine made the floor sway under her feet as she walked along the length of the table and hurried out into the moonlit courtyard. The woman she'd followed was gone. The only people around were two guards talking to each other a bit in the distance.

Sigrid took a deep breath of the refreshing air and looked up at the moon. A woman giggled in the darkness at a man's urgent voice. Groans of pleasure could be heard from the trees. Apparently celebrations had already begun for the summer festival.

Sigrid swallowed and felt the nausea come over her. With her hand over her mouth she ran into the darkness, doubled over, and retched.

"It's true, King Harald was out of his mind with drink when he drove the guests from his table, screaming that he would castrate them all," said Ingolf, who had just sat down at the table after having been away for a good, long while. "Styrbjörn the Strong of Trelleborg saw it with his own eyes and told us about it while we were pissing."

Sweyn looked at Harald with distaste. The king was half-asleep in his high seat, his mouth hanging open.

"With a lack of honor like that, he's an embarrassment to all Danes," Sweyn said.

Ingolf drained his cup and wiped his mouth with the back of his hand before he responded in a low voice, "That's why we need a strong king."

The ship captains looked at Sweyn and nodded their agreement and then continued teasing Gunnar, who had split his pants earlier that day.

"Seeing your ass through your breeches was worse than being hagridden," Torstein said, and everyone started laughing.

Sweyn silently drank his mead. He couldn't laugh with the others. Instead he stole yet another furtive glance at Sigrid, who was sitting farther up the table with Olav from Gardarik. Whenever they leaned toward each other intimately, he felt a stab in his chest. Damn it all. His desire for her was a hunger in his body. He'd never cared about any woman like this before. Even women he'd had sex with he rarely gave any more than a fleeting thought.

She must have bewitched him and cast a love spell on him that made his heart heavy. That was the only reasonable explanation.

Sweyn emptied his goblet and held it up so the servant would refill it. Sigrid turned to look at him and grinned at his torment. Damn that bitch.

"She's a witch," he grunted.

Åke looked at him with a furrowed brow and said, "How can you even think about her when all this is within reach?"

Sweyn bit his teeth together so hard that his jaws ached. Did Åke think he was drawn to her of his own free will?

"I don't want anything to do with her," he said, "and will force her to break the spell she put on me."

At that moment Sigrid stood up and walked toward the doors. Temptress or magic spell, he would make the bitch heal the damage she'd done. He put his hands on the table and pushed himself to his feet.

"Don't bring shame on yourself or your brothers," Gunnar said in a sharp voice. "Remember our code."

"I'm just going for a piss. There's no shame in that," Sweyn muttered.

The courtyard was empty, apart from the guards. There was no sign of Sigrid anywhere. She had probably sauntered off to bed, satisfied at having teased him. Incensed, he walked around the corner and stopped short. Sigrid was doubled over in the courtyard, vomiting like a cat.

"Go away," she sobbed when she spotted him. Then she retched again.

Sweyn's annoyance evaporated as if by magic. He started to back away but paused. If it had been one of his brothers-in-arms, he would have roared with laughter and kicked him in the ass, but this was something else. Sigrid was draped loose limbed over a fence and could hardly hold herself up.

There was only one thing to do. Sweyn strode over to her, took a firm hold around her waist, and held her up while he pushed aside the hair that had fallen over her face. She retched again, but her stomach was empty.

"Let go of me," she whimpered.

"Don't worry," he said, the tenderness he felt at her pitiable state practically suffocating him.

Her warm body trembled in his arms. Her waist was suspended in his hand; her back pressed against his chest; her thigh rubbed against his prick. Damn it. Too late, feeling himself harden, he quickly turned to the side. Palna would beat him senseless if he found out about this.

Sweyn cleared his throat, embarrassed, and asked, "Are you . . . better?"

Sigrid got up and wiped her mouth with the back of her hand, avoiding looking him in the eye.

"Water," she croaked.

There was a water trough a few steps away and Sweyn led her over there.

"Will that do?"

She washed off her face and rinsed out her mouth, then ceremoniously dried herself off with her cloak. Damned woman. Fresh from vomiting, she was still beautiful. Her hair looked like it had been spun out of moonlight, and her lips were blood red in the evening light.

"Well, that's embarrassing," she said, looking down.

How could anything be so genuine and beautiful? As if under a spell, Sweyn reached out his hand and caressed her warm, damp cheek. He raised her chin, and her pleading eyes met his. Sweyn could hardly breathe. Now he knew. She wanted him just as much as he wanted her. His thumb trembled as he ran it over her lips and into her mouth. A jolt of tender desire coursed through his body as she took his thumb deep into her mouth.

"I need you," he said hoarsely. "In this life or in the next, you will be mine."

ᛝ

The touch of his hand ran through her body like fire. It hobbled Sigrid with weakness and a peculiar sense of joy.

My beloved.

They were back in the meadow, alone with their child, laughing happily. She felt the promise of the life they could share. *You will be mine,* he had said. How could something that felt so right be wrong? And yet it could never happen, not in this life. Regret was like a blow to the gut, and Sigrid forced herself to turn away.

"I am King Erik's bride," she said.

The words caused his eyes to darken.

"Not yet you're not," Sweyn responded. "And never will be, if I have my way." He took a step back, pulled his hand over the back of his head while he calmed down. "Sorry, I had no right to say that."

Sigrid slowly shook her head. None of this was right. Her desire for him made her crazy. She had drunk way too much, embarrassed herself like a vagrant without family or position. Now she was lusting, like a dog in heat, after a poor Jómsvíking, who was illegitimate and had just begged his father for ships.

Why are you doing this to me, Vanadís?

She had to go, leave Sweyn, and never give him another thought. Sigrid looked around anxiously, her heart pounding, almost expecting to see Axel step out of the shadows by the wall and scream that she was unworthy of becoming Erik's bride.

"Sigrid!" Ulf's voice made her jump and take a step backward.

The next moment her brother walked around the corner of the building.

"What are you doing?" he asked. "Whoring with this Jómsvíking you've been yearning for? Have you no honor?"

Sigrid scoffed. Ulf had bedded every skirt in their village so he really wasn't one to talk in this case.

"He walked over as I was vomiting my guts out," she replied. "If you think that's whoring around, then I guess so."

"Are you following my sister?" Ulf asked, eyeing Sweyn with suspicion.

Sweyn held up his hand to stave off the accusation. "Look, I just came outside for a piss. I saw her throwing up and came over to help her. You have my word that's all that happened."

Ulf walked over to the fence and cast a distrustful glance at the evidence before coming back.

"Father will have to hear about this," he said, slurring his words.

Sigrid shuddered. She carried Toste's and the family's honor on her shoulders. Men had died on her journey to her husband in Svealand. What in the goddess's name was she doing?

"They weren't alone," a gruff voice said.

Sigrid was astonished when that seeress she'd met earlier in the day stepped out of the shadows beneath the trees. Yet again Vanadís had protected her and sent help when she needed it most.

"No one's honor was in any danger, just the girl's pride as she retched miserably," Beyla said. "You have my word on it, and I'm sure you wouldn't question that, would you?"

Ulf bowed his head to Beyla.

"Luckily I was too hasty," he said.

The seeress scrutinized him.

"Your sister needs rest and care so she will be strong tomorrow. Take her to her lodgings."

Ulf obediently held out his hand to Sigrid and said, "Come along, sister."

"We'll speak tomorrow," Beyla said brusquely to Sigrid, who humbly bowed her head in deference to Beyla.

She didn't dare even look at Sweyn as she, Sigrid the betrothed, obediently followed her brother away. All the same, Sigrid felt Sweyn's eyes on her back like a warm caress. She bit her cheek. She cursed not getting to be alone with the Jómsvíking. She cursed the shackles that bound her. She cursed the storm that was tearing her apart.

Only after Sigrid had disappeared behind the cluster of buildings did Sweyn turn somberly toward the seeress. She had seen everything and was angry, which was clear from her face. There was no doubt that she was going to tell Palna what she'd seen. She would never lie to her own brother.

"I sincerely thank you, Beyla," Sweyn said.

The seeress took his arm and led him in among the trees, away from all the watching eyes and listening ears.

"This evening I saw the most highly esteemed of the Jómsvíkings lose all sense, willing to throw away everything he had worked for, *for a wench,*" she spluttered angrily. "How could you be so foolish and careless? Don't you remember the responsibility you bear?"

You can bear no better burden on your journey than common sense; in unfamiliar places it's better than wealth; such is the comfort of the destitute. He had to get out of this.

"I swear that wasn't my intention," Sweyn said. "She put a love spell on me, bewitched me with her sorcery."

Beyla laughed a low, scornful laugh and put her hand on the necklace of sticks and bones she wore around her neck.

"Never did I think I would hear anything so pathetic. *A love spell?* Who else has wronged you? Did Thor not hold your hand nicely in battle?"

Sweyn looked down at the ground, his cheeks feeling hot. He shouldn't have tried to blame someone else.

"I beg you, please don't say anything to Palna."

Beyla sighed and then looked thoughtfully up at the moon.

"Well," she said finally. "Maybe there is a love spell. If so, my counsel would prevail over such things, not my brother's. When the moon reaches its full strength, the herons of forgetfulness will be able to break the spell. At Attil's burial mound tomorrow night I can give you peace."

So there was a way out of this. Sweyn exhaled and said, "Thank you for your silence. You have my gratitude."

"This is going to cost you considerably. Go now. Your brothers may start to wonder where you are."

ᚠ

Emma was shivering from the cold when she came to, curled up in the tent. Teeth chattering, she sat up and pulled her cloak tighter around her. The light from the tent opening stabbed at her head like needles. Her hands were washed, but there was something under her fingernails. When she picked it out, she saw that it was shreds of skin.

What had she done? Kára purred contentedly inside her, her hunger sated, but Emma didn't remember what had happened. She remembered walking to a meadow with the stranger. He was lying in the grass, his face ashen. That was all she remembered. In vain she tried to capture the memories, but they receded and dissolved like an autumn fog.

Beyla sat in the tent opening. Using a rock, she ground herbs in a bowl.

"Drink," Beyla said, placing a cup next to her. Emma's hands shook so much she couldn't lift the cup.

"Ah, so it's like that," Beyla said, and without waiting for an answer she pushed the wooden cup up to Emma's mouth and forced her to swallow the stinking slush.

Emma's stomach turned and she was on the verge of throwing everything up, but Beyla pressed her finger to Emma's throat so the nausea abated.

"You'll feel better soon," the seeress said sternly and squatted down in front of Emma.

"When did I get here?"

"I don't know," Beyla said with a shrug. "You were lying on the floor when I returned. You don't remember anything?"

Beyla gave Emma a concerned look. "Is Kára's hunger sated?" she asked.

Emma's quick nod answered the question, and Beyla started gathering her bundles of herbs.

"It is well known that dísir demand offerings when they take human form. They thirst for the life force they need to remain in this world."

Emma felt the chill from the ground once again creeping into her body while her womb ached the way it did when she was a child and Acca had had her lie with many men.

"So I have to kill people so that Kára can stay inside me long enough to sacrifice me for Sigrid's baby? That is no merry future," Emma said, trying to smile. "I wish Kára hadn't chosen me."

Quick as a snake, Beyla reached for her staff and struck Emma hard on the back.

"Silence, you abomination!" she scolded.

Emma crept away, rubbing her back where the blow had landed.

"I didn't mean that," she whispered, cowering from the next blow.

Beyla sniggered and lowered her staff.

"Be grateful to have the chance to give your unworthy life for something bigger than yourself. Do you think the goddesses give without taking? Hel chose me, and every night and day I hear the whispers of the dead. They scream their sadness and longing for this world, yet I bear it with joy, grateful at having been chosen by the Mistress of Niflheim. I make sacrifices, heal people, prophesy, and overpower the dísir to protect the warriors, all in her name. She works through me, as I am her seeress and servant." Beyla's eyes darkened. For a moment, she looked old and frail. The next, she was filled with rage. "You were a waste of a life when Kára, the Wild Stormy One, took pity on you. It's an honor granted not even to the most powerful seeresses."

Emma looked down at the ground.

"I *am* grateful," she whispered.

Her words appeased Beyla somewhat. She sank back down on the skin rug and pulled out a pouch she carried in her belt.

"The gods and goddesses choose seeresses and priestesses to interpret their will and assist them in their sacrifices and deeds. Kára chose you for something big. The Christians' darkness is closing in on our world. Scandinavia has stood strong against the cross for a long time, but with the tempting talk and promises of power and riches, the Christians are succeeding in poisoning the Vikings. The Ragnarök you saw, I have also seen. It is going to destroy us all."

She poured rocks and pieces of bone into her hand. Then she sang a spell that filled the air around them with sorcery before she tossed the stones and bits of bone on the ground in front of them.

"They give the same answer, every time," Beyla said and picked up two stones with symbols on them. "A king who heals what is broken."

Emma sat up and nodded. Beyla held up a piece of bone with symbols on it that glowed in the half-light inside the tent.

"Otherwise disaster, Ragnarök." The seeress sighed heavily and put the piece of bone down on the skin rug. "The vision you had, the savior Sigrid will give birth to, is our only hope."

Emma closed her eyes and saw how the threads wound in and out of each other in the tapestry that was everyone's life. The drink started to take effect, and her body felt lighter as the pain and hopelessness abated.

"If she lives until then," Emma said.

The seeress grabbed Emma's arm brutally. "Who threatens Sigrid?" she demanded.

"Far too many people. Both her life and the child's life are fragile," Emma said. She blinked in surprise at the seeress's alarm. How could the wise woman be so blind? "Don't you see, Beyla, this is why Kára is here?"

꜏

Sigrid walked barefoot down the fog-shrouded shore along the sea, which was covered with thin ice. The pale grayish mist swept around her as she wandered through the emptiness, through what had happened and what would happen. Sól had burned out in the sky, devoured by the wolves that chased her across the heavens.

The snake biting its own tail burned there instead, the symbol of eternity.

The little boy holding her hand led her onward to the edge of a waterfall, which gurgled and laughed as it found its way to the sea. Two bears chased each other playfully. They bickered with such joy that Sigrid began to laugh.

Then the fog thickened. Shadows, pale figures in the vast, gray mist, came and went. The boy stopped in front of three burial mounds. He pointed to the one in the middle and urged her to go to it. Sigrid wanted to stay where she was, but he shook his head and made her proceed.

Then he let go of her hand and backed away into the mists, away from time, and she forced herself to walk up to the top of the burial mound.

She again found him there. Sweyn was kneeling with a broken sword in his hand. Her head was lowered and her eyes were wary as she knelt down in front of him and stroked his cheek. They watched each other in silence, locked in time.

"My beloved," he said, undoing her clothes.

She felt no doubt as she opened herself to him and willingly let him penetrate her. Everything was as it should be.

"The summer festival is starting soon." Alfhild's voice disturbed Sigrid, yanking her out of the pleasing dream. She opened her eyes and looked with frustration at her kinswoman who sat on the edge of her bed.

"Go away," Sigrid said, rolling over.

This was the second time Sweyn and the child had come to her in dreams. Sigrid curled up under the fur pelt, her body heavy with desire.

Why do you torment me with lust, Vanadís? Are you testing my will?

Yesterday she had drunkenly vomited in front of Sweyn and shamelessly offered herself to him. She, about to become a queen, had behaved like a lewd country mistress currying her master's favor. But Freya had sent her Beyla the seeress, who had protected her honor. Soon Beyla would give her the answers she sought.

Sigrid took a deep breath and slowly sat up in bed. Alfhild came right over with a mug of milk. Sigrid looked down at the drink and turned her head away.

"Are you still feeling sick?" Jorun asked.

Sigrid shook her head as the loneliness closed in around her.

"Shouldn't Vanadís make sure our queen stays healthy and beautiful instead of putting on a vomitous show outside the royal hall?" Jorun asked, her lips curling into a smile.

"Watch your tongue," Sigrid said quietly.

Her kinswomen exchanged glances before looking down at the floor. They had put on their simple light-gray shifts for the summer sacrifice and wore their hair down and adorned with flowers.

"King Harald's priests banned the sacrifice," Sigrid said. "The old ways cannot be honored here."

Jorun's grin widened.

"Only the sacrifice is forbidden," Alfhild said, shaking her head. "The festival will still be held, and people are coming from near and far to participate. It's going to be held at the burial mounds and will be bigger than ever, even though King Harald is a cross worshipper. I can't wait for it to start! I've seen a lot of people I would gladly dance around the maypole with," she added laughingly and blushed.

"Orm told me that people were going to honor Sjofn, the goddess of love, in secret. As everyone knows, her power is too strong to resist," Jorun said. "The priests are furious, but what can they do?"

Alfhild gave Sigrid a knowing look.

"Orm tells Jorun so many things these days when they're whispering together in the darkness. It's pretty clear who she'll be honoring Sjofn with tonight."

"Shut up!" Jorun said with a laugh, pulling a simple shift out of the chest for Sigrid. "Would you like to wear this, Queen?"

Sigrid noted the sarcastic edge to Jorun's voice as she said the last word, but today was the wrong day to fight with her kinswoman.

"Gladly," Sigrid replied and stood up. It was a suitable dress since she was going to visit Beyla. "I'm going to visit the Jómsvíking camp. Perhaps your Orm would like to accompany us there, Jorun."

That would put her kinswoman into a better mood and give her something to think about besides what Sigrid was up to.

"It's not like that," Jorun replied, but she smiled her satisfied smile.

"Not yet it's not, but tonight Sjofn will reign supreme, and she allows everything that is otherwise forbidden," Alfhild said with a wink.

Here's hoping she'll bless me as well, thought Sigrid. She pulled the shift over her head and waited while her kinswomen put flowers in her hair. Soon she would finally receive the answer she so fervently needed. How appropriate that it would come during the blessed summer festival.

"Quit pacing, otherwise I'm going to cut your Achilles tendon," the giant Ax-Wolf barked.

Sweyn stopped pacing in front of Palna's tent and sneered at Ax-Wolf, who lay on his back on the ground, moaning from the effects of too much mead. His companions had had a cheerful evening in the harbor while Sweyn and the ship captains sat at the king's table. He wished he'd been off drinking with them instead. Thoughts about both King Harald and Sigrid had hounded him in his sleep, and they were still eating at him.

"There's no worse travel food to drag across field and dale than an excess of ale," Åke sneered. Then he pounded on his shield right next to Ax-Wolf's head so it boomed.

"I'm going to rip your intestines out, you damned pup," Ax-Wolf roared angrily.

Åke swore as a rock hit his arm. But then he noticed something and pointed to one of the king's servants walking through the camp. Sweyn stretched his back and hid his concern as the servant walked up to them. The man looked at Sigvard—lying on the ground and snoring—with distaste, before he turned to Sweyn.

"The king summons you to his hall."

Sweyn's restlessness receded. It was time to find out what path his and the Jómsvíkings' fate would take. He looked around for Palna but decided he must still be down at the harbor. He would have to face this alone. Ax-Wolf kicked Sigvard, who got to his feet, half-asleep, flushed, and bloated.

"You don't need to bring any warriors or weapons with you," the servant told Sweyn.

"We're not going to let him go alone," Ax-Wolf said, putting his hand on the servant's shoulder. "That's just how we work."

Soon they were walking together toward the royal hall while the rest of the Jómsvíkings called out their best wishes.

"Good luck, boy!"

"Stand tall!"

A dull rumble in the distance made them all look up at the gray clouds.

"Thor is here," Åke said. "This is going to turn out well."

The calm in Sweyn's chest spread. He couldn't have a better omen.

The royal hall was deserted except for King Harald, who sat leaning forward on his throne, speaking in confidence to an ornately dressed, beardless man and Thyre and her husband Styrbjörn, who sat on the king's right side. As Sweyn and his three fellow warriors stopped before the throne and bowed their heads, his half sister's smile was both friendly and encouraging.

The king talked to the beardless man for a long time before finally waving him away and leaning back in the throne.

The daylight was not merciful to his fat face, and it was hard to believe that Harald had once been the strongest and most feared of the Danish warriors. The eyes that looked at Sweyn with abhorrence would have better suited a pig.

"You summoned me, *Father*?" Sweyn said, waiting for whatever was going to come.

Anger clouded Harald's face darkly.

"I ought to dismember you for the mess you made *and* send you to purgatory to burn there for eternity!" he said, his cheeks wobbling. "Thank Thyre for the fact that you're still alive."

That very moment the hall was filled with the rumble of Thor's chariot rolling across the sky. The beardless servant jumped at the noise and his face went white. Even Harald cast a glance up at the ceiling, and Sweyn could sense the stench of his fear of the gods he had so infamously abandoned. As for himself, Sweyn filled with unwavering strength. Thor stood by his side so he did not need to fear Harald, either in this world or the next, and if he were to be sent to Valhalla, the Great One would meet him there.

King Harald angrily waved to the beardless fellow, who hurried over and spoke to the Jómsvíkings: "Harald Jelling, king of God's mercy, has decided in his inexhaustible mercy to give you two ships with crews."

It was one ship less than Sweyn had asked for, but Palna had warned him he should expect that. Sweyn bowed his head, unable to conceal his pleasure at this tremendous triumph. Victory! The toothless bear had finally backed down.

Another rumble of thunder, a bigger one, filled the cavernous royal hall, and the wind picked up, tugging at the doors. The servant looked around nervously and then said, "This grandiose gift, so mercifully given by the leader of kings, comes with two conditions you must swear to. The first is that you must fight at Styrbjörn the Strong's side when he retakes his legitimate place on the throne of Svealand."

Sweyn sized Styrbjörn up with his eyes. Styrbjörn looked like a decent man, and Thyre had stood up for Sweyn's birthright as her brother. It seemed like a fair requirement, and one that he could agree to.

"You have my sword," he said and received a pleased nod from Styrbjörn.

Above them, Thor struck with Mjölnir. The sharp bang of the hammer echoed through the large hall as the wind yanked and tugged on the doors.

"What is the second?" Sweyn asked.

The beardless servant cleared his throat anxiously and said, "You must swear that King Harald, the leader of the Jellings, will never have to set eyes on you again."

Sweyn grinned broadly. Age and an excess of mead had made the old king's head just as rotten as his teeth.

"I make that promise gladly," Sweyn said. The next time they met, Sweyn would thrust the sword into his fat belly and laugh at the old man's death twitches.

"Then it's decided. Leave the hall," the beardless man pronounced, turning his back to them. But Sweyn did not move. He was not going to be dismissed so easily.

"When do I get my ships?" he asked.

The beardless man gave the king a questioning look, and King Harald held up five fingers, indicating five days. Sweyn nodded.

"And when do we take up arms against Svealand?" Sweyn asked.

Styrbjörn straightened up to his full height, which was not insignificant, and declared: "Be ready at the spring sacrifice. I will send a messenger to Jómsborg then."

Now there was nothing more to discuss. Sweyn bowed his head, and the Jómsvíkings turned around and left the hall together. Thor greeted him with a thunderclap as they walked back to their camp, and his brothers thumped him on the back and congratulated him on his strength.

Victory!

Sweyn took a deep breath of the rain-laden air, raised his clenched fists to Thor, and closed his eyes as the wind tugged at his clothes.

"I thank you," he said as relief coursed through his body. "I will repay you for this forever."

He received a rumble of thunder as a response.

This morning he had awakened as a simple warrior, a mere pup with no family, dependent on the goodwill of others. He had had no possessions other than his weapons, the clothes he wore, and the golden brooch given to him by Palna.

Now he was Sweyn of Jelling, a ship captain and Jómsvíking with a noble lineage, a man to be remembered and feared. The throne of the Jellings would soon be within his reach.

"Help me achieve this, Thor," he implored, and as a lightning strike cleft the sky, he was filled with respect.

The gods were truly with him.

ᛣ

The courtyard was nearly deserted as Sigrid headed toward the Jómsvíkings' camp with Alfhild, Jorun, and Orm in tow. A servant girl with her arms full of firewood gave them a nervous look before darting off. The guards standing on either end of the courtyard stared at them wide-eyed.

Thor's chariot rolled over the clouds in the distance, and a cheer could be heard from not far away.

"Has the summer festival started?" Sigrid asked Orm, who shook his head.

"Everyone's at the thingstead to see the condemned be killed," Orm said.

"Oh, can we stop and watch?" Jorun pleaded. "It's not far from the camp."

Sigrid looked up at the heavy gray cloud cover. The sun hadn't reached its peak yet.

"For a moment," she said.

"Thing killings are my absolute favorite," Jorun said, her face beaming in delight. "Now it'll be a real summer festival."

◆ ◆ ◆

The whole region must have been gathered at the thingstead. The area was packed. Old and young, high and low class, everyone stood side by side around the hill where one of the Christian priests was praying over a man while the executioner stood next to him, waiting with his ax.

A poor woman put her arms around her daughter's shoulders, sadness and revulsion in her face. A man stood next to them, a carpenter, judging from his clothes. Like many of the others, his eyes were filled with a thirst for blood.

Sigrid reluctantly followed Orm, who led them all the way to the foot of the hill. Being surrounded by so many strangers was unpleasant, but the people they encountered quietly moved out of their way. People looked at them, stunned. They whispered and pointed at their simple shifts and the wreaths of flowers they wore over their loose hair.

"It's the three sisters," people said and gasped, looking at Sigrid, Jorun, and Alfhild. "They're back. It's a sign."

Sigrid furrowed her brow in surprise at the looks, which were filled with expectant joy.

Up on the hill the condemned man, an older man with graying hair and a pockmarked face, noticed them as he put his hand on his heart before kneeling and placing his head on the already-bloody chopping block. The executioner, a skinny man with a grim expression, raised his ax. The air grew tense with anticipation as everyone stared at the hill.

The next moment the blade fell on the back of the condemned man's neck, and his head rolled off into the grass as a murmur ran through the crowd. People nodded to each other in relief.

May he find peace in Niflheim.

Sigrid walked up to the foot of the hill, where chieftains, priests, and noblemen had gathered around King Harald, who was sitting in a chair. They all stared at her uneasily, as if she were a frost giant from Jotunheim, and whispered among themselves.

The king's merciless eyes caused Sigrid to shudder. Thyre knelt at his side and kissed her father's hand and then whispered something to him. The little venomous snake slithered around the dragon, manipulating him and whispering evil into his ear.

Ulf, who was standing with the jarls behind the king, left his spot and came over to Sigrid.

"You are causing quite a stir with your attire," he said.

"I'm wearing the clothes you're supposed to wear on this, the holiest of days," Sigrid said.

Ulf gave her an amused look.

"They say you're dressed like the three sisters who used to do the sacrifices in Lejre at the summer festival back in the old days, and that you are defying the new religion and mocking the priests. You've managed to draw attention to yourself once again, sister."

Orm wrinkled his nose at Ulf's words and said, "Svealand's queen will dress as she sees fit."

Sigrid watched an old woman dart a hand out to touch her gray homespun dress. The woman bowed to Sigrid before sneaking a glance at the king and the noblemen. King Harald and the priests had imposed the death penalty for any Danes caught worshipping the old gods, but Sigrid was entitled to honor the old gods if she wished.

"We'll stay," Sigrid said haughtily, holding her head high. Let them think what they will.

Ulf sighed heavily.

"All right, but I'm not planning to stand next to you this time," he said, leaving her.

Orm disdainfully watched him leave, and Sigrid was ashamed of her brother for having so little backbone just then, retreating and letting the cross worshippers have their way.

"This would never happen in Svealand," Orm said and then took his position behind her again.

Olav from Gardarik moved into the spot Ulf had just vacated, smiling and once again unconcernedly showing Sigrid his friendship.

"You're late. There are only two left," Olav said, pointing to the bodies at the foot of the hill.

"Did they die well?" Sigrid asked.

"Straight-backed and silent," Olav responded.

"Then the old ways are still strong in Lejre," Sigrid said earnestly.

"The next one won't be as dignified," Olav said and nodded to a young woman being led up the hill. She was skinny, and her shift was dirty and so worn that it hung in tatters around her. Her hair was matted, and her face was pale with fear as she clung to a religious man who walked beside her.

The spectators fell quiet as a fat man with a heavy chain hanging around his neck stepped forward and called out the judgment: "Sif Stensdotter is to die for stabbing her husband, Eskil, to death in his sleep. After that she drowned her two children, Rota, age four, and Torvald, age two."

People yelled their hatred.

"Behead the murderess. Kill her!"

"The ax seems too kind a punishment for her," Sigrid said. "Back home she would have been slowly hanged or stoned."

Olav shrugged and said, "They weren't entirely sure she was guilty."

The woman clung to the priest so hard he had to pry her off.

"Eskil killed them," she said, sobbing. "I stabbed him because he killed the children."

Her shrill cries echoed over the hill as she struggled in vain to get free from the men. Finally they forced her down onto her knees in front of the executioner.

"Please don't kill me," she screamed to the silent audience, tears running down her face. "He's the one who did it! He took my children from me!" Her whole body trembled as she raised her clasped hands to the sky. "Save me, dear God. I don't want to die. I don't want to die."

One of the men took hold of her hair and forced her head to the chopping block. After that he let go, took a step back, and nodded to the executioner.

The woman's screams abruptly fell silent as the blade dropped on her neck and her body collapsed to the ground with her head next to it. Blood ran over the ground, and the sacrificial offering was received by a wind that swept over the hill, followed by flashes of lightning that cut through the heavy gray clouds.

Thor, master of Mjölnir, I greet you.

Thor received his offering, and the light of his hammer striking shook the earth. Sigrid heard a few shouts and cheers from the onlookers.

"She is calling to her cross-god, but Thor is receiving her personally as a sacrificial offering," Sigrid said.

The executioner picked up the woman's head by the hair and showed it to the crowd. Just then Thor's chariot rumbled over them in the clouds. Sigrid smiled at Vanadís's lover.

Several of the spectators raised their hands to the sky and welcomed the Master of Thruthvang to the summer sacrifice. The air trembled from the giant slayer's strength.

The priests crowded behind the king's chair, waving their hands in front of their chests and looking scared to death, as if Thor himself were going to burn them to ash.

Thyre held her father's hand and looked around anxiously.

Sigrid caught her eye and smiled unkindly. *Feel the power of the old ways,* she thought as people's yells thundered around her. *Fear the punishment of the gods for turning your back on them. You'll never be queen of Svealand, and you'll never spread your cross worshipping in the most powerful kingdom of the old ways.*

"Could I give you a piece of advice?" Olav said quietly. Sigrid reluctantly turned toward him.

"Calmly leave this place as if none of this happened." His voice was both concerned and caring.

"Why?"

"You may be the spark that ignites discontent, which will not work to your advantage. I wish you well, so I ask you to follow my advice."

The priests and several of the jarls were glaring at her as if she were a monster. Around her the crowd surged like an unpredictable ocean that might erupt into a storm at any moment.

"He's right," Orm said behind her.

"Let's go," Jorun said, pushing herself against Orm's breeches. "I'm scared."

Sigrid calmly took off her wreath of flowers, and then left the Thing space with her head held high.

They bow down to your power, Vanadís. You and the Æsir still rule the Danes.

ᚴ

"Your victory is only half," Palna said with a seriousness that immediately extinguished Sweyn's joy. His foster father had listened carefully to what had happened in the king's hall. Palna sank down into a squat, his eyes on the ground.

"But I got everything I asked for," Sweyn said.

"The king won quite a bit when he got you to swear you would assist Styrbjörn in his fight for Svealand. He is going to ask me to swear the same, and I cannot refuse him. That is how he keeps us away from his shores. He wisely fears us."

Sweyn squatted down beside Palna. He had hoped for his foster father's recognition, but there was none to be found from the leader of the Jómsvíkings.

"What's wrong with fighting for Styrbjörn the Strong?" he said. "We've fought for Christians before. A Jómsvíking does not discriminate when it comes to silver. Those are your own words."

Palna looked up at the darkening clouds for a prolonged moment and then finally asked, "What were you born to do?"

"To take Harald's throne and kingdom, the way you planned."

"Who is the strongest who could help you do that?"

Sweyn sucked the air in between his teeth. Only now did he understand. Erik, the king who highly valued the old ways, could have been a powerful ally.

"I should have seen it," Sweyn said, ashamed.

"Three of the ring fortresses remain loyal to Harald. Their warriors aren't worth as much as the Jómsvíkings in battle, but there are four times as many of them. With Erik's axes and swords the victory would have been ours. Harald knew what he was doing when he made you swear to fight on Styrbjörn's side. The old boar has defended his throne for more years than most live, and he is extremely skilled at sowing discord."

"Skilled or not, when I get my ships I'm going to take what I want," Sweyn said. "Those who don't bow their heads in deference will end up kneeling to me once their warriors have fallen, their villages have burned, and their families have become fodder for eagles."

"The ships he's giving you will be old and poorly built and with incompetent crews," Palna said, scratching at the fleabites on his neck. "Still, no one will be able to say he behaved other than honorably."

He laughed softly.

"You really shouldn't have given him your answer so quickly. You should have discussed it with me."

Sweyn shook his head. Palna had taught him to tread cautiously, and even so he'd walked right into Harald's trap.

"Still, I have a name and ships. That wouldn't have been worth much to you, but for me that's a huge victory. I'll take what I want, just you wait."

"Nothing pleases me more than your anger." Palna looked toward the tents where Sigrid came walking with her retinue. "Still, I wonder if your desire for a different booty didn't make you so eager to say yes to fighting against the Svea."

Damn it, she was beautiful, dressed in a simple shift with her hair down so it billowed over her shoulders. Sweyn could hardly breathe.

"I cannot deny that I've never seen her match and would gladly have killed Erik and married her myself."

Palna took hold of Sweyn's shoulders and swiveled him roughly back to face him.

"Her father is like a brother to me. His honor is my own. You're not to go near her. Hear me and obey."

Sweyn's indignation grew into anger. He'd always done what Palna wanted without talking back, always done his best to obey his foster father, but on this he could not remain silent.

"If Toste is like a brother to you, then how is it honorable of you to allow Sigrid to naively marry a man we're planning to attack in the spring?"

Palna gave him a look so brimming with rage it filled Sweyn with fear.

"If you touch her, I will lash the flesh off your back. Do you understand?"

Cowed, Sweyn looked down. He nodded grudgingly.

"Yes, Father."

The wind tugged at Sigrid's shift as she walked through the Jómsvíking camp, past the warriors sitting outside their tents sharpening their weapons, repairing their outfits, or playing board games. She scanned the men the whole time and finally found what she'd been looking for. Her cheeks reddened.

You will be mine, he had said yesterday. *My beloved,* he had tenderly whispered in her dream. Now he made a point of looking the other way. Sigrid's heart sank in her chest. Why was he so contrarian? Had the things he had said just been a young man's drunken ramblings, full of charming lies?

"What brings Toste's daughter and her summer brides to our simple camp?" Palna asked.

Sigrid smiled at the scarred leader and said, "I'm looking for Beyla."

"You'll find my sister over there under the oak trees." Palna pointed to a solitary tent at the edge of their camp.

A gust of wind kicked up a cloud of dust and a few drops of rain fell. Sigrid turned to Orm and her kinswomen.

"Wait here," she instructed. She curiously watched Sweyn, who was still averting his gaze. "I have to do this alone."

The seeress's tent was surrounded by four oak trees, which whispered their welcome to Sigrid as she approached the grove. Dark shadows from the branches fell over Beyla's tent, where Emma sat in front of a cold fire pit.

Emma's hair hid her face, and she was filling a leather pouch with dirt and leaves as she squatted unsteadily on her toes as if extremely drunk.

Beyla was wearing a blue dress. A blue cloak embroidered with symbols lay beside her. She wore a simple necklace of bones and pieces of wood around her neck.

"Brísingamen," Beyla said, putting her hand on her necklace.

Sigrid smiled. This was a simple test, but she knew the story of how Freya had slept with the four dwarf-smiths to get the gleaming necklace that had the power to conquer her enemies. When Freya returned home, everyone else saw only bones and wood when they looked at the necklace, and they thought she was crazy. And yet Freya was able to use it to defeat the enemy, and with Thor's help they were all killed.

"Power comes in many guises," Sigrid said.

Beyla nodded, relieved. That was the answer she was looking for.

"Well said," the seeress replied and invited Sigrid into her tent.

It was small and smelled strange. Sigrid sat down on a fur pelt and looked at all the knapsacks and bags around her. The dried head of a fox hung from the roof and watched her through dark eye sockets.

Emma slipped in and curled up by a sack. She stared straight ahead but moved her lips as if she were having a silent conversation with something that could not be seen.

"What's the matter with her?" Sigrid asked.

Beyla's necklace rustled as she sat down next to Sigrid.

"Without Emma I wouldn't have taken the risk of meeting you here. Harald has warned that anyone clinging to the old religion will be put to death. Even here in my brother's camp we are not safe from the king's spies."

"Vanadís will burn them all to ash," Sigrid said.

"We certainly hope so," Beyla said with a smile. "Tell me, future queen of Svealand, what is it that you seek from a seeress?"

Sigrid took a breath and started to tell Beyla about the dís who fell as a shooting star, the wind that saved them in the Alva Woods, her dreams about the child and Sweyn.

"And then," Sigrid continued, "Vanadís sent you to give me the answers I seek. Why did I dream about Sweyn if I'm to marry another man? What does Vanadís want me to do?"

Sigrid swallowed. Her mouth felt dry after she shared her many concerns.

Beyla looked at Emma, whose head drooped as she rocked back and forth.

"Do not be silent," Sigrid urged. "Help me find the answers I so unwaveringly seek." Having waited so long, her patience was at an end.

Beyla pursed her lips and gave her a stern look.

"It's pitiable to hear you ask questions you already know the answers to. Vanadís has already said what she wants. What more do you wait for, Tostedotter? Should Freya carve your fate into a stone and hit you on the head with it?"

Emma burst out in shrill laughter. Sigrid looked at them both, taken aback. This was not what she'd been expecting.

"I've had no training at being a seeress," Sigrid said. "I have no knowledge of the Hidden."

"Tsk, tsk, tsk," Beyla said shaking her head and clicking her tongue. "A seeress is something you are, not something you become."

Sigrid gasped for breath. So this was truly who she was. She *had* been chosen, just as she had suspected—*known*—since she was a small child.

I thank you.

"Tell me, then, how I can serve the goddess," she said, her heart pounding.

Beyla shook her head as if Sigrid were some lunatic simpleton. Then she blew life into an ember in the metal warming pan. She fed it with moss until a small flame flared up.

"If you have not understood that, then you truly deserve no answers."

Sigrid looked into the flames, ashamed.

Beyla fed the flames with twigs and crumbled dried herbs. A heavy, pungent smoke spread through the tent. The mark on Sigrid's wrist heated up and burned.

"The will of the goddess and the tapestry of the Norns are not easy to interpret," the seeress said. "Brief glimpses are what we get, revealing small fragments of eternity. Who knows where they fit into the tapestry or when something will happen? The knowledge you seek is not to be found."

The heavy smoke made Sigrid's eyes tear up, and she started to feel oddly lightweight, as if she were hovering above the ground.

"You know what must happen," Emma said in an unfamiliar voice.

The hair on Sigrid's arms stood up as the air around them thickened. There was a presence in the tent that felt like something not of this world. A tunnel of light formed, connecting her to Emma, but there was someone else in the girl's face, a shapeless being that watched her with night-black eyes.

Arrows of fear shot through Sigrid as a stormy joy burgeoned in her chest.

"Respect me." The voice could be the roaring of a thousand wild animals, so terrible in its inhuman power.

"May you be hallowed, dís," Sigrid whispered.

Then the light of the tunnel bond faded and died. All that was left was Emma, rocking back and forth and staring blankly into space.

Silence filled the tent. Only the whispery moan of the wind could be heard. Sigrid pushed back Emma's hair with a trembling hand. The furious inhumanness of the dís was both frightening and alluring.

"Tell me how to serve you," Sigrid said hoarsely.

Emma laughed again and then the creature within her hissed, "Your child is mine."

At the moment she spoke those words, the wind rushed into the tent, and Sigrid felt a hand caress her hair before the tent flap fluttered closed again. The whites of Emma's eyes showed before she crumpled, loose limbed, to the ground.

Sigrid gaped at the seeress, startled, her heart pounding.

"Is she going to hurt my son?" Sigrid pleaded. Nothing must happen to the boy. Sigrid would sooner die herself. A sharp pain burned on her cheek, and Sigrid gasped for breath. Beyla had slapped her.

"Do not blaspheme!" Beyla snapped. "Kára came to protect you and the child. Be happy that your son is blessed."

Sigrid lowered her head. *Forgive my foolishness in the face of the protection and the gifts you give.* She rubbed her eyes, which burned and stung from the smoke. *Dancing bears, new ice, a bride's words in bed.* From the first moment it had all been about the child. The smoke eased, and her chest filled with certainty in the face of what must happen. Sigrid shook her head, steeling herself against the seeress's sharp look.

"I see you're starting to get it now," Beyla said with a satisfied nod.

Sigrid gulped and stammered, "I can't do it." For all her yearning and longing for the child, she was filled with horror. She would do anything for Vanadís. Except this.

Beyla leaned forward and wrapped a cloak around Emma and then awkwardly patted her hair.

"The burden Emma bears for the sake of your child is going to kill her," Beyla said.

A wave of compassion swept through Sigrid as she looked at Emma, curled up under the cloak. She didn't look very old, younger than her, and now the poor girl was forced to live with a dís inside her—for Sigrid's sake.

"I'm sorry," Sigrid said and stroked Emma's arm. She took Emma's hand in her own. The girl smiled with gray, cracked lips.

"I want to do it for him—and for you," Emma whispered and then gave Sigrid the leather pouch she had been holding in her hand.

Sigrid wrapped her fingers around the worn leather. She couldn't waver now that Vanadís had shown her will. Strength was everything.

Emma watched her, her face motionless.

"It's in the tapestry," Emma said.

An irrepressible joy filled Sigrid and swept away both doubt and uncertainty.

I am yours.

Then she nodded and said, "Then it must happen."

ᚠ

Dancing had already begun around the maypole, which was decorated with leaves to make the earth fertile, and drums boomed from the burial mounds.

"Tonight we will celebrate your great fortune," Ax-Wolf cried cheerfully, trying to be heard over the drums. He kicked a drunken farmer who was sleeping in the grass. Right next to him a couple was kissing and groping so eagerly that the woman's crotch was on display for everyone.

"Give it here," Åke said. He grabbed the strong drink from Ax-Wolf. After he'd drunk, he handed it to Sweyn, who shook his head.

"Are you still mad at Father?" Åke asked. "You'll forget about her soon enough."

Sweyn didn't answer. He watched Ax-Wolf playfully grab a woman whose hair was the same color as his own and kiss her right on the mouth. Any other day of the year she would have slapped him, but now she pushed against him affectionately. Tonight people honored the gifts of the fertility gods, and Sjofn was in charge. Anything was allowed, and many children would be born in the spring.

"Father just wants what's best for us, for us to be leaders," Åke said. Three girls danced around him, trying to pull him along with them. When he declined, they laughingly moved on to other warriors. Åke drank more and then put his arm around Sweyn's shoulders. He guffawed at a man painted blue who was juggling balls.

"Forget about Palna, Sigrid, and everyone," Åke urged. "Be happy for once."

Sweyn looked out at all the dancers moving around the flower-bedecked maypole. Many of the dancers were already topless. Soon more clothes would fall away.

Sweyn clenched his teeth. He wasn't allowed to touch Sigrid, but betraying her father and attacking her husband were fine, of course.

"There's a bull dance out by the pasture," Gunnar called, running past with several of their fellow warriors, all of them quite drunk.

A few Jómsvíkings followed them to watch the spectacle, but most stayed with the thundering drums and the dancing, lusting after what it had to offer. A laughing maiden gave Sweyn a lusty look and gestured for him to come with her.

"Put Toste's daughter out of your mind, now," Åke said. "See all the looks you're getting. You can lie with whomever you want tonight. May Thor himself hit you in the head if you don't accept what's being offered."

Sweyn twisted away to get Åke's arm off his shoulders. The love spell Sigrid had cast on him was so strong that he had no desire for any of the screaming, laughing women around him. It was as if she had castrated him.

"It'll be over later," Sweyn said. "Beyla promised to break the spell I'm under tonight."

Åke gave him a teasing grin. "You really believe you're under a spell?"

"I know I am," Sweyn responded angrily.

"As you wish," Åke said, raising his hands as if to say he'd given up and backing away, chuckling. "Uh, your spell is coming this way. If you want to drive it away, I mean."

Sweyn turned around and then gasped for breath. She was coming toward him through the crowd, proud-backed and with a smile on those lips he'd caressed. She didn't say anything when she reached him, just looked him in the eye and took his hand. With no willpower, Sweyn allowed himself to be led into the dance.

The church was built from thick wooden planks. It had a pointed roof covered in black shingles. Two torches stood in front of the door, and a warm light shone on the grass from an opening in the side of the building.

Emma squatted under the oak tree, listening to the hymns from the window. Male and female voices blended in melodies that reminded her of the monastery in Wessex. Images of her life there, the church, the hard stone floor, the strict faces of the nuns, the girls' taunting laughter, and Megan's harassment welled up in her like rats filling her with a sickening darkness.

Emma crossed her arms and rocked back and forth. The monastery didn't exist anymore. It was gone, along with the person she'd been before Kára had blessed her.

The hymn faded, and a priest's mass began. The dís filled her with dark strength, which washed through her mind, purifying her of sin.

Suddenly Emma saw the fat monk Ambrosius kneeling before her, screaming and pissing blood out of his cut-off cock. She blinked. Then the vision was gone.

The monotonous voices of the mass in the church blended with the festival drums.

Emma rocked back and forth and looked up to see two monks wearing brown cowls walking toward the church. They walked close together, conversing seriously in concerned voices. She pressed her back against the tree, hoping they wouldn't notice her, but the elder of the two glanced up and stopped at the oak in surprise.

"What's the matter, my child?" he asked kindly.

Emma eyed them, her heart pounding. The smell of fire came to her from somewhere. It grew stronger, stinging her nose and tearing at her throat, making it hard to breathe.

"She looks scared," the younger monk said. "Be not afraid, we won't hurt you."

They looked at each other in concern when she didn't respond.

"God knows what she's been through," the elder one said.

Kára hissed inside her like an animal. Emma focused on the things people used to say at the monastery, and at once Kára was gone.

Sinner.

Seek salvation.

You will burn in hell for your sins.

The hand the monk held out was clean, his fingernails clipped and neat. As if in a dream Emma took it, allowing herself to be helped to her feet. Smoke tore at her throat, and voices whispered in her head as she let herself be led to the church as if she were a passive animal. The priests spoke to her in voices filled with caring and praised her for not participating in the heathens' festival. Emma did not allow their words to draw her in. Soul trappers, that's what they were. Their words only existed to overpower her so she would become a slave to their god.

Emma stopped in front of the door of the church. The smell of fire grew stronger and stronger. The cross on the door glowed like a burning ember. Emma's heart was bursting in her chest.

"Come, child," said the elder priest, but his face was ugly and contorted, and his eyes glowed red as he lured her. Demons, they were all demons. Emma couldn't move, her feet were stone, and the screams of the dying filled her head. The demon priests walked into the church. The cross on the door burned and glowed.

"What do you want?" she whispered, looking down at her dirty hands, screams echoing in her head.

Emma bit her lip so hard that the taste of blood filled her mouth. Kára had to come back. Without her, she was nothing.

Why aren't you with me? she pleaded.

The death screams from the villagers burning in the basement echoed through her head. The smell of burning still stung her nose, and only then did Emma realize what the wonderful Stormy One demanded of her. She pulled the base of the torches up out of the ground and then laid them in last year's dry leaves under the stairs. Emma backed away and felt Kára wrapping around her like a cooling, comforting embrace. She got the flames of the fire to stick to the wood, and soon they were licking at the glowing cross. Fire rose against fire, faith against faith. The screams in her head became real, and Kára filled her mind again.

Emma ran away laughing, toward the festivities as the flames raged against the sky and swallowed the house of the God worshippers.

Feeling liberated, Emma flung herself into the dance and let the drums silence the screams in her head. Kára was pleased with her offering. Emma was in her good graces again. Laughing, she felt an arm pull her close.

"Palna," she said, putting her arms around his neck and pushing her body greedily against him. "How may I serve the leader of the Jómsvíkings?"

He smiled and pulled her away to a more private place.

Damn the future and the past. Damn the twisty prophecies of the seeresses. Damn spouses, fathers, and duties. Here and now, this was all there was: Sweyn's strong arms around Sigrid's back, his grasp on her waist, his warm breath burning against her neck.

The horns called out their greeting to Nátt as ethereal summer darkness settled over Lejre. The fires on the hills were lit, and they blazed up.

Drumbeats hammered and sweat rushed over her body. The darkness and drums made the world feel dense and trancelike.

Bare feet kicked up dust, and warm bodies pressed against each other, eyes closed, hands gripped tightly. Drums urged them on and wove gods and people into one, while the full moon watched over them in the sky and sorcery flowed through the ground. Since the dawn of time, people had danced their thanks on this night for the gifts of the gods, and the lust-filled Sjofn rewarded them richly.

Sigrid was drunk with lust and freedom.

She caught a glimpse of Jorun far away in the crowd, passionately kissing Orm. Naked breasts in the darkness, shameless caresses between parted thighs. The rumble of the drums grew and made them pulse as one, lifting them into the sacred trance. Everything was as it should be, and she wanted more.

"Now," Sigrid said.

Sweyn took a firm hold of her wrist and she was pulled away from the crowd into reality. His steps were so fast she had a hard time keeping up as he pulled her up a hill. Only when they stood alone in the darkness under an oak did Sweyn let go and wipe the sweat from his brow.

"You shouldn't be at that dance," he said.

The sound of laughter and moans of pleasure could be heard behind them among the burial mounds where the family's forefathers rested. Many people had sought seclusion in the darkness to honor the Vanir gods.

"Is it any better that I'm alone with you?" Sigrid asked, leaning against the oak.

"No," he replied, looking up at the full moon, which tempted and pulled at them.

"And yet here we are," she said with a smile, and Sweyn nodded.

Over by the royal hall, a large fire lit up the sky. Black smoke rose to the heavens. Cries and yells were audible across the hills even from their distance.

"Is the royal hall on fire?" Sigrid asked. Sweyn looked at the smoke, his brow furrowed.

Then he smiled contentedly and said, "Someone set the church on fire and surely not for the first time."

Sigrid smiled. It was fitting for the brown cowls to lose their church on this night. They gazed deeply into each other's eyes, wrapped in the moment. All they had was here and now.

"I'm taking you to your father," Sweyn said hoarsely.

"No," she said, taking off the wreath she wore on her head and looking at its drooping flowers. Her desire for him stole her breath, making her almost pant. This was just a dream; nothing she did tonight was real. "Soon I will be shackled to Erik's bed. Tonight I'm free."

Sweyn crossed his arms in front of his chest and shook his head pleadingly. She put her hand on his, and after a moment's hesitation, he took it, squeezed it hard, and then let go. The sea quietly caressed the shore while the moon played in the dark water.

"Follow me," she whispered, putting her hand on his cheek, feeling his heat as she stroked his skin. His jaw muscles tensed under her fingers. His doubt and internal struggle were visible in his dark blue eyes.

If they followed the shoreline, they would come to Atle's Hill, Beyla had carefully explained. There they would find the sacred oak. Sigrid leaned toward Sweyn's head, so close that her lips almost grazed his ear and she inhaled the bracing scent of safety.

"Assist me in offering the summer sacrifice," she whispered. *My beloved.*

Sweyn's body trembled with anticipation, but he still looked tormented.

"Don't do this to us," he pleaded, but she had already won.

Sigrid took his hand and led him toward the shore, blood coursing like fire through her body. Let her take care and not stumble.

ᚻ

This was crazy. Palna had sworn he would whip Sweyn senseless if he was seen anywhere near Sigrid, and yet here he was walking next to her like some passive farm animal.

Loving a guileful woman was like taking a poorly tamed two-year-old colt onto thin, slippery ice or traveling in a blinding storm with a rudderless ship. He could lose everything for her sake.

He who slept with another man's wife would be banished from the Jómsvíkings. That was the rule Sweyn had sworn to uphold in order to wear the oath ring he bore on his arm. To be expelled from his brotherhood and become an outlaw was the worst punishment imaginable. Still, he could not leave her.

The moonlight turned her hair to spun silver, and she shimmered in the night like the divine being she was. The heat from her hand in his strangely weakened him.

In her proximity there was nothing painful or bloody: no carcasses of men with their bellies cut open, no burned babies in their mothers' arms, no war, no death, no wounds, no pain. There was only beauty, purity, and peace in her.

He couldn't resist. She was the only thing he'd ever wanted, the most beautiful woman he'd seen. Only a castrated fool would have turned down what they had together at this moment.

The sound of the festivities grew fainter with every step. Soon there was only shimmering light on the water and the sound of the waves lapping on the shore.

The ancestors' burial mounds were visible farther along toward the sea.

"I don't know anything about you, aside from the fact that you serve as a Jómsvíking and are Harald's illegitimate son," Sigrid said gently.

"Not illegitimate anymore. He gave me ships, which makes me a Jelling."

"I'm glad you've been adopted into your family line," she said, her smile blinding him. Sweyn thirstily drank in her sincere words. "What will you do with the ships?" she asked, and he smiled wryly in response.

He was going to run with the valkyries and spread death through Svealand, kill Erik, and take Sigrid for his own wife so that she would be his always. After that he would go to war with the chieftains who remained loyal to Harald, conquering them one by one until they bowed to him. Then he would finally kill his birth father and assume the throne.

"I will fight at Styrbjörn's side. He and I will conquer Svealand together. Then I will turn on Harald and drive him from the Jelling throne, which will make me king of the Danes and the Jutes. When the throne is mine, I will attack England and take back what we lost."

Sweyn stopped abruptly. This was more than he'd told even Åke. It was lunacy to tell this to Sigrid. He looked anxiously at her, waiting for her to burst out laughing at his grandiose plans, bigger than a bastard should dream of, but Sigrid watched him with the greatest seriousness.

"Then it's decided that Harald will fight at Styrbjörn's side."

Sweyn nodded. He'd said too much.

"I know you'll be able to take everything you want," she said, and her grip on his hand tightened.

"Is that what the seeress foresaw from the offering bowl when you met her today?" he asked huskily.

She shook her head so her hair billowed around her shoulders.

"If you fight for Valhalla, the gods will grant you victory," she said in dead earnest. "Never doubt that."

At that moment he wanted nothing other than to believe everything she said. The words filled him with strength. He was Valhalla's warrior, chosen and protected.

"I'm going to come get you in Svealand and make you mine," he said seriously.

She stopped and looked at him, her eyes gentle like a caress.

"I know," she whispered.

They stood under an ancient oak tree, as big as Yggdrasil itself. There were flowers on the ground, and bits of colored cloth were tied around the trunk. Sweyn looked up at the branches, where animal offerings swayed in the breeze: two goats, a calf, and what looked like a dog, but no people.

Sweyn touched his heart and bent his head in reverence. Sigrid bowed deeply beside him and took a little pin from her dress, which she laid at the foot of the oak. After that she picked up an ornate offering bowl that seemed to be waiting for her.

Sweyn followed every move she made. She was no giggly maiden dancing in the summer night, shamelessly offering herself to all the men. She was a believer. Only the most devout had such strong faith that they offered a sacrifice in the old way on the most powerful night of the year, even though they risked a death sentence for doing so.

Sigrid pulled a dagger from the pouch she wore on her belt and whispered an incantation. Then she cut her hand and let the blood drip onto the ground.

"Erce, mother earth. Receive your daughter's offering." Her voice was husky with emotion as she spoke, and her hand trembled as she brought it to the sacrificial bowl and let a few drops of blood fall into it. "Freya, Vanadís, Ur-Mother. Protect me. Accept my body and spirit. You are my blood. I am yours."

She motioned for Sweyn to approach.

"I don't know the words," he said.

"Give your strength and your life to the gods, and let them occupy you," she whispered and set the knife blade to his hand.

Sweyn gulped and nodded. Her eyes were like a caress before she made the cut. A burning pain, and the blood ran out of the wound. Sweyn closed his hand and dripped his blood on the ground.

"Thor, I give my life for a victory in your name," Sweyn said and moved his hand to the bowl, letting his blood fall into it. "My life is yours."

Sigrid smiled. Her eyes twinkled as she raised the bowl up to the four points of the compass and then to the tree as she chanted words he didn't understand. Then she turned to him.

"The oath you swore is sealed with Kvasir's blood," she said and handed him the bowl.

Sweyn's hands trembled as he took the bowl. He looked deep into her eyes as he drank. The mead tasted bitterly of dirt and blood.

"I give my life force to Vanadís," she said.

He hoped, as a man, he had given the right response. It must have been all right, because when Sigrid emptied the bowl the leaves of the sacrificial oak shivered in the wind.

A strange presence was around them, so strong that it stung like needles in their skin. The ground throbbed like a heartbeat beneath their feet. The hair stood up on Sweyn's arms as the darkness dimmed around them. The gods they had invoked were here.

"She's arrived," Sigrid whispered devoutly, swaying.

The bowl fell out of her hand onto the ground, and her eyes rolled back until only the whites were visible. For a moment a woman so strange and yet so familiar stood before Sweyn. The spear-sharp eyes, the spirals in her forehead, the hissing snakes on her arms were as familiar to him as if she'd always been with him. He glimpsed shadows dancing around burning fires behind her back, and the drums could be heard again.

"She's blessing you," Sigrid said.

She took off a black leather pouch that had hung around her neck, and she put it around his neck. Her hands stopped at his shoulders, and her eyes locked on his.

"Show her your reverence," she whispered bashfully.

Finally! Sweyn was already hard as he pulled her to him. Her mouth tasted sweet from the mead. Her body was warm against his hands. It required all his strength and self-control not to fling himself on top of her. Instead he carefully laid her down on his cloak.

Her heavy breasts bounced as she took off her dress, and at that moment the strength of the sacrificial mead took over Sweyn, and all his lust was released.

Sigrid was floating between worlds when the goddess took possession of her body and consummated the sacred pair's ritual.

"Mine," Sweyn whispered, his mouth against hers.

His caresses left trails of fire in her body, and she willingly drowned in the sea of lust.

Take my gift, take my life, take my everything.

The pain cut through her as he penetrated her and Sigrid didn't exist anymore. She wrapped her legs around him and drank in his strength and vitality until they fell quivering back into reality.

It was done. The veils of the past grew denser while Sigrid tenderly stroked the scar on Sweyn's sweat-dampened back. The dísir played in the leaves of the sacrificial oak, content at the offering that had been made. Erce held Sigrid safely in her embrace. She had done what she needed to.

Overcome by tenderness, she kissed Sweyn's shoulder. *My beloved.* Sweyn wiped the sweat from his forehead and laughed as he lay down on his back.

"I goofed," he admitted. "If I remember the old sagas correctly, the man's seed is supposed to spill on the ground to bless the next year's crops."

"The ground gets its share, my summer king," Sigrid said, smiling at his ignorance. She could feel the life force trickling out of her body.

She lay on his chest, felt his heart beating against her cheek as he held her in his arms. If only she could stay like this forever. It must be what was intended, for it to be the two of them.

"Well, I guess I became king faster than I thought," he said and smiled. Sigrid inhaled the scent of his strength while stroking the hair on his chest. It was done. "You're bleeding," he said, surprised, noticing the spots of blood on his hand.

"It is as it should be," she said gently. The seeress had said that might happen and that it was a favorable sign.

"Why?" he asked, worried, his mouth against her hair.

"I was untouched."

Sweyn stiffened. He was quiet for a long time before he brushed a lock of hair out of her face and kissed her.

"Thank you," he whispered with such tenderness that Sigrid almost started crying. Quickly, to hide what she was feeling, she reached for her dress. She got dressed and carefully did her belt and buckles.

Sweyn was slower dressing, and she watched his muscular body as he dressed.

"Where did you get these?" she asked, just grazing the scars that ran across his back.

"Floggings," he replied. "That'll teach you to do things right pretty quickly."

Even though he was smiling, she saw a shadow come over his face. She wanted to ask him about his life, know everything he'd done. She wanted to stay by his side forever and run her fingers over his scars every evening. Even so, she had to get back before anyone missed her. She gulped and grazed the leather pouch that she'd hung around his neck.

"This contains the power of the gods. It will give you victory and make you invulnerable in battle. It is my gift to you."

She kissed him one last time before turning and starting back toward the party, walking with heavy footsteps.

"Wait!"

If she stopped, she wouldn't be able to leave him again. Sigrid kept going along the path, forcing herself to put one foot in front of the other. A moment later he grabbed her arm and got her to turn around.

"Stay with me. I'm a ship captain now, a Jelling. We could run away together."

Sigrid smiled sadly at his dreams and shook her head.

"Nothing would be so dishonorable as bringing shame to my father and my family." She kept walking, her heart bleeding in her chest.

"I swear I'll come get you," he said from behind her. When Sigrid turned around he'd taken out a gold brooch, the eight-legged Sleipnir. He put the brooch in her hand and folded her fingers around it. "Send this to me and I will come right away."

A brooch forged from Freya's tears, the ones she shed over her lost husband. Sigrid ran her finger over the expensive gold while the pain tore her apart.

"Go now," she whispered.

He hesitated. "This isn't over," he said, taking her hand.

"You have to go," she whispered.

My beloved.

Sweyn turned around and with one last look at her he walked into the woods. Then she couldn't see him anymore.

Sigrid closed her hand around the gold brooch and saw the little boy from the dream standing in front of her in the moonlight, like a pale premonition of what was to come. *My son.* Her love for the child was so strong that she could hardly breathe.

"It is done," she whispered.

The next moment the child disappeared and all that was left was the empty path that led back to her life.

Emma's head ached and throbbed. Her flesh and bones burned with an otherworldly lust, a ravenous need, as if she contained a thousand lives and they were all immolating themselves. The moonlight that fell through the foliage boiled in her blood and filled her with a restless hunger that neither fire nor Palna could slake. Back and forth she paced along the path as Beyla shot her angry looks.

"I swear I'm going to hit you soon if you don't settle down," Beyla scolded. "You deserve a thrashing anyway for the wretched mess you've made."

Emma cared very little about Beyla's irritability. Soon she would do what Palna had asked her to do and deliver the message to Skagul Toste. But first she had to see Sigrid.

A blessed relief flooded through her body when Sigrid appeared, walking down the path in a soiled dress, her head hanging. Emma was meant to be with Sigrid. She knew that for sure.

Emma cocked her head to the side and asked Sigrid, "Why do you grieve?"

She should be skipping down the path in joy at the wondrous thing that had just happened, not be glassy-eyed with tears. Sigrid brushed the hair out of her face.

"It is done," Sigrid said abruptly.

"Yes, it really is," Emma said with a giggle, Kára's howling in her head. Despite Sigrid's pale cheeks, she glowed with a divine light. Emma ran over to her side.

"What is weighing on you? Your sacrificial offering worked. I can see that clearly."

"I'll never see him again," Sigrid blurted out, pain burning in her eyes as she turned her head away.

So that was what this was about. Emma's laughter was an echo of Kára's. *Small grains of sand, small seas, small are the minds of men,* as Odin put it.

"What does that matter if he did his part?" Emma said.

"Quiet now," Beyla said sharply.

Emma didn't say any more. Instead she followed Beyla and Sigrid back to the royal hall. Soon Sigrid would understand. Emma knew that for sure.

Emma smiled at the burned-out church, where the priests were searching through the ashes and embers for anything worth saving. What had once been a church was now just a glowing heap. Thick smoke rose up into the brightening sky.

"The abomination is gone. You won't have to see it anymore," she said proudly.

"Not so loud," Beyla whispered. "You may pay bitterly for this and for the dead man whose body they found this morning."

Emma shrugged. The guards hardly looked at them. A couple of lovebirds sat whispering by the well and a man lay sleeping by the wall of the building, snoring loudly.

"It doesn't matter," Emma said. "Before the sun is at its peak, Sigrid will have left Lejre. And we must go with her."

"That's not true," Sigrid said, looking puzzled. "Father said we sail in three days."

Emma smiled wryly but said no more. They knew nothing of what was to come. They were blind, like newborn kittens.

The door to the building where Sigrid was staying was open and several men sat in the dining room, drinking mead. Their laughter echoed between the walls. Sigrid stopped at the threshold, still sad about Sweyn even though she should be singing with joy.

"I'll talk to you tomorrow," Sigrid said. "But now I have to rest." With a brief nod, she left them and entered the hall.

Emma turned to Beyla and said, "I'll meet you by Toste's ship."

The seeress gave her an uncertain look and pulled Emma in close.

"What craziness is this?" Beyla said. "I can't go anywhere away from my brother."

Emma shrugged. That didn't matter. She didn't need a seeress, not now that she had Sigrid.

"Then our paths diverge," Emma said indifferently and slipped into the hall.

The men were all very drunk. Emma watched Sigrid walk across the rough plank floor with a glance at her relatives and the strangers who were variously fondling, kissing, and drinking. Several men sat with women on their laps while others snored loudly on the sleeping benches.

"Where have you been, daughter?" Toste yelled angrily. He sat with a buxom woman on his knee with his hand up her skirt.

"I made a sacrifice, the way you're supposed to on this night," Sigrid retorted.

"By yourself?"

She shook her head and said, "Beyla was with me."

"I was there, too," Emma said, stepping out of the shadows.

Toste grunted. His eyes were bloodshot and glassy in his drunkenness, and his beard wet with spilled ale.

"I never should have let you run around on your own. People are talking about you and the girls coming to the executions dressed as sacrificial priestesses. People have been heard plotting evil against you and now you've gone and defied the king by offering a sacrifice."

"The king may reign, but my faith is my own," Sigrid said, smiling, and walked proudly to her room.

She was truly worthy of the fate the Norns had woven for her. Emma's bosom swelled with pride and love. Toste muttered something about his daughter being far too impertinent for her own good. Then he looked at Emma.

"Well, what do we have here?" he said.

Emma walked over to Sigrid's father while the woman sitting on his lap glared at her.

"I have a gift for you," Emma said so warmly that Toste sent the buxom woman off to fetch some more mead.

When the woman got up, Emma took her place on Toste's lap. She nuzzled into him as the chieftain got his tankard filled. She realized she knew the truth about Toste, the whole truth. Palna had explained before he sent her to speak to him. At the time, she didn't think much about what he said.

"Olav's people ended up in a fight with the Obotrites down at the harbor," one of the Svea said.

Toste laughed.

"I had better luck with my men last night," he said.

A woman sitting with the Svea recounted how angry the king had been because he hadn't managed to sleep with his mistresses and how he tried to get the priests to bless his manhood. While the woman spoke, Emma rested her head on Toste's shoulder and played with his beard. She twisted it around her fingers and inhaled his scent. Toste's rough hand wandered up her thigh.

"What is this present you wanted to give me?" he said in a low voice, moving his hand all the way up to her crotch.

Emma moved as one of his fingers penetrated her and leaned closer to him, so close that her lips grazed his ear.

"Palna would like you to come to his hearth immediately," she whispered, so quietly that no one else would hear.

"Whatever it is can wait," Toste said.

Emma bit her lip as his finger pushed deeper into her.

"At the spring sacrifice, King Harald is going to send the Jómsvíkings to fight with Styrbjörn for the throne of Svealand. Your old pal Palna is now your enemy and your daughter is in danger."

Toste let go of her as fast as if she were a glowing cinder. His blood-shot eyes widened and filled with disbelief.

"Palna would never do that," Toste exclaimed.

"What I say is true," Emma whispered, carefully hiding her satisfaction. "Palna told me that tonight when I shared his bed."

That was only a small lie, but it worked.

"I don't believe a word. Your snake's tongue can't sow dissention between me and my brothers-in-arms."

"I swear in the name of your guardian spirit that I am telling you the truth. Ask Palna, he is waiting at his hearth."

Toste stood up so fast that Emma almost fell on the floor. He grabbed her hand so hard it hurt.

"If you're lying, I'll send you to the afterworld."

"You will soon realize that I never lie," Emma said, shaking her head.

Someday the truth would catch up with Skagul Toste.

†

He had had her. Sweyn closed his fingers around the leather pouch, and Sigrid was with him again in all her resplendence. The most beautiful woman in the nine worlds performed the sacrifice with him, and Thor himself had granted him his strength. Sweyn smiled at the strange pleasure that sped through his body.

She said he could never be wounded in battle.

Harald had given him ships during the summer festival. The most transcendently breathtaking woman had offered the sacrifice with him. Sweyn took a deep breath, his strength growing. Only now did he appreciate the great fate the gods had in store for him. Loveliest Sigrid, dís of the dísir, nothing could compare to her pure beauty and strength.

He stopped on the outskirts of the camp. His brothers-in-arms snored loudly beside their now-cool fire pits. Only one fire still burned.

Palna sat there by the hearth, staring into the flames, brooding. Sweyn really didn't want to talk to him. Palna was very perceptive. He would surely notice right away that something had happened. But when Sweyn sat down, his foster father didn't even look up. Melancholy weighed on Palna's shoulders like a cape, and his eyes were locked on the dancing flames.

"You shouldn't have let your brother drink himself senseless," Palna said.

Sweyn looked at Åke, who had passed out drunk on his skin rug.

"He went off on his own," Sweyn said.

Palna grunted in dissatisfaction. He was quick to anger tonight, which meant nothing would go well, no matter what Sweyn said. Sweyn had received far too many beatings during Palna's bad moods. It would be better to wait until tomorrow.

"Only a man without honor lets down his brother-in-arms," Palna said.

Sweyn stared hard at the fire.

"Sometimes a man has no choice," he finally responded.

The fire crackled quietly. A few men were just going to bed, their noisy laughter growing quiet.

"All the same, wicked deeds must be atoned for," Palna said and then sighed heavily. "King Harald made me swear to fight with Styrbjörn the Strong, so you won't be going north alone."

"I'm glad," Sweyn said, shooting a questioning glance at his foster father. Something was wrong, but he couldn't put his finger on what.

"I'm sure Harald is going to take Jómsborg from me after we've fought in Svealand, in revenge for my sticking to the old ways and for my bringing you to his court."

Sweyn was surprised. Without Palna, Jómsborg wouldn't be the sharp spear that had brought silver and victories to the king of the Jellings. Yet now the king thought he could just toss Palna aside like a worn-out shoe.

"The brothers will stand by your side," Sweyn said.

"We will be good to our word and fight in Svealand," Palna said. "After that, with the help of your battle wolves you will conquer King Harald's jarls one by one, until you've brought that dragon to his knees."

They eyed each other grimly.

"I'm ready," Sweyn said. Never in his life had he been so sure of anything. He would fight Harald and win, and Sigrid would be his queen.

They heard voices from the outskirts of the camp. Sweyn's heart stopped in his chest when he saw Toste approaching with Sigrid at his side. What in Balder's name did this mean? Why was Toste coming to see him? Had Toste heard about the sacrifice and come now to demand payment for his daughter's honor? If he knew, he would consider her to have been violated before her wedding.

Sweyn got up, his sword in his hand, and watched the two walk through the camp. Sigrid was his, having offered the sacrifice to the gods for him. He would fight for her honor and his own until the gods sent him to the afterworld.

"Relax," said Palna, who was still sitting calmly.

When Toste got close enough, Sweyn realized that it wasn't Sigrid at his side but Emma. He slowly exhaled. Emma's blond hair must have played a trick on him in the darkness of the summer night. Even though they were similar, the castratrix could in no way compare to the beautiful Sigrid.

Had she told Toste about their encounter? Damn it. Sweyn was still standing with his sword in hand when Toste reached their hearth.

"Is she telling the truth?" Toste asked, pointing at Emma. He was drunk, the smell of mead very evident.

"She is," said Palna.

"Have you turned your back on me and become my enemy?" Toste said, shaking his head in disbelief.

Sweyn gripped his sword tightly. Every muscle in his body was tense and ready for an attack.

"This was not my choice. Nor did I want it to be this way," Palna replied with a heavy sigh. "If I didn't promise Harald my sword, he swore Jómsborg would burn. I cannot stand up to the king alone. You'd have made the same choice."

Sweyn slowly lowered his weapon. They were talking about the coming war against Svealand, not his encounter under the oak.

"What you say is true," Toste said, scratching his beard thoughtfully as his rage evaporated.

"We each have to stand on our own side of this. Still, I honored our friendship by sending the girl to fetch you," Palna said. Only now did he get up and stand face-to-face with Toste, his longtime battle ally. "Now I will tell you the rest. King Harald and Styrbjörn are planning to take your daughter captive tomorrow. You must leave Lejre tonight."

"I have fought for Harald since we were lads," Toste said, looking incredulous. "I wear his oath ring. It's hard to believe he would take my daughter captive and draw arms against me."

Light and shadow fell over the aging warriors' faces as they looked grimly into each other's eyes.

"Nothing is the way it usually is in King Harald's court," Palna replied. "The battles we fought for him are long forgotten. We're hired hands from the past, condemned to be driven away."

"Now I know for sure that the pact with the Svea was meet and just," Toste said, slowly stroking his beard. "It hurts me that we're not on the same side of this, my friend, but your warning is honorable."

"I'm bound by the oath I swore to join the battle in Svealand, but it is the last time my sword will serve Harald," Palna said. "I hope a more honorable king will take Harald's place on the throne of the Jellings."

Palna glanced over at Sweyn, his foster son.

"I wish you all success. Soon we will drink mead again together, in Jómsborg or in Valhalla," Toste said, putting his hand on Palna's shoulder.

They nodded solemnly to one another before Toste swiftly left the Jómsvíking camp. Sweyn hoped Toste and his crew would escape Styrbjörn's men, because if Sigrid were taken captive Sweyn would not be able to sit quietly by.

"Will they make it out in time?" Sweyn asked.

"Toste hasn't unloaded his ships," Palna said. "They can easily be out on the sound before daybreak."

Sweyn swallowed his concern and said simply, "It was honorable of you to warn them, Father."

"Twice Toste has saved my life. It was time I repaid him."

Palna turned to Emma, who was still standing, hesitant and listening, a short distance from them. He said, "You did that well, even if you took your time."

Emma padded up to Palna, got up on her tiptoes, and kissed him on the mouth.

"Good-bye," she said and then turned to Sweyn. "I will watch over your Sigrid until the next time we meet, king of the Danes." Then she ran off between the tents and sleeping warriors.

Sweyn closed his eyes and cursed Emma the castrator. He should have realized she couldn't be trusted.

"Toste's daughter is *yours*?" Palna asked.

Sweyn grimaced. He couldn't remain silent about what had happened, and lying was against the Jómsvíking code. The scars on his back were evidence of that.

Sweyn grasped the leather pouch he was wearing around his neck and looked his father in the eyes like a man.

"This night Sigrid served as my priestess during the sacrifice. Thor and Freya blessed us. I am going to be victorious in the battle."

Anger and surprise came over Palna's face.

"I told you to stay away from Toste's daughter, and yet you defy your father and chieftain." His voice was a low growl. Sweyn gritted his teeth. No amount of trouble could make him wish the whole thing away.

"Yes, and she gave herself to me," he added.

The blow came so fast that Sweyn didn't have time to duck. A sharp smack on his cheek, and he practically fell over backward. When he regained his footing, he looked his father in the eye, ready for the next blow.

His whole life he had quietly taken the beatings he had coming to him. But not for this, not after what had happened. Sweyn grabbed Palna's hand in midair and held it still without breaking eye contact.

"I'll take the whipping you promised I'd get if I went near her, but I will not be slapped around like a kid."

He could see Palna's surprise, but only for an instant before he struck Sweyn in the mouth with his left hand and then got in a kick to the stomach. Sweyn was ready for him. He twisted free and caught his father's other hand. Palna couldn't writhe himself free, although he tried his best.

"Let me take my punishment like a man, not like a son," Sweyn said, his heart pounding like a drumbeat in his chest.

The noise woke the other Jómsvíkings, and half-asleep, they watched what was happening. Gunnar came out of the tent and asked why Palna was beating Sweyn.

Palna looked Sweyn right in the eye and declared, "At dawn, Sweyn will dance beneath the cane."

Then he broke Sweyn's grip and punched him in the face so hard that Sweyn fell to the ground, half knocked out from the pain. Palna kicked him in the gut, so he curled up, moaning.

"Did I not say that I would whip the flesh off your back if you didn't stay away?" Palna roared.

Sweyn nodded, grunting.

"Am I a man who keeps his word?" Palna continued.

Sweyn forced himself to nod once again.

"You won't be so impertinent tomorrow."

Sweyn moaned as Palna gave him one last kick in the gut. The bitter taste of warm blood filled his mouth. The ground danced beneath his feet as he tried to get up. His body ached, and blood ran from both his nose and mouth. But a man had to take a licking. Sigrid was worth it. Not even Palna's wrath could make him regret what had happened. Sweyn wiped his chin on the back of his hand and dragged himself to bed.

His ribs ached but seemed intact, and he still had all his teeth, so things weren't that bad.

"Of all the passionate wenches you could've picked this night, you picked the only one you weren't supposed to touch," Åke said.

Sweyn laughed painfully, spat out more blood, and then squeezed the leather pouch that still hung around his neck.

"It had to happen," he said simply.

"How could you defy Father after all he's done for you?" Åke said with deep disappointment. "How could you turn against us? Did the king's recognition and the ships you got inflate your head so much you lost all sense?"

Sweyn felt his split lip and avoided making eye contact with Åke. Sigrid's scent was still on his fingers and he could still feel himself inside her.

"Maybe the whipping will beat some sense into you again."

Sweyn gulped and looked away at the first hint of dawn on the horizon before he groaned from the pain and lay down on his bed. He hoped Sigrid would get away from Harald and Styrbjörn's men. Nothing else mattered.

Sigrid hurried through the twilight on her bare feet, quite out of breath. The battle gear rattled as the warriors walked by her side, their hands at the ready on their swords. Axel was closest, and the anger was deeply etched into his face. Ulf kept looking around fearfully the whole time. At any moment someone could run up and take them captive.

Sigrid had already been settled in her bed for the night when the door was flung open with a bang and Toste had rushed into the room and said they needed to get to the ships.

He said, "Harald is taking Styrbjörn's side against Svealand. They're going to take you captive." Then warriors had entered the room and carried out their chests. Alfhild and Jorun had packed up their things and now they were hurrying to the boats.

A skinny, elderly servant, staring with his mouth open, guarded the courtyard in front of the royal hall.

"Where are you going at this hour?" he sputtered.

Sigrid's heart froze in her chest. If he sounded the alarm, King Harald's warriors would come running, bind her like an animal, and drag her off.

"The movements of free men are their own business," Toste said authoritatively, eyes fixed on the guard.

The guard conceded and took a step back as they hurried past, onto the road that led down toward the harbor.

"He'll go to his supervisor and tell him what he saw," Toste said. "So we won't have long until they're after us."

Sigrid's hands trembled as she clutched her cloak. Never in this world or the next would she become Harald's captive. Resolute, they reached the small village at the harbor, and several villagers pointed to them as they hurried down the slope to the harbor itself. A few drowsy men stood in the square and watched them rush by.

"What's your hurry?" one of them asked.

Toste took Sigrid by the arm and made her run the last little bit across the square toward the water. Three of the ships were already out in the water. Her father's biggest ship waited in the breakers for them to arrive. The warriors were already sitting on the rowing benches, half-asleep and frowning.

Four men held the prow, so that Toste's party could easily climb on board before the boat was pushed off into the water. Emma stood next to them with a big bundle in her arms. She had said this would happen. Never a doubt entered her mind, since she prophesied their departure from Lejre.

"She's coming with me," Sigrid said.

The water was cold as she waded out to the ship and was lifted onboard. As soon as the last of the warriors had climbed in, the ship pushed off, and the men rowed away from the shore at Lejre.

Out of breath, Sigrid sank down in her spot by the mast, with Emma beside her. Anxiously she looked around for warriors on land and sea, but all was quiet. A favorable offshore breeze was picking up, and it filled the sails as soon as they were unfurled. Soon the four ships were leaping over the waves, out to sea. Sigrid shivered beneath her cloak.

"King Harald won't be seeing you in his hall, either as his guest or his captive," Toste said grimly.

"This is Thyre's doing," she replied.

That poisonous snake had hated her from the first moment. Surely Thyre had dripped her venom into her husband's and father's ears, urging them to take Sigrid captive. Thyre would pay bitterly for that.

"It wasn't Thyre," Axel said, shaking his head in disagreement. "Styrbjörn bears the blame for breaking the peace between the Svea and the Danes. I tell you this: we Svea will not back down in the battle he seeks in Svealand. Let him come with whatever of Harald's warriors he wants. They will become eagle food on our plains. He's dead already, doomed and soon to be forgotten by everyone."

The men mumbled their agreement, and Toste put his clenched fist to his chest.

"The Scylfings will fight at your side. After this night, Harald and Styrbjörn are our enemies as well."

Both men nodded grimly at each other.

Sigrid watched gloomily as the Danish coastline grew smaller in the dawn light. She had been given to Erik as a peace bride but instead of guaranteeing peace, she was dragging the Geats into yet another war. Her sacrifice was for naught and would only lead to more death. The cloak of grief she wore since she'd parted from Sweyn ached heavily on her shoulders.

This cannot be your choice, Vanadís.

Sweyn had said he would accompany Styrbjörn to Svealand. She had thought his talk of battle might be dreams made out of desire, but he had spoken truthfully about everything. It was her own mind that had been darkened by her lust for the Jómsvíking.

Sigrid had a hard time breathing when she fully understood what she had done. Not since Rovald the Strong had refused to save her father and her three brothers when their ship sank had anyone failed the family so badly. She curled up remorsefully as the regret stuck knives in her belly. She had lustfully bedded the enemy, a man who wanted to kill her betrothed.

"I'm going to be damned by future generations," she whispered to Emma, who cuddled against her like a dog.

Emma contemplated her regret with deep surprise.

"You will be celebrated in song through the ages for your courage and your greatness," Emma whispered, her lips to Sigrid's ear. "You have humbly bowed to the will of the goddess, and she will repay you generously for it."

She stroked Sigrid's hair tenderly.

"They're going to fight each other," Sigrid said.

Sweyn would oppose her husband and fight to the death for Svealand. There was no other place where the old ways were as strong as Svealand's Aros, where the gods rested and people went on pilgrimages to the sacred temple of the ancestors. Styrbjörn was a cross worshipper and he would never be allowed to win there. But if Styrbjörn was killed, Sweyn could be killed as well. Sigrid sighed heavily. Whatever happened, it wasn't going to be good.

Emma shrugged, as if none of this mattered.

"Men's friendships are fickle, like the winter weather in the mountains; one moment they're fighting, the next they're kinsmen. Forget Sweyn. He has a different destiny in the tapestry."

Sigrid stared at her shoes glumly, wet from wading out to the boat. How was she supposed to forget the most precious thing that had happened in her life? Her longing for him tugged at her heart.

"Why do you dwell on such somber thoughts when you have so much to be happy about?" Emma asked. "The chosen one will be here soon. He is king of kings, the most important ruler."

Emma smiled calmly and then began to hum a song that Sigrid had never heard before. Sigrid swallowed and then nodded. She had done the unthinkable, for her son's sake. Whatever happened, it was a small sacrifice to make.

My beloved, Sweyn had said. *I will come get you.* Sigrid put her hand on her belly and caressed it tenderly. Their story wasn't yet over.

Sweyn was hanging by the ropes that held his arms outstretched. His back was bare, and warm blood ran down his back and his legs. He moaned in pain as the blow of the whip pulled off a bit of flesh. That was the thirteenth blow. Only two more to go. He had to endure this. She was worth it.

Palna stood in front of him with his arms crossed to make sure Sweyn took his punishment like a man. No trace of emotion showed in his foster father's face. He had kept his word, and Sweyn couldn't contradict that.

Fourteen. This blow was worse than the others and higher up on his shoulders. He stifled a scream and immediately cursed himself for his weakness.

All the Jómsvíkings stood around him watching him take his punishment. Most of them bore traces of the whip on their backs, but few had ever taken more than ten lashes. And yet they grinned when he moaned. Sweyn took a deep breath and waited for the final blow.

Fifteen. It cut through his body like a knife. Palna nodded briefly and walked away. Sweyn fell forward onto the grass when the ropes were untied.

"You foolish boy," Ax-Wolf muttered. "It could have been your greatest day. You got everything you'd striven for: ships, crew, and the king's recognition. Yet you had to run off and hump your way to unhappiness."

Sweyn lay still on the ground while the giant Ax-Wolf looked him over.

"You won't be able to sleep on your back tonight, that much I can say," Åke said, looking worriedly at Sweyn.

"Did she get away?" Sweyn croaked.

The men exchanged glances before Åke nodded.

"Toste's ships are gone, and Harald is furious. His men are looking for the person who tipped them off."

Sweyn's cracked lips hurt when he smiled. Sigrid was safe, and soon he would go find her and make her his own.

PART TWO

ᚤ

Sweyn stared in disbelief at the two ships that were pulled up onto the beach. They were the oldest ships he had seen in his whole life. Many of the planks were so rotten that it was a wonder the ships hadn't sunk. Barely half the oars were left, and most of the rowing benches were cracked and broken.

The crew was even worse. The men who were supposed to serve him were either advanced in years or underage, looking like they could scarcely hold a sword. The few who were of a serviceable age were either feeble or sickly.

"My damned birth father collected the worst men the Danes have," Sweyn told Ax-Wolf, who was close to bursting out laughing.

"It's probably going to be quite a task to make warriors out of this crew. Half of them are going to die of heart attacks if we force them to row."

Åke, who stood next to them with his arms crossed, chuckled.

Sweyn raised his hand up over his head and grimaced as the wounds on his back burned. Beyla had applied an ointment to his skin and then put meadowsweet leaves on the wounds before wrapping them up. The pain was diminished but not gone completely, which put him in a rotten mood.

Palna was having just as much trouble keeping from laughing as the others.

"I warned you you'd be tricked, didn't I?" Palna said with a grin, as a pale youth started coughing so his lungs rattled.

Sweyn had received what he was due and had been recognized as a Jelling, but he was not going to be able to win any battles with these ships and crews.

"Will the ships even make it to Jómsborg?"

Sigvard and Ax-Wolf scrutinized the vessels, knocked on the wood, and stuck their knives into the worst of the planks. Then they exchanged glances.

"Probably, if we mend the ragged sail and procure some oars."

Well, that settled that. He could move on to the next thing. Sweyn walked up to the men who were standing on the beach holding their bundles and weapons. None of them had swords. They all carried axes. The oldest one looked like he was over sixty, and judging from his scrawny arms it had been a long time since he had rowed a boat.

"Go home," Sweyn told him.

The old man thanked him and practically ran off the beach and back to Lejre, clutching his bundle of clothes. Sweyn also excused the young coughing man—he didn't need someone with a weak chest—along with most of the oldest and youngest. One by one the men fell out until not even half were left.

Sweyn looked down at a boy he recognized from the day he came ashore in Lejre. The kid had said he wanted to become a Jómsvíking as he was shooed away.

"How old are you?"

"Fifteen," the boy said, stretching to make himself seem taller.

Sweyn exchanged an amused look with Åke, because they could both see that he wasn't a day over eleven.

"Don't lie!" Åke growled.

The boy cowered, as if he expected to be hit, but there was no fear in his face, just determination.

"I'm almost eleven, but I'm strong, and I've been practicing with a wooden sword," he said.

Sweyn couldn't help but smile. The boy was skinny and flea-bitten, wearing dirty, patched clothes, and he stank of manure. Still, the boy reminded Sweyn of himself at that age. He had the same defiance and fearlessness about what was to come.

"Your name is Ragnvald, isn't it?"

The boy nodded. He had lively eyes, and both his legs and his mind seemed healthy. That was more than could be said for the rest of the men.

"Do you understand what serving me would entail?"

Ragnvald nodded eagerly and began to enumerate: "Training day and night, getting beaten if I make mistakes or don't listen. If I break any rules, speak ill of my brothers, or don't report everything I know, you'll kill me. If I'm worthy, I'll get to fight with you until I die on the battlefield, the best death a warrior can have."

The words tumbled out.

Åke raised an eyebrow and said, "He knows more than most."

"You can stay," Sweyn told the boy, who lit up in a huge smile. The other men had listened carefully to the boy's words, and Sweyn saw uncertainty on several of their faces. "You heard Ragnvald. I offer you only fighting until the death. If you are not willing to give me this, you are free to go."

Four men took their knapsacks and left, and now there were only seventeen men left on the beach, half the crew for one ship.

"This isn't much of a hird you're left with now that the losers have gone," Palna said.

"Better to have a few good men than a bunch of worthless ones," Sweyn said. "Sigvard, go find men who want to serve the Jómsvíkings while we load up here in Lejre. There must be some capable fighters."

Sigvard turned away from the boat he was examining and departed directly.

"They shouldn't be hard to pick out," Sweyn said. "I'll ask the ship-wright to come look over our ships. I know him well, so he'll probably help us."

Palna nodded in approval and asked, "How will you pay them?"

Sweyn patted the pouch he wore on his belt and said, "My share of the spoils from the monastery will be enough to feed the men over the winter."

Åke put a hand on his shoulder and added, "My share should cover it if you come up short."

Palna looked more than satisfied now.

"You'll get the ships I promised you in Jómsborg," he said, and left them standing on the beach.

Sweyn looked at his ships and remaining crew. They may be pathetic, but they were his. He clutched the pouch Sigrid had given him and felt his confidence growing.

"This is going to go well," he told Åke, and for the first time he believed it himself.

ᚻ

Jorun placed the last flower into Sigrid's hair and straightened her necklace and dress.

She scanned Sigrid for flaws before bowing and taking a step backward. "You're ready," Jorun pronounced.

Sigrid raised her chin. Her enemies had tried to kill and capture her,
but she'd traveled through forests and across seas to elude their grasp.
Her body had been taken over by Vanadís, and she'd received the greatest of gifts in return. Only ash and stone remained after she lost what
she loved most. She didn't need to be afraid any longer, not even about
the approaching meeting with King Erik. Sigrid looked out over the
lush foreign fields heavy with rye and flax.

"Go," she told her two kinswomen. "I want to speak to Emma."

Jorun and Alfhild pouted. During all the days they spent sailing
to Svealand, they had made it clear that it was tough for them to put
up with Sigrid always wanting to have Emma by her side night and
day. They were blind and deaf to the ties that bound Sigrid and Emma
together. They were ignorant of the strength and the calm that Sigrid
got from her protector. Jorun and Alfhild reluctantly left Sigrid while
Emma calmly remained by her side.

Sigrid gulped before she began speaking.

"How will I manage to smile lovingly at another man when I am missing Sweyn so much it rips me apart?" she asked.

Her worry paled in comparison with the thoughts of Sweyn and what they'd done during the sacrifice, which never left her day or night.

"You are poisoned by desire," Emma said disinterestedly. "Turn your darkened mind to how you're going to tempt your husband into your bed. There mustn't be any doubt about who's the father of the child you're carrying."

Sigrid made a face as aversion burned in her gut. The whole voyage she'd prayed to the goddess, fervently hoping she was carrying Sweyn's baby so that everything would be like in the dream, but she received only hollow silence in response.

"All that matters is what they believe is true," Emma said with a giggle.

"Are you ready?" Sigrid's father yelled impatiently. "We're waiting."

He stood with Axel, Ulf, and the other men on the shore where the ship had been beached. Behind them lay the glittering water that had carried them for days past foreign coastlines and monster-filled depths, far into Svealand with its burgeoning fields and meadows where plump farm animals grazed. Signs of the Sveas' deep faith in the gods were everywhere. They saw altar stones and temples, processional routes and sacrifice locations as they moved toward the hub of the wheel. And soon she, Sigrid Tostedotter, would become queen of these families and land. Her stomach ached as she stood at the edge of this precipice.

"Before dark I will lie in the king's embrace," she said.

"Then everything is as it should be," Emma said, smiling cheerfully at a butterfly that danced by in front of her.

Grant me strength, Vanadís. Sigrid walked up to the men waiting and forced herself to smile.

"Do you remember what's going to happen and what to say?" Axel asked kindly.

Sigrid tried to swallow, but her mouth was too dry. She said, "My only concern is that I won't please the king."

"Well, then you have nothing to fear," Axel said with a grin.

Toste cleared his throat. He looked uncertain, as if he were having second thoughts at the last minute.

"You were sent here as a peace queen," Toste said. "But you will meet Erik as a war bride. Styrbjörn the Strong and the Jómsvíkings are going to attack at the spring sacrifice."

Sigrid smiled sadly and said, "We've been on the verge of war since I was born. I fear these battles as little as I feared the others."

"Erik will keep you safe," Toste replied.

I'm sure you believe that, Sigrid thought, giving a somber smile and holding out her hand. Her father took the handfasting ribbon and tied it around Sigrid's and Axel's wrists to symbolize the betrothal made back home uniting the families.

"Are you ready to meet your husband?" Axel asked. The Svea warrior's eyes were full of friendship and joy.

Sigrid took a deep breath. Was she ready to meet the people the Geats had been fighting for two generations? Was she ready to meet the man behind her own mother's death? She would be forced to live with this man instead of the man who had stolen her heart.

She looked at the Svea who had gathered along the road that lead past the gray timber houses and large farms up to the royal hall at Kungsgården.

"I want nothing more," she replied.

None of the people lining the road cheered or shouted words of greeting. The eyes watching her were filled with both distrust and loathing. Two women, both with their hair wrapped up in cloth, whispered to each other and pursed their lips as if she were an outlaw on her way to her execution. An older man with a leather apron shook his head and watched her with skepticism.

"She comes with war and has death in her wreath," another said.

Sigrid forced herself to walk with pride even as her courage wilted in her chest. They hated her, like an enemy and a stranger. Her heart pounded as she stared stiffly straight ahead.

"Go home, Scylfings," someone shouted from behind her back.

"Why do they harbor such ill will toward us?" she whispered to Axel, who seemed unmoved by the whole thing.

"I encountered the same wariness when I first entered your lands," Axel said, unconcerned. "And yet I forged many bonds of friendship. Give them time. You'll win them over with your charm and strength."

He led her up the hill to an enormous royal hall built of dark logs, with winding dragons on the roof. A large party waited in front of the courtyard around an ornate bower decorated with leaves and flowers. Axel had explained that welcoming a wife as she stepped into her new home and presenting her with an oath ring was very serious business to the Svea. People read a lot into what happened at the threshold.

Sigrid looked at the unsmiling group awaiting her. While there had been many well-dressed young people, priests, merchants, and strangers in King Harald's court, here in Svealand there were only warriors and chieftains. Stern and powerful, they watched her expectantly with their heads held high. They were all tattooed and wore silver oath rings on their arms.

The women were just as severe-looking. Draped with expensive jewelry that gleamed around their necks and arms, they sized her up with piercing eyes.

Sigrid gulped as one of the men stepped forward to stand under the flowery arch.

It was Erik.

Her mother's murderer was both older and shorter than she'd expected, and he was neither handsome nor ugly. His beard was short and brown, his hair so long that it came down to his shoulders. The tunic he wore was made of rough homespun with embroidery around the edges. His leggings were the same color, and his leather boots

stretched halfway up to his knees. His hand rested on the richly ornamented hilt of the sword he wore at his hip, and he was studying her
attentively. For a brief moment she saw the same chill in his greenish-
gray eyes that she had seen in his villagers. Reluctance was like a flock of
flying birds in her chest. Sigrid clenched her teeth. She was a descendant
of Vanadís, and she had Kára's protection. She would do this for the
sake of the Scylfings.

"My king, allow me to present your wife, Sigrid Tostedotter," Axel
announced ceremoniously as they held out their hands together, bound
by the handfasting ribbon.

Sigrid and Erik regarded each other in silence for a long time.

"I accept her," the king of Svealand finally said in a voice that was
deeper and manlier than she had expected.

He took the ribbon off their wrists, and Axel immediately backed
away. In his place, an aged temple priest wearing a gray gown with a fox
head hanging over his shoulder came hobbling over to them. He held an
ornate silver oath ring that was more beautiful than any Sigrid had seen.

He read an incantation over the ring before Erik took it from him
and held it up to Sigrid. She cleared her throat and put her hand on
the ring. It was important that she not make a mistake now. Axel had
been careful to explain that. The slightest misstep would be interpreted
as a bad omen.

"On this oath ring I swear my faithfulness to you, Erik of Svealand,
and that I will bear you many strong sons and honor you in thought
and deed," Sigrid lied in a loud, clear voice without taking her eyes off
Erik. "May Eir and Odin kill me if I break this oath."

A spark of approval was visible in his eyes, but only for a brief
instant before he grew serious again. There was a grim sternness about
him, as if this were something he was being forced to do. And if that
was the case, then they had something in common.

"With this ring the oath is sworn," the priest said and fit it over
her wrist.

It was heavy and so big that it didn't sit securely until it was pushed to her upper arm.

"You will enter my hall and my kingdom as my wife," Erik said and bowed his head.

The priest held the ax over their heads and again read an incantation. Then he pronounced, "The oath that has been sworn cannot be broken."

An older woman with beautiful gray hair and keys hanging from her belt stepped forward with a horn made of blue glass. She was the king's mother, who ran the estate and certainly wouldn't be happy about giving up this status.

Sigrid accepted the horn, raised it to Erik, his mother, and then the guests before she drank the cool wine. She then passed the drink to Erik.

The priest gave them a contented look and said, "It is done."

At that moment three flutists began playing a melody and the guests around them shouted their congratulations. The austerity they had displayed thus far was now completely gone, and they laughed and talked together. Sigrid took a deep breath. She was Erik's wife, and soon she would be Svealand's queen. No other woman ranked above her. Power boiled in her blood, and her cheeks flushed in the summer heat.

"They weren't lying when they said you were beautiful," Erik said quietly. "That's a relief."

Sigrid forced herself to smile. Axel and Orm had described Erik as the most handsome of men, and that certainly was not the case. She leaned toward him.

"I'm delighted that I please you," she whispered.

She was immediately rewarded with a lustful look. This seduction was going to go well, after all.

"This is my mother, Haldis," Erik said.

"A warm welcome to you, Sigrid Tostedotter," the queen mother said. "I've been looking forward to your arrival."

Anyone could hear that her voice was dripping with duplicity. All the same she smiled and held out a beautifully embroidered head covering, the symbol that Sigrid was now a married woman.

Women and men came forward and greeted her. The names and faces melted together, and she had no idea how she was going to remember them all. Two beautiful young women with blond hair stared at her so spitefully before greeting her that Sigrid realized they must be Erik's mistresses. She greeted them indifferently, eager not to show the slightest weakness.

"Allow me to show you around your new home," Haldis said.

Sigrid looked questioningly at Erik, who stood engrossed in a profoundly serious conversation with her father.

"You'll meet your husband at the feast tonight," Haldis continued.

Sigrid took a deep breath and went with the king's mother. Emma, Jorun, and Alfhild joined them. Emma's presence was reassuring.

The hall was large, and every bit of wood was decorated with twisting patterns that had been painted in bright colors. Amazed, Sigrid stopped in the middle of the hall and looked around at the brilliantly colored splendor. The long table in the middle was so big that a hundred men could sit at its benches. The throne was as big as King Harald's in Lejre and so ornate it made Toste's throne back home seem like a simple stool by comparison.

At the two short ends of the vast, rectangular room there were stairs leading up to landings where the highest-ranking residents had their rooms, just like back home.

But Haldis did not go up either of those staircases. Instead she led Sigrid toward a door in the wall next to the stairs. Sigrid followed her into a small room with benches and weaving looms. There were several doors around them and Haldis opened one of them. Sigrid saw a plain room without tapestries on the walls. It was furnished with a simple bed, without posts, and two chairs.

"I hope you'll be comfortable here," Haldis said.

This was a downright insult, and Sigrid absolutely would not tolerate it.

"The mistresses back home live in nicer quarters than this!" Alfhild exclaimed in surprise from behind Sigrid's back. "Why would you give the queen of Svealand such a plain room?"

"It's what we have to offer," said Haldis, blushing.

"Who lives in the rooms upstairs?" Sigrid asked.

"The king and his companions live there."

"In *all* the rooms?" Sigrid asked, incredulous.

Haldis cleared her throat and said, "They're all taken. This is the king's will."

Sigrid carefully studied the woman as the silence in the room grew awkward. She had to teach them now, right from the beginning, who was going to be in charge.

"I will make the decisions about who stays where in my own home. Let us see the other rooms that are available. Then after that I'll decide where my chamber will be," Sigrid announced, turned on her heel, and left.

The servants did a double take, startled when she quickly strode back out into the hall, eyeing the two sets of stairs that led up to the landings where the rooms under the ridge of the roof were located.

"Where's the king's room?" she asked an older servant, who pointed to the stairs next to the throne.

Sigrid thanked him and walked toward the opposite staircase, with Haldis hurrying along behind her.

"Those rooms are occupied," Haldis said, panting.

Sigrid didn't respond but just climbed the stairs. She didn't stop until she reached the two doors.

"Open them," she ordered Jorun, who without hesitating opened the doors wide.

It was just as Sigrid had thought. Both of the rooms were big and airy and furnished with beautifully decorated beds and comfortable pelt rugs on the floor. Two dresses lay on a chest, and on a table there were several pieces of jewelry. There was a doll and a wooden top lying on the floor in one of the rooms.

"Is it the custom in Svealand for the king's mistresses to live better than his queen?" Sigrid asked.

Haldis looked down without responding.

"Alfhild," Sigrid said, "ask the men to bring up my chests. Jorun, you can empty these things out of here." She sat down on a chair, and Emma stood behind her. "Send a servant with some water so I can wash off the travel dust," she said while Jorun tossed all the items in the room into a chest, which she then dragged out.

The king's mother looked like she wanted to scratch Sigrid's eyes out.

"Was there anything else?" Sigrid asked her kindly.

"The king is not going to allow you to be domineering," Haldis finally said.

Sigrid got up.

"Maybe I should go back home and tell everyone that you value mistresses above the daughter of the chieftain of the Scylfings. That is an insult the Geats will not tolerate."

Haldis sternly sized her up, but Sigrid did not back down. This Svea matron was nothing compared to the harshness of her own grandmother or the spitefulness of her stepmother, Gunlög, which she had been fighting against all her life.

"You can be as impudent as you like and buck and rear, but other customs prevail here than among the Geats. You will soon see, once my son reins you in."

"I will have the respect my family and position merit," she said with a calm smile.

Sigrid held out her hand, and Emma gave her the leather pouch she carried for her. When she opened it, she saw the Sleipnir brooch that

Sweyn had given her, although that wasn't the gift she took out now but rather a silver brooch inlaid with red stones.

"If I receive what my lineage entitles me to, I look forward to becoming friends with my husband's highly esteemed mother. Take this gift as a sign of my hope that you will look after me and teach me the ways of the Svea, like you would your own daughter."

Haldis's eyes gleamed as she accepted the brooch.

"I thank you, and it is also my hope that you will become like a daughter to me," she said in a softer voice.

Sigrid smiled kindly as Haldis pinned her new piece of jewelry to her dress. Haldis smiled with delight and ran her hand over the finery.

"We both want the best for your son, your highness," Sigrid said.

Haldis nodded to herself, as if she had made the decision at that very moment to stand beside Sigrid.

"From what I've heard and what I've seen today, you may be worthy of Erik," Haldis said. "Rest for a while. I'll send a girl up to fetch you for the feast."

When the door closed, Sigrid flopped down onto the chair.

"It's like stepping on a snake's nest. They all hate me. Did you see that?"

Emma smiled and said, "As long as they fear you, it doesn't matter."

"I can't stand the Svea," Sigrid said and pursed her lips.

Emma shrugged and said, "All the same, it is woven that you will save them."

ᚻ

Sigrid got up when she heard heavy footsteps on the stairs. She watched the door expectantly. Soon there were two knocks, and without waiting for Sigrid to answer, the door opened and Erik entered.

Again they regarded each other in silence.

"Have you settled in?" he finally asked.

"Once I kicked out your mistresses, the rooms became sufficient," she responded.

Erik sniggered and looked down at the floorboards, like a little boy who'd been caught being naughty.

"I was not aware that better preparations had not been made for your arrival," he said. Either he was just blaming his mother or perhaps Haldis was actually the one responsible for the whole thing. Sigrid looked out the window at the farms and fields.

"Where are your mistresses now?" she asked.

Erik cleared his throat and said, "I sent them away."

Sigrid nodded, even though she didn't believe a word of it. He would keep them somewhere nearby so he could visit them, but to her that didn't matter.

Erik sat down on the chest by her bed.

"It pains me that you weren't welcomed better after your long trip, and that you were forced to flee from Lejre."

Sigrid managed to keep her irritability in check. Erik was Svealand's king, the one the Svea chieftains had chosen to lead them. He had married her to create an alliance with the Scylfings, and what she thought or felt didn't matter in this game.

Sigrid sighed heavily. Her longing for Sweyn burned in her loins.

"This isn't easy for any of us," she said.

"No," Erik responded. "And yet it must be done."

They looked at each other, not with pleasure but with understanding.

"What do you want me to be, husband?" Her decisiveness made him smile.

"You must be beautiful and charming. You must also get along with the womenfolk, otherwise your life among the Svea will be hard."

Sigrid straightened her back and said, "Aren't they the ones who should get along with me, the queen of Svealand, descendant of Vanadís? Without my family's support, Svealand will be weak when Styrbjörn stands at the fence with the Jómsvíkings on his side."

Erik pulled his hand over his beard and gave her an amused look.

"Respect isn't something that just comes automatically. It must be earned. We Svea are a proud people, and anything unfamiliar is regarded with skepticism, even if it be a divinely beautiful Scylfing maiden."

"To insult me is to insult my husband," Sigrid responded so fast that Erik started laughing.

"Axel warned me of your sharp tongue and your quick mind." He got up from the chest and stood close to her. "He also said that you were beautiful like a summer morning, but that you needed to be broken. He spoke the truth on every count."

Sigrid swallowed her irritation and looked up at the man whose heart and support she had to win.

"Perhaps," Sigrid said. "So tell me what else you wish of me, my husband and king."

Erik looked more than content as he ran his finger over her cheek and then let his hand continue down to her dress and the outline of her breast.

"I would like you to be heavy with child when the Svea chieftains gather for the midwinter sacrifice. Everyone will see your fertility and know that I am expecting a son and heir. Can you do this for me?"

Sigrid reluctantly realized she was blushing.

"I would not wish it any other way," she lied quietly and looked down modestly. "Whenever my husband wishes, I am ready."

Erik did not need much urging. He undid her dress and let it drop to the floor. Sigrid shivered, standing naked before him, allowing him to fondle her with his eyes and hands.

"A body made for birthing babies," Erik said contentedly, sliding his hand down her belly and on down between her legs.

Sigrid reluctantly flinched with pleasure as his gentle stroking caused her to open.

"I am sworn to Frey," he told her, laying her gently back on the bed and starting to take off his breeches. "Do you understand what that means?"

She nodded, knowing full well that Frey was the defender, the fertility god, and Freya's twin brother. It meant that he had sex with as many women as he could. That was a relief.

Erik was already hard as he came down over Sigrid and pushed deep inside her. She whimpered with pain and stifled her reluctance. No one should accuse her of not having been a virgin. Sigrid wrapped her arms around him and caressed him as he groaned in pleasure. If she bore a child, it would be Erik's. They were safe, and that was all that mattered.

All this I do for you, Vanadís.

Ψ

It felt like an eternity since Sweyn had left Jómsborg. During all the days he'd worked to get the ships into seaworthy shape, there had been moments when he doubted he would see home again. Nevertheless he had succeeded in putting together a relatively decent crew and readying the ships.

He had returned to Jómsborg in triumph and received cheers, but there was one person missing from his homecoming. Now Sweyn followed the footpath through the meager patches of arable land outside of town. He stopped in front of the fence, concern burning in his chest.

The cabin looked more tumbledown than it had when Sweyn had left it. Several of the fence posts were broken, and the smoke hole in the sod roof looked like it had caved in. The little garden, on the other hand, was meticulously tended and seemed to be growing well.

Sweyn squatted down and petted Gray who came running to meet him, tail wagging, barking so enthusiastically that the chickens flew up into the trees. The door to the cabin was ajar, and he pushed it open.

"Mother, I'm home," he called, his heart filled with pride.

She was sitting on the sleeping bench. She pulled her hand over her gray hair as if he'd bothered her.

"My boy, I didn't think you'd be here so soon."

She had only the single room with the hearth, a loom, a sleeping bench, and a table where she did her needlework. But everything was neat and clean, and although her dress was patched, it was made with the finest stitches.

"Are you sick?" he asked worriedly.

It wasn't like her to take a nap in the middle of the day, and she had dark circles under her eyes.

"Nothing too bad," she said with a calm smile. "I just needed to lie down for a bit."

"I was worried when you weren't out to welcome me and my ships back to Jómsborg."

Everyone had been at the beach when they landed, staring open-mouthed at Sweyn's ships and the men who now served him. It was his finest hour, and he had wanted his mother to see it. He had wanted her there when, his heart swelling with pride, he led his men through the gates in the log wall that formed Jómsborg's defensive palisade.

"You should have seen my crew when they set eyes on Jómsborg."

They'd stared with their mouths hanging open because of the town's strong, unparalleled defenses. The fortress sat on a hill well out on a peninsula, and you could see for miles in all directions. The yards-high walls were made of logs, with towers for archers. The training grounds that every Jómsvíking learned to fear lay around the fortress. That was where Sweyn and his fellow warriors would train the men who crewed his new ships. Several of them were skilled and experienced. Some of them might even become proper Jómsvíkings if they were lucky. They'd be able to make some of the others into warriors before the winter was over.

As soon as he had found shelter for his men, he had hurried out of Jómsborg to his mother's cabin at the edge of the woods outside the palisade. Now that he was here, he realized she wasn't doing well at all.

"I saw their surprise and how proudly you stood as you led them through the gates," his mother said. Then she had a nasty coughing fit. "I didn't want to disturb your big moment, so I never approached you."

She ran her hand over his arm and looked at him, her eyes beaming with pride. Sweyn set his knapsack on the table and hugged her.

"You shouldn't live out here in the cold anymore. My luck has turned, and you can live inside the fortress, sleep in a soft bed, and eat meat and sweet bread every day."

She shook her head and laughed in embarrassment. "That won't do. How would that look?"

Sweyn smiled. Finally he could say the words he had longed to say since he was a child.

"The shame you carried is gone. King Harald acknowledged me and gave me ships. Your son is a Jelling and a ship captain, so it isn't suitable anymore for you to live out here. I have silver to pay with."

He took out the pouch with his share of the monastery loot.

His mother never had to live in poverty again. He would make sure she had only the best. Sweyn dropped down onto his knees in front of the old woman and looked into her gentle eyes.

"Your good name was restored at the throne of the king."

Although his mother was highly esteemed in Jómsborg for her honor and sewing skills, Harald's denial had been a heavy burden for her all these years. Being raped by a king and then called a liar and a loose woman had worn on her even though she had striven not to let Sweyn see it. He took her skinny hand and felt the pride swelling in his chest again.

"Everything will be fine now."

She turned her head away and wiped the tears from her eyes.

"Ever since the first time I held you in my arms, I knew that you were going to do something great. No mother could be prouder of her son."

She coughed again, so hard that it tore at her lungs. Sweyn's eyebrows went up.

"Gather your things now and come live with me in Jómsborg. You'll never have to sew for other people again."

"What would I do during the day?" she exclaimed with a serene smile.

"You'll rest and eat until you're fat," he said with a grin and started gathering her things.

"I can't leave my house. What about my chickens and goats and my garden patch?"

"Everything will be well looked after. And Gray is coming with you."

As a ship captain, Sweyn had his own room in the fortress. They could stay there until he found something bigger.

"I want to hear all about your trip. Is there any other reason you're so cheerful?" his mother said, eyeing him intently as he filled the sack with her things.

Sweyn chuckled at her astuteness but shook his head.

"No, there's nothing else to tell."

She would get to meet Sigrid soon enough, but until then there was no point in worrying her.

There would be a small banquet to celebrate her becoming his bride, Erik had said, after having lain with her again and again and finally left her bed. It would not be anywhere near as big as the one they would have at the midwinter sacrifice, when all the Svea chieftains met at the temple.

Sigrid looked out at the drunken, laughing guests lining the long tables that had been arranged outside. There were many more people than she'd seen in Harald's royal hall, so there must be some truth to what people said, that the Sveas' midwinter sacrifice was the largest in all of Scandinavia.

Pigs were being roasted around all the fires, and women and men danced boisterously to the musicians' playing. Erik sat in the throne beside her. He had handed out expensive gifts to chieftains, warriors, and other noblemen, who were now contentedly examining what they'd received. The priestesses and the priests who sat at the table had also received presents.

"You are a generous king, my husband," she said.

"It's my duty." Erik smiled broadly at her and took her hand. "Tell me, are you satisfied with what you've learned about Sjofn's delights?"

Sigrid couldn't help but smile at the memory of how he'd made her cling tight to him, screaming in ecstasy.

"You are truly dedicated to Frey, my husband," she replied modestly.

"I'll visit your bed often," Erik said with a contented smile, standing up. "You will bear my child this winter."

He gave her belly a pat before walking away to warmly greet an older man with a braided beard and a tattoo on his forehead.

All eyes watched Erik with devotion and admiration. Axel hadn't lied when he said the king was respected and honored by the people of Svealand. It would have been easier if she could hate him, but there was nothing to dislike about Erik.

Sigrid put her hand on her belly and felt the longing burn in her body: the king of kings, the most important ruler, and the leader among warriors. May she soon hold him in her arms.

"You look lost in thought for a festive evening like this. Aren't you pleased with your husband?"

Sigrid looked up and saw Axel coming over to her with a beautiful woman.

"He's everything you said and more," she said warmly. "I welcome you, my friend and companion."

"You honor me, Queen," he said, and gestured to the bowing woman. "This is Solveig, my wife. I offer her to you, to have at your side, to serve you."

Sigrid smiled at the woman. There was a calm, friendly demeanor to her, and her expression was charming and sincere.

"Your husband has taken good care of me, and I would be grateful to count you as a friend. There is much I want to know about the Svea."

"Then I'll leave you to it," Axel said and walked over to the king.

The two women smiled at each other.

"My husband told me about the hardships of your voyage. I'll do everything I can to assist you." Solveig looked around and then leaned closer to Sigrid. "Do you understand why you were received the way you were?"

"Haldis didn't seem pleased that Erik had acquired a wife," Sigrid said with a smile.

"Haldis isn't the one you should be afraid of. She lives solely for her son, and the shortcomings in her welcome were to assess whether you're strong enough to earn respect." Solveig knelt down beside Sigrid. "Worse are those who speak ill of the king's honor because he took a foreigner for a wife." She spoke so softly that her words were scarcely audible.

Sigrid looked to see what Solveig was looking at. A priestess with black makeup around her eyes was standing with two tall young women. All three were looking at Sigrid with spite.

"The youngest is Aedis, Erik's mistress who's borne him two daughters. You kicked her out of her room this morning."

Sigrid nodded. She would keep her eye on that one.

"The mother, Hyndla, is a powerful seeress, and the sister is married to Sacrifice-Sven, who wants Erik's throne as much as Styrbjörn does."

Sigrid couldn't help but laugh.

"Nothing like making powerful enemies right from the start."

There didn't seem to be any end to the ill will she encountered every way she turned. People she'd never talked to were ready to stick a knife in her just because she breathed. Among these strangers she was forced to move as if on thin ice. Solveig, too, might be a false friend who wanted to get close to her for her own gain.

"You're not concerned at all about what I just said?" Solveig asked in surprise.

Sigrid followed Emma with her eyes. Her protector walked between the clusters of people talking to each other and listened wide-eyed as a little child to the words that were being said. No one had any idea of her formidable power.

"My life is in Freya's hands," Sigrid said calmly. "My only fear is displeasing my husband or Freya, not the disputes and evil machinations of other people."

She stroked the mark on her wrist with her finger and smiled at Hyndla, who stared at her angrily. If the old woman realized how loyal Sigrid was to Freya, surely that would placate her ill will.

"I need to visit Svealand's holy temple and talk to Hyndla."

Solveig looked at her.

"You and Erik will face the gods in the temple when the night is at its darkest. Axel must have mentioned that to you?"

Sigrid nodded. What he'd told her were tidbits and half-sung songs about her bowing before the gods. She didn't know what the whole thing meant, but just getting to visit Svealand's temple was enough.

"Do you know what will happen there?" Sigrid asked.

Solveig looked away and replied, "No one can speak of that."

Sigrid smiled. "Then I must leave my destiny in Freya's hands."

Axel's wife hesitated. Then she said, "You won't be facing the goddesses. You will face the judgment of the Æsir: Thor, Odin, and Frey."

The old ways were strong in Svealand. Kára sang with the gods who filled the country and radiated from the sacrifice places, altar stones in temples, and graves that were strewn over the vast plains like stars in the sky. Emma squatted down and picked up a fistful of dirt that she smelled before she let it sift through her fingers. Valhalla's presence was strong around her, and behind that there was something older. Ull and Nerthus, the All-Mother who had ruled the earth since the birth of time, filled the ground with peace and good crops. The Svea truly had every reason to be arrogant given the sorcery they had in their country.

Emma stood up and walked among the swaggering mead-drinking warriors, past people who enthusiastically praised Erik for filling their stomachs and then turned to speak ill of Sigrid, who had ensnared their king with her love charms. When she approached Sigrid's kinswomen, they turned their backs on her. Blind and deaf to everything except for their pathetic lust, they were now united in their dislike of her. *Small grains of sand, small seas, small are the minds of men.*

Emma wandered on, watching the foreigners, who revealed their standing in the flock through their gestures, clothing, and jewelry. As if she were invisible to everyone, she walked between the groups of people and stopped near Haldis, the king's mother, who was surrounded by agitated women.

"If that Scylfing bitch thinks we're going to dance to her every whim, she's going to be surprised," said a young blonde.

"Calm yourself, Frigda," Haldis said, calmly stroking her hand. "You know Erik. Once he's won his victories, he'll be back in your arms just as he's always done. He needs a legitimate son, and you can't deny him that."

"Even so, it's a disgrace that he married a Geat," a dark-haired beauty said.

"He did what he had to," said an older woman, her belly great with the baby she was expecting.

The blond mistress pursed her lips and said, "All I ever wanted was to be with him."

"Frigda, Erik is dedicated to Frey," Haldis protested. "His duty is to spread fertility and strength among everyone in Sveastand, not just in his own family. Be happy for the moments you've had. It is an honor for a farmer's daughter to be the king's mistress."

The blonde nodded and wiped the tears from her cheeks. She obviously didn't find that very comforting. Haldis's brow furrowed and she gave the girl a warning look.

"I'll find you a husband so you can have your own hearth. Then you'll have something else to think about when Erik can't come to your bed as often as before. Don't you want that?"

Frigda bowed her head obediently and conceded, "Yes, Venerable One."

"Good. Then it's decided." Haldis clapped her hands contentedly and surveyed the men. "Who shall we choose? Who's good enough?"

Emma continued her wandering. A short distance away two warriors were saying they'd really like to screw that Scylfing bitch bloody, and what a shame it was that they couldn't get close to her.

Emma stopped short of the tables where the most important guests were dining on roast pork. Hidden in the shadows, Emma was relieved to see Sigrid smile at Erik. Emma had sat outside Sigrid's door and listened to them having sex to secure the baby's future. Everything was as it should be. Erce's presence was like a slow heartbeat in the ground that filled Emma with warm security. The pain that Kára inflicted was gone now that she was keeping watch over Sigrid. There was nothing to worry about. Everything was going to be fine.

Emma wandered down to the beach, where the boats were pulled up and resting on the sand. She sat down there and leaned her back against a ship, looking out at the dark river water. Her belly was full of the food she'd managed to get ahold of. The night was warm, and her eyes were heavy with sleep. She curled up contentedly and yawned tiredly.

"What do you see?" a hoarse voice said.

Three women with walking staffs, older than time itself, came wandering toward her. Their faces were wrinkled, with cheeks so sunken they were like skeletons. Their heads were topped with wispy silver and white hair, and animal claws and ravens' feet hung around their necks.

"I see a *fylgja*, a guardian spirit, in human form," another of them said with her toothless mouth.

They were all wearing the simplest homespun cloth, which hung frayed and dirty from their stooped bodies, but their strength was so great that Emma felt their power throbbing in her body. She sat up and looked at the three in surprise.

"I see the vessel that bears the dís we prayed and sacrificed for."

The three women waited for Emma's response. She gulped and wondered whether they were of this world.

"Blessed am I by the storm dís, Kára, guardian spirit of my mistress, Sigrid Tostedotter. Who are you, Venerable Ones?"

They watched her in silence for a long while.

"We are they who see what was, what is, and what will be," they responded in unison.

Seeresses. Emma humbly bowed her head in reverence to the three old women. The staffs they used for support were covered in symbols and topped with finials: a falcon with outstretched wings, a dragon, and a sow.

"She is the vessel, she who will be sacrificed for the child, but still she does not see clearly," the second said. "The one she waits for will be late."

The third shook her head.

"She may die before she's completed what will come. The thread is thin."

And suddenly they backed away from her, as if they feared her destiny.

"What do you see?" Emma cried behind them. "Where can I find you?"

The eldest stopped and answered, "Seek us in the sacred grove. Maybe we will answer you."

Then the three of them were gone, as if they'd never been there. Emma pulled her fingers through her hair and looked out at the empty beach where the reeds bowed to the wind and the shadows lingered under the trees. What did they mean? Kára was silent and as distant as the memory of England. *A thin thread. The one she waits for will be late. Maybe she would die.* A cool wind swept in over the river and made her shiver in the summer night. Maybe they weren't even real. Maybe they'd come from the afterworld, and yet they had warned her.

The beach, which had felt so safe before, suddenly felt dark and menacing. She got up to hurry back to the party but had only taken a few steps before a dark figure staggered out of the woods. Emma sighed heavily. Toste and his boys were walking toward her. The chieftain was very drunk and looked at her with a covetous sneer.

"I've been looking for you, goldilocks," Toste drawled.

Uneasiness crawled up her back. She was wary of the danger and started running in the opposite direction. The next moment a pair of strong arms grabbed her from behind and a beard tickled the back of her neck.

"Why do you run?"

It was one of the warriors. She recognized his voice from the ship. He grabbed her breast and squeezed so hard she squealed.

"Good catch," Toste yelled, approaching.

Fear started prickling through Emma like cold needles. She closed her eyes and called out for Kára. *Come to me. Save me.* Emma tried to break the grip around her waist, but Toste picked her up in his arms.

"You part your legs, yearning and enticing," Toste said with a laugh and tossed her on the ground.

The laughing warriors tore off her dress, then held her so tightly she couldn't move. Now she was really scared, her heart beating so hard it was going to burst out of her chest. Toste pulled her to him.

Mistress, I beg you. Help me!

The blow struck her right in the mouth, hard hands held her arms, drunken laughs echoed as Toste lay down on top of her, so heavy she could hardly breathe.

Fear washed over her like cold waves. It froze and paralyzed her. She couldn't move or escape from his wet mouth, which pressed against hers.

Kára, help me.

"You'll get what you yearned for after you part your legs and offer yourself up."

Emma screamed and kicked, but Toste hit her in the face again, this time so hard he almost knocked her out.

"Shut up!" he growled and dug out his prick.

"I beg you," she whispered as the men's sticky desire all but suffocated her.

"You'll get what you're asking for."

Toste's eyes were glassy and vacant. Emma whimpered with pain as he pushed his way into her. It felt like a knife driving in between her legs. He panted and grunted on top of her, as she now knew he'd done to her mother. Palna had told her everything that evening in Lejre. Chafing beard against her mother's face, stinking lust mixed with mead. Her own father was thrusting into her, puffing and panting. His sweat dripped onto her face. She closed her eyes as he emptied himself deep within her with a moan.

"You liked that."

Toste pulled out of her and right away another man took his place. The pain tore at her loins. A half-stiff cock was shoved down her throat so deep that she was on the verge of vomiting. Emma was yanked to her feet, tossed back and forth between laughing men who forced themselves into her in every conceivable way. Stinking groans in her face, pain like knives cutting apart her body. When she tried to stagger away from them, they hit her so hard that blood poured down her chin. They weren't laughing anymore, but taunting her as they filled her with their disgusting, stinking pricks.

Emma screamed inside her head: *Kára, I beg you. Save me. Take them away.*

And then Kára was back. Like a windstorm she filled Emma's mind with divine rage and drove away all weakness. But it was too late. The men buttoned up their pants, chuckling and satisfied.

"She'll do."

"We ought to bring her on the boat so we don't get bored."

Emma stood next to herself, and as if in a dream she watched as the enraged Kára stood her nearly naked, bloody body up on its feet. Then Kára stretched out her arms and guffawed at the warriors' frailty. They smiled fearfully, looking as though they thought she was out of her mind.

"Do you enjoy screwing your own daughter, blood violator?" Kára said with a growl, pointing at Toste.

His drunken smile, so full of contentment, hardened into a mask of doubt.

"Who did you enjoy most, the mother you raped in Mikklavík or the daughter you begot then and just screwed?"

Kára's growling summoned a north wind, which clawed and tore at them.

Toste's smile was extinguished, like a fire someone had pissed on. The warriors looked up from the pants they were buttoning and watched Emma apprehensively.

"What lies are these?" Toste said.

Emma smiled and shook her head, then walked up to her father and took a firm grasp between his legs.

"Palna told me how you had your way with my mother. When he saw Sigrid, he knew for sure that you were my father. Don't you see how similar we are, my sister and I?"

Toste's drunken face stiffened in disgust, and he flung her aside. She fell hard to the ground.

"Get out of here with your lies."

Emma crawled across the ground, fortified by her hatred.

"What is it, Father? Don't you want to screw your daughter anymore?"

Toste straightened his clothes, but she could tell from his face that he, too, saw the likeness between her and Sigrid.

"Shut up, whore."

Emma got up and laughed. It was her blood tie to Sigrid that had saved her from the flames in the monastery and made Kára bless her. Only a sister can watch over a sister.

"Come, Father, screw me some more," she howled. "Give it to me again."

"You're insane," Toste said and gasped, backing away from her. There was no arrogance in him anymore, just disgust.

"Come back, Father, take me again."

Emma stretched out her arms to the sea. Kára's wind raced onshore, forcing the bushes on the beach to bend.

"I curse you all. I curse your cocks. May they be limp and useless until the ends of your miserable lives."

The wind whipped sand at them, and even the trees were bending now. She saw the fear in their eyes as they hurried away from Kára's wrath.

Emma tipped her head back and laughed until tears poured down, the tatters of her torn dress whipping against her body, and her father's seed running down her thighs.

Then the abyss opened, and she fell down into the darkness.

Torches lit the procession route. A sacrificial priest stood before them with his head shaved and black makeup painted around his eyes, like a dís. He was wearing a light tunic and bowed first to Erik and then to Sigrid before gesturing with his hand that they should follow him.

Sigrid's anticipation rose as they strode toward the sacred temple, where the real ceremony would be held. When she had asked Erik what would happen, he laughed in an almost scornful way and whispered in her ear. "We must do this to keep the priests satisfied. Put on a good face, my lovely, and look like you're filled with respect."

Those disrespectful words chafed at Sigrid. Did Erik not honor the gods? Maybe she had misunderstood him.

You would never let Svealand's king blaspheme against Valhalla, O dazzling Radiant One.

The hair stood up on Sigrid's arms as she followed the burning torches toward the ancient place where Odin himself had his throne. Strange shadows were dimly visible in the night. Maybe they were spectators, beings from another realm. There were many stories about Svealand's giants as well as the dwarves who lived in the mountains and in the rocky slabs who watched over the descent to the realm of Hel.

Grandmother knew many of them by heart and would tell them on long winter evenings.

The sound of drums was soon audible, guiding them through the night. The smell of wet summer fields and burning fires mixed with an unfamiliar scent. Sigrid's heart pounded as they approached a round palisade with a lavishly ornamented gate painted blue.

Sacrificial priests and priestesses dressed in white, with black paint around their eyes, waited for them like the gods they served. The mark on Sigrid's wrist grew hot, and it burned as she stopped devoutly before the gates.

I greet you.

This was Valhalla on earth. Drums echoed rhythmically and soon a song could be heard about Svealand's kings, who had been blessed by the gods. The voices rose and intertwined with each other so that the song almost reached the clear, starry heavens. Sigrid's eyes welled up. She'd never heard anything so beautiful.

At her side, Erik held out his arms, and the priests removed his belt and sword, as well as his cloak and his shoes. A priestess carefully removed Sigrid's shoes so that she could step onto the blessed soil. After that they pulled back.

Erik's face was stern and unreadable as he held his hand out to Sigrid. She took it expectantly and followed the king of Svealand through the gates.

The pictures on the temple walls moved in the torchlight. The cool air was filled with the most delightful aromas. The stones were cool under Sigrid's bare feet. With every step she took, she felt lighter and lighter, as if she were leaving everything worldly behind her and floating into the realm of the gods and goddesses.

The big doors were covered with golden symbols and pictures, and when they approached, the doors opened as if by themselves with a muffled creak. Sigrid trembled as she entered the most sacred place, and the power of Valhalla enveloped her.

The hall was large, as if it had been built for giants, and featured white walls covered with bronze discs. At the far end there was a raised dais with three thrones on it from which Odin, Thor, and Frey watched them.

The priests and priestesses stood along the walls holding torches as Erik led Sigrid forward to the powerful gods. Finally. Her joy at being in the presence of the gods made her weak.

I serve you, mighty Æsir.

Thor's throne was the biggest. Svea held the god of farmers and warriors in the highest esteem. Thor, the protector of mankind, wore a linen cloak, and his hammer, Mjölnir, sat beside him on his throne. Odin, the All-Father, who gave mankind the runes, sat beside him. His arm ring Draupnir hung at his side, and his spear Gungnir was leaning against his chair. Frey, the Vanir god, protector of fertility, brother of Freya, was wearing a wreath weighed down with wheat, and his erect penis was large, like he was. Blood from the animal sacrifices ran over the three wooden gods, and the smell of the offerings lingered heavily in the hall.

Three stone altars, dark with blood, stood before the dais. Three priests in masks waited there, each with the sign of his god: Frey, Odin, or Thor. They were the gods' human forms in this world. Sigrid nervously bowed her head.

Find me worthy.

The priests stepped forward, inviting veneration with their wooden masks and embroidered cloaks and belts, and intoned, "We greet you, Erik, protector of the gods, champion of Svealand, chosen by Frey."

Erik bowed his head, put his hand on his heart, and replied, "I serve you in everything. My life is yours."

The three expressionless masks watched them.

"I give you my wife, Sigrid Tostedotter, to bless or reject," Erik said. He turned his head and gave her an indifferent look, as if he didn't care which way the gods judged her.

Sigrid's legs became so weak that she could hardly keep herself upright. Erik should have told her this was going to happen so she could have prepared herself. Her heartbeats echoed into eternity. The three blood-spattered gods regarded her in silence, inscrutable in their infinite power. Sigrid could scarcely breathe in their presence.

"I live to serve Valhalla," she said and sank onto one knee before Thor's priest.

She held out her tattoo, which burned softly on her wrist. He *had* to bless her. She had served Valhalla her whole life, had been chosen by Freya, and was protected by her dís.

Sigrid gasped for breath as Thor loomed before her, alive and strange in his sublimity. Then he nodded his approval. He dipped a twig into a bowl of blood and splashed the blood over Sigrid. Without thinking, she took hold of the edge of the priest's long tunic and kissed the coarse cloth.

Odin's and Frey's priests stepped forward now and blessed her. Bliss surged through Sigrid. She had been blessed in the most sacred of temples. Spellbound, she looked up at the priests as tears of happiness mixed with the blood from the sacrificial animals running down her face.

Vanadís, thank you for your favor.

Never before had she felt so happy.

ᚷ

The knives of pain sliced slowly through Emma as she came to her senses again, tormented. The taste of blood filled her mouth, and every part of her body ached and hurt. Then something cool was wiped across her cheek.

"Be still."

A slave girl sat beside her, gently cleaning her wound with a bit of wet cloth. The girl was hardly more than a child, skinny, wearing a patched shift, with dark hair so short it sat like a helmet on her head.

"It will heal," the girl said seriously. "Can you stand up?"

Emma sat up slowly and looked at her bloody thighs. Nausea rumbled like thunder through her head as thousands of waterfalls of pain washed through her body.

Kára had allowed her own father to violate her the same way he'd violated her mother. How could she? How could she let her down like that?

"I thought you were dead," said the girl.

Emma put a curse on them, which was the last thing she remembered. That curse had used up the last of her strength, which explained how weak she was now. In vain she tried to cover her body with the torn dress. Why had Kára left her alone? A poisonous darkness came billowing toward her, whispering. Emma gasped for breath and struggled to remain in this world.

"What's your name?" she asked the girl.

"Soot. Haldis owns me." She held up the basket she had in her hand. "I was supposed to be out fetching mussels when I found you. At first I was sure you were dead, but then you moved."

Emma swallowed and looked at the filth all over her body. Sticky semen ran from her crotch, over her legs, and onto her belly.

"Help me down to the water, Soot. I have to be clean again."

"The king was so magnificent, and you were so gorgeous by his side," Alfhild said with a smile, pulling the comb through Sigrid's freshly washed hair.

Sigrid smiled sleepily at the memory of the temple and the people who were waiting outside when the ceremony was over. The crowd had followed them back to Kungsgården cheering.

"You husband is truly the finest of men," Jorun said. "Can you properly honor him sufficiently and rouse his lust and affection?"

Jorun put all the jewelry Sigrid had been wearing into the jewelry box and snapped the lid shut.

Sigrid gave Jorun a piercing look and snarled, "My husband is none of your concern, maidservant."

Envy flared in her kinswoman's eyes before she turned to put the jewelry box back into one of the chests. It had been too long a day for Sigrid to tolerate Jorun's little jabs. All the same, her doubts about Erik had already begun to sprout.

I'm pleased with you, he had said, leaving her at the door to her room. *But you should never have kissed the priest's outfit. That old goat already thinks far too highly of himself.* Sigrid had been amazed at his irreverent words. *Sleep now. Tomorrow I will visit your bed again.*

Then Erik had turned his back and gone down the stairs without waiting for her response. Sweyn would never have spoken that way about a priest. He would have slept by her side, and they would have spoken tenderly about the events of the day. She would have lain on his chest and listened to his heartbeat, the way she'd done in the grove after they made the sacrifice.

Sigrid had lain down in bed with her longing for the Jómsvíking aching in her body.

She swallowed, feeling melancholy.

"Where's Emma?" she asked.

She wanted her seeress close. Only Emma could understand her longing for Sweyn and what the priest's blessing had meant to her.

Jorun shrugged and then turned to Alfhild and sarcastically quipped, "Who knows? She's probably running around humping warriors."

"Find her and bring her here," Sigrid commanded.

Jorun and Alfhild exchanged a look that Sigrid couldn't interpret.

"It's dawn, and we don't know our way around the estate," Alfhild said. "She could be anywhere."

"It's not suitable for us to be running around looking for someone who's hardly more than a slave," Jorun said.

Sigrid gritted her teeth. She'd had enough of their defiance.

"I will decide what's suitable for you," she said, sitting up in bed. "Go and find Emma! I want her with me."

The two woman exchanged looks again. Alfhild clutched the cloak she was holding in her lap. Her cheeks flushed red, and she stared angrily at the floor. Jorun's mouth was pursed, her chin raised in defiance.

"We are tied by blood and have been close to you since we were children," Jorun said. "How can you prefer a stranger of lowly birth over us?"

How dare they question her will, especially now that she was queen of Svealand? Did they think they were all still back home, where they could casually tease her, almost like equals? Didn't they see that everything had changed? Her aunt Ylva had been right about the incompetence of them both. It was time for Sigrid to put them in their places once and for all.

"Find her, or I'll have you whipped. You must learn to show respect for the queen of Svealand."

They looked away, bowed their heads humbly, and left her alone to ponder their ill will and envy.

Sigrid lay back down on the bed and let herself be enveloped by the aching solitude. Hopefully they would find Emma soon. No one else could ease her sorrow and longing.

The guard on duty at Kungsgården had looked at Emma as if she were hardly worth stepping on. He had been reluctant to let her go up the stairs to the queen's room, but Soot had convinced him that he would be severely punished if he didn't let Sigrid's maidservant go to her chamber.

"You're going to pay for it if I get a scolding," he told the slave girl.

"No scolding. You'll be rewarded," Emma slurred flatly.

The guard raised his hand, then knocked on Sigrid's door. A voice immediately responded that they could enter. Emma was leaning heavily on Soot when she stumbled into the room.

Sigrid sat up in bed and looked at her with an expression that Emma had never seen before. *She sees the stinking heart of me,* Emma thought, shuddering. *She sees that I'm sullied, no better than a worthless slave. If she turns away from me, there won't be any point in living anymore.*

"Leave us," Sigrid told Soot, who immediately slipped out.

Emma swayed back and forth. She would have fallen over if Sigrid hadn't helped her sit down on the bed. Sigrid put a cloak around her shoulders, and Emma pulled it around her, shivering.

"Who did this to you?"

Emma's lower lip trembled as she shook her head. She couldn't tell her. The shame sat like a noose around her neck, and if she told the truth she would be banished.

"Speak," Sigrid said. "I demand it."

Emma hesitated at the order and said only, "It's better if you know nothing."

"That choice is mine, not yours." Sigrid's voice was like the crack of a whip.

"I was alone down by the river." The words swelled up in Emma's throat and were hard to get out. "A bunch of warriors . . ." The laughing faces danced in front of her as she remembered their breathless, sticky lust. And then came the pain, the cursed, shameful pain.

"Who were they?"

Emma whimpered. She couldn't tell about the incest and hurt Sigrid like that. That was a burden she had to carry herself.

"He who sullies my servant sullies me as well. You can't keep quiet about this." Sigrid looked Emma straight in the eye, compelling her to answer.

Shame poisoned every part of Emma's body. Her belly ached. She felt sick. She had washed herself again and again and rubbed her skin with wet sand until it was covered in painful sores, but even the sea could not wash away the filthy thing that had happened. Emma whimpered again when Sigrid grabbed her arm, which was covered in bruises.

"I swear I'll banish you if you don't tell me who did this to you."

Emma couldn't imagine a worse fate.

"It was Toste and his men," Emma whispered. She studied Sigrid's face, looking for any sign of acknowledgment, but her face was a stiff mask in the dark. Emma was drowning in shame and despair. *She's going to banish me now,* she thought. *First Kára failed me, now Sigrid is going to turn her back on me. Please let me die soon, because I can't live with this.*

"Father will have to pay," Sigrid finally said. "He does not have the right to violate my domestic staff."

Emma started to cry in relief. She would get to stay. With the tears running down her cheeks, she curled up.

"There, there—dry your tears. Your wounds will heal."

Emma gratefully closed her eyes as Sigrid stroked her hair. She was safe here with her and could tell the truth. She didn't need to hide anything.

"It was incest," Emma whispered.

Sigrid grabbed her chin and tilted Emma's face to look in her eyes. "What are you saying?"

"Toste raped my mother." Emma gulped, forcing the words out. "He's my father. That's why I was chosen to carry the dís and serve you."

She looked away, her tears stinging her wounds. May she die as soon as she'd done what Kára demanded. Then it would all finally be over.

A sister. Sigrid looked with disgust at Emma's feeble sobs. Surely if she had Scylfing blood in her, she wouldn't be crying like a slave. What a wretched protector—the girl couldn't even protect herself and was complaining, loudly, about what had happened. Still, Father's incest was hard to swallow. Sigrid squirmed uncomfortably. If Emma really was her sister, it was just as bad as if Father had forced himself on *her*. Just the thought of that turned her stomach.

Emma rocked back and forth, sobbing, her arms crossed over her belly. Her lips were cracked and swollen. Her face was full of bloody scrapes and bruises. They'd really been rough with her.

A sister, even if only a half sister. Sigrid bit her cheek. The one sister she had known had died before her first birthday.

Father's mistress Åse had been forced to put two newborn daughters out in the woods, but the third one she was permitted to keep since she was beginning to get on in years. Father even adopted the girl so she wouldn't have to be a slave. Sigrid had been pleased, because she was fond of Åse, and she'd been able to play with charming little Helga.

Blood ties were powerful, and Sigrid had felt a connection with Emma from the beginning. Emma carried the dís who came to protect Sigrid's unborn son, and she did so at considerable cost to herself. The dís was eating away at Emma's mind.

Did you give me a blood kinswoman? Is it the blood that makes her ready to sacrifice her life for me?

Sigrid's head hurt. So many things were happening that it felt like she was tumbling down a hill, loose limbed, ricocheting and bouncing off boulders as she fell. Emma's cracked lips trembled from crying, and she hung her head in misery. *A sister.*

Sigrid pulled Emma's head onto her knee and stroked her hair. Emma's hair was wet, but she felt warm in her lap.

"Why didn't the dís protect you?"

"Kára failed me," Emma whispered. "She didn't come to save me as her vessel until I was dying, but then we put a curse on them."

"A curse?" Sigrid's hand stiffened midstroke. Toste was the chieftain of the Scylfings and her own flesh and blood.

"Freya made their pricks soft," Emma whispered.

Sigrid sat in silence for a long while, struggling to stifle the laughter that was percolating through her like a playful spring brook, but soon it poured forth. She laughed at everything that had happened, at the great sorrows and burdens she and Emma were being forced to bear. She laughed until tears were streaming down her cheeks at the warriors' limp cocks, Erik's vanity about his manhood, the Sveas' hatred of her, the approaching war, the fates of Sweyn and Emma. It was insanity from beginning to end.

Emma lifted her head and looked at her in surprise. Then Sigrid caught a glimpse of mirth in her eyes, too.

"Maybe I wasn't the best choice for their diversion," Emma said.

"You can say that again," Sigrid said and then doubled over with laughter. Her stomach ached, and tears were pouring down her face. "Oh, Emma," she finally said. "What kind of destiny have the Norns woven for us?"

Emma stiffened as a shadow came over her battered face. When she looked up at Sigrid, it was no longer the girl there. Coal-black eyes with splashes of silver stared vacantly at her.

"He's here," she said in the whining, unfamiliar voice of Kára. The next moment Kára was gone.

Emma swayed and fell down on the bed unconscious. Sigrid swallowed, consumed by tempestuous joy. She was pregnant.

Your greatest gift, Mistress of Folkvang, blesser of mothers.

Sigrid tenderly placed her hand on the warm skin of her belly, felt the germinating life that grew deep inside. It was her son. Soon she would hold him in her arms, close, and protect the little one until he reached his full strength and could conquer the world.

Sigrid curled up next to her sister, feeling her warmth. She needed her now more than ever.

ᛗ

*Freya, I thank you for the ample gifts and the protection you give me, your
descendant and servant. Our lady, give of your strength so that my words
will be obeyed and these foreign people will show me high esteem. Help me
to act justly so that I can sanctify the valuable gift you've given me.*

Sigrid felt Freya's strength fill her after she finished her prayer, and
she smiled at Emma.

Emma's swollen face was turning black and blue. She was half-
unconscious from wound fever, and Jorun was having a hard time getting her to drink the decoction of boiled willow bark, lady's mantle,
elder, and masterwort that Haldis had given them.

"Rest," Sigrid said gently to Emma. "Jorun will take care of you in
the best way possible."

Sigrid silenced Jorun with a look before she had a chance to protest.
Jorun hadn't even asked what had happened to the girl. Nor had she and
Alfhild obeyed Sigrid and gone to look for Emma as instructed. They
would pay for all of it.

"I'll look after her, my queen," Jorun said quietly.

"Yes, you will, and if she's not better by tonight, I'm going to hold
you responsible."

The hall was almost entirely empty when Sigrid came downstairs. A slave woman bowed to her and then hurried away, surely to inform someone that Sigrid had left her chamber. Sigrid walked out into the courtyard, where she found what she was looking for.

Father was inspecting a horse along with Ulf and some other men. He was wearing an embroidered white linen tunic and a cloak trimmed with beaver fur, although it was a hot day. He had a new belt, embroidered with silver thread, around his waist, and his beard was combed and braided. Toste laughed merrily when the steed reared up on its hind legs and kicked its hooves. Then he spotted Sigrid and walked over to meet her, smiling.

"You slept long and well, my daughter," he said, his eyes twinkling with mirth.

Sigrid hesitated. The rage she felt faded in the sunshine. He was her father, the chieftain of the Scylfings, and he had always treated her with the greatest respect. Toste had taught her everything a nobleman's daughter needed to know and more. Still. Sigrid ran her hand over her belly and remembered her obligation and her responsibility.

"Walk with me, Father," she said.

Doubt briefly flickered in his eye, and then he nodded.

They left the courtyard and followed the path that wound through the foreign farm fields that undulated around them like a lush ocean. Sigrid stopped by a gate and inhaled the scent of soil and flowers.

"This kingdom I gave you is magnificent," Toste said contentedly. "I kept my word."

Sigrid looked at her father. She'd sat by many times as he mediated between farmers, and she shared his loathing of people who didn't just come out and say what was at the heart of things.

"You injured something that belongs to me," she said.

"You shouldn't worry your head about things like that on a day like this," Toste said, his eyes widening. "Your husband will hold a feast soon. You have to make yourself beautiful for him."

The guilt was visible in his eyes, hidden beneath his cheery, friendly demeanor. There was no doubt about what he'd done: incest. Sigrid made a face of revulsion.

"Emma is my sister. When you raped her mother, you gave her Scylfing blood."

"Daughter!" Toste said sharply. "Many people falsely claim they belong to our family. You should have the girl whipped for her lies."

Sigrid shook her head. She had looked up to Toste her whole life, respected him in thought and deed. All of this crumbled when she saw him standing in the summer sun, an aging man wrapped up in expensive cloth but without honor.

If she hadn't seen Kára in Emma's eyes, maybe she wouldn't have believed the girl, but Freya herself vouched for the truth of what Emma said, and not even Father could blaspheme against the goddess.

"I see your blood in Emma," Sigrid maintained.

Toste shook his head. "Even if she is mine, she is still nothing, not even a mistress's child. She's worth less than my dogs. The gods give us our place in this world. She is a slave, and you are the queen of the Svea. Don't bring calamity over us all by breaking the gods' system of order."

Sigrid smiled joylessly at Toste's evasive words. She did not intend to let herself be deceived by his ploy.

"Emma is a seeress, a prophetess, and my sister. She serves me, and you injured my property."

"Enough with your silliness," Toste said with a laugh, pulling his hand over his beard. "The girl has been spreading her legs and enticing me since I first spotted her in Lejre. She got what she's been so lewdly begging for, and there's nothing wrong with that. She rode me with passion and pleasure, and if she says otherwise, she's lying. You have my word and my honor on that, daughter."

Sigrid's decisiveness faltered. He spoke as if only his words were sensible. Then she put her hand on her belly and took strength from her child. Emma was more important to ensure protection for Sigrid's son than Toste was. In choosing between Valhalla and her own family, she needed the strength to choose Vanadís.

"The gods punish incest harshly," Sigrid said, looking between her father's legs.

Only now did he look at her with apprehension.

"Don't believe her lies. She's an outsider, a slave. Do you give her words more weight than your own father's?"

Sigrid sighed heavily. She would never get him to admit guilt, no matter what she said. But Toste had other weaknesses.

"You won't have any more sons with the curse she put on you. I recommend you reimburse me amply for the damage you caused." She left him to return to the hall.

"Stop, daughter!" he bellowed.

His words were like a whip crack on her back. Suddenly she was a little girl cowering from her father's anger all over again. Then she stood up taller and turned around.

"I am the queen of Svealand, and as such I must be addressed with greater respect. I await your reimbursement for the incest."

Sigrid left him standing by the meadow. She was carrying the child of Scandinavia's greatest king in her womb, and she did not plan to let herself be bullied by anyone, not even her own father.

↕

Sweyn carefully led the horse through Jómsborg's open wooden gates and onto the main street. Mother clung on tight, unaccustomed to riding as she was, and bashfully accepted the greetings and congratulations she received from the warriors, housewives, and craftsmen they met. None of them looked unkindly upon her.

"See how they respect you?" he said, pride swelling in his chest.

His mother smiled meekly. She looked even paler now. In the daylight, her skin was almost gray. A messenger would have to be sent for Beyla. Surely she could give his mother her strength back.

Sweyn stopped outside the ship captains' row and led her to the room that was now his. There were four sleeping benches, a hearth, a table, and a narrow bench for sitting.

"It's very nice," she said and sank down onto one of the sleeping benches.

"You're sick," he said solemnly.

She shook her head and said, "All I need is some rest."

A knock made him turn around. Åke stood in the doorway with one of Palna's slaves, a thin, young woman who politely averted her gaze.

"Father gives you this as a gift," Åke announced.

Sweyn gave his brother a look of gratitude. He hadn't had time to buy a slave, even though he really needed one. Every waking minute was taken up by all the commitments he had.

"Do the men have barracks to live in?"

"Yes, they're waiting. Food and wood need to be procured, and we need to decide who will stay where."

Sweyn squeezed his mother's hand and stood up.

"Take good care of her, or I'll whip you to death," he told the slave.

"Yes, master," the thin woman said and bowed deeply.

With one last worried glance at his mother, Sweyn left the room and followed Åke to his men.

ᛘ

Sigrid slowed down on the path when she saw her brother coming to meet her.

"Why this anger, sister?" Ulf said. "Are you in trouble so soon? If so, more awaits you in Kungsgården. Your presence is desired there."

Sigrid breathed in with relief. She had never felt lonelier than when she turned her back on her own father. Ulf was her only brother.

"That can wait," she said, sighing heavily. "I have something important to tell you. I have learned that we have a sister: Emma, my own maidservant."

"Father's mistresses have many children," Ulf said with a shrug, unimpressed.

"Does he screw them, too, with his men and then beat them to a pulp?"

"Sigrid!" Ulf said quietly. His voice was both admonishing and somber.

"Were you in on the whole thing?" Sigrid spat out the words. That thought hadn't even occurred to her until now, and it filled her with revulsion.

"No. Father's escapades don't tempt me."

"So this wasn't the first time?" Sigrid rubbed her hand over her forehead. Her head felt like it was splitting in two from everything going on—with Erik, the temple, the dís in the guise of Emma, her own uncertain position as queen of Svealand.

She sat down on a boulder.

"It's what people do," Ulf said.

"It's incest," she whispered.

Ulf sat down next to her and looked out over the village below Kungsgården. She could tell that behind his beard he was disgusted, and now she sensed his silent anger.

"Will she live?" he asked.

"I think so."

He looked down at the ground and interlaced his fingers with a heavy sigh.

"Father is a good man, but he makes mistakes just like we all do. You've usually only seen what you wanted to see. You've always held him in such high regard."

"It really opened my eyes when he married me off to Mama's murderer," she said with a snort. "And when he humped my sister and beat her half to death."

She would never be able to stand by her father again, never give him the benefit of the doubt.

"I'm far from home, and everyone wants to kill me. The Svea hate me, and to Erik I'm just a broodmare that he can't impregnate quickly enough. Jorun and Alfhild defy me in everything." She stood up and paced back and forth, despair raging in her chest. "My only comfort and strength is Emma, who's possessed by the dís Freya sent to protect me. And now my sister is almost dead, half-fornicated to pieces by our own father. Is it any wonder I'm going crazy?"

Sigrid stopped and looked at her brother, her heart pounding.

"It could be worse," he said.

"How could it possibly, in any reasonable way, be any worse than this?"

He held up his hands, laughed glumly, and said, "Yrsa was queen of Svealand when she was captured by Helge Halvdansson and they had a son together. When the child was three, Yrsa found out that Helge was her own father. And then Tok-Harald slit both the mother's and the child's throats because gnomes told him to. That's the kind of stuff we do in our family."

He was giving her such a gentle look that she couldn't help but smile a little.

"You're crazy," she said. But she used a calmer tone and felt like laughing.

"No, not yet, I'm not," he said with a shrug. "And you aren't either, sister. You'll rise to meet their expectations. You're strong, and your faith will help you."

Her brother's words meant a lot to her. She ought to tell him about the baby she was carrying, how the dís had appeared to her and told her that her son was in her body.

"Father made a mistake, and whenever he does that he feels deep remorse and tries to pretend he's innocent," Ulf said. "He'll reimburse you for the injuries he caused your maidservant."

"Our sister," she corrected him.

"No, she'll never be our sister," he said, noting the fierce look in her eye.

Their moment of closeness was over.

The deceit and the incest were wounds that would always gall her. If her father reimbursed her, she would forgive him. Even if Sigrid could never forget, she would be satisfied with that. Emma had cursed her father's manhood, so he would surely pay quite a bit of silver to get that spell removed.

They started walking back to Kungsgården along the sun-warmed path.

"Repayment or not, it seems like you're going to have to part with Emma anyway," Ulf said.

He nodded toward the courtyard, where an oxcart was being tended by a tall man with the symbol of the temple on his goat-hide apron.

"They've come for her."

Sigrid looked at her brother in astonishment. Why would they care about Emma?

"They don't have anything to do with domestic servants."

Ulf gave her a concerned look.

"The temple priests have more say than even the king. Tread cautiously, sister. Your enemies are using Emma to hurt you."

Sigrid tried to swallow, but her mouth was parched from fear. She wasn't afraid of worldly power, but the priests and priestesses were another matter.

"They're just people," Ulf said.

"No," Sigrid said, slowly shaking her head. "There's nothing human about the gods."

The hall was full of people when Sigrid stepped in with her brother by her side. Those who had assembled fell silent and turned to look at her, their eyes unfriendly. It didn't bode well.

Erik sat on his throne, talking to the three priests who had blessed them during the night. They were still wearing their light tunics and the black paint around their eyes, but they were no longer wearing masks. Ergil, the royal family's ealdorman, was also there. Erik had said that the old man, with his thinning beard and the age spots on his face, was only summoned for serious matters.

Erik got up from his throne and waved to Sigrid.

The mark on her wrist grew warm, and it burned as she walked through the hall. Solveig watched her uneasily, which frightened her. When she got closer to the throne, she saw Emma kneeling nearby.

Her head hung disconsolately, and she didn't even look up when Sigrid arrived. What was the meaning of this? Had Father transferred the debt onto Emma, or was Ulf right that someone else wanted to use her to make trouble for Sigrid?

"How may I serve you, my king and husband?" Sigrid asked, nodding her head in deference.

Erik watched her, his eyes rimmed in red from exhaustion, but there was no sign of reconciliation in them.

"Accusations have been made," he said in a loud voice.

Sigrid shivered as the three priests eyed her as if she were a sacrificial animal. They could talk to the gods and see the Hidden. If they accused her or Emma, she had every reason to fear them.

"I don't understand. Did I do something to vex my husband or the gods whom I so faithfully venerate?"

She almost succeeded in sounding indifferent and innocent. Wide-eyed, she looked at the priests and her husband. Arngrim, the eldest of the priests, began to speak. His face was painted with thick white paint that had cracked in places. Still, he was just as awe inspiring as Thor, who had animated him during the nighttime blessing.

"You have a false seeress as a maidservant. A liar who poisons people with unholy sorcery and puts curses on good men."

Sigrid and her brother exchanged glances. So he'd been right that they were going to use Emma to hurt her. But who was behind this? Toste had entered the room. He stood in the background and contentedly watched what was happening. Jorun and Alfhild stood with the women, seeming pleased, as if this was the best thing that could possibly happen. Other people were also relishing watching the priest, and neither Erik's mistresses nor Haldis seemed to think that this was a bad outcome.

Emma raised her face, disfigured from the swollen bruises. Her eyes were bloodshot. The wave of tender rage Sigrid felt made it hard to breathe. *My sister, Vanadís's gift.* Not even the priests should be allowed to touch her.

"That is a serious accusation," Sigrid said loudly, looking around the room. "It's extremely fortunate that there's no truth in it. Emma is carrying the dís Kára within her. Freya herself has blessed me with this gift. He who defies Freya defies Valhalla. Certainly that is not the priests' will."

She stood up taller as a murmur ran through the hall. Sigrid realized too late that she'd gone too far. She had challenged the priests even though that hadn't been her intention. Their eyes were as cold as fish eyes and Erik looked profoundly displeased. Sigrid wiped her sweaty palms on her dress.

"The gods speak through us, Scylfing woman. Their will is ours," said Frey's priest, but he stopped talking when Arngrim held up a hand.

"We venerate Our Lady Freya and our queen," Arngrim said. "Let us leave it to the gods to decide if this girl Emma is acting on their behalf. If she carries Kára within her, we will honor her."

Damn it. Sigrid had walked right into a trap.

She looked at Emma, sitting there with her eyes closed, sad in her wretchedness. Why couldn't the dís come to her now? Kára had just been there at dawn to announce the presence of the baby. Why did Emma just sit there, huddled and vulnerable, leaving Sigrid to bear this shame alone?

"Well said," responded Erik. "Let us test this maidservant's truthfulness right away. If she's lying, I want her gone before the day is done."

The three priests bowed to Erik and got up. Sigrid saw the triumph in their faces. Then she understood. The test they were going to put Emma through would kill her.

"I want to see my maidservant tested and triumph," Sigrid said quickly. "If she lied, I will send her to the afterworld myself. But if she told the truth, I want her respected as a great seeress."

Arngrim smiled faintly and then bowed his head.

"So it will be. If she survives, she will be respected."

♃

They couldn't just take Emma and kill her. Sigrid had to have hope, maintain confidence. She followed the procession through the crowd outside the temple. Visitors crowded around booths where merchants with scales and weights were selling everything conceivable: jewelry, mead, bread, and chunks of roasted meat wrapped in leaves. Chickens, pigs, and goats were crowded into cramped pens. A man carrying a sheep with its legs tied together stopped and watched Emma with disgust as she walked at the front of the procession with the priests by her side.

Sigrid gulped. This had to go well.

In a stall a man was selling small clay statues of the gods and goddesses. Freya wore a long dress and raised her hand as if she were casting a spell, a sword at her side. Thor held the hammer in his hand. There was also Erce, who sat in her chariot decorated with flowers, symbolizing her power to grant peace and a good harvest.

"A half daler," said the woman selling the figurines. "You could certainly use Erce's blessing."

Sigrid walked on, filled with disgust at having had to see the goddesses desecrated. With a shudder she followed the procession through the tall gates that were guarded by two young men with hammers like Thor's.

It looked different from how it had looked at night. The building looked smaller, and priests with shaved heads and priestesses with staffs were visible through the open doors. That's not where the three priests were leading them, though, but rather to the grove of trees behind the temple.

"They're taking her to the holy oaks," Sigrid whispered to her brother, looking toward the ancient grove, where people had been making sacrifices since the dawn of time.

A priestess waited by a bonfire. Hope sank in Sigrid's chest when she recognized Hyndla, the seeress whom Solveig had warned her about.

They were going to burn Emma. If Kára didn't help her this time, she would surely die.

Jorun giggled behind her back. When Sigrid turned around angrily, Jorun looked down, but Sigrid had already caught the gleam of ill will in her eye.

"Are you taking pleasure in Emma's pain?" Sigrid asked, offended.

Jorun quickly shook her head while Alfhild pressed her lips together to keep from laughing. Had her kinswomen, her own flesh and blood, really come to the temple to watch Emma get cleared out of the way?

"Is this your doing?" Sigrid asked.

"No, Sigrid," Jorun said. "We would never hurt Emma, no sooner than we would hurt your dogs or Buttercup."

She was lying. Sigrid recognized the look in her eyes all too well.

"If I find out that you went behind my back, I'm going to skin you and salt your screaming, bleeding bodies."

Sigrid was so angry with her traitorous kinswomen that she wanted to eviscerate them. She turned her back and clenched her fists so tight that her fingernails dug into her palms.

Kára would help Emma survive. Freya would not let her maidservant down.

"Soon they will all kneel down in submission before the Wild Stormy One," she told her brother.

"May you be right, sister," Ulf said with grave wonder. "May you be right."

Emma eyed the bonfire with resignation. It towered in front of her. She had avoided one death by burning, only to encounter another. No one could escape his or her destiny, and she was already dead, after all. This would allow her to go to the afterworld, to the big void where the goddess ruled and there was no pain.

Hyndla didn't even glance at Emma, just turned to the three priests and asked, "Who is she?"

"She says she's a dís. She has put a curse on free men," said Thor's priest.

Hyndla's lips curled in scorn.

"Tie her by the fire. Let the flames determine whether she's blessed by the gods or a liar."

Hard hands dragged Emma up to the bonfire and tied her to the pole in the middle. She moaned with pain as the rope cut deeply into her wrists and waist. Kára was silent, as if she'd never been there. Emma must have completed her destiny. The dís had no more use for her and was going to let her die the same way she had been saved. In sadness, Emma watched the people who came running to see her suffer. They longed for her death. Every direction she looked there was just eager curiosity. Then she caught Sigrid's eyes, filled with pleading. *My sister.*

Emma pursed her lips and almost started crying. She so wanted to take care of Sigrid and her son. How could she do that in the afterworld? She looked up at the now-overcast sky. Who would look after them now?

Hyndla loudly chanted spells as she raised a lit torch. Without hesitating, she set fire to the twigs that flamed up with a roar.

Emma felt the heat approaching. The billowing smoke tore at her lungs. She started coughing and soon the pain came as the fire licked at her feet.

"Where is your dís now?" Hyndla screamed at her, her eyes wide.

The three priests beside her watched Emma with anticipation. They were enjoying her pain. Sigrid's face was white as snow, and her lips moved in prayer. Emma moaned in pain as the fire cut at her feet like knives. Her dress caught fire. Now she would die, seared by scorching flames. The fear ripped her wide open, and she tumbled down into an abyss. She was back at the monastery, locked in and screaming with those demons, who were so willing to die in the flames.

My destiny is not yet completed! Roaring, she ordered the dark smoke to part for her. She overpowered the gods, bent their will to obey her. *Kára, Wild Stormy One, obey my will. Dísir, I summon you!*

Emma screamed so loudly that her voice echoed over the earth, down to the afterworld, and all the way up to the heavens. The sky rumbled as it rushed to aid its sister, and a burst of wind suddenly blew through the grove of trees.

A heavy raindrop fell on Emma's face. She looked up at the sky, where shrieking beings, terrible in their veil-draped strength, swept through the clouds.

Sisters, I greet you.

The rain started gushing toward the ground as if the gates of the sky had opened and Hvergelmir itself gushed down from the black clouds. Sizzling and sputtering, the flames were extinguished at once. Emma raised her face to the sky and laughed at her sisters, the dísir in the sky, as the rain washed away her sin, doubt, and pain.

The eternal spiral kept spinning through time, and she was still in this life. The humans, so pathetic in all their weakness, took cover beneath the oak trees as the rain came down in torrents. A moment later it was over.

Drenched, Sigrid stood before her, rain dripping from her face and clothes. As if she hadn't noticed how wet she was, she smiled in relief. Hyndla, who had so willingly tried to send Emma to the afterworld, stared at her. The priests looked just as bewildered.

"Release the girl!" a sharp voice ordered.

The three old seeresses whom Emma had met on the beach came walking laboriously toward them, supporting themselves on their staffs. Hyndla and the priests sank, crouching down in the wet grass.

"The sacrifice has been refused," one of the elderly seeresses said.

"They let themselves be governed by vindictiveness and a desire to dominate," the second said with a disgusted look at Hyndla and the priests, who paled in the face of her stern gaze.

They knelt on the wet ground before the three aged women, and there was fear in their eyes.

"The punishment is severe for those who tear the tapestry and disturb the fate of everything," said the eldest of the seeresses.

Housecarls climbed onto the bonfire and cut the ropes that bound Emma. She was alive. The pain from her feet radiated through her legs, and she couldn't stand upright. Emma sank down before Sigrid's feet, shivering from the cold.

Sigrid knelt beside her, wrapped her own cloak around Emma's shoulders, and then ran her hand over Emma's hair.

The three old women stared vacantly at them.

"Thank you, Venerable Ones," Emma whispered.

"You live to complete your destiny," one said.

Emma lowered her head and put her hand on her heart. She understood. The time would come soon for her final sacrifice. Her destiny approached relentlessly. She moaned in fear and leaned into Sigrid's comforting warmth.

"I bow to your will," Emma replied.

The three seeresses nodded in satisfaction at her response.

Sigrid looked in astonishment at the three ancient women. They were more shabbily dressed than anyone else in the temple, and their wispy gray hair was like cobwebs around their heads. Their sunken faces were filled with warts and scars, and their eyes were nestled inside deep wrinkles. But one of them carried a falcon on her staff—Freya's animal form. These seeresses who looked like they had lived since the dawn of time must be powerful.

"Venerable Ones, I do apologize, but who are you?" Sigrid asked, moving her hand to her heart.

The eldest of them turned to Sigrid and said, "The mother of the king is blind."

Another chuckled throatily and added, "She does not recognize those who mete out the terms, change people's lots in life, and measure out the fate for the children of mankind."

The hair on Sigrid's arms stood up, and she dropped to her knees before Verdandi, Urd, and Skuld, the three Norns who controlled the fates of everything. Now she understood the priests' fear. In the face of the three great ones, they were all nothing.

"All-knowing spinners of destiny, I serve you," Sigrid said, panting.

The three Norns, guardians of the font of knowledge, who dwelled at the foot of Yggdrasil, nodded.

Without saying anything more, they left Sigrid and Emma crouching on the ground and walked, supported by their staffs, into the grove of trees. The next moment they were gone, as if they'd never been there. All that was left were the rain-wetted leaves dripping on the lush soil.

Sigrid put her arm around Emma's shoulders and held her tight.

I thank you so tenderly for your protection.

The onlookers and the temple servants who only a brief moment before had so eagerly hungered for Emma's painful death now backed away from them, filled with fear and respect. Even Ulf's mouth hung half open, as if he couldn't believe what had just happened. Sigrid rested her cheek against Emma's wet hair and inhaled the smell of smoke and sour hemp. This was victory, magnificent and mighty. They had made the journey together from desperation to respect.

"No one will dare come after us again," Sigrid said and cautiously stroked Emma's sooty cheek. "We're safe now."

ᛏ

It was crowded around the mead barrel where men played backgammon, drank, and listened to music so upbeat that few could sit still on the benches. Young women danced with drunken warriors, and they roped everyone into the song's refrain.

> *His grave was the ship,*
> *that ferried him home,*
> *home to the All-Father's dwelling*
> *where the valkyries poured*
> *the mead he adored. Sing hey!*
> *Sing ho, for Kvasir's reward!*

Sweyn drank the sweet mead and leaned against the wall while the smiling Gunn tried to sit on his lap.

"I've missed you, my handsome."

They had been attracted to each other before, and she was one of the most beautiful women in the hall, with an ample bosom, but she was acting drunk and he found her unappetizing.

"Not tonight, beautiful," he said politely.

After Sigrid, other women did not much appeal to him. He hadn't even enjoyed the house slave even though she'd offered to warm his bed. If you'd had the most beautiful of young women, it was hard to feel any desire for anyone else.

Gunn sat down next to Åke instead, who willingly pulled her onto his lap.

"Don't refuse the gifts that are offered in this life," Åke chastised. "Soon enough we, too, will be drinking in Valhalla."

Gunn laughed coquettishly when Åke put his hand on her breast.

"Is Sweyn not interested in women anymore?" she asked, and nibbled on his ear.

"Get out of here!" Åke said, standing up so quickly that she practically fell on the floor. "No one speaks that way about my brother."

Gunn's laugh was shrill and mocking as she sauntered away from the table.

"Sweyn, you've got to stop turning the ladies down. People are starting to question your manhood and say you'd rather sew with your mother than screw."

Åke nodded toward their fellow warriors, who were whispering together and giving them knowing looks. Sweyn sighed heavily. This was the first evening he'd had time to drink mead in a long time and it vexed him that he couldn't find any peace even here. But he would not abide rumors about his manhood!

"I'm tired of the selection here. I've enjoyed all of them far too many times," he said loudly so that many could hear.

Sweyn emptied his cup and nodded to a blond wench who walked over with pitchers of mead in both hands. She looked faintly like Sigrid, although much plainer.

"I could go for that new one, though," Sweyn said.

Åke laughed in relief as Sweyn waved to the blonde, who thrust out her chest for him.

"You look good, but are you expensive?" he asked her. When she grinned, he noted that she was missing one tooth.

"I'm sure we can come to some agreement," she said.

"This one's on me, brother," Åke said.

Sweyn did not find the young woman very enticing, but there wasn't a single set of eyes in the hall not trained on him. A single man was compelled to show his manhood. Without saying anything, he flung the blonde over his shoulder and carried her to an available sleeping bench on the long side of the hall. She immediately pulled up her skirt and parted her legs. Sweyn resolutely pushed the thoughts of Sigrid out of his mind as he loosened his breeches. Then he lay down on top of the mead wench. *Might as well get this over with so I can be left in peace.*

ᚼ

The wind brought a tinge of fall with it as Sigrid grimly accompanied Erik to say good-bye to her father and the Scylfings. Nausea burned in her belly as they strolled along in the late summer heat between the farms that lay on the slope by the little river. She would never have believed that you could feel this sick when you were expecting a baby.

The loaded ships waited by the river. The men were eager to get home to their families. She would be left behind and alone among strangers, waiting for the war that would be upon them soon.

Toste stood on the beach and looked Erik steadfastly in the eye, then put his hand on Erik's shoulder.

"I'll be back for the spring sacrifice with the best of the Scylfing warriors. You have my word on it. We'll fight together, like brothers."

Erik put his hand on his heart and said, "Together we'll win."

The two men smiled at each other.

"At the spring sacrifice you will hold your grandson," Erik said. "You will understand then how strong the bond is between the Sköldunga family and the Scylfings."

Sigrid swallowed and carefully hid the distaste she felt for her husband. At least he hadn't visited her bed in the last month and a half, which was a relief.

In the beginning he had come to her bed at least once a day, often twice. Then he started questioning her about her monthly bleeding and feeling her breasts, looking for signs of a baby. Even though she said she was carrying his son, he didn't trust it to be true. It wasn't until there was a full moon and she hadn't had her monthly bleeding that he believed her. Erik had given her a bracelet of the finest silverwork, and after that she had hardly seen him. The few times she had tried to talk to him, she had been quickly brushed aside. Erik preferred the company of men and advisors by day, and he warmed the beds of other women at night.

Sigrid put her hand on her belly and looked at her father. The chill between them had not broken, but rather expanded as the seasons progressed.

"I leave you with the most honorable of men," Toste said to her.

The broodmare was pregnant, and everyone was happy. Father had offered her silver in payment for Emma's injuries and demanded that the curse that had been put on him and the men be removed.

"I haven't had sex in weeks. You can't let your father suffer this way," he'd said. "Not even the priests in the temple can break the spell she put on me."

"Ask her yourself, and make up for your actions," Sigrid had replied, but her father refused.

"I'm not planning to go anywhere near that abomination."

After much hesitation, Sigrid had accepted the silver and said that she would discuss the matter with Emma. Emma had laughed and said that of course she could break the spell that had temporarily castrated her father but that it was probably mostly in his head.

Sigrid smiled stiffly to Toste and said, "May Rán carry you safely over the sea, Father." She put her hand on Erik's arm. "Tell them at home of my great happiness."

Sigrid fought her nausea as Jorun and Alfhild said good-bye to their kinfolk. Somberly, Sigrid turned to her brother to say her toughest good-bye.

"Keep an eye on those two," Ulf said and nodded at Sigrid's maidservants. "I've heard some things."

He'd asked Sigrid to send the two women back, and now he looked so worried that Sigrid almost wanted to cry.

"They're all I have left from home."

Sigrid couldn't send them away and no longer had any reason to. She had given them a stern talking-to and they hadn't defied her again since. Now they feared Emma instead and fawned all over both Emma and Sigrid to gain their approval.

"Promise me, then, that you'll be on your guard when they're around," Ulf urged.

She nodded and smiled at him. When they had left home, he had been annoying, a kid she'd grown up with but hardly knew. Now he stood before her as a full-grown man and the only person who seemed genuinely to care about her.

"You've really changed during this trip," she said and patted his cheek.

"You used to be a kid," Ulf replied with a smile, "who was hard to put up with and used to getting your way in everything. Now I see a young queen who will soon be a mother. I'm proud of you, sister, and I envy your deep faith. You may need it in the face of the storm that will descend upon us soon."

He said the last few words with such a miserable face that Sigrid could hardly bear it.

"Will you be back in the spring?"

He nodded and said, "Yes, with news from home."

Then he was gone, and Sigrid was left standing by herself, surrounded by cheerful good-byes and congratulations.

Her heart was torn to pieces when the Scylfing ships set out, rowing down the Fyris River to the sea.

She wanted to run after them, to yell to her father to take her away from here so that she could live with Sweyn for the rest of her life. Instead she forced herself to smile as Erik took her hand and led her back to the hall. He did not speak a single word of comfort to her or even deign to look at her. But the villagers they encountered greeted them kindly and with deep respect.

"Bless us with peace and fertility, beautiful Queen," a young woman with a round blemished face cried out.

Everyone knew that she'd been blessed with a dís by Freya and also had the blessing of the Norns. Ever since what happened in the grove, women thought that Sigrid could imbue them with the goddess's fertility.

"You are truly blessed," Sigrid said with a smile.

An old woman bowed deeply and put her hand on her heart.

"The rain in the grove was fortunate," Erik said with a contented grin. "Now they see you as Freya and me as Frey. Songs about us, the sacred couple, are being sung throughout Svealand, as is the song about my future prince being sent from the gods. It will help me win the chieftains over to my side for the battle against Styrbjörn. You serve me well and strengthen my position."

Sigrid walked slowly up the hill, her feet swollen and aching in the summer heat. Sweat trickled down her back and nausea heaved within her. She had never felt so far from Valhalla.

"Surely you have something to do with the fact that they're singing songs about us," she replied.

Sigrid forced herself to smile at a woman who proudly displayed her own pregnant belly. Erik's soft chuckle confirmed her suspicions.

"It would be dumb of me not to avail myself of this opportunity," he said and then picked up the pace, paying no consideration to her condition.

"I'm leaving early tomorrow," Erik told her. "Mother and her warriors will watch over you and the baby."

It wouldn't make much difference, given how rarely Sigrid saw Erik these days.

"When will you be back?"

"Each of the Svea chieftains must be persuaded to mobilize Svealand for war so that we can defeat Styrbjörn."

"You can use the songs about the sacred couple when you talk to Sacrifice-Sven, and—"

"I can handle Sacrifice-Sven. You don't need to trouble your head about the affairs of men." Erik's voice was so sharp she thought he might hit her. "While I'm away, you will sacrifice at the temple every seven days. Appease the priests! I need you to turn those old goats' minds so they are filled with goodwill toward me. Visit the farms and bless the young women and children. Talk to the old people, farmers, and noblemen. Wear your most beautiful clothes, put up your hair, and hang jewelry around your neck. You are Svealand's Freya and must spread your radiance and fecundity to all the farms. Will you obey me in this?"

Sigrid nodded.

"Good. Farewell, my queen. Don't worry. I'll be back before the midwinter sacrifice." He kissed her cheek and left her standing there in the courtyard.

Sigrid clenched her teeth. Erik seemed to think she was his hired hand. It was a disgrace how he talked about the temple's sacred workers as if they were a necessary evil that he dealt with only reluctantly.

All the same, she had no choice. The broodmare had to be dressed in a golden harness and trotted around to all the farms with its mane and tail braided. Sigrid sighed heavily.

"Don't look so glum. You don't need to fear for Erik's life right now," Solveig said and took Sigrid's arm as they walked toward the hall. "And you're carrying his son, sent from Valhalla."

They could see Erik, out by the pasture, having a serious talk with Axel and several of his other men.

"It won't be easy for Erik to persuade the chieftains to come and bring their warriors," Solveig continued. "Several of the powerful ones secretly support Styrbjörn. You're the weight that will tip the balance over to our side and bring us victory."

Sigrid put her hand on her belly. Erik had to win so that her son would become king and the temple would remain untouched in all its strength.

It is your will.

Then she remembered Sweyn's words, that he would defeat Erik and make her his own. Some days when she woke up just before dawn, she felt like he was lying beside her, so close she could feel his breath on her cheek, and her heart burst with longing. Then she prayed that he would keep his word and come take her away from here, no matter what happened. This was her desire, even though her beloved would have to fight her father, her brother, and her husband. It was treason to want Sweyn to win, and it filled her with shame. Still, she couldn't extinguish the flame of hope, and she wanted nothing else but to be with him, even if only for a short while.

Other days she wished she'd never met the Jómsvíking, so she could better go along with the bitter lie that she and Erik were a sacred couple. Then she wouldn't be ripped apart by these wishes and doubts.

Give me a sign.

But Freya was silent, and Emma had no answers to give.

Sigrid sighed heavily.

"I don't know what I'm going to do," she said half to herself.

"Give him a sign of your affection," Solveig said kindly. "Give him a piece of jewelry or needlework that he can take on his journey to remember you by."

Sigrid almost started laughing. Solveig had so little insight into her thoughts.

"That's good advice, which I will follow," she replied.

Haldis was waiting for her in the hall with her court of ladies. It took Sigrid a little while to make her way over there. The pregnancy left her so tired sometimes that she worried about keeping up her strength. Her body ached all the time.

"Come and eat with me and we'll talk," Haldis said. The queen mother had been more than kind since it became clear that Sigrid was expecting.

Sigrid followed her from the hall out to the herb garden, where they sat down on a bench. The meal was already laid out. She helped herself to a piece of cheese and hoped she would be able to keep it down.

"It's auspicious that you're carrying the king's son and that the Norns and Freya have blessed you," the queen mother said and looked out at the river, which wound its way through the greenery like a shimmering snake.

Sigrid watched the older woman carefully, wondering where this was leading.

"In the way your son speaks, he does not appear truly to respect the temple," she said cautiously.

"He has his reasons," Haldis said, giving her a pointed look. "You should know that the Thor worshippers control the temple. Odin used to be held in highest regard, and his hall was the most beautiful that had been seen. But Thor's priests fought with Odin's and eventually they burned down the hall. A lot of people are still angry about that."

Sigrid had never heard of fighting between Valhalla's priests. That was a blasphemy that couldn't be allowed.

"But Erik is consecrated to Frey," Sigrid said, struggling to understand.

Haldis laughed quietly and bitterly and said, "Yes, I suppose it's for the best that Frey chose my son. Otherwise none of us would be alive today. None of us is immune to a drop of poison or a noose around the neck. Nobleman or not, whoever comes into the priests' sight seldom lives long."

Sigrid faltered as the terrible weakness returned. It was as if it took over and filled her body with sickness. She hoped it would be better when the baby got bigger.

"But the priests follow the will of the Æsir," Sigrid said, managing to keep her voice steady.

"I fear that they mostly follow their own will," the queen mother said somberly, shaking her head.

What should she say to that? Such a blasphemous statement, and from Erik's own mother! The priests had willingly tied Emma to the bonfire. Could they not sense Kára's presence in her? And yet the priests had knelt fearfully before the Norns, so presumably they were able to perceive their true nature. Sigrid didn't know what to make of it.

She swallowed the cheese with difficulty and drank a little water.

"Is Freya not worshipped in the temple?" she asked. She hadn't seen any trace of the most important of the goddesses.

"At one time she had her own hall, filled with seeresses and dressed in the purest gold. But now she is honored only in the groves. The all-knowing Norns also rule there."

Rage seething inside her, Sigrid inhaled slowly and then said, "Our Lady is the most important." *Those bloodthirsty priests ought to learn that.*

"I know that your faith is profound, and I also honor her each day," Haldis said, putting her hand on Sigrid's mark. "Do you fully grasp the significance of what I've just told you?"

Sigrid swallowed. Fighting between the priests about which of the Æsir was most powerful was a bad sign. It portended Ragnarök, when Valhalla would be shaken to its core.

"Was Styrbjörn sworn to Thor before he allowed himself to be baptized?" Sigrid asked.

Haldis nodded briefly.

"That's why you have to give birth to a son, to show that Frey is strong in Erik," Haldis said, and Sigrid saw the desperation in her eyes.

She nodded. The new life had already taken root in her. Her son was living and growing stronger with every breath she took.

"No one will be disappointed on this point," Sigrid affirmed.

"Then you also have my support and assistance, both as queen and Freya priestess," Haldis said.

The women looked at each other in silent agreement. Sigrid realized to her astonishment that she had formed an alliance with the queen mother.

2

The formation of soldiers started slowly walking across the muddy field toward the row of warriors waiting with swords and raised shields. The soldiers advanced rhythmically, holding their shields out like a protective wall.

When they were a stone's throw from the waiting warriors, Ax-Wolf barked, "Spearhead!"

The men in the center of the formation increased their pace while those on the sides slowed so the formation took on a wedge shape that could drive into the row of warriors awaiting them. But the ones in front went too fast and the lines of men following stretched too thin. One of them tripped, and when the others tried to avoid stepping on him, the whole formation broke up.

Sweyn shook his head, clearly distressed.

"Stop! Right now!" shouted Ax-Wolf, bright red in the face. "I've never seen a worse group of ball-licking good-for-nothings! A slave is better than any of you!"

Sweyn pulled his hand over his face and swore softly. They had been practicing these maneuvers for weeks and still couldn't achieve the wedge. The warriors took up their positions again, weary and muddy, shivering in the north wind.

Some of the Jómsvíkings who were gathered by the field watching the training, doubled over laughing at Sweyn's men.

"Your warriors seem a little heavy on their feet," cried Urban from Eyvind's phalanx. "Walking and fighting at the same time seems like it might be too much for them."

Sweyn laughed softly without showing his anger, but retorted, "You, the man who fell down drunk right in front of Gunnar, ought to know."

Urban remained indignantly quiet while the other men laughed more and more. No one would ever forget the night when an incredibly drunk Urban had tripped, landing facedown in front of Palna's brother.

"He's still right that half of them are useless," Sweyn told Åke.

The Jómsvíkings who served on the two ships Palna had given him were good at everything. But the warriors he'd gotten from Harald and the others he had hired in Lejre weren't suitable to take into battle.

"Ax-Wolf is likely to get them into shape," Åke said. "There's still time before we sail for Svealand."

"Nowhere near enough time," Sweyn said glumly. How patient were the Jómsvíkings? That was the question. Some of the men from Lejre had already been beaten up, one so badly he still couldn't stand.

The men moved back into formation on the field to try yet again.

It would be Yule soon, and training was taking all his time. In addition, he'd spent a fortune in silver on food and on the smith who had armed them all. And still, the men were so pathetic they'd be killed in their first battle. And his aspirations would die with them.

They had to learn. Even if he had to whip the skills into them, they were going to become fearsome warriors.

"Don't let them leave the field until they can do it," he said sternly. "I'll be back before dark. Palna wants to see me."

The north wind tugged at Sweyn's cloak as he walked toward his foster father's house. It was the biggest in Jómsborg, built of logs that had been chinked with mud and then whitewashed, with a thick thatch roof where the smoke rose from two chimneys.

Sweyn knocked on the door and waited until Valdur, the limping, old warrior who served Palna, opened the door.

"He's expecting you," Valdur said and led Sweyn down the hall into Palna's room.

Sweyn's foster father was sitting on a stool in front of the hearth, looking into the flames. Sweyn stopped in the middle of the room and took a deep breath of the smoky warmth. It did not bode well that his father wanted to speak to him alone.

"Have a seat," Palna said, gesturing to a bench beside him.

Sweyn sat down, his legs aching with fatigue. Gratefully he warmed himself in the heat of the crackling fire.

"How's your mother doing?" Palna inquired.

"Better. Beyla has been attending to her with healing drinks. I hope the evil in her will be driven away."

"You take good care of your mother. It does you credit," his foster father said and nodded contentedly.

"You deserve my thanks for the slave you gave her. She's good."

"Good, good. I hear things aren't going so well with your warriors."

"They'll be ready by the spring." Something would work. He would show his father that he could lead men and be victorious in battle.

"I'm sure they will. That's not why I summoned you." Palna cleared his throat before proceeding. "You're not a child anymore but a Jelling nobleman, a chieftain in charge of four ships. You need a wife at your side. If you have a son, your name and your position will live on. My Valfrid is of marriageable age, and she is both accomplished and beautiful."

Sweyn watched his father and waited. So this was the old wolf's plan? Sweyn laughed somberly at the thought of sharing a bed with any of Palna's three daughters.

"She's my sister," Sweyn objected.

"Not by blood. Valfrid can give you many splendid sons and she's familiar with a Jómsvíking's life. It would be wise to take her as your wife."

Sweyn stared into the flames with distaste. Valfrid's head was so empty it echoed, and she never had anything sensible to say. She was nothing compared to Sigrid, and he would rather have tied a boulder to his back than take her as his wife.

"I'm going to be the king of the Danes, and Valfrid is no queen."

A shadow came over Palna's face, and he said, "Are you saying my daughters aren't good enough?"

"They're my sisters," Sweyn replied calmly. He wasn't planning on letting himself be scared into something he didn't want.

"That Tostedotter woman still poisons your mind, I see. But you should give up on her. Sigrid is already heavy with Erik's child. That's what that tradesmen from the North said when they were unloading their goods last month."

A baby! Sweyn's heart skipped a beat. "How far along is she?"

"It's Erik's baby," Palna said with a sigh. "She's lost to you. Take Valfrid as your wife and forget Tostedotter."

Sweyn shook his head. Certainty took root in him. Sigrid had been untouched when they lay together during the sacrifice, and now she was carrying his child.

"In the spring I will fetch her and the baby from Svealand and bring them to Jómsborg. She is my wife and queen. There is no other."

He was going to be a father. That knowledge lifted his spirits. He would win in Svealand, and his men would be more than ready. He had to get back to the training grounds, and push the men harder than he had been. They had to succeed, for the sake of both the baby's and his own destiny.

"You are weaving wishes and dreams out of a cloth that does not exist. Take Valfrid. That is my wish."

"I respect you and honor you in everything, my foster father," Sweyn said, standing up. "But I am a Jelling and the son of a king, and on this matter I make my own decisions."

As Sweyn strode through Jómsborg, he pulled out the pouch he wore on a cord by his heart and stroked the worn leather. Sigrid and the baby were his. Neither Erik nor Svealand's warriors would keep him from taking what he wanted. In the spring his wait would be over.

H

Icy winds swept through the hall. The wind tugged at the doors, which banged on their hinges. Outside, the frost giants reigned. They had covered the fields in a gray chill, and snow lay knee-deep around the buildings.

Sigrid pulled her fur-trimmed cloak around her swelling body. The flames in the hearth could not drive away the cold, even though everyone had gathered in the women's small room, which held the heat better. Solveig and Haldis sat at the loom, where images of Erik's victories against the Obotrites were revealed by their labor. Several of the women were embroidering another part of the tapestry. It would hang in the great hall soon, along with others that told of Erik and showed that he was the greatest of Svealand's kings.

The women regarded their responsibility to record the great heroic deeds in pictures with the utmost seriousness. Haldis paid close attention, deciding which warriors would be included in the weaving, what they would be doing, and whether they were alive or dead.

"Saga herself, the most eloquent of the goddesses, wants each matron to pass on the stories by weaving her own cloth, like the Norns," she'd explained, as if Sigrid came from a distant land.

Sigrid stared gloomily at her own needlework and sighed. Erik's horse looked mostly like a big pig, and she was so tired she could hardly sit upright on the bench.

She should have demanded her right from Haldis, should have stood up and declared that from this moment on she was the one who made the decisions about tapestries and stories. But she didn't have the strength. The baby drained her and gave her swirling dreams about monsters and giantesses who put a baby in her belly and waited around to steal it from her, once it was born. Sigrid shuddered and looked at the women sitting silently, leaning over their looms.

Because of her weakness she had barely been able to visit any farms lately. Still, with Emma by her side, she had forced herself to visit every home in Svealand, or at least that's how it felt. Poor, wide-eyed farmers had shyly offered her porridge and then asked her to touch their young daughters' bellies—and the same with their goats, cows, horses, chickens, and even an ox—so that she would make them fertile. Proud matrons, the wives of warriors and chieftains, had asked the same, although the food they'd offered her was better. She'd even been offered meat.

She'd visited drafty longhouses where snotty-nosed children sat in straw beds with their dirty mothers, as well as ornate halls with domestic servants in courtly clothes. Everyone had accepted her basket, filled with dried meat, eggs, honey, cheeses, berries, and sweet buns, with the same pleasure. After that they had asked the same questions: Had she been blessed by Freya or was she the Lady herself? Could Kára reveal herself to them? Could they touch her belly and be blessed? Humbly, Sigrid had complied in every way.

For your sake, so that they will see you and revere you.

She even found Erik's cast-off mistress, Aedis, when she visited an old farm with a leaky thatched roof and scrawny farm animals. There was a lot of animosity toward her among the household servants, and Sigrid hadn't understood why until she spotted Aedis trying to hide herself behind some women. Aedis had run out of money when Sigrid kicked her out of Kungsgården. Her mother, Hyndla, couldn't help her since she'd been expelled from the temple after trying to kill Emma on the bonfire. Now Aedis and her children lived with relatives who could scarcely feed them, and no man would marry her because they were all afraid of getting on the king's bad side.

"Didn't Erik give you silver and jewelry to ensure the well-being of you and your children?" Sigrid had asked.

"I had to hand those over the day I arrived here," was her bitter response.

Sigrid looked at Erik's two daughters, who were gray in the face and skinny as twigs. This was shameful of Erik. He was no better than her father, who took what he wanted and then went on his way. They were dishonorable rogues to let their children live in hunger and privation.

"You must come with me to live and serve on my staff at Kungsgården."

Sigrid's offer amazed Aedis and her household servants, but she turned it down.

"I'd rather starve than let you make a fool of me."

The mistress's hatred and pride didn't surprise Sigrid, and she hadn't actually thought Aedis would take her up on it.

"Well, but the king's children shouldn't live in poverty. Accept this token of my friendship, the first of many." Sigrid put one of her silver bracelets on the table in front of Aedis and then left the farm. Word of her magnanimous generosity toward Aedis had spread quickly, and Solveig praised her for her benevolence.

Every Freyaday, Sigrid had gone to the temple with offerings, which were sacrificial animals from the king's own flocks. She'd gotten to know the priests better, but she gave most of the animals to the priestesses, who in turn showed her genuine friendship. At each visit she prayed to Freya and the Norns in the sacred grove, and for this she gained respect in the temple. It was a pleasure for Sigrid to get to pray at the site where the old ways were strongest.

Everything had truly worked out well, and wherever Sigrid went she was met with admiration and joy. All of it would benefit her son when he arrived.

"Tell me about how Queen Elfrida murdered King Edward and put a child on the throne, Emma," cried Virun, Orm's young wife. Several of the Svea women chimed in right away, also eager to hear the story again.

People loved Emma's stories from far away England and never tired of hearing them.

Emma stood up and wiped her palms on her dress. She pushed aside her blond hair, which seemed impossible to tame, and looked out at the noble women on the benches.

"The crops were failing in England, and most people were sure it was because God was dissatisfied with young Edward having been chosen as the king. Several of the chieftains came to Corfe Castle and sought the advice of the king's stepmother, the dowager queen Elfrida, who lived there with her son Æthelred. Every time one of the chieftains stepped into the queen's room, she said that if God wanted her to intervene, then she would receive a sign."

They were enthralled as Emma told them how King Edward rode alone into Corfe Castle after getting away from his hunting party and how Elfrida met him in the lower courtyard, where she was pouring mead. When he went to get off his horse to take the welcoming cup, the dowager queen's servants murdered him.

"Did the king die well?" Virun blurted out.

"He took a sword in the back and didn't manage to say very much."

"He didn't make any poetry about his death or give any advice to his young half brother?"

Emma shook her head.

"When the blow landed, the king's horse ran away, dragging his body out of the castle, and he wasn't freed from the horse until it reached a poor, blind woman who lived below the castle. When the blind woman walked up to the body and touched him, she immediately got her sight back. That was the first sign that the crop failures were over."

Jorun and Alfhild were the only ones not listening eagerly. They appeared unmoved.

Sigrid faltered when she noticed them, the pain in her belly getting worse.

"Erik should be home soon now that the giantess and goddess Skaði has covered the water with ice," Solveig said without looking up from her embroidery.

Sigrid looked into the flames. She could hardly remain upright on the bench. The baby in her belly kicked as if he were trying to break her back. Sigrid moaned, and Haldis gave her a look of disapproval.

"Childbirth is the battlefield of women," Haldis chastised. "They must withstand it just as bravely as men do battle."

The Svea women all nodded in agreement, as did Alfhild and Jorun, who sat sewing with the others. It annoyed Sigrid that although neither of her kinswomen had ever given birth, even they seemed to find Sigrid a little too delicate.

Sigrid clenched her teeth in anger. She really had no use for know-it-alls, not now, when it felt like she was going to be split in two. And this was one of her better days. Lately she had been so weak that she sometimes hadn't been able to leave her bed and couldn't stomach anything more than the warm milk Jorun brought in the mornings.

"I couldn't eat for several moons when I was pregnant with Virun, and it took two days of labor before she was born, but I didn't complain about it," said Haldis's sister Ingrid.

"The king's son kicks with the strength of Thor," Haldis said, and everyone laughed.

Curse them all. Sigrid doubled over as a jab of pain cut right through her belly. Emma came over next to her right away and held her hand.

"Something's wrong," Sigrid whispered, her forehead breaking out into a cold sweat.

"It's not time yet," Haldis said in an attempt to comfort her.

"I'll take you to your bed," Emma said, trying to help Sigrid stand up.

The floor swayed beneath her, and everything went blurry.

"Help me," Emma hissed to Jorun, who methodically set her needlework aside.

Alfhild and Solveig responded more quickly to Emma's plea and helped Sigrid toward the stairs. Something was wrong with the baby. Sigrid knew it. She forced herself forward, step-by-step, while the jabs of pain just got worse. Finally she fell into the darkness.

ᛢ

Sweyn stopped in the doorway in surprise, seeing his mother sitting up and sewing his battle flag even though it was the middle of the night.

"You're still awake?" he asked, undoing his sword belt.

His body ached after the long cold days on the field where he was training the men. Still, it was worth it. The archers weren't as good as they should be yet, but the warriors had eventually learned to form a wedge shape.

"I want to finish your pride," she said, looking up from her needle-work with a smile.

The light from the lamp danced over the deep wrinkles below her eyes.

"You should rest, not work so late," he said.

"Nonsense. Are you hungry? Gren can get the fire going and heat you up some food."

The slave got up and waited, her eyes down. Sweyn shook his head and walked over to his mother and looked at the light-blue flag, his heart swelling with pride. He'd been wondering for a long time what symbol he ought to adopt as his own. The flag was the symbol his men would follow in battle and would be displayed behind him one day when he sat on Harald's throne. It was something to choose with care. Mother was sewing up the last of the brightly colored pattern with the finest of stitches. It twisted around the hammer of Thor, which was being held by a howling wolf. Sweyn had never seen anything like it. The handwork was so well done and colorful that he couldn't take his eyes off it.

"It's a masterpiece," he said, running his hand over the embroidery work.

His mother smiled, pleased.

"Every stitch has been a pleasure. It will go with you as you conquer the world. When your standard bearer holds it high and thousands of warriors follow you into battle, a part of me will always be with you, my son, my pride and joy."

Sweyn put his hand on hers and firmly grasped it.

"You'll see it happen."

She burst into a hacking cough that went on for a long time, and then their eyes met.

"I'll be dead soon."

Sweyn stared down at the floor. He'd known it for a long time, but even now he didn't want to believe it was true.

"I'll go to the afterworld with honor and my name restored. Don't grieve for me, Sweyn, not even you with your strong will can do anything about it. Be happy about this last bit of time we've had together, when you made me prouder than any mother could be. I've gotten to watch you take your first steps toward the greatness you will achieve, so I can die in peace."

Sweyn stared at the floorboards in silence.

"No," he said firmly. "You're not going to die yet. You'll see me take my place on the Jelling throne."

"Not even you can change my fate."

The silence between them grew.

"Are you planning to tell me about her, or are you planning to remain silent until it's too late?" his mother finally said.

"Who?" he asked, running his hand over his head.

"The girl you carry here." With an amused grin, she put her hand on his heart and then went back to her sewing. "A mother notices these things, even if you try to hide them. I persuaded Beyla to tell me a few things, although hers is not an easy tongue to get wagging. Tell me now, because I've been waiting a long time for you to say something."

Sweyn nodded to the slave, who set out a plate of bread and cheese on the table along with a cup of small beer.

"You'll meet her in the spring after I fetch her and my child, who will have been born by then."

Just saying those words filled him with a rare sense of warmth. It would be a son to raise, a copy of himself, or a girl who was like Sigrid. A whole clan of smaller versions of themselves would eventually come, but this would be their first.

"My son is going to be a father. You couldn't give me better news."

His mother looked so happy that Sweyn regretted not having told her sooner.

"Now you see that you can't go and die," he said. "Sigrid is strong and of noble birth, blessed by Freya herself. She is unmatched among women. She is my queen."

His mother nodded to herself and sewed another stitch before fixing her eyes on him again.

"If this is your will, then I know it will happen."

Sweyn took a piece of bread from the plate, feeling content. Finally there was someone who understood that he was going to have Sigrid no matter the cost.

"It must be bad sorcery. Only a curse can work this fast," Solveig said, uneasily eyeing Sigrid, who was lying in her bed in a fever trance, tossing and turning and mumbling senselessly.

Haldis sat on the edge of the bed and nodded grimly before pointing to Virun, who stood in the doorway.

"Go to the priestesses. Take a couple of the men with you."

The girl nodded and left right away while Haldis anxiously wiped the sweat from Sigrid's forehead.

"You have to survive. Erik needs his son."

Emma watched, paralyzed, as Sigrid slipped away toward the afterworld. The room stank of rot and death, and the dark shadows of the corpse eaters moved menacingly around the bed, ready to extinguish her sister's life. *Get thee gone, cursed darkness.*

Emma dug her fingernails into her face and whimpered in pain as she dragged them over her skin. This couldn't happen. Kára was inside her and protecting Sigrid and the baby, and yet she had no idea what to do. Emma had prayed and pleaded for Kára to intercede, but the capricious dís wasn't responding. Powerless, Emma was forced to watch the glow fading from the protective charms that had been carved into the door frame. The iron under the bed did make the shadows hesitate, and yet they still gathered expectantly around Sigrid's weak body. Sigrid grew increasingly tired and ever weaker, as if some evil were slowly poisoning her, her beloved sister. The blood trickled from the gashes Emma had dug in her cheeks, and her body trembled. Sigrid was dying before her eyes, and she couldn't do anything about it.

"You've seen enough. Get going," Haldis yelled at the women who crowded around the bed and the doorway.

The Svea women and Sigrid's own kinswomen reluctantly left the room. They were anxious, as if they feared both for her life and their own.

"Why don't you protect her?" Haldis angrily demanded of Emma. "You, who can summon the rain and predict the future, save my grandson."

Emma had no answer to give. She crawled over to the bed, took Sigrid's hand, and held it to her bleeding cheek. *Beloved sister, come back to me,* she prayed. *Don't leave me.*

The queen mother scoffed and took off a leather pouch she had been wearing around her neck. She put it on Sigrid's belly and whispered something into her ear, an ineffective spell. Sigrid tossed her head from side to side. Her face blazed red, and her eyes were glassy, staring vacantly into the hidden world.

"Nothing's working," Haldis said in exasperation and turned to Emma. "Save my grandson, or you'll hang to death in the oak tree at dawn. I swear it."

Just then Kára percolated back to life inside Emma. She had only a faint intuition, but it was enough.

She took a firmer hold of Sigrid's hand and sent all her strength into Sigrid. Closing her eyes, she stretched herself deep into her sister and felt the poison that was coursing through her blood. Though

Sigrid's mind was deep in the hidden world, Emma was almost able to reach her with the tips of her fingers, but then the connection was broken, and Emma fell out of the spirit world and back onto the bed beside Sigrid.

"Well, did you succeed?" asked Haldis and snorted in dissatisfaction when Emma shook her head. "Let us hope, then, that the priestesses can save our queen, because otherwise we're lost."

ᚴ

The grayish-black fog closed in around Sigrid like a damp embrace, and yet she wasn't cold, and the pain was gone. All that remained was the blessed emptiness and the foreboding she knew so well from the dreams she'd had. She had never realized before that she was wandering through the afterworld, so different from Freya's glittering golden Folkvang that she had anticipated. But all that had little meaning now; nothing was important anymore.

Sigrid looked blankly at the pale shadows wandering past in the mist—emaciated children with sunken cheeks, stooped old people, women with babes in arms, old warriors with bent backs—who could be glimpsed and would then disappear. They were all walking east, enticed by the sound of a huge river that drew them toward it. A distant voice, quiet as a whisper, called to her from far off, but she couldn't turn around. Nothing had any meaning anymore. Without any will of her own, she followed the stream of dead people into the void, toward Hvergelmir's spring in Niflheim. Her life dissolved away with every step, like fog on a summer morning when a breeze sweeps in off the sea. Sweyn and the baby were the last to leave her. Apathetically, she let them run off and disappear as if they had never been there. Emptiness was reflected in the pale bodies that wandered beside her. *Small grains of sand, small seas, small are the minds of men.* There was no suffering here, no joy or sorrow. They were all liberated by the vast emptiness.

Sigrid looked up at the gate to Hel's nine realms, which towered above her. Gigantic and made of bones and human skulls, the gate was wide open so the dead could wander into the afterworld. The voice called to Sigrid, this time even more faintly. The noise from the bubbling cauldron of Hvergelmir, the source of everything, where the rivers had their torrents, drowned everything as it called to her. Sigrid couldn't do anything but obey the pull. With no will of her own, she kept going and barely thought of the unknown being that was approaching.

Sweyn looked up at the sun, which was covered in its winter garb, concealed in the darkening sky. Something was wrong—he could feel it in every bone in his body. His worry for Sigrid had been aching like a wound in his chest all day, and now, as he watched the sinking sun, his foreboding grew into certainty. The link between them had broken. Her presence—which otherwise was constant, as if she were standing beside him, so close that he could smell her and feel the warmth from her skin—was gone. Something must have happened to her and the baby, otherwise she wouldn't have vanished.

Sweyn rubbed his fist over his heart to quiet the pain, as real as if he'd been stabbed in the chest. If anyone hurt her, he would flay the skin off him or her, piece by piece. He swore it.

"Vanadís, Thor, I call on you. Protect my Sigrid."

That moment, the sun went behind a cloud, and darkness fell over Jómsborg. Sweyn shook his head in distress over this bad omen as worry ached throughout his body. Damn it that he wasn't with her, that he couldn't protect her. His powerlessness ate at his body.

Just let her still be alive. He looked back up at the sky. Sigrid had to live and give birth to their baby. She was the only pure and precious thing in his life, and without her there was no meaning to anything he did. Everything was for her sake.

He clenched his fists and looked despondently at the mud under the rags he had wrapped around his frostbitten fingers. If only he could be by her side. Then he could protect her and keep her safe from everything and not let anyone hurt her. He should never have let go of her in Lejre. The thought that Erik of Svealand was enjoying her company tortured Sweyn night and day.

Damn it all!

A cry made him look up. Åke came running across the muddy field, waving to him.

"They're fighting again," Åke cried, panting. "I think there might be some fatalities this time."

Sweyn looked up at the sky one last time and then walked over to Åke, his heart heavy. The fully qualified Jómsvíkings who served him were still having a hard time putting up with the less-well-trained men, which was easy to understand, but they were pushing the new recruits too far and beating the worst among them too severely.

"They're not going to improve if they have broken legs," Sweyn bellowed angrily and started running toward the men's training grounds.

↑

Sigrid regarded the stranger who was disturbing her journey with apathy. As the dead were walking toward Hel, a young woman, not much older than herself, came walking toward her, away from Hel. She stopped in front of Sigrid, shrouded in gray fog.

Her face was half burned away, like the mistress of the kingdom of the dead, and her clothes hung charred on her frail, thin body. But her eyes were filled with such tender love that they pierced Sigrid's apathy, all the way to the woman she once was.

"Mama?" Sigrid whispered so quietly that the words were drowned out by the thundering waters of the source of everything, Hvergelmir.

Her dead mother's smile was just a ripple on the woman's lips as she reached out her arm, frail and transparent, to stroke Sigrid's cheek. This gentle caress burned Sigrid's skin and made her apathy crumble away to dust. She was in her mother's arms again, safe, being sung to sleep.

The veils that lay over her mother lifted, the burn injuries faded, and her mother stood before her, young and beautiful, with rosy cheeks and wavy blond hair just the way Sigrid remembered her.

"I've missed you so much," Sigrid whispered, tears streaming down her cheeks.

Her mother smiled gently, and her eyes filled with such a loving sorrow that Sigrid could feel her yearning. Then her mother took her hand, and the next moment they were back in Sigrid's childhood nightmare. The burning wooden hall was filled with the screams of the dying, who lay side by side with the dead. Three women tugged at the locked door. A baby lay next to them, its skull crushed.

Her mother lay lifeless on the floor, bleeding from a gash in her back, and Sigrid lay underneath her. She was three years old. Screaming and crying, she pounded on her mother with her little clenched fists, trying to get out from underneath her heavy body. Sigrid gasped for breath under her mother's body as fear tore her to pieces. She cried for her mother and pummeled her as the flames came ever closer.

Then her mother lifted her head and looked around at the flames and the smoke. Her face was chalky white and blood was pouring from her back. She forced herself, coughing, to her feet. She took Sigrid by the hand and dragged her over to the wall. She was dying; she shouldn't have had the strength, but with her face locked in determination, she pulled her toward a narrow window, step-by-step. It was only an opening to let in light, too small for a grown-up, but enough for a child. With a scream of pain, her mother picked Sigrid up in her arms, and the child clung terrified to her neck.

"No, Sigrid, you're going to live," her mother said and, sobbing, kissed her hair.

The flames were close now. With a roar they consumed the floorboards, racing toward them.

Her mother yanked Sigrid's arms away from her neck. Bellowing with pain, she shoved Sigrid through the window opening. She held on to her hand and let her fall softly the last little bit of the way onto the grass. The child Sigrid looked up at her mother, still standing at the narrow opening where the smoke was billowing out.

"Run, Sigrid! You have to hide. Run, now!"

The child Sigrid hesitated, then turned her back on the building and ran toward the woods. Inside the building her mother collapsed to the floor, and with a smile she leaned her head against the wall as the smoke and flames killed her.

The vision disappeared and they were back on the path that led to the kingdom of the dead.

"It was you!" Sigrid said, wiping away the tears that were running down her cheeks.

Her whole life she had wondered who had saved her from the flames. She had never realized that it was her mother who had defied death for a few moments so that she could live. Nor had Sigrid realized that her mother was still watching over her from the realm of the dead.

"Thank you," she whispered.

Her mother smiled and took her hand again. Without a word she started to go, but not toward the rushing waters of Hvergelmir. Instead she was leading Sigrid away from the realm of the dead, through the gate, and back to the borderland.

The voice that had called to her before could be heard more clearly now, and her mother was leading Sigrid toward it. The mists started to ease up, and it grew lighter and lighter. Finally her mother stopped. Sigrid understood. Her mother couldn't come any farther. She opened her mouth to tell her everything that was on her mind, how she missed her and how grateful she was, but her mother put her finger to her lips and shook her head, smiling. She already knew everything, and Sigrid didn't need to say a word.

With one last caress of her cheek, Sigrid's mother sent her on her way into the light, toward life. Sigrid took a wheezing, gasping breath, and she was back in her pregnant body.

◆ ◆ ◆

"Thank Vanadís, thank all the goddesses in Valhalla," Emma said.

Emma's face floated like fog above her. Her mouth was moving, but Sigrid couldn't hear what she was saying. Sigrid closed her eyes and could feel that the knives of pain were no longer cutting at her belly. She had seen her mother. Memories swept through her body, washing away the poison that had almost killed her. She swallowed and noted the bitter taste of vomit in her mouth. Her mother was watching over her and protecting her in everything.

"I thought you were gone for good," Emma said.

"The baby?" Sigrid whispered, moving her hand to her belly.

"He's alive," Emma said somberly.

Emma helped her lift her head and drink water from a cup. The cool drink washed a little of the taste from her mouth. Sigrid coughed and realized she really needed to pee. She looked around. The room was empty apart from Emma, who sat by the bedside. A pitcher of water and a bowl sat on a stool by the bed, and next to that there were several rags.

"You've been unconscious for three days and nights," Emma said gently. Her eyes were rimmed in red, from exhaustion and tears. Her face was ashen, and her hair hung uncombed on her shoulders.

"Not even Kára could reach you in Hel's borderland, nor the priestesses, who cast their most powerful spells over you. I thought you were lost, that you were both going to die."

The baby moved in Sigrid's belly, as if to let them know he was still alive. Sigrid swallowed with difficulty and drank a little more water.

"I was almost there when my mother made me turn around." She smiled and knew that she'd never be able to explain what had happened to anyone, not even Emma. Becoming aware of her mother's love had healed something deep inside her. Her mother had given her her life and then saved it twice. No love was greater.

Aside from yours, All-Mother.

"Did your mother say anything?" Emma asked.

"Not a word," Sigrid said sadly, shaking her head. Then she trained her eyes on Emma and asked, "Were you the one calling me?"

Emma looked down and nodded.

"I called to you for three days and three nights."

"I heard you. You made me come home," Sigrid said. "Do you know why I fell ill?"

Emma made an awful face.

"All I know is that you had poison in you, but I don't know who gave it to you."

Sigrid inhaled and felt the weakness creeping through her body. But she had to be strong. They would punish whomever was guilty, so severely that he or she would die screaming in pain.

Only two of the spears hit the stacked straw bales they had set up in the field. An instant later, more archers' arrows thudded into the straw. Sweyn watched the warriors with pride, shivering in the cold on the snow-covered training ground. Lean and sinewy, like strong wolves, they were all grinning. The long days of training had succeeded in making warriors out of them in spite of all the challenges.

"You have fought long and well, and for this you will be rewarded," Sweyn yelled, grinning at their hopeful faces. "During Yule you will rest. And now, two pigs will be slaughtered to fill your plates tonight."

The men cheered at the gift. It was important to reward hard work, and the extra food was worth the silver it cost.

"Go, and may your gods bless you," he said.

The line of warriors broke up as they left the field.

"We may make men out of them yet," Sweyn said, turning to Ax-Wolf, Sigvard, and Åke.

"I'm not so sure about that, but at least they're not completely incompetent," Ax-Wolf said, obviously feeling relieved at the work that had been accomplished.

Sigvard raised an eyebrow and said, "A quarter of them are good warriors. They're the valuable ones. Half of them are eager kids who want to make a name for themselves in battle. They'll be the first to fall."

"And what about the last quarter?" Sweyn asked, watching his soldiers wandering across the field, joking and talking.

"They lack the will for battle and stick to the rear of the line. They never do any more than they have to."

Sweyn nodded somberly and said, "Then they must be tempered so as not to feel fear."

"Let them do the hoarfrost dance," said Åke, grinning. "That really drove the fear of death out of us."

Sweyn couldn't help but smile at the memory. When they were nine, he and Åke had been put out in the woods in the middle of the freezing winter, each with a knife as his only weapon. For three days and three nights they were not allowed to approach any farm or people. They had to survive on their own in the dark among the giants.

"If you hadn't managed to make a fire, we'd be wandering around in the afterworld right now," Sweyn said, laughing.

"Well, that rabbit you snared helped, too," Åke said.

"It's decided, then," said Ax-Wolf, and together they headed toward Jómsborg's gates. "After Yule, we'll start putting them out."

Ragnvald, the boy Sweyn had hired on the beach in Lejre, came walking along with his fellow soldiers, and when he spotted Sweyn he grinned. He looked older and stronger, but he had a terrible limp.

"What happened to your foot?" Sweyn asked.

"Nothing," the boy replied stoically.

His shoe leather was worn shiny and there was straw poking out of a big hole in one of his shoes.

"Don't lie, boy," Sweyn barked. "You won't be any good with frostbitten feet. You need new shoes. Next time speak up."

"Thank you, chieftain," Ragnvald said, bowing his head.

"Get him some new wool clothes, too," Sweyn told Åke as they watched Ragnvald hurry away after his buddies.

"The chest of silver is almost empty. Your and my share of the plunder from England has been gone for a long time. Only a little bit of what Ax-Wolf gave us remains."

"Can we make it to the spring sacrifice?" Sweyn asked.

"Not even if the men do well with their trapping in the woods."

The cost of keeping his own men was greater than Sweyn could have dreamt. Ships and crews gobbled up silver at a ridiculous pace, and everyone always wanted something from him. Life had been so much easier as one of Palna's warriors.

"I'll get more money. Buy what Ragnvald needs and don't worry. In Svealand we'll bring in a real haul, and then silver won't be a concern anymore."

It would have to be so, otherwise he was going to wind up in massive debt. But hungry wolves hunted best, and Sweyn would be victorious against the Svea. He had to believe that.

"You could borrow some from Father," Åke said, teasing him.

Sweyn nodded. Palna would demand again that he marry his own sister, but even if Sweyn refused he would get the money. He was sure of that.

They walked through the tall gates and onto the main street where the market was in full swing. The ground was frozen, and the air was so clear and fresh that it bit at their faces. However, Jómsborg's streets were filled with off-duty warriors and farmers who crowded the market stands. Most of the men were gathered around a dark-haired merchant from the North, who had an animal pelt covered with Thor hammers, crosses, sun crosses, and other amulets with foreign symbols on them honoring unknown gods. There was freedom of religion in Jómsborg. Palna was careful to see to that, and the merchant was doing good business.

"If we have the cash, we ought to gather around the mead barrel tonight," Åke said, stopping in front of a stand and inspecting some sturdy leather shoes.

"We surely will," Sweyn said, smiling at his brother.

It would be a good Yule, and everything would work out for the best. He didn't even worry about Sigrid anymore. Whatever he'd felt must have simply been in his imagination.

"Master." He turned and saw the house slave standing next to him, shivering with cold, her head bowed.

"Palna sent a messenger for you. You are to go to his house immediately."

Sweyn and his brother exchanged glances. For once things were going as they should, so hopefully there was no mischief afoot.

Father's hall was filled with strangers when Sweyn stepped into its warmth. As he walked over to the fire, he carefully inspected the faces, but he didn't recognize any of them.

Palna stood with a nobleman with a gray beard and the eagle eye of a scarred warrior. His tunic was made of silk, and his wool cloak was trimmed with beaver fur. He was clearly a powerful man of great wealth. Sweyn bowed his head humbly.

"We've never met, but I'm Valdemar," the man said in the voice of a commander. "I've come to assist you in the battle against King Harald, the dog who was once my brother."

A bulge was visible in the vast surface of Sigrid's enormous belly, as if the baby were trying to push his way to freedom right through the front of her body. Sigrid smiled and ran her hand over the stretched skin. The tenderness she felt took her breath away. *My beautiful boy, my beloved son.*

"Calm down, your time hasn't come yet," she chided him. Her words seemed to quiet him, because he settled down, and she was able to breathe freely again and go back to getting dressed.

"The Scylfing blood must be strong in him," Alfhild said, helping her pull her dress over her head, the dress that had been restitched to fit her swelling body.

Her belly was so big that the women kept saying they'd never seen anything like it, that it seemed like she was carrying a whole mountain around.

"Well, Erik's family aren't really wallflowers either. That's one thing I know all too well after carrying and giving birth to eleven of them," Solveig said as she sat on the foot of Sigrid's bed, sewing. She looked up and gave her daughter Fridborg, who had also started waiting on Sigrid, a knowing look. She got a smile in response.

"A lot of kicking means a healthy baby. That's what my grand-mother used to say," said Sigrid, taking the cloak Emma held out to her and wrapping it around her shoulders. "I'm looking forward to showing the king how his son is thriving."

Erik had returned in the middle of the night with his entire retinue after being away for months. Sigrid had been afraid he would visit her in her room and had lain in bed listening for his footsteps. Instead his men's laughter had echoed through the hall until dawn. Now she could no longer put off the discussion she needed to have with Erik.

Ever since her mother had rescued her from the afterworld, she'd been thinking about how to protect herself and the baby from the unknown enemy who had almost put an end to her life. Now she'd found her answer, and she truly hoped Erik would welcome it.

But her words about visiting Erik had caused the women to stiffen and Alfhild to look away. Sigrid knew all too well who was missing and had an idea what she could expect. She buttoned her cloak and left her chamber with her head held high.

Both Axel and Orm were in the king's retinue, who were eating breakfast when she went downstairs to the hall. They stood up right away and despite their fatigue, they greeted her with pleasure.

"Erik's son will truly be born big and strong," said Orm, looking admiringly at her belly.

"We received word of the evil deed that almost ended your life," Axel said somberly. "I swear on my honor that the guilty party will be found and made to pay."

Sigrid had no doubt he would keep his word.

"Where is my king?"

A shadow came over Axel's face.

"The king is still resting and shouldn't be disturbed," Orm said quickly.

"Surely he'd like a visit from his queen after his long absence," Sigrid said and smiled pleasantly at the men.

Axel stood up, gave her a pleading look, and said, "Wait, my queen. Let me fetch him."

It was obvious that Erik wasn't alone in bed, but Sigrid did not intend to allow them to stall her. Her errand was too important for that.

"I decide where I go in my own hall," she said, climbing the stairs with difficulty.

She recognized the woman's laugh she heard from inside the bedchamber right away. It was as she had thought. Sigrid opened the door without knocking.

Jorun lay naked on Erik's bed, her legs spread and her hair a mess. She sat up, but her face was not filled with horror—more a triumphant gloat. Erik rolled off her and stared at Sigrid in astonishment.

"By Odin's fist! Why, you're as big as a boulder, wife!"

Sigrid looked at Jorun. Erik had sex with all the womenfolk. Still, she did not plan to tolerate her own kinswoman and maidservant willingly parting her legs for her husband. Jorun had finally gone too far. In silence she watched Jorun pull her dress on over her head with a smile and put her shoes on without any sense of urgency. Then Jorun nodded her head in parting to Erik, who leaned contentedly back in the bed, following her with his eyes as she left the room.

Sigrid did not speak until the door was closed.

"So, you've taken Jorun as your mistress?"

Erik laughed, unconcerned, and said, "Oh, she'll never occupy that role. I just wanted her. Come have a seat, wife, so I can look at you." He patted the bed with his hand. "You look like a swelling flower bud about to bloom."

Sigrid remained standing, filled with contempt for her husband.

She had been chosen, had created a life, and had traveled into the afterworld and back. Three times people had tried to kill her, and still she had managed to stay alive. Erik had scarcely been wounded in battle, and in some ways he couldn't measure up to her in strength. And yet she was forced to serve him as wife and queen. Sigrid swallowed. She had never wished more fervently that Sweyn would dispatch him to Niflheim.

"Did you receive the chieftains' support?" she asked. It took all her self-control to keep her voice civil.

A shadow came over Erik's face, and it was clear that things hadn't gone as well as he'd wished.

"That's none of your concern. Let me feel your breasts. They're the biggest I've seen."

Sigrid clenched her teeth. Her back ached, and the baby was moving, making her need to pee. Still, she had to let Erik do what he wanted.

"I know how you can unify more chieftains under your rule, husband."

"I'm grateful for the success you've had here at home," Erik said, giving her a disinterested look. "You've played the role I gave you splendidly, but that doesn't mean the king is going to listen to advice from a Scylfing wife."

Give me strength.

Sigrid tried in vain to halt the rage that erupted from her in a torrent. She'd put up with everything that this wretchedness had subjected her to, but now this was enough.

"Someone nearly murdered me and your son, and still you are thinking more about sleeping around than about protecting those nearest you."

"Bridle your tongue, woman. You are speaking to your husband and king."

"Who are you to call yourself king when you don't even protect your unborn child?"

Erik leapt out of bed and reached her in only two steps.

"Now you will be silent!" he said so fiercely that spittle hit her face.

Sigrid smiled at his ridiculous rage.

"I can see why the chieftains are leaving you in the lurch. A wimp of a man who can't defend his own farm can never protect a whole kingdom."

Erik's fist struck her on the cheek so hard that she almost fell. The pain reverberated through her head, burning through skin and skull. Sigrid stood up taller and calmly looked him in the eye.

"The truth hurts you so badly that you have to hit someone defenseless, you poor cockless creature."

Erik's face was bright red with rage when he raised his fist again. The veins in his face bulged, but Sigrid wasn't afraid. Every blow showed what an unmanly wretch he was. With the cool of a frost giant, she looked him in the eye. They sized each other up in silence. Then Erik screamed out his rage, a loud, crazed howl, and then turned away.

Sigrid's lips curled as she rubbed her hot cheek. Erik paced back and forth across the floor, still naked.

"Don't you understand the burden I'm carrying to save Svealand, woman? Why won't you support your husband?"

Had she done anything but that? Sigrid put her hand on her enormous belly. She had very little energy to listen to him whining about how heavy his cloak was. It was his turn to listen.

"Protect your son's life," she demanded. "Proclaim him king at the midwinter sacrifice while he is still in my womb. Then the dynasty of Erik has an heir even if you fall in battle. It will strengthen you as king and secure your son's life."

It was the wisest move Erik could make, yet his eyes were filled with scorn.

"Like a loose woman, you screwed a common Jómsvíking before you came to my bed. Now you want your bastard proclaimed king. It'd be hard to find anything more disloyal than this."

This was bad. Sigrid bit her cheek. Now she understood why Erik showed her such contempt. If she wavered now, both she and the baby would die.

"That is a malicious lie and you know it," she said calmly.

Erik's laugh sounded like a growl.

"I do? I don't remember any blood when we first lay together."

"I do," she lied, without breaking their staring contest.

Jorun must somehow have found out what happened and told Erik about the sacrifice. Her kinswoman's treachery was greater than she'd thought. Sigrid took a deep breath and forced herself to keep her voice steady.

"Anyone spreading such lies about me is clearly serving Styrbjörn. Surely it's the same person who poisoned your son and me. Are you planning to assist this spreader of lies or stamp out the enemy who advances Styrbjörn's cause?"

Erik pulled his pants over to him from where he'd slung them on the floor. He put them on and reached for his dagger, which was on the clothing chest, and slowly pulled the blade out of the sheath.

"If I am right, my honor requires me to kill you."

He really meant it. Erik's eyes were vacant as he moved the blade through the air just in front of her throat and then down over her belly, gently, almost lovingly. Sweat trickled down Sigrid's spine.

Turn his insanity around. Give him some of your rationality. Don't leave me now, I pray you.

"A rumor that your queen is carrying another man's son comes from Styrbjörn or disloyal Svea chieftains to taunt you," she said. "Few will want to fight at your side, and you'll lose everything you have. You will be remembered forever as the man who lost Svealand to the cross worshippers."

Her voice almost broke when she saw the look in Erik's eyes. He was teetering on the edge of madness, and if he fell, he would plunge the dagger into her.

Please don't let him hurt my son. Take my life, but save my child.

In vain she held her hands over her belly.

Madness still in his eyes, Erik said, "I married you to secure the borders in the southwest and because I needed a son. I couldn't have made a worse mistake, because your duplicity and bloated body make me sick. Fools might believe that you were chosen by Vanadís, but neither you nor the priests are fooling me with your Valhalla. It's all empty pretense spun of air, serving false gods, made up by lying, greedy priests who covet sacrificial gifts."

Sigrid flinched. Svealand's king could not renounce the gods!

"Don't blaspheme," she pleaded.

Erik put the blade to her throat again: cold metal against skin and just one heartbeat from death.

"I hope you die in childbed and that my son survives. That would be the best."

The baby kicked so hard that Sigrid could hardly stand upright. She felt the shivers coming.

Give me the strength to overcome this denier.

"You need both me and your son for the chieftains to want to fight Styrbjörn," she whispered. "Proclaim the baby king at the midwinter sacrifice. Then the chieftains will willingly fight for you, and you will kill the lies. They will hail you as a manly king and not mock you as a weakling."

"I would rather die than be fettered to you and your bastard."

Sigrid closed her eyes. This was it. She was going to die here now by her own husband's hand.

"The baby I carry is yours, your own flesh and blood. Do you trust a Scylfing maidservant of low birth, a foreigner, more than the daughter of a chieftain, your queen?"

The darting look he gave her confirmed Sigrid's suspicion. Jorun was the one who had turned Erik against her.

"I have no reason not to believe her words," he said, the blade trembling in his hands.

"Yes, you do, Erik," said a calm, male voice.

Relief flooded through Sigrid. It was over. *Thank you for protecting me from his insanity.*

Axel had stepped unnoticed into the room, and he walked right up to the king without showing any concern.

"Leave us," Erik ordered. "Without you I'd have been free of her."

But Axel shook his head and said, "Without her you wouldn't have a son to present or have the Scylfings on your side. Lower your dagger. Proclaim the baby king. Put your dynasty and Svealand before yourself."

The true power behind the king was speaking.

Erik looked grim.

"How can you stand by her? She's a foreigner. Her people killed your son. Have you forgotten that?"

Axel's face remained completely calm.

"I'll do anything for Svealand, as should you if you're worthy of your throne."

The look Axel gave Erik seemed to rein him in. Erik sat down on the bed, glaring at them in disgust.

"Is this going to lure the Fredes and Hågvard's people to the battlefield?"

"I don't know that for certain. But I do know that if you let the rumor spread that your queen is carrying a bastard, everyone will turn their backs on you."

Erik clenched his fists so hard that his knuckles went white. He sat there in silence for a long time before he finally nodded.

"Then that's what we'll do," he said, his voice choked with anger. "Damn you for binding me to this duplicitous woman."

For the first time since he'd entered the room, Axel looked at Sigrid.

"It is decided," he said.

Sigrid had won. The baby's life was saved. She nodded briefly and walked calmly to the door so as not to show how frightened she had been by the king's insanity. Only once her back was turned to them did she permit herself to smile.

"Indulge your husband," Axel said. "Support him in his hour of difficulty."

Sigrid turned around.

"Of course," she replied. "I apologize for leaving you. I'm having some difficulties with my domestic staff that I need to attend to."

She had won, but rumors were hard to quash. They spread like weeds, nourished by people's ill will. The baby wouldn't be safe for sure until Jorun's poison was completely obliterated.

Axel bowed his head.

"It does you credit that you maintain control over your domestic staff. Don't hesitate to ask my wife for help. She is quite skilled in this domain."

They exchanged a look of mutual understanding, and Sigrid could not have felt any more grateful to Axel.

"I will do as you suggest," she replied and was finally able to leave the king's room.

Sigrid shut the door and leaned against it while Emma regarded her weakness with concern. This was no time to curl up in misery, not yet, not now, when she needed to fight for her honor and the life of her child.

They had to find out what had happened. Someone had put a curse on Sigrid, and she had been so weak from poison that she'd almost died. Emma needed to find out everything she could about the night when Toste raped her. Sigrid would have to talk to Haldis and Solveig herself. Without them on her side, she couldn't weave the web that would be needed to catch Jorun.

"We have a lot to do," Sigrid said sternly.

This time that bitch would get what she had coming to her.

ᚾ

Sweyn stared into the fire, still moved by the news Valdemar had brought to Jómsborg. King Harald had murdered Henning, Valdemar's only remaining son. One night Henning was helping a very drunk Harald into bed and, for no reason, Harald pulled his knife and stabbed Henning to death. The act was so shameful no one had heard its like. Sweyn swallowed his hatred for his birth father as desire for power surged through his veins. Harald's shamefulness would turn out to be his own lucky break.

"If you fight against the king, I will stand with you," Valdemar told him.

"Why don't you fight him yourself?" Sweyn asked. "Doesn't the throne of the Danes entice you, leader of the Jellings?"

Valdemar smiled joylessly at the insubordinate question.

"I've laid four sons on funeral pyres, and now Harald has heinously extinguished the hopes I had for Henning. All that remains for me before I drink with my sons in Valhalla is revenge."

Sweyn eyed his birth uncle with respect. Valdemar was an honorable man, the leader of the Jellings, sent by the gods. With Valdemar's support, Sweyn's claim to the throne would be taken seriously, because Valdemar had both the men and the money to back up the campaign.

"I am so grateful that you choose to fight with me," Sweyn said.

"Everything my brother built in his youth will be gone soon. Emperor Otto has conquered Danevirke. The ancient earthwork fortifications no longer protect the Danes' and Jutes' lands. Of the five ring castles, once filled with dreaded warriors who guaranteed peace and free passage, only Jómsborg remains strong. Harald, foolish and filled with the incompetence of insanity, can't hold together the kingdom he took from our father, Gorm the Old. Danish and Jutish lands are being torn apart as people fight for pieces of what Harald once built but can no longer hold on to. Petty chieftains are fighting each other, brothers against brothers, believers against cross worshippers."

Valdemar stared into the flames. Light and shadow danced over the old man's face as he remembered days gone by.

"I know that the gods fed your anger in Lejre's royal hall, where you demanded your birthright, unafraid and without weakness," Valdemar said, studying Sweyn closely. "From that moment, word of your strength has spread. Of all Harald's sons, you are the only one who was raised to be strong in the face of iron, ice, and death. Only a young warrior, so full of hunger for power and victory that he is not afraid, has the strength to take and to hold the throne of the Jellings."

Sweyn bowed his head, carefully concealing how much the old man's words pleased him.

"If you back me up," Sweyn said, "I will kill Harald in the name of your son Henning."

Relief flooded Valdemar's face, lined with age and grief, and he said, "Let's have a seat and discuss how this can best be accomplished."

Jorun smiled arrogantly as the housecarls led her into the women's room. Wearing a clean dress, her back straight, and her dark hair braided in a wreath on her head, she clearly had no idea what was going to happen, but she was going to face it with dignity.

Alfhild was not so calm. She was wringing her hands and looking around anxiously as she sat down on the bench that had been placed in the middle of the room.

Sigrid sat on the throne that had been placed before the bench. Solveig and Haldis stood by her side and a double row of noblewomen crowded around the perimeter of the room. They had come from near and far to attend the midwinter sacrifice and when Sigrid summoned them, they joined in willingly. Three of the temple's foremost priestesses also stood among them, and they bent their heads graciously before their queen. Because of the crowd it was already hot and stuffy in the room, but it was important that a lot of people witness and discuss what was about to happen.

Sigrid looked at the kinswomen she had known and trusted since she was a child. She had been blinded by the blood ties and by her affection for them, but now her eyes were wide open.

"I accuse you, Jorun of the Scylfings, of spreading false lies about the identity of my child's father," Sigrid said. "With malevolence, you dripped poison into the ear of my beloved husband, the honorable king Erik, to sow dissention and ruin my honor."

Jorun's lips curled in scorn.

"The honor you speak of has never existed," Jorun retorted. "You went off into the woods in Lejre to sleep with that Jómsvíking, Sweyn. You spoke together tenderly and exchanged lustful looks. I saw it happen. I saw it with my own eyes. By Freya and all the goddesses, I swear I am telling the truth."

The noble-born but gossip-hungry Svea ladies whispered excitedly among themselves, gobbling up these words. No accusation could be worse than that their queen was expecting another man's baby.

You foolish bitch. Sigrid clenched her hands in contemptuous rage. Bitterness and envy must have rotted Jorun's mind if she thought Sigrid was going to sit by and let her spread her poison over Svealand.

She nodded to Emma, who was waiting, eager to stick the first dagger into Jorun's back.

"Everything you say is a lie," Emma said. "Sigrid and the Jómsvíking were never alone in Lejre. The seeress Beyla and I were with them. The four of us went to the oak grove to make a sacrifice in secret, to avoid Harald's ban on the old religion." Emma, her face contorted, pointed at Jorun. "Shame on you for insulting the honor of your queen and kinswoman with filthy lies when she was honoring Valhalla on the most sacred day of the year."

For a brief instant, Jorun's eyes flashed uncertainly. Then she turned to the noblewomen present and said, "You can't believe what a stranger with no family says. This woman is Sigrid's lapdog and lies willingly for her mistress."

"Emma is a dís sent by Freya herself," said Haldis in a voice cold as a winter storm. "One of the leaders can vouch for her honor."

The queen mother nodded to the housecarls, who opened the door. A murmur ran though the room as Hyndla stepped in, awe inspiring with her staff, the magnificent blue cloak trimmed with embroidery, and catskin gloves at her belt. Without looking at either those gathered or the accused, she stepped forward to Sigrid and knelt down before her.

"I venerate you, my hallowed queen," Hyndla said. Her voice was loud, so everyone in the room could hear her words.

Sigrid watched contentedly as Jorun paled. Helping Aedis and her children with gifts and silver had paid off. Erik's consort stood by her, owing a debt of gratitude, and so she had been willing to arrange a clandestine meeting between Sigrid and her mother. After that, making a deal had been a simple matter. Hyndla had been driven out of the temple when Kára saved Emma's life from the bonfire and had suffered gravely from the loss in reputation it had earned her. She had willingly gone along with Sigrid's request in order to restore her good name.

"I greet you, mighty seeress," Sigrid said. "You are esteemed by the goddesses. You are honored by your queen."

Hyndla put her hand on her heart, stood up, and walked over to Emma, who was still standing in front of Jorun. To Emma, Hyndla said, "Esteemed Kára, leader of the valkyries, I humbly bow down to you. My life is yours. Let me serve you."

She knelt before Emma and bowed her head.

Emma's eyes glittered silver, and her face looked like it had been carved in stone.

Sigrid was clenching her fist so hard that her fingernails were digging into her palm. Now if only Emma would forgive the seeress. There was complete silence in the room. The temple's priestesses had stepped forward, tensely watching what was happening. Sigrid hoped and believed that her sister, Emma, would do what she had to, but she could never be completely certain.

"You have my respect," Emma finally said.

Sigrid slowly exhaled, and the temple's priestesses nodded to one another in contentment. Then Hyndla got back up onto her feet. She raised her staff at Jorun and said, "I curse you, who have denied Kára threefold. May your lies cause your tongue to wither away. May your loins never bear fruit, and may your heart quit beating."

Jorun stood as if frozen solid, her mouth half-open. Sigrid contentedly wiped away a drop of sweat as it ran down her forehead. Now finally Jorun was beginning to see what Sigrid could do.

Hyndla walked over to the priestesses, who greeted her warmly and smiled gratefully at Sigrid. Sigrid put her hand over her heart as a gesture of respect to them before turning back to address Jorun.

"Your blasphemy against Emma is not your only shameful action."

Sigrid nodded to the housecarls, who opened the door and let in the slave girl Soot, who had found Emma on the beach. Emaciated and dirty, she stood in the middle of the room and looked around uncertainly as the stench of filth and pee spread through the room.

"Tell everyone what you said to Emma," Sigrid said kindly, leaning forward as far as her pregnant belly would allow.

Soot brushed a lock of hair aside and cleared her throat.

"That woman there"—she pointed to Jorun—"showed the warriors the way and said that Emma had asked them to come and have sex with her. But Emma didn't want to have sex, so they beat her up and did it anyway. That one was standing in the trees, watching and sneering."

Jorun stared down at the floor. She realized she'd been beaten.

"What happened then?" asked Sigrid, not letting on from her voice how furious she was.

Soot cleared her throat.

"They beat Emma unconscious, and when they left I went over and helped her."

"Why did you do that?" Haldis asked coldly.

"Because I was afraid she was dead," Soot said, hanging her head.

"You managed this well," Sigrid said with a nod of approval. "Go to the cookhouse and eat your fill. Ask Ägdis to wash you and give you new clothes. As of today, I own you."

Soot opened her mouth but couldn't think of anything to say. Instead she bowed her head so deeply she almost tipped over. Sigrid sent her out with a wave of her hand and then leaned back and looked at Jorun again.

"Well?" She did not conceal the disgust in her voice.

"Surely you don't believe what she says? A slave's word isn't worth anything. We're kinswomen, relatives. Why would I want to harm your servant?"

"Confess and keep what's left of your honor," Sigrid advised. She felt only revulsion for Jorun's fawning.

Jorun flung up her hands and looked beseechingly at the women present.

"Never will I admit to something I didn't do. Sigrid is just jealous because the king prefers me to her."

"Shut up and know your place. You are speaking to the queen of Svealand, consecrated by Freya," Solveig said angrily.

Sigrid almost started laughing. She could hardly believe what she was hearing. Jorun was a lowborn kinswoman, and yet she seriously believed that having sex with the king gave her power to defy the queen? Only now did Sigrid begin to understand that Jorun's perception of her own status was built on feeble dreams.

Sigrid trained her eyes on Alfhild, who hadn't said a word. She sat huddled on the bench, her face white and her hands trembling. She had never had a weak mind, so it was hard to understand why she had thrown her fortunes in with Jorun.

"I never would have expected you to betray me," Sigrid said.

Alfhild's lower lip quivered, and a tear ran down her cheek.

"I didn't mean to. I wanted to tell you, but I didn't dare because of Jorun."

"That's not true," Jorun said quickly. "You were just as angry as I was that she turned her back on us."

"Forgive me, Sigrid. I didn't intend to harm you. Forgive me." Alfhild held out her hand to Sigrid, who looked away. The pathetic weakness of her kinswomen was shameful to behold.

Haldis sniffed scornfully beside her and said, "This is what happens when simple farm girls try to serve in the king's court." She stepped forward, honorable with her gray hair and strict face. "Your repulsive actions don't end there. We found poison in Jorun's chest. The same poison you gave Queen Sigrid to take her life and the life of the unborn king of Svealand."

The words reverberated between the walls and instantly elicited the anger of the watching women.

"Traitor!" cried Orm's wife, Virun.

"Kill those curs!" said Aedis, and the noblewomen nodded to each other.

359

"Burn her!"

Jorun started quaking with fear. This was the most serious of the accusations. It wasn't true that they'd found poison, but Sigrid and Haldis had decided together that Jorun should be punished for the deed so that the matter could be put to rest.

"It's all lies," Jorun whispered while Alfhild cried and cowered on the bench.

"Are you accusing the queen mother of lying?" Solveig bellowed. She stepped forward, staring at Jorun. They had decided that Solveig, who came from the oldest and most powerful of the Svea families, would sentence Jorun. That way, no one would doubt the sentence, and Sigrid would be forever exonerated.

"She who harms the queen of Svealand must pay with her life," Solveig announced. "Such is the law. At dawn you will be hanged until dead."

The women around the room nodded contentedly and cried out their approval.

"May it so happen," said Sigrid, nodding to the housecarls, who pulled Jorun onto her feet.

Only now did Jorun realize what was going to happen. Gray in the face, she looked pleadingly at Sigrid.

"Don't let them kill me, I beg of you, my kinswoman. Don't kill your own flesh and blood."

"I neither want to nor am able to defy the law of the Svea," Sigrid said simply. She couldn't dredge up the least bit of compassion for her kinswoman.

"Toste will punish you for this," Jorun said.

Sigrid shook her head. Even now, Jorun didn't understand the damage she had wrought. She who had been raised in the same family ought to know that if you showed weakness, you would be killed. Jorun had to be sacrificed so that Sigrid could uphold her own and the baby's honor.

Besides, it was her own doing. If Jorun hadn't gotten caught up in her own bitterness, scheming, and spreading poison, this would never have happened.

"You've brought shame to the family and betrayed your own kin. If your father were here, he would have put the rope around your neck himself. Go, and die with dignity." Sigrid gestured with her hand, and Jorun was dragged screaming out of the room.

"Please, don't kill me. I'll never fail you again. Let me make it up to you," Alfhild said, sobbing and quaking in fear.

"What trust you had with me has been destroyed and can never be made whole," Sigrid scoffed, her chin up. "You serve me no longer and have no place on this estate."

Alfhild looked at her in horror. "Where will I go?" she whispered.

"That's up to you. You must leave this house immediately. You may not take anything with you."

The housecarls dragged Alfhild to her feet. They had to hold her up so she didn't collapse.

"Isn't there anything I can do to appease you?" Alfhild pleaded in a whisper.

"If you want to show loyalty to your queen, you can go to the grove and beseech the gods to choose you," replied Solveig.

Alfhild's eyes widened when she realized what that would mean.

The housecarls led her out, and Sigrid watched as the door closed on the last remnant from home. If Alfhild chose to live, she would have to find someone to serve, otherwise she would soon freeze or starve to death. But no one would want her. The respect and prosperity she had had as Sigrid's maidservant were gone forever. Sigrid could have had Alfhild killed, but it was better to show magnanimity.

"I honor you, my queen," Haldis said, getting up, her expression one of pure respect. "May peace now reign in your hall."

"Justice has been done," Solveig said, nodding with dignity.

Sigrid straightened up, stretched her aching back, and looked around the room at the leading women in Svealand.

"I'm ready to sacrifice everything, even my own blood, to protect my husband, his son, and Svealand. Know this: in these times of misfortune—when Styrbjörn longs to kill your sons and husbands and wants to force you to kneel to his false god—I am ready to die for you, daughters of Svealand. Bear this in your hearts when misfortune comes to your farms."

Everyone in the room bowed her head to Sigrid with a respect she had never encountered before. Only now did they fully accept her as their queen. Surely that was worth sacrificing her kinswomen for.

ᚦ

"Svea, chieftains, relatives," cried Erik, looking out over the large band of men and women who stood gathered in the grove. "Thor has promised us victory in the battle. Thor sent a sign that I should crown my unborn son king at this sacrifice. Should I perish, his mother, the queen, will reign until he is of age!"

A cheer ran through the crowd. Erik placed his hand on Sigrid's swelling belly and looked out over the sea of Svea dressed in furs and thick cloaks, surrounding him as far as he could see.

Most of them held up their weapons and hands to show their approval while a few turned to look at each other with skepticism. These were the chieftains Erik had to placate. Sigrid forced herself to smile at her husband. The veins in his forehead swelled, and beads of sweat appeared even though it was a cold day. No one had ever crowned an unborn child before and if he didn't win the Sveas' approval, he was sunk. Still, he had no choice. Sigrid had seen to that.

Thor's priest, Arngrim, stepped forward and raised his blood-spattered staff to the sky.

"We follow the will of Æsir-Thor, Alda Bergr, the protector of humanity. He swears the Sveas will be victorious if the child is crowned in the name of Valhalla."

People, still blood-spattered from the sacrifice, started yelling their war cries. The shouts grew into a thunderous roar that filled the plain and echoed over the snow-covered hills and the bodies of the sacrificed animals hanging in the grove.

Sigrid swayed as the power filled her body. The baby kicked in her womb, as if responding to the cries of the people. She was pleased. This was what she'd been chosen for. She smiled at the Sveas. She was strong and worthy. She reaped their approving looks.

Thank you for the fate I have been given.

Sigrid hadn't slept the previous night, but instead merely waited sadly for the day to come. Erik had been angry when he heard about the sentence, but there was nothing he could do to save Jorun's life. He'd swallowed the scheme she'd carefully woven. To begin with, Sigrid had gloated over the victory, but as evening fell, her desire for revenge and her fervor for battle had faded and given way to remorse and anguish.

She had lain awake in bed with Emma by her side. When the darkness was at its peak and the howls of the wolves could be heard on the wind, she'd curled up under the animal skins and whispered the most forbidden of questions: Who is the father of this baby? Half of her hoped and prayed every night that it was Sweyn, but she was the queen of Svealand. Could she really betray her people and put a bastard on their throne?

Emma had stroked her hair and told her that she was the mother of the baby and that the Norns had arranged the rest.

"Feel no blame. Rejoice instead in your strength. Your honor is saved, and Erik is forced to do as you wish. Everyone speaks of you with respect and says that you are a blessing sent by Freya. Kára honors you for your victory."

After that she kissed Sigrid on the forehead and embraced her tenderly from behind with her arm around Sigrid's belly.

Without Emma's strength, Sigrid would have been forced to fend for herself. Only Emma understood the longing and the fear she bore.

"I tremble at the thought of what will come in the spring, but I welcome it."

"Everything is in the hands of the goddess; there's no reason for concern," Emma had said. "Tomorrow you will become the most powerful of the Svea women, and your son will be proclaimed king of Svealand. You are already adored by everyone in this country. Take delight in the lofty role Freya has given you."

"*Happy is the one, who receives praise and kind words; less certain is it to own something that dwells in the chest of another,*" Sigrid mumbled, quoting Odin's maxim.

Emma laughed sadly and tenderly stroked her arm. "True, but yet you're safe, my lovely."

In the morning Solveig and Haldis came and adorned her with the dress and cloak that the queen mother had worn at her coronation. Her hair was braided and put up in the ingenious way the noble Svea women often wore it.

"Now you look like one of us in everything, my queen, not a stranger anymore."

Sigrid's mind had frozen to ice, but she was careful not to show how heavy her heart was as she descended the last of the stairs into the hall.

Erik awaited her with Axel at his side. Behind them stood the rest of the court, magnificently dressed and ready for the midwinter sacrifice, the biggest event of the year.

"I greet you, my respected husband," Sigrid said with a forced smile.

He could hardly look at her as he took her arm and led her to the waiting sleighs.

They sat quietly side by side under the furs, bound by their shared fate, while the driver urged on the horses, which set off energetically through the winter landscape. It was the most beautiful of winter days. The snow lay thick on the fields and ornamented the branches so they glittered white in the sunshine. Sun on the darkest day of the year was a good sign, guaranteeing the sacrifice would be well received by the gods. On this day the gifts to Sól and Dag would persuade them to leave the underworld so that the mother and son could spread warmth and life to the fields of Midgard.

Members of each dynastic line and family came to the midwinter sacrifice, because such was the law of the Svea. They came from every direction of the compass, on foot, on skis, and in sleighs. Fires had been lit and tents set up everywhere around the three burial mounds.

Sigrid wanted to look away when the sleigh stopped by the meeting grove not far from the temple. Three bodies hung, each from its own oak tree. Two of them were skinny slaves who'd tried to escape from their masters. With a gulp Sigrid forced herself to look at the third body. Jorun's arms and legs were tied behind her back, and she was swaying in the wind and covered with the snow that had fallen overnight. Her dark hair, which Sigrid had brushed and braided so many times, hung frozen around her white face.

This was the same Jorun, whom she had played with as a child, who had been like a sister to her. Her kinswoman who had turned her back on her and betrayed her in the worst way. Sigrid forced herself to take a breath as she looked at the dead body. She ought to be happy at the punishment Jorun had received and spit on her frozen body.

"Did she die well?" she asked. The words almost stuck in her throat.

"No, she cried and screamed for mercy," Erik said stiffly. He turned his head and for the first time looked at her with a loathing that neither the animal skins nor the baby could mitigate. Frost covered his beard, and his face was frozen.

"Are you satisfied?" he asked, and Sigrid understood that he would never forgive her or fully believe that the child was his.

The distrust between them was too great.

Sigrid nodded and fixed her eyes on the driver, who turned around, waiting for instructions.

"You can drive on. I've seen enough," she said. With a sudden cheer, the procession of sleighs set off for the midwinter sacrifice.

As if from nowhere a large marketplace had been constructed outside the palisade that surrounded the temple. Fires burned between market stalls, where handicrafts, food, and clothing were being sold. There were pens of pigs, cows, goats, and shaggy animals with big antlers on their heads, and crowds of people everywhere. Men with weapons and fur-trimmed cone-shaped hats and women in long skirts and fur-lined cloaks milled around. Even the slaves, filthy and skinny, shivering in their shabby clothes, walked around wide-eyed, staring at the endless market wares and animals. Erik pleasantly greeted both chieftains and free farmers, and when the sleighs stopped outside the gates, people crowded around them. Erik stood up in the sleigh and greeted the people with dignity. Then he stretched his hand out and pulled Sigrid to her feet. A murmur ran through the crowd when they saw the size of her belly.

"Then it's true."

"Freya's chosen one is carrying his son."

"The sacred couple has been reborn."

Sigrid forced herself to smile at everyone. A queen's role was to spread peace and life to her people. She was Freya, the one whose noble blood caused her to stand tall over them. It was her duty to live in riches and happiness with their king and bear him children. She stood over them all in rank and birth, and today her son would become king.

Nothing was more important. Distaste tightened around her throat like a choking noose.

Erik led her around the sleigh, and then they walked up to the closed temple gates together.

Three times he knocked on the ornately carved wood before a voice called, "Who goes there?"

"The king of the Svea is here to sacrifice to the gods and swear his loyalty to them."

"Then you must enter," said the voice, and the big gates opened wide.

The three gods waited for them with their sacrificial knives in their belts and masks over their faces.

Torches lined the path to the sacred grove.

Sigrid gulped and prayed silently that what she feared would not happen, after all. Without hope, she stepped in among the sacred trees and sank down onto her knees in deference to Odin, Thor, and Frey, who had been positioned in the middle of the grove.

The three gods regarded her emptily as the sacrifice began. Nine dogs and nine horses were given to them, three to each. For each offering, the priests and priestesses dipped a branch in the blood, which was then splashed over the gods and those gathered while they chanted the blessing incantations.

The drops of blood ran down Sigrid's face, and she held out her hands and felt how the air vibrated with the power of the gods.

The rumble of the drums echoed like thunder when the priestesses led in the nine human sacrifices.

Three were of noble birth—two men and a woman—three were farmers, and three were slaves.

They had all chosen of their own free will to sacrifice themselves so that the world could turn out of the darkness and Sól could return. Then the Svea would gain the protection of the gods and fertility would reign in the fields and among the animals and humans. This had to be done every nine years to appease the Æsir. The chosen heroes and heroines unselfishly gave their lives for the others.

Sigrid gasped for breath when she spotted Alfhild. Her head was shaved, and she was wearing the simple shift of a seeress. Her bare feet were blue with cold in the snow, and her eyes were filled with the fear of death, although she was bravely attempting to smile. Being cast out of Kungsgården and stripped of everything, she had chosen to dedicate her life to the gods. It was an honorable decision. Sigrid felt a stab in her breast. She was proud of her kinswoman, who chose to go to the afterworld so gloriously.

Alfhild slipped and slid on the bloody snow as she walked up to the sacrificial priestess. She almost fell down and then, gaining her footing, she prayed for forgiveness. Sigrid could smell her fear when Alfhild stopped in front of her and put her hand on her heart.

"My queen and dearest kinswoman, tell them back home that I died well," she said, her voice weak.

Her lips, which were turning white, quivered as she tried to smile and her eyes were empty of all life; little Alfhild. A part of Sigrid wanted to take her kinswoman in her arms and comfort her as she'd done when they were children, but all she did was nod quickly.

"I'll do as you wish," she said.

Alfhild started wandering away from Sigrid and the grove as if she didn't know where she was. The priestess beside her had to take her by the arm and lead her to the waiting angel of death. The rumble of the drums grew and then went completely silent as the seeress turned Alfhild's head to the side and sliced open her throat so the blood ran into the bowl that a young priest was holding up, while the drums began thundering again, and those gathered called out the gods' names. The blood gushed, steaming, out of Alfhild as the noose was placed around her neck and she was hung from the branches of the sacrificial oak. Her body jerked as the life ran out of her. Then the angel of death raised the dagger and stuck it into her heart. The threefold death was complete. Alfhild's bleeding body swayed in the wind. Things would be better for her in the afterworld.

The next sacrifice, a smiling man, was led up to the next altar. Sigrid jumped when the angel of death came forward and splashed Alfhild's blood in her face. *Welcome her in Folkvang, my mistress.* The darkness hid Sigrid's tears. Everything had to be paid for. Nothing happened without sacrifice.

Sigrid looked at the Svea who had gathered around the hill, which was covered in the blood from the offerings. Arngrim spoke a magic formula over the child and then pulled away so that Erik could take his place.

"My son and heir's name will be Olaf!"

The cheers echoed between the snow-clad hills all the way up to Valhalla. It was done. Bittersweet triumph filled Sigrid's chest. The king in her womb had been given the name Olaf. Sigrid turned her head, looked at the nine bodies hanging in the grove, and then raised her bloody hands to the sky. This was her son's first step toward greatness. Triumphantly she drank in the cheers of the Svea. Victory to the king of kings, honored be Olaf Skötkonung the Lap-king.

ᚠ

Styrbjörn the Strong's messenger had come, and Jómsborg obeyed his call. Every man in fighting shape hurried to the harbor. Women and children followed to say good-bye, and together they formed a river of people flooding the muddy road and streaming out of the gates.

Sweyn increased his pace as he walked against the flow of the crowd back into Jómsborg. For a day and a night he'd supervised every step of the preparations, and there was nothing more he could do now.

The ships had been stored away for the winter rest period and were more than seaworthy. The men were well trained and hungry for battle. Sweyn's men all had good weapons, and their shields were painted red and gold, his colors. Few of them had armor, even fewer of them helmets, but many had padded clothes and at least two weapons. Thanks to Valdemar's support and silver, he'd been able to give the men what they needed and more. He wore the most expensive gift himself, a suit of armor of unimaginable value made of small iron plates joined together. His uncle had taken it as spoils during his youth when he'd been on a campaign in the south and had given it to Sweyn with the admonition to wear it visibly so that everyone could see that he was a worthy king.

Sweyn couldn't be more grateful to his uncle, whose support brought him closer to the Jelling throne.

Sweyn slowed when he saw that the door to his room was open. That didn't bode well. With a heavy heart, he pulled off his helmet and went in.

Women with white mourning veils over their faces stepped aside as he walked over to his mother's bed. It was over. His mother looked so peaceful, lying there with her mouth half-open and her eyes closed. Sweyn pet Gray on the head. The dog was standing watch, whimpering over his mistress's body, and shared Sweyn's sorrow.

His mother had been alive when he went down to the harbor to supervise the loading of the ships. He had said he would come say good-bye before they sailed at dawn.

"You should have sent for me," he told Beyla, his voice choked up.

"She didn't want it," the seeress replied. "Sleep-Åsa felt you'd said everything that needed to be said and that she was leaving this world with her mind at ease and her heart filled with pride for her son."

The stabs of grief that pierced Sweyn were so painful he could hardly breathe. His mother was dead. He leaned forward and tenderly ran his hand over her cheek. She'd given him everything in this life.

"*Sweyn will be victorious* were her final words," Beyla said. "You honored her well."

The seeress held out the banner his mother had so painstakingly embroidered for him.

A part of me will always be with you, she had said. Sweyn hugged the fabric to his chest. "She knew she was going to die," he said thickly.

He had known she was clinging to life for his sake, but he hadn't wanted to admit it. Sweyn sighed deeply when the horns sounded, summoning the warriors to the harbor.

"It's time to go," Beyla said softly.

Ingbritt, the wife of Palna's brother, Gunnar, put her hand on his arm and reassured him, saying, "We'll give her an honorable burial."

"Thank you," he said, still sounding choked up. "Look after Gray and my slave until I come back."

"It will all be done," Ingbritt said. "Fight well."

His helmet felt heavy as stone when Sweyn put it on. Then he put his hand on the hilt of his sword and drove the all-encompassing sorrow out of his mind. His mother was in the afterworld. All he could do was conquer this one.

"Torstein's clan is arriving from the North this morning," Orm said to Erik, who had gathered those nearest to him around the long table in the royal hall. "Their ealdorman will swear fealty to you during the day."

Ynge, an old warrior whose face had been disfigured by a sword blow, took a shield from a small pile and set it with the others on the long table. The shields showed which chieftains, families, and warriors had obeyed the burning cross that summoned the Svea to battle with Styrbjörn.

"There's only a handful left in the pile of shame," Orm said.

Erik stood leaning over the table, dressed for battle in his armor and with his sword at his side. He looked at his men, in their glossy armor and byrnies, all carrying axes or swords. Their helmets and gloves sat on the table, which also held a dish of bread and meat they had been eating during the long hours they had been planning the battle.

Sigrid swallowed and put her hand on her unwieldy belly. The wolf time was upon them. Soon Sweyn would be here, and they would fight to the death over Svealand and the temple of Valhalla. If the Svea lost, the darkness of the cross worshippers would swallow them all.

The baby kicked. During spring Sigrid's belly had grown enormous, and she had a hard time standing or sleeping. The men said King Olaf was going to be born in full battle regalia with his sword raised and plunge into the battle against Styrbjörn right away. The women tried to hide their worried looks, because a big baby meant a difficult delivery.

Sigrid shivered as fear snaked down her back.

"Knut and Halvdan are the most powerful of the men from the south," Erik said. "If they haven't arrived before morning, they're on Styrbjörn's side. The Scylfings' ships haven't arrived either, even though my queen's father swore a sacred oath."

Erik looked over at Sigrid where she stood by the wall with her retinue and gave her a contemptuous look. She swallowed with difficulty. It did not bode well that her father hadn't kept his word in these times of misfortune when the darkness neared and the battle in Valhalla's name was about to begin.

Erik's loathing had grown even more intense since the midwinter sacrifice. He didn't talk to her, and when he did look at her, his eyes were filled with contempt. Everyone in the household could see how disrespectfully he treated her, and if her father didn't come through, he would use that as a way to get rid of her.

"There's still time," Orm said to calm things. "Toste is an honorable man, and the priestesses said that the signs are auspicious. Svealand will win."

"We'll see how it all turns out," Erik said with a stern look at Orm. Then his and Sigrid's eyes met.

"Your son, King Olaf, will be born any moment," Sigrid said, running her hand over her belly. "I ask permission to leave Kungsgården with my women to give birth to him in safety."

Heavy with child and defenseless, she feared the sharp battle blades. The baby was fragile, and his life could easily be extinguished. Even if Sweyn won and hurried to her side, there were countless other warriors who would kill them without hesitation if he didn't get to them in time. All she could do was protect herself and the little one. Time after time she had asked to take shelter at another royal home farther from the fighting, but Erik had refused her.

"Svealand's women do not flee from a battle. They stay and spur their men to victory. You, who are carrying the future king of the Svea, will remain."

That was the same answer he had given her each time she asked. Sigrid wrung her hands, and at that moment she hated him more than ever.

"I need you," Erik said. Without looking at Sigrid, Erik gestured for her to follow as he headed toward the door. With footsteps so heavy it was hard to walk upright, she left the warm hall filled with the stench of many days of sweaty agony and followed her husband out into the courtyard.

Wolf time, blade time. The ravens swooped over them, hunting for food. All the same, the trees were dressed in their airy summer attire, and the other birds sang merrily among the spring flowers.

The Svea warriors who had pitched camp were so numerous they filled the plain. Farmhands, hirdmen, and free farmers had set up tents by their chieftains. Still, Erik wasn't satisfied. He positioned himself next to Orm, still furious at the chieftains who had remained at their farms, thus turning their backs on their king.

"The priestesses and priests demanded silver and cattle, yet they couldn't foresee which of the chieftains would betray us. Styrbjörn's Christian priests walk around bragging that their god is so strong that he can defeat mighty armies, that he elected Styrbjörn king, and that no one in this world can question his divine right. I wish I had that power over my chieftains."

Sigrid looked around nervously, but Orm was the only one who had heard the blasphemous statement.

"Not many will follow you into battle if they hear what you're saying," Orm replied uneasily.

Erik shrugged.

"Baptized kings have a divine right and don't have to stoop to insolent farmers. If you don't obey a baptized king, you burn in hell for all eternity," Erik pointed out. "I wish I had that power."

Forgive him for his insanity, for he knows not what he says.

Sigrid walked up to the king and noticed that Orm mercifully stepped away to give them space.

"Are you profaning the old ways before your big battle, husband?" she said when they were alone.

His words had truly frightened her. Valhalla's champion couldn't waver. The gods would punish both him and Svealand for that.

"When your father keeps his word, then you'll have the right to open your yapping mouth," Erik said, not even looking at her.

A gust of wind caused his cloak to lift, so he looked like a bird of prey. The silver fittings on his armor gleamed, and he held his iron helmet in his hand, making him look like Frey, the god he was sworn to. Sigrid wrapped her cloak around her and changed the position of her feet because the dampness from the mud was seeping through her shoes.

"Let us stand united," she pleaded. "Remember that I am your son's mother."

Erik leaned his face in so close to hers that she smelled his foul breath.

"I hope you are," he said quietly. "If he doesn't look like me, you won't live until summer."

"Swear that you are not giving in to the cross worshippers," Sigrid replied, swallowing her fear.

"I won't swear anything to you. You don't control me."

Sigrid felt the darkness closing in around them. He was truly crazy.

"Let's get this done now," he said and waved his retinue over. Together they walked down to the plain.

"Svea warriors, brothers, kinsmen," cried Erik in a voice so strong that it reached the rear echelons. "The wolves will be on Svealand's beaches soon, led by the treacherous Styrbjörn. They come for the golden prize of Svealand."

He slowly pulled his sword out of its leather sheath decorated with silver and held it up to the sky.

Just then a flock of ravens flew over them, a sign that made Erik laugh with pleasure.

"Send the foreigners to the afterworld in the name of the old gods!" he yelled. "For Valhalla!"

"For Valhalla!" the warriors cried back in a deafening rumble. A forest of spears, axes, and swords was raised to the heavens.

The force of the cry was deafening. Not even the Jómsvíkings could best the mighty army of the Svea. They were already confident of victory. They would loyally follow Erik to defend their farms and fields. But what if they knew what their double-tongued king had just said? Sigrid took a deep breath.

Vanadís, Thor, All-Father: Guide Erik back to the true path. Don't let him be lured by the promise of a false god. Keep his nature in mind and grant him victory, in Valhalla's name.

She raised her hands to the sky and shut her eyes as the spring sun caressed her face and the warriors' bloodthirsty howls echoed across the plain.

Even now she ached with a shameful desire for Sweyn to take her away from here so they could be together. But if that happened, it would rob Olaf of his kingdom and future, and Valhalla would be annihilated. Sorrow lay so heavy over Sigrid that she could hardly stand.

Erik stepped down from the stone he had been standing on. He was accepting praise from Axel and the men nearest him when a shout was heard from among the army. Warriors pointed to the sea, where five ships were spotted sailing toward them.

Relief flooded through Sigrid when she saw the mark of the Scylfings on their full sails. Her father had kept his word. He was coming with his warriors.

"So there was honor in the Scylfings' word, after all," Erik said contentedly. "Take Sigrid away from here. Your farm will do, Axel."

Sigrid took a deep breath. She could finally flee the battle and give birth in safety.

Axel nodded.

"My men will escort you there," he said and gestured to four warriors in the hird, who walked over to her crossly.

They were probably afraid they would miss the battle.

"I said he'd let you go, sooner or later," Solveig whispered.

Sigrid took her arm, and they walked back toward Kungsgården. The priests and priestesses were arriving at the courtyard, dressed in their best cloaks and with their war drums in their hands. The priestesses' faces were painted black, frightening as valkyries. They were ready to unleash war charms and battle witchcraft on the enemy. Hyndla raised her staff in greeting and walked over to meet her.

"It's close now," Hyndla said. "Your son will be born in death and blood."

Sigrid glanced at Solveig beside her and then took Hyndla's arm and led her away from listening ears.

"I want to say something that's been weighing on my mind," she said quietly.

Erik's disloyalty to the gods worried her and when she saw the seeress in her battle garb, she knew instantly what she had to do.

Hyndla nodded in a dignified way.

"I owe you my loyalty," Hyndla said.

"Vanadís sent me a warning dream last night. If King Erik, my revered husband, swears loyalty to Odin, he will be victorious in this battle. If he does not, the All-Father will turn his back on him."

"Are you sure it was Odin?" The surprise was evident in Hyndla's eyes.

Sigrid nodded somberly. No one would know this was a lie, but if Erik was forced to do this he couldn't turn to the white Christ. If he swore his loyalty to Odin, the status of Thor's priest, Arngrim, would crumble, which would be convenient revenge for his having turned against Emma and Sigrid.

Sigrid hadn't forgotten. She never forgot anything.

"The dream was true and clear."

Hyndla's lips curled, and she said, "I'll take care of this. Don't you worry."

"You have my deep gratitude," Sigrid said and then moaned as a band of pain cinched her belly, stronger and more biting than the weak pangs she had been feeling from time to time.

"What's the matter?"

Sigrid stared at Hyndla in horror.

"The baby's coming."

ᚱ

This battle would be recounted for generations, and women would weave the most important heroes into tapestries. The ships that filled the sea and waited to land on the coast of Aros were so numerous that only the oldest could remember an army so mighty.

Styrbjörn had gathered fifty ships, and the Jómsvíkings had twenty-five dragon boats. More had joined them as they journeyed to Svealand. Many chieftains were ready to go to war against the Svea. People said a hundred and seventy-five ships and more than seven thousand warriors were gathering in Fýrisvellir, six miles from King Erik's dwelling. Sweyn would lead his own warriors into battle in the midst of this grand fighting force.

He pulled the armor over his head and carefully tightened the buckles. His men were waiting, tense and eager to go ashore. Hundreds of warriors around them were leaving their ships, pouring over the Sveas' fields like a wall of iron and strength, seeking honor.

Sweyn's heart swelled with joy and pride as he waded ashore and took his first steps toward Sigrid.

◆　◆　◆

My baby. Sigrid moaned in pain on the bed. All day she had been fighting for Olaf, who clung to her womb.

"You couldn't have picked a worse day to give birth," Haldis said.

Sigrid clenched her teeth so hard her jaws ached. She had never felt a torment like the fiery band that was pulling tight around her belly.

"Fetch the water and towels," Haldis called to the servant girls.

Sigrid screamed as yet another wave of pain tore at her.

This wasn't the best place for a battle. Chieftains in battle gear, a couple of them wearing impressive ring mail, surveyed the battlefield that Styrbjörn the Strong had chosen. Danes, Jutes, East Geats, and West Geats all stood side by side, distinguishable only by the heraldic markings on their shields. Two Gotlanders had even joined their northward campaign.

"Erik's men will stand here ready for battle when morning dawns," Styrbjörn said, looking out at his grim-faced warriors.

The Fýrisvellir plain stretched all the way to the edge of the woods in the distance, with water on either side. On the third side there was a large marsh. Styrbjörn, wearing a valuable suit of armor with a large silver cross on his chest, took off his helmet and pointed toward the pine trees at the edge of the woods.

"Those woods are a mile wide, and beyond that lies Aros. That's where Erik's men are gathered. They're going to attack from the woods."

And if things don't go our way, they'll drive us down into the sea, thought Sweyn. Fighting without an escape route was madness. Anyone who knew anything about warfare knew that.

"How many of them are there?" Palna asked quietly.

Styrbjörn smiled and put his hand on the broad-shouldered boy who had approached the camp, which had been set up behind them on the beach, and almost got his throat slit before he managed to convince the guards that he was a relative of Styrbjörn the Strong.

"Östen here says we outnumber them. The strongest of Erik's chieftains didn't answer his call, so they're on our side."

The beardless boy smiled and seemed beyond proud to have been mentioned by Styrbjörn.

"The Svea know that Erik calls himself their king unjustly. With God's help, tomorrow we will retake what he controls."

The chieftains nodded to each other and started asking Styrbjörn about the warriors they would encounter and how skillful they were with the weapons they carried. Sweyn looked toward the pine trees, whose tops bowed to the wind. She was so close. He could picture her sitting in her room with their baby in her arms. *My Sigrid, my queen.* He clutched the leather pouch he wore around his neck.

"Frode, I want you at my side, because I've seen how you and your men stand firm in battle," Styrbjörn continued, putting his hand on the Jutish chieftain's shoulder. Frode nodded, content to be given such an honorable position. "Åsmund and Ärre, I'd also like to see you in the advance guard."

The two chieftains from Scania stood tall at the prestigious assignment.

Then Styrbjörn turned to Palna and said, "Erik is likely to send men to approach through the marsh. I want you and Sweyn to meet them with the Jómsvíkings."

"Jómsborg's warriors could do more good by your side," the dissatisfied Palna said, scratching the scar on his cheek.

"You are the wolves that strike the beast in the flank and give me victory," Styrbjörn said to Palna with a smile.

The chieftains seemed both surprised and pleased that Styrbjörn wanted to keep the Jómsvíkings away from the glorious part of the battle. But at the same time, Styrbjörn's failure to make use of the Jómsvíkings' skills showed that he was not a capable commander. Only a fool would give his best warriors a spot in the rear echelon. Sweyn and Palna exchanged glances, but they bit their tongues until they were walking back to camp alone.

"You'd think we were ragtag farmers begging to fight in his hird with shoddy axes. Not much of a battlefield he picked either," Sweyn said and received a grunt in reply.

In the Jutish warriors' camp, the men were sitting with their bellies full, drinking mead and playing backgammon. At the next fire, the battle-hardened Norwegians were attending to their weapons.

"I have a bad feeling about this," said Palna.

Sweyn couldn't do anything but agree as they walked through the crowded encampment.

"Still, there are a lot of men willing to follow Styrbjörn," Palna pointed out.

"How many men you have and how skilled they are doesn't mean a thing if you position them in the wrong place on the battlefield," Sweyn said, objecting.

Palna turned to Sweyn and studied him for a moment and then said, "This morning I found out from a reliable source that Harald gave Jómsborg to Styrbjörn and that Styrbjörn has been bragging about how we're going to be serving him from now on. He's putting us at the back to denigrate us before he takes our warriors away."

Sweyn seethed, burning with hatred for Harald. He could hardly believe it.

"Without you, Palna, there is no Jómsborg. No one's going to follow Styrbjörn," Sweyn said.

"Men's loyalties are fickle and they'll follow whoever pays them best. Don't you believe otherwise," Palna said with a gloomy smile. He fell silent and nodded his head in respect to a chieftain with braided hair and a beard, who, along with his retinue, was proudly forcing his way through the crowds of men between the tents. Only after he had passed did Palna begin speaking again. "I told you this could happen, and the sign has come that your time is now. We have to sail south and force Harald's chieftains to their knees, one by one. If you're going to seize the Jelling throne, it's now or never."

Sweyn stopped and closed his hand around the hilt of his sword, fervor boiling in his blood. Palna was right. Harald's betrayal invalidated the oath they had sworn to fight for Styrbjörn. To stay and squander good men's lives in a battle that wasn't his own was madness. All the same, he had given Sigrid his word that he would come fetch her.

"You can't have any weakness if you want to conquer your father," Palna said, his voice justifiably brimming with anger.

They stepped into the camp where the battle-hungry men eagerly rose to find out what the plan of action was. Sweyn stopped and pulled his hand over the back of his head. Giving up on Sigrid was like having his heart cut out of his chest. But it would be unthinkable to let Palna down and not succeed at shouldering his fate. He would become the king of the Danes and Jutes.

"If you hesitate, you are not worthy to sit on the Jelling throne," Palna said, turning away in disgust.

Sweyn nodded grimly. He had to make the right decision, no matter how hard it was.

Sweat poured down Sigrid's trembling body as a force greater than anything she had ever experienced tore her body apart and forced the baby toward birth. He was almost here now. The band of pain around her stomach cinched tight and she clung to Emma's hand, screaming, as she fought to get the baby out. Solveig stood, leaning over her legs, while Haldis yelled to the serving girls that they should fetch a length of cloth. Soon, soon it would be over. Sigrid gasped for air and with one last painful shudder, she pushed the baby out. Exhausted, she sank down on her back. There was a brief moment of silence, and then a pitiful cry was heard.

"Give him to me," she panted. She'd longed for this moment. She would finally get to hold Olaf in her arms now.

But the women around the bed stood silent, looking down at the newborn between her legs. Something was wrong. She could see the astonishment and fear on their faces.

"Give him to me!"

Fear was like an icy hand around her heart. Emma leaned down and wrapped a piece of cloth around the baby. Then she handed the newborn to Sigrid.

"It's a girl," she said feebly.

Sigrid panted as she watched the baby crying and floundering in Emma's arms. It couldn't be. She was supposed to bear a son, the king of Svealand, he who was going to become the king of kings.

Disappointment and distrust spread through the room.

"This couldn't have happened at a worse time," said Haldis, her voice dripping with displeasure.

The baby whimpered in Emma's arms, searching for the breast with her mouth open and waving her tiny fingers around.

A girl. How can you give me a girl?

Milk started running down Sigrid's chest as Emma placed the girl in her arms. Reluctantly she closed her arms around the baby, who found Sigrid's nipple. Then the girl closed her little mouth and started greedily sucking on the breast. *My daughter.* Sigrid was filled with such love that she could hardly breathe. *My baby.*

She smiled sadly at the girl, who suddenly fell asleep with her mouth open, unaware of the catastrophe she brought into this life with her.

Just then the door was flung open and Erik hurried in, cheerful and full of anticipation.

"Give me Olaf so I can show him to the chieftains," he cried.

Haldis reached over and pulled away the cloth that lay between the girl's legs.

"It was a girl."

Erik stared in disbelief at the slit between the baby's legs before his face contorted in rage.

"A curse on you, Scylfing. A curse on your bastard," he said, drawing his dagger.

Sigrid put her arm around the baby, protecting her with her own body.

"We can pretend she was stillborn," Haldis said.

Sigrid shook her head, looking around horror stricken. The girl was so little and defenseless. They couldn't hurt her. Erik watched them both.

"They both died in childbed," he announced coolly. "That'll be best."

Mother of All, save us!

Erik left the room, slamming the door behind him. Sigrid held on to the baby desperately.

"Why is it a girl?" she whispered to Emma, who shook her head in response.

"I don't know," Emma said.

Then came the pain.

Sigrid's body shook as the band of pain cinched tight around her belly again. She embraced the pain with joy.

Her mistress hadn't failed her.

It went faster this time. She tilted her head back and screamed in triumph as she pushed out the baby. Roaring, she gave birth to yet another baby, who cried loudly and clearly. Haldis cut the umbilical cord and wiped away the blood and grease before she held up the newborn boy.

"Olaf Lap-King, I welcome you to life," Haldis exclaimed and placed the baby into Sigrid's arms.

Sigrid sank back exhausted onto the bed's bloody sheets while tears of joy ran down her cheeks. They were saved. The boy was smaller than his sister and his face was pinched, but his tiny cry was full of the will to live. *Welcome, my son.*

The women smiled and expressed their best wishes, but there was still concern in their faces and they whispered to each other, quietly so that Sigrid wouldn't hear them.

"The boy is strong," said Haldis. "But twins are still a bad omen."

Sigrid stiffened and looked around the room. Had they taken her daughter away from her? A newborn's life wasn't worth much. They set them out in the woods to become ghost mylings, or drowned them, suffocated them, or set them on dung heaps to die.

"Give me the girl," she cried, fear making her voice shrill.

"She's here," Emma said calmly and laid Sigrid's bathed, sleeping daughter in her arms, wrapped up in the finest linen.

Relieved, Sigrid hugged the baby to her chest. The little girl slept, breathing gently against her arm. The boy whimpered and then settled down. Sigrid was bursting with joy. This was everything to her, the will of the goddess, the reason she was alive.

If anyone tried to harm them, she would tear them to shreds and then destroy their families. No one in this world or the next was going to touch her children.

"Twin-born children are sacred, blessed by the dísir," Emma said, eyeing the women sternly. "Kára will protect them as a guardian spirit. That is the valkyrie's promise to the Svea."

Sigrid stroked the boy's wrinkled face. He yawned and then looked around shakily. His blue eyes and nose were very familiar to her, for she had seen them many times before. The worry that nagged at her grew into fear.

It was Sweyn. Her beloved was the boy's father. Vanadís had given her the children during the sacred couple's sacrifice in Lejre. Everything was as she had seen it in the dream.

Sacred mother, wash away his likeness and save our lives.

Sigrid jumped when Haldis carefully lifted Olaf from her arms. She washed the boy's face and then wrapped him in a blue and gold garment with the king's family's dragon embroidered on it in silver thread. The door opened and Erik stepped into the room again.

"I give you your son, King Olaf, ruler of Svealand's families," Haldis declared.

Erik took the child and held him aloft while he carefully inspected him. The king was stone-faced, and Sigrid's heart almost stopped. He knew.

"This baby was sent from Valhalla to ensure your victory over Styrbjörn and the Christians," Sigrid said. She couldn't keep her voice steady as Erik's and her eyes met. Olaf was so little and frail in his hands. One light blow to the back of the head and the little one would be dead. Sigrid clutched the girl to her bosom.

Protect your gift, I beg you.

"The chieftains will rejoice and fight for your victory when you show them your son," Haldis said.

Sigrid reached for the newborn. Then Erik turned around abruptly and walked toward the door with the baby in his arms. Sigrid exhaled slowly. He was going to show off the boy. The threat to Olaf's life had been averted, for a while. Exhausted, she sank back in the bed. Cries of hurrah could be heard from the hall where the men were honoring their new king.

"Bless Olaf the Lap-King," someone cried, and everyone chimed in.

"It's a good omen," someone else said.

Sigrid stared straight ahead vacantly with the little girl in her arms as the women cleaned her up and made her ready.

"Even the Jómsvíkings won't give Styrbjörn the victory," a voice cried out in the hall below them.

Sigrid gasped for breath. The Jómsvíkings were here. Sweyn was here. Her heart started hammering in her chest. Her beloved was near.

"You need to rest now," Solveig said and spread a clean comforter over her. "We'll bring little Olaf back to you soon."

Sigrid couldn't even look at the women as they left the room. What should she do? The children's lives were flickering flames in a raging storm. If Freya didn't protect them, they would soon wander to Hel's caves. Her daughter looked at her with eyes the same dark blue as the sea itself. *Guide me, I beg you.*

Then she saw the answer, deep in her daughter's ancient eyes. Sigrid wiped away a tear and then smiled, filled with sorrow. What she had to do now was terrible, but there was no other way. Now she understood.

I hear and obey.

Sigrid had to wait a long time for her opportunity. After Haldis returned with Olaf and then left, Sigrid was finally alone in the room with Emma. Then Sigrid asked Emma to fetch a bit of charcoal and a piece of bark to write on.

"There are no words for how much it pains me to ask you this."

Emma accepted the wood with the runes that Sigrid had laboriously written in the dark and then smiled sadly.

"I know," she whispered.

Sorrow at the decision she'd been forced to make tore Sigrid to pieces. Still, she had no choice. Tomorrow her beloved would fight Erik and no matter who won, her life and the children's lives would be in danger. Erik would kill them if he won, she was sure of that. If he won, he would no longer have any use for them.

If Styrbjörn won, Valhalla's final foothold in this world would be gone, and the old ways would collapse. The new king would kill her babies to wipe out their claim to Svealand. No matter where she turned there was nothing but death for the two tiny lives she had just brought into this world.

She leaned back in the bed and looked sadly at Emma. There was only one way out of all this, and it was tenuous and fragile. Sigrid took a deep breath.

"You must give this to Sweyn and to no one else," she whispered.

Emma leaned forward and tenderly brushed aside the hair that had fallen into Sigrid's face.

"I know," she said again.

No one had stood vigil by Sigrid's side as loyally as Emma. Kára had to protect Emma now. Nothing could happen to her. *I know you're watching over her.*

"Fetch my jewelry box," Sigrid instructed.

Emma got up and retrieved the ornate box. Sigrid opened the lid and took out Sleipnir, the gold brooch that Sweyn had given her in Lejre. She kissed it tenderly before placing it in Emma's hand.

"Give this to Sweyn, and then he'll know that the runes are from me."

"Anything else?" Emma asked, closing her fingers around the eight-legged horse.

The sorrow in Sigrid was going to boil over. She wanted to say that she thought about Sweyn every morning when she woke up and every night before sleep came, that the best and worst part of her life was the brief time they had had together, and that she couldn't imagine a life without him. But she couldn't ask Emma to say any of that. The babies had to live, even if she had to die.

"Tell him that I hold him in high regard, and that I implore him not to enter this battle."

"What should I answer about the children?"

Sigrid gave a sob and said, "Tell him they're Erik's."

The words were so difficult for her to say she barely got them out.

Emma stood up with a nod. Sigrid held out her hand and firmly squeezed Emma's.

"Come back to me," Sigrid told her. "Without you we're alone and defenseless."

Emma kissed her hand and then walked over to the cradle, where she ran her finger over the babies' cheeks.

"I will always watch over you," she told them.

The next moment she was gone.

X

Emma snuck down the stairs and into the royal hall, where Erik's closest chieftains were putting on their swords and adjusting their armor and other protective gear. The Svea stood straight-backed in groups, readying for battle. No one noticed her walk through the room. It was as if Kára were hiding her from their view.

"Well," Orm said, tickled with amusement, "you definitely succeeded in appearing angry that the Södermanland chieftains hadn't shown up. Styrbjörn's spies will definitely have passed on word of their betrayal to Styrbjörn. He will have no idea of the size of the force that's hiding in the woods, the force that will come from behind to break his back like a hammer."

"Styrbjörn will bitterly regret the battle at Fýrisvellir," Erik said, picking his helmet up off the table.

Emma slipped outside into the courtyard as Erik and the chieftains started heading toward the doors. The night air was cool as she crossed the field, sticking to the shadows, and making her way toward the woods. She wasn't the only one on the move. Farther away, in the cold moonlight, she saw unit after unit of warriors passing through the trees. Horses whinnied, and the rattling of armor echoed through the night. When Emma started running, there was no fear in her chest, only firm determination. She knew now that she would fulfill her destiny.

Kára propelled Emma's feet forward. Noiselessly, like a warm breeze, she swept between the trees toward Styrbjörn's camp. The light from the enemy's fires guided her as she made her way. At the edge of the woods she stopped and looked out across the vast field. The warriors' campfires were as numerous as the stars in the clear night sky. In raising her hand Emma paused and smiled tenderly because she caught a whiff of the scent of the two babies still on her fingers. Without hesitating, she headed straight across the field as Kára's whispering voice grew stronger.

No one stopped her as she wandered between the warriors' tents, all with banners hung above the flap openings.

The warriors sat around the fires, resolute, their emotions unreadable, sharpening their weapons or staring into the flames as they awaited the next day's battle. They prayed to their crosses, seeking courage and comfort from their god. Others sought strength from mead and talked loudly. Emma giggled at the stench of their fear of death. None of them would live until the next night. They all had the mark of death on their faces.

Onward. Forward.

By one fire a woman lay on her back, waiting patiently for the warrior groaning and thrusting between her legs to finish. A pockmarked older woman took silver from the next man in line. The crowd around the fire was large, so they must be making quite a profit.

Emma looked away. Long ago Acca had taken her to a camp like this, where she had spread her legs for a pittance. But that was before she had been blessed by Kára and joined Sigrid, her beloved sister, the only one who had ever given her joy and safety in this life. The small bundle containing the gold Sleipnir brooch and the piece of bark with the runes written on it hung around her neck. She would faithfully deliver the message that was going to shatter Sigrid's happiness but save the babies.

Emma hurried along the path, carefully scrutinizing each flag and banner: griffins, dragons, crosses, and crossed axes. There was no end to all the symbols and colors that waved in the gleam from the fires, but nowhere did she find the roaring wolves of the Jómsvíkings.

She smoothly stepped aside for a hirdman in a conical hat, who stopped and stared at her in surprise.

"I can't find my way back to master Palna, the chief of the Jómsvíkings," she said.

"They're all the way over there," said the hirdman with teeth so rotten that his jaw stank.

Ah, finally. Emma started running, but she hadn't gone many steps before a shadow emerged from the darkness and grabbed her roughly by the arm.

Ax-Wolf came up to the fire and squatted down in front of the flames. The red-haired giant looked grimmer than usual. The men were quiet, and there was neither anticipation nor hatred in their chests, as there should have been.

Sweyn exchanged a glance with Palna, who was waiting impatiently for him to give the orders Palna wanted to hear. And yet, he couldn't do it, not yet. His weakness for Sigrid paralyzed him.

"What's weighing on you, brother?" Sweyn asked.

Ax-Wolf scratched the back of his head and made a face.

"I've fought on every shore in the world and faced both Franks and giants in battle. Never have I backed down. But I have a bad feeling about this battle. I can't deny it. A black bird fell dead from the sky, as if Odin himself were sending me a warning."

His brothers-in-arms nodded. They obviously all had some doubts about standing beside Styrbjörn. Just before sunset, Styrbjörn had strolled through the camp dressed in his showy armor and promised them victory in the name of his god.

"The godless heathens will be slaughtered," Styrbjörn the Strong had shouted. "The demons will no longer poison Svealand, and those who fall by the sword will be rewarded with an eternity in the kingdom of heaven."

A priest had walked around and splashed water on them. Very few of Sweyn's men or the other Jómsvíkings had enjoyed receiving the white god's sorcery.

Sweyn fished out the leather pouch he wore around his neck and held it in his hand. Sigrid was so close he could feel her; only the woods separated them, and if Styrbjörn won, he would hold her in his arms before the next day was over. Sweyn sighed heavily and looked up as the guard Trond approached, dragging a woman through the darkness.

"I found a spy creeping along in the shadows," Trond said and shoved her into the light from the fire.

Sweyn recognized Emma immediately as she fell flat on the ground.

"Let her be," he said, watching the girl scramble to her feet.

Sigrid must have sent her.

"Do you have a message?" he asked.

Emma pushed her hair out of her face and looked at Palna, Beyla, and the others around the fire before she responded.

"I have a message, an ominous one," she said, handing Sweyn the piece of bark.

Sweyn snatched it and squatted down near the fire. Slowly he deciphered the symbols that had been written on the wood. *Leave Svealand. Leave me.* That was it. He closed his hand around the wood as the hope that had nourished him died and everything became a charred wasteland. It was over.

"She implores you to forgo the battle," Emma said. "All that awaits you is death." She took out the gold brooch that Sweyn had once given Sigrid and put the piece of jewelry in his hand. "Many times more Svea are hiding in the woods, waiting to attack your flank during the battle. You will all die. The men's faces all bear the mark of death from Odin, the All-Father, who has promised to make Erik victorious. Turn around. This isn't a battle. It's a slaughter. You are destined for something else."

Sweyn looked down at Sleipnir and ran his thumb over the gold. She had risked everything to warn him. *My beloved.*

"Did Sigrid have my baby?" he asked, choked up.

"She had a son and a daughter today," Emma replied, shaking her head. "Both are the very image of Erik."

Not his? The last hope drained from Sweyn. He angrily threw the piece of bark with the runes into the fire. Sigrid had given birth to another man's children. She had turned her back on him and asked him to leave Svealand. How could she forsake him like this?

ᚹ

Kára swept over the meadow into Emma's mind. Emma reeled as the Wild Stormy One filled her with engulfing flames, devouring fire. Sweyn's campfire flared up, kicking up a cloud of sparks. Emma nodded to the storming dís. The destiny she had twice avoided needed to be fulfilled. She understood that now.

"Summon your men. Prepare your ships for launch. Only death and despair await you here," Emma cried out as the wind tore at the men's tents and cloaks.

She had shattered Sweyn's hopes with her lie, yet still he hesitated to do what he needed to do. He was blind and deaf to the signs he had received.

"Flee from here. Kára will fill your sails. Listen to Sigrid's appeal."

It was true that the Jómsvíkings had a bad feeling about this battle site. They all felt a sense of foreboding about the darkness that towered over them, and yet they remained, hesitant, standing at the precipice. Kára's whispers increased in strength. She had to drive them from this land. Their lives must be saved. Emma turned to Beyla and grabbed her arm.

"What I have said must happen," Emma said.

The seeress lowered her head in acknowledgment. "I hear you."

"Then sing of my name so it will live on forever," Emma replied.

Emma let go of Beyla's arm and turned around and ran, away from the fire, through the tents with their flags and banners waving and their burning fires where men hunkered down in the wind. Kára carried her toward the ships bearing Styrbjörn the Strong's colors. Only when she was there did Emma stop and hold her hands up to the sky, where the valkyries were swooping around in the night, coveting the blood that waited by the beaches.

Kára greeted the valkyries with a roaring shriek, so powerful that it echoed between the nine worlds. *Fire Giants, I summon you and conjure up your devouring might.*

She grabbed a burning log and jumped onto one of the ships. She set fire to a pile of cloth and laughed loudly as the fire giants spread in every direction. Quickly she leapt over to the next boat beached there and spread the flames further.

The fire was like a living being. It consumed each ship and jumped from one to the next, each of them blazing up in the night. Emma rolled over the gunwale and backed away from the ships. Laughing, she watched the roaring inferno. *Consuming flames, radiant devastation, most lethal of forces, I conjure you.* Then suddenly the all-consuming fire was far too close. Screaming, she saw it climbing from the hem of her dress up toward her chest. Burn, they were all going to burn.

Men came running from every direction trying in vain to put out the flames. Emma held up her burning arms to the sea of flames on the beach. Her skin bubbled and scorched, her hair burned away, and her flaming dress clung to her body. She embraced the screaming pain as it consumed her. Burn, they were all going to burn and she had to die.

But not yet.

Styrbjörn the Strong and his men stared at her in horror.

Emma's legs scarcely held her as she staggered toward the cross Styrbjörn wore on his chest.

"I curse you, cross worshipper," Kára roared at him in a mighty voice. "You who profane the Most High will all die."

Emma's dress and cloak blazed and she sank to her knees. Smoke filled her lungs as she wheezed and coughed, struggling for breath. Sigrid and the babies must live. The torment was insufferable as her flesh burned and her skin became charred.

"Kára!" she bellowed in her pain.

Soon you will be with me, the dís whispered gently.

With a shudder of pain, Emma closed her eyes as the darkness released her. It was finally over.

Sweyn stood up like a new man, filled with contempt. He had been a sniveling fool, caught up in false hopes, fawning like a lapdog over another man's wife. He had disgracefully allowed dreams to stand in the way of strength and had faltered when so many men were relying on him and supporting his cause. But no more.

He stared vacantly at the flames that raged in the distance, by the shore. Just then Ragnvald came running, all out of breath.

"Styrbjörn is burning his own ships," the boy screamed breathlessly. "People heard him say he would be victorious or die on these shores."

So, madness had finally consumed the cross worshippers. Sweyn looked at his men, saw their uncertainty about what was happening, and then smiled broadly.

"This isn't our fight," Sweyn said. "Tell the men we're boarding our ships immediately. A richer plunder awaits where we are headed, far greater than what Styrbjörn has to offer."

The words set the men in motion. They snatched up all their things and rushed to the ships.

"It's time to take what I have coming to me," Sweyn stated with a nod to his inner circle as they left the camp.

A yearning for battle ached in Sweyn's body as he stood at the prow of his ship and watched the flames spreading through Styrbjörn's ships like a wind-driven wildfire. He wanted to beat someone to a pulp, kill every man he saw, and hear their death screams as they fell to his sword.

Ragnvald waded out into the water with his knapsack in his arms. He was the last of the warriors who had hurried to the ships. The boy flung his pack over the gunwale and was pulled aboard as the men began rowing away from the beach, where scores of ships were burning. The flames rose into the sky with a roar all the way up to Valhalla, turning night to day for the Jómsvíkings.

"Styrbjörn sure picked an expensive way to instill courage in his men," Åke said.

Their own ships a lost cause, Styrbjörn's warriors lined the beach pointing at the departing Jómsvíking ships and screamed that the Jómsvíkings were deserters. In vain Styrbjörn's men shot burning arrows after them, hoping to share the devastation.

"Row!" shouted Sweyn. "Row us all the way to Valhalla!"

At that moment Sweyn saw everything clearly: Sigrid, Svealand, Styrbjörn's battle. They were all delusion. There was only one path to take.

"By Thor!" he cried to his men sweating on the rowing benches, as the sails filled with Kára's favorable wind. "We sail to the south and we'll burn and plunder any village or farm that serves Harald Bluetooth. Men, I promise you riches and glory, or an honorable death."

The men's loud shouts only fueled Sweyn's rage. Sigrid might be lost to him, but he would claim the kingdom that was his.

ᚺ

The babies slept calmly at Sigrid's breasts, safely dozing, unaware of how fragile their lives were. She held them in her arms, unable to let go of them. She wanted to protect every breath they took and safeguard the time they had together. However short it would be. Muffled screams were heard from the hall. Sigrid wiped away her tears and listened carefully for the news she hoped for and feared.

"The Jómsvíkings are deserting! They're leaving Svealand!"

"Styrbjörn is burning his own ships!"

She had succeeded. Sweyn had listened. Sigrid lowered her head as sobs shook her. Her beloved was gone.

Thank you, Vanadís.

Her tears fell on the two little ones while her grief at the sacrifice she had made stabbed daggers in her heart. Without the Jómsvíkings, the Svea could win. She had given up the happiness and safety she and the children could have had with Sweyn for Freya's sake, so that the power of the gods would endure, to prevent the Christian god from swallowing the world. All she could hope for now was that Freya, the shining Radiant One, would have mercy on and protect their lives from Erik. Sigrid's cheek was wet, and she wiped it with the back of her hand.

Freya had sent Kára to watch over the babies and had protected her in everything. She had to trust that she wouldn't desert her now that Olaf, the king of kings, was here.

A quick knock on the door made Sigrid look up. To her relief, when the door opened she saw Ulf step into the room, looking singularly manly in his battle garb, fully armed.

"What's wrong?" he asked Sigrid in surprise as she quickly wiped away her tears.

She shook her head and said, "Nothing, now that you're here."

"Father is still back home fighting Anund's men. Soon even their land will belong to the Scylfings. He sent me with five ships to make good on his promise to Erik."

Things must be bad if Toste sent Ulf, who has no interest in combat.

"I brought good men with me," Ulf said as though sensing her thoughts. He walked up to the bed and studied the babies. "Oh, look at the poor little thing."

Sigrid lifted up the girl, who lay closest to her, and placed the baby in her brother's hands.

"Is this Olaf?" he asked, giving her a look of concern.

"That's the girl. Erik won't adopt her. He says she's to be killed. He wants to do away with all three of us."

"I know."

"How can you know?" Sigrid said, raising her eyebrows.

"I have people who tell me things," Ulf said, smiling at the baby, who gave a big yawn in his hands.

Carefully he put her back in Sigrid's arms.

"If Erik won't adopt her, I'll take her home as my own," Ulf said calmly. "No Svea is going to spill Scylfing blood."

Sigrid's eyes filled with tears again, but this time out of relief.

"We share blood and lineage, sister," Ulf said. "I have to leave you for the battlefield now. Erik is going to swear himself to Odin before the battle and once we've been victorious—with the All-Father's help—I will return to your side."

Standing tall, he strode over to the door and put his hand on the carved handle.

"Estrid," he said.

Sigrid put her arms around the girl.

"Yes, her name will be Estrid," she said and forced a smile. "Come back victorious."

He nodded and left them, looking resolved. Sigrid lay back in bed and took a shaky breath. There was still hope. The darkness wasn't over them yet.

The thunderous beat of the war drums echoed through the morning mist as the mighty army of the Svea stood ready to face Styrbjörn's warriors. Row upon row of grim-faced men with their shields raised and weapons in hand waited to fight to the death. The banners fluttered in the wind. Horses whinnied and stamped uneasily. In the sky the valkyries waited, ready to bring home the finest of the fallen. Like birds of prey the wondrously beautiful dísir—with their flowing hair and bared fangs—shrieked.

Emma swooped forward over the grass, filled with the empty serenity she had been blessed with. The ground pulsed in expectation and anguish at the battle that was about to take place.

Sweat ran down the warriors' faces as they waited to wage the battle of life and death. They shouldn't feel any fear. There was only stillness in the afterworld, and soon their torment would be over.

On the far side of the meadow Styrbjörn the Strong rode ahead to the front line on a white horse. The banner with the white cross billowed over his head. Emma looked at his empty future with indifference. The darkness at the top of his head was the sign that his time would soon be up.

The drums quieted, and Erik moved forward with Odin the All-Father at his side. The one-eyed god carried his ravens, one on either shoulder, and his back was stooped beneath his dark cloak.

Erik put on his helmet and firmly grasped a battle spear, feeling strengthened by the watching presence of the mighty god beside him. The king of Svealand raised the spear to his people before turning and throwing it over the battlefield.

"Odin owns us all!"

His battle cry was answered by all the warriors, and like a wave of fury the Svea surged across the meadow, down toward the intruders at the beach. The steady rumbling beat of the war drums triggered unit after unit of lethal men, brimming with the rage of the valkyries.

Styrbjörn's warriors raised their shield walls and spears as the Svea arrows approached their units. Showers of arrows rained from the sky, drilling into the wooden shields and into the men, who fell screaming. A moment later the two forces met in rage, pain, and death: ax blade against ax blade, sword against sword, long spears through soft bodies, crush, chop, shred, shriek. Emma circulated through the fighting and watched man after man fall to sharp blades. Youths who dreamt of making a name for themselves as warriors, fathers seeking glory and riches, men with no choice but to obey their master's orders. They were all doomed.

Emma smiled at Kára, who with a howling shriek swooped down from the sky like a black shadow. The valkyries, horrifying in their bloody insanity, harvested the fallen warriors. They took some of them into their arms and whisked them into the afterworld, the best for Freya in Folkvang, others to Odin's Valhalla. They imparted their blessed fury to some of them so they were filled with such strength that their blows could easily cleave a shield in two, and a select few they protected fiercely. Mjölnir flashed as Thor, the mighty thunderer, fought at the Sveas' side. Thor, the magnificent protector of mankind, knocked down enemy after enemy, and the Svea warriors beside him were filled by his strength. A brilliant light shone over Styrbjörn and the cross bearers, dazzling in its purity. It carried them forward and filled their hearts with courage. Soon they would cross swords in this world and the next.

Emma squatted down and stroked the cheek of one of Styrbjörn's dying warriors, no older than herself. Trembling with fear, he clung to life with his hands pressed over a bleeding, fetid wound in his belly.

"Feel no fear, my friend," Emma counseled with a smile. "Let go. It will be easier that way."

The young man turned his head and when his eyes settled on her, he started shrieking in sheer terror. Emma looked down at her own scorched feet. If he didn't want her comfort, he could just lie there and die by himself. He would have plenty of company soon enough.

Styrbjörn's men backed toward the water, step-by-step. The rage of the Svea hammered mercilessly at Styrbjörn's lines, knocking warrior after warrior down and grinding them up like a millstone. Erik's sword flashed in the battle, guided by Odin at his side. Splashed with blood he reaped his enemies under the waving banner of Svealand as he fought his way toward Styrbjörn.

Styrbjörn fought bravely against the Svea shield wall, and he urged and incited his men to gain ground. Then the loud warning cry of a horn penetrated the din of the war drums. Ship after ship pulled ashore. They were the chieftains from Södermanland, who had finally arrived to attack Styrbjörn's forces from the flank.

Emma giggled at the desperate struggle of those marked for death. Trapped between two armies and the water and the marsh, Styrbjörn and Harald's Danish fighters had nowhere to flee. With desperate courage, they fought bitterly against the superior armies. The ground shook with death screams and despair. The sky darkened from the valkyries' hunger. Emma swept across the meadow, which had now been baptized in blood, over toward Styrbjörn the Strong, who was fighting, staunchly defended by a close ring of men around him. His standard bearer lay by his side, already dead, an arrow straight through his neck. The Svea cut down Styrbjörn's hird one man at a time. Axel and Orm, side by side, were leading the battle.

Then Erik rushed forward to Styrbjörn, his own nephew, and their swords met. The combat was intense as they slashed at each other with their swords, relative against relative, Valhalla against the cross. Sweat poured down their faces, and their exhaustion showed in their fighting as evening fell over the battlefield.

Styrbjörn was bigger and stronger than the king of Svealand. With his strong arms, Styrbjörn managed to split Erik's shield. Erik, smaller but able to move faster, caught the shield Axel tossed to him and continued fighting with Odin's ecstatic rage gleaming in his eyes.

Emma lowered her head in deference to Odin as the stately old man came walking through the battle in his broad-brimmed hat and dark blue cape. The one-eyed All-Father bore a staff in his hand.

"Odin by your many names," Emma said, "Vakr, Farmatýr, Baleyg, the Most High, Awakener, God of Burdens, Flaming Eye, I honor you."

Odin didn't look at her as he raised the staff toward the light radiating from the cross that Styrbjörn wore on his chest. Styrbjörn advanced even more fiercely and landed a blow on Erik's sword arm, but he kept fighting even with blood pouring from the wound. The cross on Styrbjörn's chest blazed with burning purity, and he grinned like a mighty god as he drove the weakening Erik backward.

Odin, the War Father, again raised his staff, and Valhalla rose like a red wave toward the shining light, god against God, strength against strength. The valkyries swooped through the darkness into the light, where they ripped the light bearer to pieces. Then the red wave crashed over Styrbjörn and extinguished all his light.

Erik was infused with a new courage. He tossed aside his shield and drove Styrbjörn backward with his sword in one hand and his dagger in the other. Then Erik succeeded in stabbing the dagger into Styrbjörn's throat. Smiling, he looked into his nephew's eyes as he choked, sputtering in his own blood.

Styrbjörn fell down dead on the ground. The flag with the cross lay by his side, trampled into the mud. Odin gazed in satisfaction at the man who had failed to conquer Svealand.

"Odin owns us all!" Erik shouted, raising the dagger high above his head. Gleaming blood red, it sent its strength over the battlefield, and at that moment every Svea warrior knew that they'd achieved victory.

Styrbjörn's people had lost. Young and old had fallen to the Sveas' blades and piercing spears. Priestesses' war charms had paralyzed many of the rest of Styrbjörn's men so they couldn't move. Those who still could huddled together, fearing the horrendous sorcery.

Many fled across the marsh but were pulled down into the quagmire by their armor. They drowned, embraced by Rán's daughters who dwelled in the water there. Only a few made it to the land on the far side and ran for the woods.

Emma smiled at a dead man who was wandering among the wounded still screaming in pain.

She pointed to the east where the immense gates to Hel stood open, but he didn't seem to see her or even understand that he was dead. Confused, he was still wandering around among the spirits who had fallen in battle.

Emma raised her arms and danced with the valkyries on the battlefield of the fallen until night came. Their blood had flowed across Fýrisvellir, and finally peace did settle over the meadow.

Odin owned them all.

ᛣ

Victory for Valhalla.

Sigrid was numb with gratitude and relief as she looked out across the hall where the freewomen, servants, and slaves were tending the wounded. The men suffered from mutilated arms, sliced-up bellies, and bleeding wounds. Svealand's victory came at a painful price. The priestesses chanted over the dead, who were then carried away, new wounded immediately brought in to take their place.

Sigrid swayed on her feet, still weak from childbirth, but she couldn't just lie in her bed as the screams of the dying filled the hall. Her chest was burdened by her worry for Emma and her brother. Her sister should have been back ages ago. Maybe she had stopped to watch the battle. Maybe she was watching over Ulf to make sure he returned unharmed.

"Rejoice, my queen," said a warrior sitting on the bench with one leg bandaged. "Styrbjörn's head is stuck on a stake out in the field. Your son's kingdom has been secured."

Valhalla's victory was also her son's. He had been born amidst blood and death. Sigrid forced herself to smile.

Thousands of torches burned on the hillside. Erik was being carried around on a shield while the Svea cheered and praised their king, defender of Svealand. The shouts of hurrah mingled with the screams of pain in the hall.

"Erik the Victorious! Erik the Victorious!" people were chanting.

Haldis looked up from the young man she was tending, wiped the blood off her hands with a cloth, and smiled.

"He didn't let us down, my esteemed son," she said, her voice filled with pride.

Sigrid forced herself to smile yet again. "Odin has blessed the king of Svealand," she said hoarsely. "Loved and honored be his name."

Haldis gave a slight nod and said, "The funeral pyre will burn high tonight. Now, now, quiet your howling."

She walked over to a screaming boy who was bleeding from a spear puncture. She gruffly patted his sweat-sodden hair and then started bandaging his wound with nettle cloth.

Hopefully Emma and Ulf weren't lying wounded on the field crying for help, alone in the night among the beasts and other beings. Worry was like a bleeding wound in her chest. It ran through her body and poisoned her blood. She looked at the men's vacant stares, as if they had looked into the deepest darkness and still carried it in their chests. Sigrid shared their despair. She stood at the precipice herself, she who ought to be the honored queen of Svealand.

Then a familiar shadow filled the doorway, and Sigrid breathed in relief. Ulf stepped into the hall, grim, his armor blood-spattered. Without even looking at the wounded, he walked straight over to her with his shield in one hand and his helmet in the other.

"Victory," he said succinctly.

She grabbed his arm and squeezed so hard her knuckles whitened.

"How many of ours died?" she asked.

"Eight Scylfings," he said grimly. "An expensive price for Erik's power."

He practically spat out the words. There was no joy in his eyes, just brooding and resolve. Sigrid faltered.

"You're going to faint," Ulf said.

He grabbed her arm and led her back to the room where Soot was watching the babies. With a tired sigh he sat down on the footstool beside her bed and put his sword on his knees. Sigrid inhaled the smell of blood and sweat as her gratitude for her brother's life burned in her blood.

"Aren't you going to celebrate your victory, look after your men, and drink with them after the battle?" she asked. "It is customary, after all."

Ulf gave her a piercing, gloomy look and said, "Calm down, Sigrid the Haughty. I know what I'm doing."

Sigrid didn't ask any more questions. Exhausted she curled up on the bed and finally fell asleep.

Sigrid heard Emma's voice like a song. It was talking about things so beautiful that mortals couldn't appreciate their beauty.

"Wake up, my sister. I have returned as promised."

Sigrid opened her eyes and saw Emma leaning over the babies' cradle. Her back was scorched from fire, and parts of her hair were charred. All the same, she was here and babbling to the babies. Sigrid slowly exhaled as the worry let go of her heart.

"I was so afraid I'd lost you forever."

Emma laughed, straightened her back, and said, "I would never leave you and the children."

Sigrid jumped in sheer horror when Emma turned around. Her face was charred black, her lips scorched, only a blackened bit of bone was left of her nose, and her eyes were gone—only empty sockets remained. She was horrific to behold, and her death must have been gruesome.

Sigrid swallowed and remembered how Emma screamed with pain on the bonfire before the rain put out the flames and how, filled with her own powerlessness, Sigrid had pleaded for the life of her beloved sister. Now she was responsible for sending her to an excruciating death.

"I'm so sorry," whispered Sigrid, tears running down her cheeks. "I hoped and prayed nothing would happen."

Emma leaned forward and stroked Sigrid's hair. The flesh on her hand was burned away, her fingers like claws.

"My borrowed time ran out; my fate was done."

Sooty teeth peeked out from behind charred lips as Emma's face contorted into a smile. Sigrid leaned her cheek against Emma's hand and cried over her sister and her own loneliness.

"You always knew I was going to die for you," Emma said. "I accomplished what you asked of me. Sweyn left Svealand, and Valhalla stands strong. Rejoice in our victory."

Her voice was as gentle as a caress, but Sigrid would not be comforted. No one had so loyally protected her and shown her such sisterly care. She should never have sent her out there. Now Emma had died all alone, a grisly, horrific death.

"It's not fair!" Sigrid cried. She lost everyone she cared about: her mother and Emma. There was only death and suffering.

"Calm down," Emma said, looking at her with her empty eye sockets. "You still need to fight for your life and the babies."

The noose of sorrow around Sigrid's throat tightened. *My sister.* She fumbled for Emma's hand, but her sister pulled away, straightening up. Sigrid stared at Emma's scorched, ghastly face and empty eye sockets looming over her bed.

"Run, sister, run," Emma warned. "He's coming for you."

Sigrid woke with a start to screaming and heavy footsteps. Ulf stood by the edge of her bed, his sword dripping with blood. A slave lay on the floor, breath rattling in the throes of death. Sigrid started trembling when she saw the pool of blood spreading across the floor.

She gasped. "The babies?"

"They're alive," her brother said.

Soot stood by the babies' cradle with Olaf in her arms. The slave girl's eyes were wide with fear, but she nodded.

"Nothing's happened to them," Soot confirmed.

"A murderer was sent to end their lives," Ulf said with suppressed rage, bending down to take the dagger out of the dying slave's hand.

Sigrid could scarcely hold Olaf when Soot put the baby in her arms. Soot was back in a flash with Estrid, who yawned wide when she was placed beside Sigrid in the bed. *A murderer, in my bedroom.* Sigrid stared into her daughter's eyes. They wanted to murder her babies. It was as she'd feared.

The dark forces rumbled back and forth menacingly. They wanted to devour her. If Ulf hadn't been there, they would all have died in their beds. How could a murderer be in the king's house, when no one could even approach the estate unseen?

"You knew this was going to happen?" Sigrid asked, puzzled.

Ulf nodded tiredly and said, "On my way back from the battle I heard a rumor that you had died in childbed. I was afraid Erik wanted to help you along into the afterworld, which he might have gotten away with on a night like this with the battle victory to celebrate and the funeral pyres burning."

Sigrid ran her fingers through her hair.

"What am I going to do?" she said, gasping, feeling darkness descending around her.

The bed rocked beneath her. Erik wanted to murder her and the children. Everything around her disappeared: Emma, Alfhild, Jorun, Sweyn.

She got out of bed and started gathering her things. She had to pack immediately, flee with the babies, and get far away from here. Emma stood in the doorway in all her gruesome, singed ghastliness, watching her calmly.

"Did Erik burn you?" Sigrid whispered. "Is he going to put me on the bonfire, too?"

Emma shook her head. The next moment she was gone.

Gracious Mother, help me.

Sigrid paced back and forth in the room, unable to find anything she was looking for. Her sack was gone, and she had no way to carry the babies. How could they escape if she couldn't find anything to carry the babies in?

"Pull yourself together!" Ulf said and slapped her. The pain of his blow brought her back to her wits. She rubbed her cheek and looked into her brother's pleading eyes.

"We can't run away," Ulf said. "Erik will follow us and after he burns our ships, he'll come take the Scylfings' land. You have to find another way."

Sigrid gasped for air. *Forgive me for my weakness.* Soot stood leaning over the babies, protecting them with her scrawny body. Ulf's face was filled with repugnance and pleading. Sigrid pulled her fingers through her hair again.

Ulf was right. Erik's honor was everything to him and he would never let them leave alive. Now that he was victorious, chosen by Odin, he was the darling of everyone in Svealand. Sigrid shuddered as she looked at the dead slave's blood. Erik could easily snuff out their lives and no one would speak ill of him. They were all doomed.

"I don't know what to do," she whispered.

Ulf took her hand and squeezed it firmly. He said, "You'll find a way. You always do."

O Mighty One, guide me. Give me strength.

Sigrid crossed her arms over her chest and rocked back and forth, staring blankly at the wall. The walls were made of rough logs, sealed with tar, and then hung with colorful tapestries. One of the tapestries depicted a Svea king killing a warrior holding a foreign shield. Could this be the answer? Sigrid shivered, suddenly filled with an icy chill.

"Will you support me in anything?" she asked her brother.

"How can you doubt your own flesh and blood, sister?" he said, giving her a concerned look.

She nodded grimly.

"Good. Then I know what has to be done."

I

Ravens and carrion feeders feasted on the dead bodies in front of the open gates of the Trelleborg ring fortress. Behind the timbered walls smoke rose into the sky, which was filled with the devouring, terrible winged valkyries.

Harald Bluetooth's men hadn't had the strength to withstand Sweyn's men, who decimated everything in their path, wolflike and drunk with strength. Now Sweyn's men were enjoying their reward, plundering the fortress of all it was worth. They showed neither mercy nor compassion to those who hadn't managed to escape.

This was Sweyn's greatest victory. With his retinue he walked down the line of defeated, kneeling soldiers. One of them impudently looked him in the eye, defiant to the death, but the rest of them hung their heads and stared at the ground.

They knew he wouldn't show them any mercy. Ruthless was the name of the cloak he wore over his shoulders and which filled his enemies with fear. He had burned the last of his weakness to ashes in Svealand when he was freed from Sigrid. Since that day, no man in this life or the next, be he king or warrior, could withstand him. They had slaughtered Harald Bluetooth's kinsmen without mercy. Sweyn took the fate the gods had given him with swords and axes, and now the gods wandered by his side—screaming for more victims.

"Word of Trelleborg's fall has already spread far and wide," said Valdemar. "We received a fiery cross from Eskil Erlandsson. He swore his loyalty to you and is sending fifty men. The chieftains are abandoning Harald and are crouching in your shadow and looking to you now."

The old man by Sweyn's side, with his graying beard and his silver-studded armor, nodded in satisfaction at this news.

"Your assistance makes me victorious, Elder," Sweyn replied humbly. He still needed the support of these jarls.

"It was opportune that the Svea slaughtered Styrbjörn's army," Palna said. "You won't have to deal with those who didn't make it out of Fýrisvellir."

The Svea had killed them all, chieftains and warriors alike.

"Without your wisdom we would have been killed in Svealand as well," Sweyn replied, noting that Palna appreciated this recognition.

"After your victory here Harald can't refuse to meet you in battle," Valdemar said. "Before the summer is over you will have conquered the king and avenged my son's death."

Sweyn stopped, bowed his head in respect, and said, "May I be worthy."

"You are."

He might have been Harald's bastard son, but everyone hailed him and respected him. Sweyn found the power sweet and intoxicating as he looked out at his army's encampment. The tents stretched farther than the eye could see and a forest of chieftains' banners fluttered in the wind. The clan leaders came to him, obsequious, coveting a share of the riches and the land he seized. The sea sparkled beyond the tents. It was the only thing separating him from his birth father now.

Sweyn was so close to the throne of the Jellings he could almost touch it.

Since they left Svealand's shores, Sweyn had attacked every village and farm that was loyal to Harald. He had mercilessly conquered any chieftains who fought him and forced them to swear their allegiance to him and promise to aid his fight by contributing warriors, silver, and supplies.

Only four of Harald's jarls had refused, and he had punished them in the worst possible way. They were hung from a tree and forced to watch their sons being filled with glowing coals and their women and daughters being raped and then skinned. Only then did Sweyn himself slice open their bellies so they slowly went to the afterworld, shrieking and floundering.

Palna's advice to be ruthless had been extremely wise. Word of Sweyn's cruelty spread like wildfire and filled his enemies with fear. Their victory was already won even as they approached the battlefield. Many chieftains laid down their weapons and swore allegiance to Sweyn, respecting his strength and ruthlessness.

Others welcomed him with friendship from the beginning. Anger at Harald's high taxes and his crusade against the old religion was greater than Sweyn could have imagined. Often Sweyn was welcomed with joy, as a liberator.

By the time they reached Scania, his reputation had grown so strong that the chieftains sought him out on their own to pledge their loyalty to him. Having Valdemar, the Jellings' ealdorman, on his side gave him the legal right to challenge his father. Sweyn was already being called the king of the Danes and Jutes. Ship after ship of warriors joined his army, which grew so strong that few dared to fight them.

Now they had taken the Scania ring fortress, the last of Harald's strongholds. His birth father had to fight him. If he didn't, he would be forfeiting his right to call himself king.

"Well?" Sigvard asked, nodding at the prisoners who had survived the battle. "Will they live or die?"

Sweyn looked with indifference at the twenty conquered men who were still waiting on their knees, robbed of hope and livelihood. They had all refused to swear allegiance to him. They were pale souls who clung to the wooden crosses around their necks and the false religion it represented, blindly and loyally following Harald, that old fool of a king. And for what?

One filthy boy, no older than ten, trembled pathetically and was so scared he had wet himself. An elderly man with a gray beard, possibly the boy's grandfather or a foster father, whispered something to the kid, who stared down at the ground.

Sweyn sighed heavily.

"Behead them, but spare these two here," he said, pointing out the boy and the elderly man. "Put them in a boat and let them bring the sacks containing the dead men's skulls to Harald with the message that he will meet me here to die."

Sigvard smiled grimly and gestured to his waiting men. They dragged off the two that Sweyn had pointed out, and then a warrior started slaughtering the other prisoners. It took him three blows with his ax to sever the head from the body of the first. Sweyn turned to Palna, who nodded with satisfaction.

"Harald can't hide in Jelling after that indignity."

"Let him hurry here and meet his fate," Sweyn replied.

As he walked back to the camp, Sweyn inhaled the stench of death and fire. The men stripped the dead of their clothes, shoes, and valuables, and then let flocks of ravens and gulls feast on the bodies. Warriors came from the open gates of the fortress carrying armloads of plunder. Others had found wheelbarrows that they loaded full of things, and a few had found slaves to lug their newly seized loot for them.

Jutes and Danes, side by side with Scanians and Jómsvíkings— they had all rallied by his side. But it came at a price. At the feast that night Sweyn would have to give the best of the spoils to the chieftains and jarls, and this always proved tricky. Sweyn despised the noblemen's bickering and how carefully they watched to see whom he favored most. But since he needed them, he had to honor each one like an impartial father treats his sons.

It had truly been easier when he was a lone warrior. He walked into the camp, where the boys were divvying up big piles of loot and praising him, flushed with victory.

"Victory!"

"Our king!"

The aroma of the meat from the butchered pigs and sheep roasting over the fires lay heavy over the camp. Two men were fighting over a buckle, pummeling each other with their fists. They rolled around in the dust, eagerly cheered on by their buddies. A drunken youth with a cross around his neck staggered around with a jug of wine in his hand, and when he spotted Sweyn he offered the jug to him.

"Drink with me, King," the youth said, grinning stupidly as he wobbled back and forth.

Everything went immediately silent.

"Who are you to think you're the equal of your king!" roared Palna.

Sweyn raised his hand. If they were in Jómsborg, the drunken youth would have been slapped for his disrespect, but these men had fought hard for Sweyn's victories so he took the jug and raised it to the cross worshipper.

"I honor you for fighting on my side." Then Sweyn raised the jug to the other men around him. "I honor all of you. You have my great pride and respect."

When he took a long draft of the sour wine, the men cheered. Their loyalty to him shone from the battle-hardened men's filthy faces, and at this moment they esteemed him most highly of anyone in this world. Victories, knapsacks full of loot, and full bellies bound them to his cause. Sweyn handed the jug back to the drunken youth and patted his shoulder.

"Your god has served us well."

Valdemar nodded contentedly. Several of the chieftains who had come to fight on their side were Christian, and Valdemar had urged him to show that he respected both the new and the old ways. As long as they were fighting for Sweyn, why should their religion matter? After all, he knew which gods were in charge.

The shouts of hurrah echoed as he proceeded through the camp. Sweyn knelt down by a young man who lay wounded on the ground. His shoulder was bleeding, and he was shivering and feverish, pale and in sorry shape.

"I see that you fought well," Sweyn said.

"I killed two men and drew the blood of a third with my ax," the warrior replied, gray in the face from fever. "But I was too slow with my shield and now here I lie."

"Bear these battle wounds with honor," Sweyn said and stood up. "I thank you for your courage and grant you relief."

He nodded to Palna who immediately gave orders for the wounded man to be picked up. Beyla would attend to his wounds, and then there was a good chance he would live to see tomorrow.

Sweyn walked on, greeting warriors, inquiring about their wounds, and praising their courage. After every battle he had made these rounds, acknowledged each and every one of those who had been killed. He had learned from Palna when he was a child that nothing gives warriors as much strength as loyalty to their leader. He took care to conceal his own weariness.

Only when he reached his own tent was he able to wash his hands clean of the blood and mud in the bowl that Ragnvald hurried over with. The boy handed him a towel and followed Sweyn when he went into the tent and took off his sword.

"What else would you like, my king?"

Sweyn dismissed him with a gesture and sat down heavily on his bed. His muscles ached with fatigue, but the victory, the somber celebrations, burned in his blood and filled him with a strength he'd never imagined.

Thor must have put his magical power belt, Megingjörð, around his waist because he hardly needed to sleep or eat and still did not feel tired.

Sweyn stared vacantly at the tent wall, where he saw the dead bellowing in horror. The jarls' sons, some of them no more than children, screamed through their charred mouths as the glowing coals made their bellies boil. He saw women with torn faces, slain enemies, Harald's thanes with their bellies sliced open. They all screamed day and night from the afterworld, lost souls that thronged around him no matter where he went.

Sweyn turned away in disgust. They couldn't hurt him. He had been chosen by the gods and had made the sacrifices they demanded. Victory was all that mattered.

The tent flap fluttered, and with relief he noted it was Åke coming in with a drinking horn in his hand.

"Eskil Hardrade is having trouble with the Jutes again. I sent Ax-Wolf to mediate."

Sweyn nodded. He accepted the mead and emptied the horn in one go. Instantly the cries of the dead faded a bit.

"Magne Toke, a chieftain from the border with the Geats, has arrived to swear his allegiance to you," Åke said, shaking his head in awe. "They're coming from every direction, bringing you gifts and paying tribute to you like you were a god."

Behind Åke stood the pale shadows of former comrades: Eyvind, who had fallen at the battle in Lund, and other warriors, whose names Sweyn no longer even remembered. They had been so full of courage and vitality, and now they stood side by side, row after row, following his feats from the afterworld.

Sweyn clenched his fist.

"Chieftains are afraid of not being on good terms with the victor and thereby missing out on the favors he can dole out. I speak fairly to my men, promise them glory and the freedom their ancestors had of thought and belief, and they swear their allegiance to me, but the day I lose they will immediately crawl to Harald, groveling for mercy."

Their fawning disgusted Sweyn. He could only trust the ones who had been on his side from the beginning.

"You will never be defeated," Åke said earnestly.

At his feet lay the memory of the young maiden from Eklunda, the one with the curly blond hair. The blood gushed from her mouth, and her body shuddered in the throes of death.

The valkyries' triumphant shrieks drove away the shadows and filled him with their dark intoxication. He had been chosen by Thor. The ruler of Thruthvang wandered at his side, and he had to show that he was worthy.

"I swear I will rule over the largest kingdom Scandinavia has ever seen. All of the land from Thule in the north to Rome in the south, from the land of the Rus in the east to England in the west will be mine."

Sweyn smiled at his own clenched fist. Like the names of Alexander the Great, Caesar, and Gorm the Old, his own name would echo through the ages. Only the most ruthless could take what they wanted, and Sweyn was one of them.

"When the Jelling throne is mine, I will make friends with Erik of Svealand. They say he has sisters. I'll take one of them as my wife. The kingdom of Valhalla will be unified."

Åke looked at him in surprise.

"Then you really have forgotten Sigrid Tostedotter."

Sweyn smiled bitterly as he pictured her smiling, reaching out her hand to caress his cheek. He was grateful for that bitch's treachery because he achieved his full power only after he had given up on her.

"She's not important," he said, a jab of pain tearing at his chest.

The valkyries' dark power grew in strength until a firestorm raced through Sweyn, burning souls and memories to ash. There was only the present. He got up and looked at Åke.

"Neither she nor anyone else can stop me from taking what I want."

"Are you ready?" Ulf asked.

Sigrid ran her hand over the babies' downy heads one last time, feeling their warmth. The little ones lay close together. They only slept peacefully when they were close to each other, as if brother and sister found solace and safety in their togetherness. Sigrid, too, had found support from her own brother during the dark months that Erik had been away.

The day after he won at Fýrisvellir and tried to murder the babies and her, he left Kungsgården. The Svea chieftains who had turned their backs on Erik were going to pay dearly for their betrayal, she had learned, and there was no doubt that she, too, would meet her destiny. All summer she had feared the king's return as ill will around her grew. Crazy rumors abounded. For instance, that she was sleeping with her brother and that the children were really his. The same people who had once thought so highly of her and asked for her blessing now whispered that she had murdered her own innocent kinswomen and was secretly aligned with Harald Bluetooth. Others swore they had seen her praying to a cross and insisted that she was actually Christian. Sigrid had struggled against the lies that were being spread, but none of the friendship she'd known before remained. One by one they turned their backs on her, even the priestesses at the temple. Of all the betrayals, there was nothing that stung more than the priestesses turning away from her. They knew that no one was a more dedicated servant of Our Lady Freya than she was, but it didn't matter.

Worried that it might put them on Erik's bad side, no one dared get close to her. They were spineless, false, and useless. Even Haldis eyed her with suspicion. Wherever she turned, she was met with a chilly silence.

It took its toll on her. Every night she watched over her children, certain that someone was going to try to kill them. She jumped anxiously at every sound, and she could scarcely eat. Without Ulf and the Scylfings she would have lost her mind in her loneliness.

Blood really was thicker than water.

Sigrid caressed the babies one last time.

Please let me return to my children with my life intact, I pray you.

Yesterday she had received word that the king was coming back to hold her accountable. Her hands trembled as she secured her cloak with a pin. Before the day was over she might be wandering at her mother's side in Niflheim, but she would do everything she possibly could to make sure that didn't happen.

Sigrid nodded to the Scylfing warriors guarding the cradle.

"Fight to the death for my babies," she said, choking up.

She caught just a glimpse of pity in their expressions before they nodded deferentially. With Ulf at her side, she walked, head held high, toward the hall where her husband and judge awaited.

"This isn't over," her brother whispered, but she could tell he was worried.

Sigrid forced a smile but wasn't able to reply.

All I can do is ask for your protection.

Erik turned his head away in disgust when she entered the hall. Axel and Orm stood beside him, as did Ergil, the family's ealdorman, who listened to everything but rarely spoke. The three priests stood by the fireplace, their expressions unreadable. Haldis and Solveig were also there, and there was no kindness to be discerned in their faces.

So these nine would decide if she lived or died.

"I can't look at that abomination," Erik muttered.

A welcome iciness filled Sigrid at the sight of her husband. He had her to thank for his victory over Styrbjörn. She had selflessly sacrificed her own happiness even though he had wanted to take her life twice, once with the dagger in the bedchamber, the second time with the slave he sent to her room. On this third attempt, he was determined to see it done no matter what.

Axel stepped forward, and she saw that even he had turned away from her. There was neither kindness nor understanding in his expression as he began to speak.

"Sigrid Tostedotter, you are accused of having maliciously induced the ruler of Svealand to proclaim your bastard child the king of Svealand, a crime so shameful it is punishable by death."

So it was decided. She was to die. The fear in her chest gave way to grayish-black emptiness. They knew the truth, and she was going to have to pay with her life for following the will of the goddess. She had sacrificed everything for nothing.

Sigrid raised her head and looked at each person in the hall. All that remained was for her to fight to the death, like the Scylfing she was. She would fight bravely for her children, and then go under.

"Lies have been spread about me since I came to Svealand. Unfounded rumors spread by jealous enemies have been repeated so often they're taken as the truth."

Haldis and the men watched her in disgust. She spoke the truth and they heard lies, convinced as they were of her guilt. They were loyal to Erik, and she was being sacrificed just as she herself had sacrificed Jorun.

Sigrid took a breath.

"These rumors are a crime against our king and against Valhalla. Arngrim, our revered priest, would never have proclaimed Olaf king when he was in my womb if he wasn't Erik's son. Odin, the wisest of the gods, would have objected if the blood of Erik's family line were not strong in the child."

With relief Sigrid saw a shadow of concern come over Arngrim's face. When Erik had changed his loyalty from Thor to Odin, Arngrim lost his prominent status to Odin's priest. Arngrim couldn't deny the power of Odin without denying Odin's priest.

"A witch can twist the most powerful men through delusion and wickedness," said Frey's priest.

Arngrim nodded seriously. "The child I crowned in your womb was Olaf. The ones lying in the cradle are changelings. Twins are a sign of evil. Only the All-Father knows what you did to Erik's true son. Your maidservant could have sacrificed the child to the darkness you poisoned Svealand with, before taking her own life."

Sigrid hid her rage as the priests prevented her from escaping the accusations. They were spineless, with their twisted minds. They couldn't wait to see her hanged. The hall reeked with their desire.

Is this the Valhalla you got me to sacrifice everything for?

Sigrid turned to Erik.

"Erik, hear my oath. The children are yours. All I've ever wanted is to serve you and help you to victory."

He looked at her for the first time since she had entered the room. The king had become emaciated during his absence, and his beard was sprinkled with gray.

"How dare you claim any part of your king's victory?" he said. "How can you claim the victory that good men fought and died for? You're insane, woman, a giantess in a human body, spreading lies and poison."

"You're talking about my sister," Ulf said calmly.

"I no longer believe a word of what the Scylfings say," Erik said, putting his hand on his carved throne.

Ulf's face darkened. This was a declaration of war against his family, the spark that would cause the war between their two peoples to reignite.

Sigrid's hand trembled as she adjusted the hood over her hair and prepared to tell the truth about what had happened.

"I sent my servant to the Jómsvíkings with a message. I beseeched them to leave the battle, in the name of Vanadís, and they obeyed me, which gave you the victory. I did all of this for you, my beloved and highly esteemed husband. I willingly serve you and Svealand in everything, and nothing pains me more than to see you angry."

Doubt was etched deeply on the faces of those listening. They didn't believe a word she said, but Erik laughed and turned to Axel, who stood with his arms crossed in front of his chest.

"Now she talks as if she were a man. If the Jómsvíkings listened to you, that proves that you slept with them. Jorun was right. You killed her because you were afraid she would spread the truth."

He waved his hand, dismissing Sigrid as if she didn't exist.

"Take the bitch away and hang her."

Suddenly the fear clutched her. She should never have persuaded the Jómsvíkings to leave the battle. She should have let Styrbjörn win. Of all the mistakes she had made, the worst was that she had given Erik more power.

There was only one way out of this.

"I know how you can become the greatest of kings in Scandinavia," she said.

Erik leaned back in his throne.

"You've said enough. Your life is used up."

"Wait," ealdorman Ergil said quietly to Erik. "I want to hear what she has to say."

Sigrid looked at the shriveled old man in surprise. She had never heard him say anything in all her time here, and yet he was the one who spoke up for her cause. Sigrid took a breath.

"Repudiate me," she said.

The words silenced the room as they stared at her in amazement.

"Repudiate me and let me return to Geatland in shame with the children. Then the peace between the Scylfings and the Svea will endure and remain strong. Let me rule Geatland for you in your son's name, and I swear by Freya and my dead mother I will follow your will in everything. Repudiate me and take an Obotrite princess for your wife. Then Svealand will be protected in the east and west, and your kingdom will increase and become stronger."

The silence that followed was oppressive. This was her last chance, the only thing that could save them. If Erik didn't see it, then Axel, the most sensible of the Svea, ought to. Sigrid looked at her brother, who nodded encouragingly.

"If you find no likeness in Olaf when he's seven years old, you can disown him. By that time you will have more sons and can choose another as king."

Relieved, Sigrid saw a spark of interest in Erik's eyes. This was a way out that preserved his honor intact. Svealand's laws permitted Erik to have multiple wives, and if he followed her advice he would get to keep everything and lose nothing. Heartbeat after heartbeat dragged by while Sigrid waited.

"The idea is worth considering," said Axel.

The other men backed him up, and even the priests nodded their assent.

Ulf put his hand on his sword and somberly said, "I speak for my family when I say that we will honor this. My father Toste has conquered Anund. Geatland is almost two times larger than it was when you married Sigrid, and you would rule over all this land. We Scylfings will honor Sigrid if she rules in your name. But if you kill her, each and every one of us will seek to avenge her death."

Sigrid held her breath as she watched those assembled. They had to accept the deal she and Ulf were offering them. It was too good to refuse.

"It is a worthy agreement," Axel finally said to Erik. "You receive more than you give."

The ealdorman nodded his agreement. Erik was half turned away from her, but she could still tell how angry he was. After an eternity he nodded slightly.

"The boy stays here. You can take the girl," he said.

Sigrid clenched her fist. Never in this life or the next would he take her son.

"In the agreement between the Scylfings and the Svea, it says that Sigrid gets to keep the children until their seventh birthday, as is customary," Ulf said calmly. "To refuse to let her keep Olaf is to break your oath."

Erik took two steps toward the long table where the jugs of mead and dishes of food were laid out. Enraged, he swept everything onto the floor so the dishes shattered.

"She tricked me into proclaiming a bastard the king of Svealand!"

"If you can prove what you say, then do so here and now," Ulf said, his hand on his sword hilt.

If Erik drew his sword, they would all die: Ulf, the children, and her. The Svea would attack the Geats, and the Scylfings back home would erupt again.

"Enough now!" roared Haldis, stepping out to the center of the room. "Our family honors its agreements."

She scowled at Sigrid and Erik.

"Your animosity is poisoning both this household and the kingdom. I see you in the boy, Erik. He looks like you did when you came into this world. Quit denying him and make a deal that is favorable to us."

Sigrid looked at Erik's mother in astonishment. She had expected Haldis to fight hard for her son, not to be on her side. Haldis gave Erik a stern look, and he finally nodded.

"All right, until the boy is seven. But I want my own people there, a man who will let me know if the bitch doesn't obey."

Victory. Sigrid's stomach ached with apprehension, and she hardly dared breathe as Erik and Ulf each drank from the treaty horn to conclude the deal. She was going to get to go home, with her children. The fearful nights were over. Haldis took the ornate horn with the silver fittings and drank before passing the horn to Sigrid. The mead was sweet in her mouth, but not as sweet as the relief.

"When do you leave Svealand?" the queen mother asked when Sigrid handed Solveig the horn.

"Immediately."

"I suppose that's best, yes."

There was nothing more to say. With Ulf by her side, Sigrid held her head high and left Erik and the Svea forever. Every step away from the hall filled her with joy.

They got to go home.

She ran into her chamber, picked up Olaf from the cradle, and hugged him tight, breathing in the heavy sweet scent of a sleeping baby.

Teary-eyed, she leaned down and stroked Estrid's cheek.

She was going home, returning as queen of the Geats. Sigrid embraced the triumph and allowed joy to race through her body. The nightmare she had been living was finally over. There would be no more sweaty nights of fear, and no more kissing up to that simpleton of a stranger she had been married off to.

With a smile, she looked at her brother.

"Without you, I'd have gone off to my noose, marked for death and soon a shadow forgotten by everyone. My gratitude is infinite, therefore everything you want you shall have. Become my jarl, and if Ingeborg from Haglaskog still wants you, I'll pay off her husband so she can become your bride."

Ulf was delighted, but her offer was a trifling repayment for everything he had done for her. Still, she enjoyed his happiness, being all too familiar with the agony of living apart from your beloved.

"If you can do that, then I will serve you loyally."

Sigrid nodded, smiling. She could do all that and more, because from this moment on she was in charge.

ᛋ

"He's here," Palna yelled, pointing to the Jellings' royal standard, which rose above the other flags.

Harald's warriors stood in a formation three men deep on the muddy plain that sloped down toward the sea. A cold autumn wind blew in over the warriors, tugging at their cloaks. This was Sweyn's greatest moment, the beginning of the stories that would be told about his feats. This was the day when he would kill his father.

Silence hung heavy over the battlefield, where hundreds of warriors waited to win or die.

The Jómsvíkings stood in the first row along with Sweyn's own hird, their shields up and the spearmen behind their backs, ready to pierce the enemy.

The warriors who loyally followed Sweyn waited like hungry wolves for his sign under the standard his mother had embroidered for him before she died.

Next to them stood the Scanians and the Danes, with a forest of flags flapping and snapping in the wind. Ax-Wolf smiled in anticipation. He wore his bear teeth around his neck for strength from his totem animal. Sigvard sneered, as if he were inspecting maidens at a slave market. Åke stood resolute, his hand on his sword, ready to fight. Hatred and pride swelled in Sweyn's chest as he put on his helmet and grasped his shield. This was his moment of destiny, when he would take the place he was born to or die.

"Several Jelling flags are missing from the king's side," Palna said.

Valdemar nodded, eyeing his brother's standard with an unreadable expression.

"They have left my son's assassin," Valdemar confirmed.

"They'll soon kneel to my supremacy," Sweyn said.

He looked up at the falcon circling above them in the gray sky. Freya in her bird form shrieked along with her valkyries. Freya had never left his side. He knew that, now that the mists had been pulled away from his eyes and he understood the true significance of the sacrifice in Lejre.

A message had come from the North that Sigrid had been repudiated by Erik and had returned to the Geats to rule there in Svealand's name. It was rumored that the babies weren't Erik's, but rather that a Jómsvíking was their father. The children were his, begotten by the gods to rule in the kingdom he had been born to conquer. Sigrid had lied to save his life because she knew Styrbjörn's men were going to die at Fýrisvellir. She had served him well.

The triumphant courage of victory filled Sweyn, and with a nod to Ragnvald, his mother's banner was raised.

"Men, warriors, brothers!" he shouted, and more than a thousand men turned their faces toward him. "For decades, Harald Bluetooth's terror has tormented the Scanians, Danes, and Jutes. He prohibited the faith of our forefathers. He took your seed in taxes so you've gone hungry while he's been rolling in wealth. He stole the ancient freedom of the men of the North. This is the day when we take back what's been lost. Overthrow Harald Bluetooth! Kill the enemy!"

The warriors answered his battle cry with such force the ground shook.

"Kill the enemy!"

Sweyn drew his sword and nodded to Palna. His foster father took two steps backward and then flung his spear, which consecrated the battlefield.

"Odin owns us all," he yelled.

The muffled rumble of the war drums blended with bellowing horns as Sweyn and his men marched toward the enemy. Like a relentless wave of raised shields, they poured toward Harald's men. The first swarm of arrows cut through the air. Sweyn crouched under his shield, hearing the dull thud as the arrowheads hit the wood. Without hesitation, he kept moving forward. A moment later the two armies met.

Sweyn ducked away from a spear and immediately struck at the enemy in front of him but missed.

A motion at the very periphery of his field of vision made him raise his shield. The ax almost cleaved the wood, and he felt the strength of the blow all the way up to his shoulder. He struck back at the spear bearer immediately, and this time, his blade cut into the gap between the man's hood and battle tunic. Bleeding, he remained on his feet and pulled back among a jabbing forest of spears.

Sweyn turned toward the ax wielder who was fighting Åke now, took the biting iron in a two-hand grasp, and swung. The blade cut through the man's skull, and he instantly fell down dead. *A curse on Harald's eagle food!* Winded, Sweyn turned his head to follow the battle that undulated around the hird fighting to protect their king.

The shield wall pushed Harald's warriors backward toward the sea, step-by-step. The spearmen behind the shields lanced down warrior after warrior who were then trampled by the men continuously refilling the ranks. *A curse on the condemned devoured by his power.*

"Spearmen, forward!"

"Surround him!"

Confident of victory, they met Harald's men, Sweyn's men relentless in their strength. Their wedge formations cut into Harald's defenses and ripped open his line. The entire hird around Sweyn was engaged in battle.

Palna fought at his side, thrusting his dagger into a warrior, and then tossing the body aside, only to rapidly dispatch a spearman. Harald's banner billowed in front of Sweyn, luring him, enticing him onward.

Sweyn tilted his head back and shrieked out his rage: "Forward!"

The hird responded to his roar, and soon the wolves howled their bloodthirstiness. Iron struck steel. Iron smashed bones and ripped apart bleeding flesh. A quick charge and Sweyn lopped the arm off an ax-wielding man, who dropped to his knees screaming.

Blades clashed, men screamed, spears impaled warriors. Sweyn hacked his way forward blow-by-blow. He felt something soft under his feet, a fallen warrior who hadn't died yet, and chopped into the back of a farmer without armor.

One blow almost broke his shield, but he proceeded ahead, fortified by the ecstasy of battle. Quick as a viper, Sweyn stabbed a warrior in the neck, between his helmet and armor. The man fell to the ground, blood gushing, while Sweyn met the sword blade of a big man in expensive armor. The warrior took a step to the side and attacked with a speed Sweyn had never encountered. He raised his sword, and it was almost knocked out of his hand. Then their blades locked. The warrior's helmet covered almost his entire face, and the eyes staring through the eye slits were icy. Sweyn's arms quivered as he struggled to hold out. He took a step back, then two. He tried to knee the warrior, who twisted out of the way at the last second and then hit Sweyn with his shield and his sword simultaneously. The pain that burned in Sweyn's arm was worse than anything he had felt before. The shield fell from his hands, and only at the last possible moment did he counter the blow with his sword.

He couldn't lose this battle.

Step-by-step he was driven backward, his sword arm aching more and more from fatigue. Winning was his destiny. He grabbed his dagger with his free hand, but accidentally dropped it on the ground. The warrior's strength was too much for him. A kick caused him to sink to one knee, but he managed to counter the blow aimed at his throat. Their swords locked again. Sweyn couldn't withstand the strength pushing his arm down. His whole body trembled with fatigue. Sweat poured down his face, and everything went silent. He could hear no valkyries screaming, no war cries, no death wails.

He was going to die now.

The enemy combatant let go of his shield and grabbed his dagger with his free hand. In the flash of this moment he could lose it all: the Jelling throne, the victory, the conquest, and Sigrid. The combatant's sword arm pushed relentlessly on Sweyn's chest even though he fought against it with all his might. Then the warrior raised his dagger. Pain seared like fire as Sweyn raised his injured arm. Defenseless, he prepared himself to die.

At that moment the pressure from the combatant's sword eased up, and the combatant sank to his knees screaming. Without thinking, Sweyn thrust at his eyes and felt the crunch as his blade entered the man's skull.

It was over.

Winded and bleeding, Sweyn clambered to his feet.

"Achilles tendons, boy," Ax-Wolf said with a grin from behind the fallen combatant. "I told you that's the place to cut, right?"

Sweyn was still alive. He pulled his sword out of the man's head and took a deep breath. The bleeding wound on his arm was deep, exposing bone, but it wasn't lethal.

He couldn't die in battle.

Sweyn laughed triumphantly and raised his sword.

Just then he heard the sound of a battle horn across the field. Harald was calling his men back. Harald's boys turned around and ran toward their ships while Sweyn's men followed them, slashing at their backs. A bit of cloth was wrapped around the wound on Sweyn's arm. Palna slapped him on the back, and they ran forward together.

The next moment it was over. Sweyn stopped, gasping for breath, sweat running down his body. Harald stood before him, once king of the Danes and Jutes, surrounded by his most loyal men, who stood blood-spattered, weapons drawn, in a circle around the old man. The king wasn't wearing a helmet and looked confused, as if he couldn't believe what he was seeing. He had a big potbelly under his golden armor. His face was beet red beneath his braided beard. He was a pitiful sight.

Sweyn yanked off his helmet and tossed it to Ragnvald.

"Kneel to your king and ruler," Sweyn yelled, striding forward to the small group of warriors around Harald.

The stench of fear lay heavy as Sweyn's warriors closed ranks in a ring around Harald and his men.

"Stop there," yelled Harald Bluetooth. "Stop where you are or die."

Sweyn smiled at his birth father's shrill voice, triumph seething in his blood. Harald, the father who had only mocked and humiliated him, wasn't so haughty now.

"Put down your weapons and swear your loyalty to me and you may live," Sweyn said.

Harald's hird hesitated. They exchanged glances and then eyed the superior forces that had them surrounded.

"Fight!" their king yelled. "God will reward you in paradise."

Sweyn watched their agony. It didn't matter to him whether they chose life or honor.

Then a young man in Jelling colors lowered his shield and strode up to Sweyn like a man and tossed his sword at Sweyn's feet. Then he took off his helmet. Sweyn recognized his half brother Erik right away, the only man in the whole family who'd greeted him kindly in Lejre.

"I honor your decision," Erik said.

"God will punish you for your disloyalty!" yelled Harald. "You're snakes that I nourished from my loins!"

Erik looked at Harald's wretchedness and then turned to Valdemar, who was guarding Sweyn from behind.

"I was close to your son, ealdorman," Erik told Valdemar.

Valdemar nodded with dignity and then said, "Then do what's right."

Erik took a deep breath, bowed his head, and said, "I swear you loyalty, half brother. My sword is yours."

A ruler had to be magnanimous. Sweyn leaned down and picked Erik's sword up off the ground and put it back in his hand.

"Then you may keep this valuable item. Come to my tent tonight and we'll talk, as brothers."

Erik leaned forward and confided, whispering into Sweyn's ear, "Father's out of his senses. Kill him."

Sweyn turned back to Harald, who was swearing at his warriors as, one by one, they set their weapons on the ground and abandoned him. Soon Harald was alone.

"You ought to grovel in gratitude at my feet because I gave you life," he shouted, pulling out his sword.

This was the man Sweyn had hated and feared his whole life. This was the moment he had dreamt of, but he felt no triumph or joy now, just hollow disgust. Without a throne and sycophantic chieftains, his father was just a yawning heap of skin and fat, a poor, pitiful wretch of a fool lacking manhood and strength.

"Come on then, lad. Don't you dare to fight me?" Harald sneered and showed his stinking blue teeth.

Sweyn was next to him in two paces and without hesitation plunged his sword underneath Harald's armor. It slid through Harald's flesh with ease, between the ribs.

"Say hello to my mother Åsa in the afterworld."

Sweyn smiled in surprise at his father's eyes. Harald rattled and shrieked as the blood poured over Sweyn's hand.

"Die, you fat pig. May you agonize in the caves of Hel."

Harald rasped and rattled as his lungs filled with blood. His eyes were cloudy, and a dark trickle ran from the corner of his mouth. Then he collapsed. Sweyn pulled his sword back out and looked at his bloody hand. It was over. The king of the Jellings, the most powerful of men, his dreaded father, was dead.

Sweyn raised his sword to the sky and looked out at his men.

"Victory!"

One by one they sank to their knees in silence and bowed their heads, their hands on their hearts. No matter which way he turned, Sweyn saw men showing him respect. Only the sea and the wind could be heard in the vast silence. Sweyn looked up at the sky, where the screaming falcon soared, resting on the wind. Sweyn was the ruler of the Northmen, and his will was law. He, the bastard, had fulfilled his destiny and taken the power and riches he wanted. Palna raised his head and looked at him, his face filled with pride and respect. Valdemar stood up and raised his hands.

"Stand up for Sweyn, king of the Danes, Jutes, and Scanians, leader of the Northmen. All hail!" Valdemar shouted.

The warriors stood up, and their roar of victory made the ground tremble. Sweyn raised his hands, their respect and esteem making him invulnerable as the intoxicating joy of victory almost made his chest burst.

"Welcome to the throne of the Jellings!" Palna exclaimed.

Sweyn raised his arms yet again, accepting the adulation of the warriors with laughter as sweet power coursed through him. He was indomitable, the greatest of rulers. But this was just the beginning of his story. He hadn't taken everything he wanted yet.

ᚲ

Sigrid looked out over Skagulheim's formal hall, where the Scylfing chieftains crowded around the long table. Torvald Scylfing with his red-haired son Harald, Tibrand from Alfheim with his brother Isar, the cheerful Annfinn, and all the others chatted together merrily as they stuffed their bellies full of the two pigs that had been slaughtered especially for this occasion. Her grandmother sat by the wall looking not at all displeased, having drunk more wine than she could take.

Ulf whispered something into Ingeborg of Haglaskog's ear, and they laughed together. That bride had cost a fair amount of land, but it was worth it when Sigrid saw how happy they were.

The light from the torches danced over the tapestries on the walls. The slaves darted back and forth with pitchers of wine and mead.

Everything was the same as it had always been, ever since the night she walked into the hall to meet Erik's ambassador. She had been such a young girl, who hadn't known anything. And yet everything was different.

The hall she had once believed, wide-eyed, to be the biggest in the world now seemed simple and narrow. And she was no longer a young girl who ran around in the woods without a care or any knowledge, believing she had the answers to everything.

Sigrid leaned forward in her throne, rocking Olaf on her knee.

The little one was wearing a battle tunic that Toste, filled with admiration and tenderness toward his grandchild, had made for him, a gesture of reconciliation for the bad blood that had flown between father and daughter. Sigrid's homecoming hadn't been as simple as she had thought it would be. Gray and worn after the war with Anund, her father had lost a lot of his standing, but kneeling to his own daughter was the last thing he wanted to do.

The victory he had won had been costly in terms of lives and farms, and Sigrid now knew the personal price her father had paid.

"Never will I give up my land to a woman and a child. That would be a disgrace for the leader of the Scylfings."

She had listened quietly to her father's rage and hidden her satisfaction at learning that his wife, Gunlög, had turned out to be a traitor. Her stepmother had moved from Skagulheim when Toste was in Svealand, and no one knew where she had gone until she was captured with Anund's brother.

She had been sending her lover messages about what the Scylfings were up to for a long time. Gunlög was the one who had told the enemy that they were on their way through the Alva Woods, where Anund attacked them with warriors and battle sorcery. The woman who had tormented Sigrid as she grew up had turned out to be the most treacherous of the Scylfings' enemies. Toste had killed her with his bare hands, and Sigrid wasn't at all sorry about that.

"This is not your treacherous wife speaking, but your own daughter," she had said. "You will kneel to me and to your grandson, your own flesh and blood. This strengthens the family's power and keeps together the lands you have so honorably conquered."

The negotiations between father and daughter had taken a whole day, but Sigrid did not back down. Her father was the one who had sold her to Erik to strengthen his ties to Svealand. Surely he could swallow the outcome of that decision like a man. Ulf stood firmly at her side, and in the end Toste consented.

"You're still going to have to convince the other noblemen to agree."

"With your support they will kneel to their king, Olaf," Sigrid had replied, and she had been right.

She had been forced into a lot of flattery to win the noblemen over, and it had cost her quite a bit in gifts of silver, livestock, and land, but in the end they had all sworn their loyalty to her and Olaf.

She kissed the boy's head and got up from the throne. The men stood and nodded their heads.

"I thank you all, respected countrymen and warriors. The privilege of serving you as queen, in the name of my husband and son, is the greatest honor that could befall a woman. I swear on my life that your land will be protected from this moment forward, defended by Vanadís."

The chieftains raised their cups and proclaimed their loyalty.

"Leader of the Scylfings!"

"We serve you, Queen!"

Sigrid smiled at their professions of respect. The victory was sweet, like the sweetest wine, but it came with a bitter taste. *Happy is the one, who receives praise and kind words; less certain is it to own something that dwells in the chest of another,* Sigrid thought. They could turn against her at any time, but for the moment she held them all in her hand. And she knew all too well how she would ensnare them further.

"Tonight you will eat and drink, and tomorrow King Olaf will give you gifts to remember this day," she proclaimed. This was met with the cheers she had anticipated.

Sigrid nodded to Åse, who stood behind her throne with Estrid in her arms, and then she left the formal hall, standing tall. Only one thing remained, the thing she had feared and longed for most.

◆ ◆ ◆

The full moon bathed the autumnal fields in its cold light as Sigrid walked up her mother's burial mound.

She brought the children with her, carried by her father's mistress Åse and Soot, the slave who had served her so well in Svealand. They stepped aside when they reached her mother's grave to give Sigrid some privacy. Only when she was completely alone with the little ones did she raise her eyes and greet Folkvang and the valkyries in the sky.

"These are my children, Olaf and Estrid, your descendants."

She smiled as her mother stepped forth out of the shadows, airy like the mists in a field at dawn and just as beautiful as she had been in life.

"Our lives are your legacy," Sigrid whispered.

Without her mother, she would have remained in the afterworld, wandering lost in Niflheim. Her mother had shown her the way back to life and given her the strength to fight for her own sake and for her children.

The evanescent shadow of the woman, who had once given birth to Sigrid, caressed the babies' cheeks.

Sigrid closed her eyes and felt her mother's hand on her own cheek, soft like a summer breeze. Thirstily she drank in her mother's tenderness and let it heal a lifetime of missing her. Then her mother grew paler in the moonlight. Summoned back to the afterworld, she dissolved before Sigrid's eyes.

Everything was as it should be. The family line was unbroken.

She smiled at Olaf in her arms, the king of kings, born to a glorious destiny. He was so like Sweyn that there was no doubt who his father was.

Day and night, Sweyn was with her. She saw him in the children that Vanadís had given them during the sacred sacrifice in Lejre. He was with her in the evenings when memories of the brief time they had shared together were so vivid that she could picture his face. *My beloved.*

Word had come from the south that Sweyn had defeated his father and been crowned king. He had achieved everything he had striven for.

And so had she. Sigrid hugged the babies and felt the warmth from her precious darlings.

It felt like a lifetime had elapsed since she had stood on this burial mound, no more than a child herself, and received the greatest of promises from Vanadís. Now that she had traveled the world and down into the underworld, she knew what was real and what was woven from her own hopes and beliefs as a young girl.

"I still miss him," she said.

Emma, always watching over them, emerged from the shadows and said, "Who knows what's in the tapestry?"

"You know, my sister," Sigrid said, smiling sadly.

Emma looked seriously at the babies.

"The darkness grows stronger. The battle isn't over yet."

Sigrid swallowed her fear as the shadows thickened around her. Nameless people, now passed on, stood beside Jorun and Alfhild. Even Gunlög could be seen at the back of the ranks. The valkyries sparked in the sky. A bird cried in warning from Sigrid's moonlit fields, which spread as far as the eye could see, and beyond.

"With Vanadís's help, you will protect us," Sigrid said.

Her sister's smile was inscrutable.

"Enjoy this peace. It will soon be over," Emma said gently and then allowed herself to be swallowed by the darkness again.

Life was a circle without end. Sigrid took a deep breath. It would never end. She turned her back to the shadows and looked toward the estate.

Four times, enemies had tried to kill her. She had descended to the underworld, given birth during a raging war, and been slandered. Her honor had been violated, and people had tried to take what was hers. She had overcome all of this. She was mightier than ever and had been rewarded with the most precious of treasures.

Olaf slept soundly, breathing safely in her arm, and Estrid looked at her with her infinitely wise eyes. Her love for them was stronger than a thousand beasts of prey and stretched higher than the vault of heaven and deeper than the caves of Niflheim. There was no strength more awesome in these nine worlds, and not even death could overcome this, the greatest of Freya's gifts.

Head held high, Sigrid left the past behind and walked down the side of the burial mound with her babies, back to the estate and the dark future that was hiding in what had been woven. Whatever it held, she would face it with strength.

"Don't worry," she told the babies. "Mama will protect you."

APPENDIX

IMPORTANT PEOPLE

SKAGULHEIM

Skagul Toste—nobleman and chieftain of the Scylfing clan, father of Sigrid and Ulf

Sigrid—daughter of the Scylfing chieftain, Toste

Ulf—Sigrid's older brother

Gunlög—Toste's wife

Allvis—Sigrid's paternal grandmother

Åse—Toste's mistress

Rune—Toste's brother

Ylva—Rune's wife

Jorun—Sigrid's cousin and maidservant

Alfhild—Sigrid's kinswoman and maidservant

Allfrid—Sigrid's mother

JÓMSBORG

Palna—chieftain of the Jómsvíkings, an elite force of mercenary soldiers, and Sweyn's foster father

Sweyn—Harald Bluetooth's illegitimate son, Palna's foster son

Åke—Palna's son and Sweyn's foster brother

Ax-Wolf—legendary berserker

Gunnar—a Jómsvíking, Palna's brother

Sigvard—a Jómsvíking, Ax-Wolf's brother

Ingolf—one of Palna's captains

Beyla—a seeress, Palna's sister

Emma—an orphaned girl who is looked after by Beyla

Sleep-Åsa—Sweyn's mother

LEJRE

Harald Gormsson, aka Harald Bluetooth—king of Denmark

Tova—Harald's wife

Thyre—Harald's daughter

Styrbjörn the Strong—Thyre's husband, nephew of Erik of Svealand

Erik, Haakon, and Torgny—Harald's sons

Valdemar—Harald's brother

Olav Tryggvason—warrior from Gardarik, the states of the Kievan Rus

AROS

Erik of Svealand—king and leader of the Svea

Haldis—Erik's mother

Axel—Erik's confidant and main military leader

Orm—Erik's closest friend and a Svea warrior

Solveig—Axel's wife

Aedis—one of Erik's mistresses

Hyndla—Aedis's mother, a seeress

Soot—Haldis's slave

GLOSSARY

Æsir—one of the two main tribes of deities (cf. *Vanir*)

Brísingamen—a necklace belonging to Freya

Dag—god of day

Danelaw—the portion of England ruled by the Danes

dís (plural: *dísir*)—a goddess associated with fate, who sometimes intervenes in the lives of mortals and clans

ealdorman—the chief officer of a district

Eggthér—a giant who plays his harp as Ragnarök begins

Einherjar—people who have died in battle and have been brought to Valhalla by valkyries

Erce—an earth or fertility goddess (used chiefly as an interjection)

Folkvang—a meadow ruled by Freya where those who do not go to Valhalla go instead

Frey—god of virility and prosperity

Freya—goddess of love, sex, beauty, fertility, and gold

Garm—a wolf chained at the mouth of Gnipa Cave

Geats, the—a tribe living south of the Svea

Geatland—the south-central portion of modern Sweden, home to the Geats

Hati—the wolf that chases the moon across the sky

Hel—goddess of the underworld

Hidden, the—unseen spiritual realms

hird—a retinue of armed companions

housecarl—a royal bodyguard

hundred—a medieval unit of land

jarl—a Scandinavian nobleman ranking just below the king

Jómsborg—home to the Jómsvíkings, on the southern coast of the Baltic Sea

Jómsvíkings—brotherhood of Viking mercenaries

Kára—a valkyrie also referred to as the Wild Stormy One

lay—a narrative poem, ballad, or song

Loki—god of evil and mischief

Máni—personification of the moon

Mjölnir—Thor's hammer

myling—a soul of a dead child who was not given a proper burial

Nátt—personification of night

Niflheim—the realm of the dead

Norns, the—the three goddesses of fate: Verdandi, Urd, and Skuld

Odin—the All-Father, king of the gods, god of wisdom

Ragnarök—aka the twilight of the gods, the final destruction of the universe after the war between the Æsir and Loki

Rán—a goddess associated with the sea who has nine daughters

Scania—the southern part of modern Sweden near Denmark

Sköll—the wolf that chases the sun across the sky

Sleipnir—Odin's eight-legged horse

Sól—personification of the sun

Svea, the—a Scandinavian tribe, aka the Swedes

Svealand—the central, core region of modern Sweden

Thing—an early parliament

thingstead—the place where the Thing was held

Thor—god of thunder, protector of mankind

Valhalla—a great hall where warriors slain heroically in battle are received in the afterlife *valkyrie*—a maiden of Odin who helps choose those fallen in battle to be taken to Valhalla

Vanadís—another name for Freya

Vanir—one of the two main tribes of deities (cf. *Æsir*)

Yggdrasil—the ash tree of life that binds the realm of the gods, the realm of men, and the underworld

ABOUT THE AUTHOR

Johanne Hildebrandt is an award-winning war correspondent and author. Her breakthrough came with the bestselling trilogy Sagan om Valhalla (The Story of Valhalla) and her horror novel, *Fördömd* (*The Condemned*). In 2002, she was awarded the prestigious journalist award Guldspaden ("the Golden Shovel") for her book *Blackout*, which describes her ten years as a Bosnian War correspondent. She was also nominated for the Grand Journalist Prize following her accounts of the war in Iraq. In 2012, she was elected a member of the Royal Swedish Academy of War Sciences and is the first woman admitted to the academy, which was founded in 1796. *The Unbroken Line of the Moon* is her first novel translated into English.

ABOUT THE TRANSLATOR

Photo © 2006 Libby Lewis

Tara Chace has translated more than twenty-five novels from Norwegian, Swedish, and Danish. Her most recent translations include Martin Jensen's *The King's Hounds* trilogy (Amazon Crossing, 2013–2015), Sven Nordqvist's *Pettson and Findus* books (NorthSouth, 2014–2016), and Jo Nesbø's *Doctor Proctor's Fart Powder* series (Aladdin, 2010–2014).

An avid reader and language learner, Chace earned her PhD in Scandinavian Languages and Literature from the University of Washington in 2003. She enjoys translating books for adults and children. She lives in Seattle with her family and their black lab, Zephyr.